He Knew He W

Vol. I

He Knew He Was Right
Vol. I

by

Anthony Trollope

CAMBRIDGE
SCHOLARS
PUBLISHING

classic texts

He Knew He Was Right vol. I, by Anthony Trollope

This book in its current typographical format first published 2008 by

Cambridge Scholars Publishing

12 Back Chapman Street, Newcastle upon Tyne, NE6 2XX, UK

British Library Cataloguing in Publication Data
A catalogue record for this book is available from the British Library

ISBN (10): 1-84718-705-6, ISBN (13): 9781847187055

CONTENTS

CHAPTER I. SHEWING HOW WRATH BEGAN

When Louis Trevelyan was twenty-four years old, he had all the world before him where to choose; and, among other things, he chose to go to the Mandarin Islands, and there fell in love with Emily Rowley, the daughter of Sir Marmaduke, the governor. Sir Marmaduke Rowley, at this period of his life, was a respectable middle-aged public servant, in good repute, who had, however, as yet achieved for himself neither an exalted position nor a large fortune. He had been governor of many islands, and had never lacked employment; and now, at the age of fifty, found himself at the Mandarins, with a salary of 3,000 pounds a year, living in a temperature at which 80 in the shade is considered to be cool, with eight daughters, and not a shilling saved. A governor at the Mandarins who is social by nature and hospitable on principle, cannot save money in the islands even on 3,000 pounds a year when he has eight daughters. And at the Mandarins, though hospitality is a duty, the gentlemen who ate Sir Rowley's dinners were not exactly the men whom he or Lady Rowley desired to welcome to their bosoms as sons-in-law. Nor when Mr Trevelyan came that way, desirous of seeing everything in the somewhat indefinite course of his travels, had Emily Rowley, the eldest of the flock, then twenty years of age, seen as yet any Mandariner who exactly came up to her fancy. And, as Louis Trevelyan was a remarkably handsome young man, who was well connected, who had been ninth wrangler at Cambridge, who had already published a volume of poems, and who possessed 3,000 pounds a year of his own, arising from various perfectly secure investments, he was not forced to sigh long in vain. Indeed, the Rowleys, one and all, felt that providence had been very good to them in sending young Trevelyan on his travels in that direction, for he seemed to be a very pearl among men. Both Sir Marmaduke and Lady Rowley felt that there might be objections to such a marriage as that proposed to them, raised by the Trevelyan family. Lady Rowley would not have liked her daughter to go to England, to be received with cold looks by strangers. But it soon appeared that there was no one to make objections. Louis, the lover, had no living relative nearer than cousins. His father, a barrister of repute, had died a widower, and had left the money which he had made to an only child. The head of the family was a first cousin who lived in Cornwall on a moderate property, a very good sort of stupid fellow, as Louis said, who would be quite indifferent as to any marriage that his cousin might make. No man could be more independent or more clearly justified in pleasing himself than was this lover. And then he himself proposed that the second daughter, Nora, should come and live with them in London. What a lover to fall suddenly from the heavens into such a dovecote!

'I haven't a penny-piece to give either of them,' said Sir Rowley.

'It is my idea that girls should not have fortunes,' said Trevelyan. 'At any rate, I am quite sure that men should never look for money. A man must be more comfortable, and, I think, is likely to be more affectionate, when the money has belonged to himself.'

Sir Rowley was a high-minded gentleman, who would have liked to have handed over a few thousand pounds on giving up his daughters; but, having no thousands of pounds to hand over, he could not but admire the principles of his proposed son-in-law. As it was about time for him to have his leave of absence, he and sundry of the girls went to England with Mr Trevelyan, and the wedding was celebrated in London by the Rev. Oliphant Outhouse, of Saint Diddulph-in-the-East, who had married Sir Rowley's sister. Then a small house was taken and furnished in Curzon Street, Mayfair, and the Rowleys went back to the seat of their government, leaving Nora, the second girl, in charge of her elder sister.

The Rowleys had found, on reaching London, that they had lighted upon a pearl indeed. Louis Trevelyan was a man of whom all people said all good things. He might have been a fellow of his college had he not been a man of fortune. He might already, so Sir Rowley was told, have been in Parliament, had he not thought it to be wiser to wait awhile. Indeed, he was very wise in many things. He had gone out on his travels thus young, not in search of excitement, to kill beasts, or to encounter he knew not what novelty and amusement, but that he might see men and know the world. He had been on his travels for more than a year when the winds blew him to the Mandarins. Oh, how blessed were the winds! And, moreover, Sir Rowley found that his son-in-law was well spoken of at the clubs by those who had known him during his university career, as a man popular as well as wise, not a book-worm, or a dry philosopher, or a prig. He could talk on all subjects, was very generous, a man sure to be honoured and respected; and then such a handsome, manly fellow, with short brown hair, a nose divinely chiselled, an Apollo's mouth, six feet high, with shoulders and legs and arms in proportion—a pearl of pearls! Only, as Lady Rowley was the first to find out, he liked to have his own way.

'But his way is such a good way,' said Sir Marmaduke. 'He will be such a good guide for the girls!'

'But Emily likes her way too,' said Lady Rowley.

Sir Marmaduke argued the matter no further, but thought, no doubt, that such a husband as Louis Trevelyan was entitled to have his own way. He probably had not observed his daughter's temper so accurately as his wife had done. With eight of them coming up around him, how should he have observed their tempers? At any rate, if there were anything amiss with Emily's temper, it would be well that she should find her master in such a husband as Louis Trevelyan.

For nearly two years the little household in Curzon Street went on well, or if anything was the matter no one outside of the little household was aware of it. And there was a baby, a boy, a young Louis, and a baby in such a household is apt to make things go sweetly.

The marriage had taken place in July, and after the wedding tour there had been a winter and a spring in London; and then they passed a month or two at the sea-side, after which the baby had been born. And then there came another winter and another spring. Nora Rowley was with them in London, and by this time Mr Trevelyan had begun to think that he should like to have his own way completely. His baby was very nice, and his wife was clever, pretty, and attractive. Nora was all that an unmarried sister should be. But but there had come to be trouble and bitter words. Lady Rowley had been right when she said that her daughter Emily also liked to have her own way.

'If I am suspected,' said Mrs Trevelyan to her sister one morning, as they sat together in the little back drawing-room, 'life will not be worth having.'

'How can you talk of being suspected, Emily?'

'What does he mean then by saying that he would rather not have Colonel Osborne here? A man older than my own father, who has known me since I was a baby!'

'He didn't mean anything of that kind, Emily. You know he did not, and you should not say so. It would be too horrible to think of.'

'It was a great deal too horrible to be spoken, I know. If he does not beg my pardon, I shall I shall continue to live with him, of course, as a sort of upper servant, because of baby. But he shall know what I think and feel.'

'If I were you I would forget it.'

'How can I forget it? Nothing that I can do pleases him. He is civil and kind to you because he is not your master; but you don't know what things he says to me. Am I to tell Colonel Osborne not to come? Heavens and earth! How should I ever hold up my head again if I were driven to do that? He will be here today I have no doubt; and Louis will sit there below in the library, and hear his step, and will not come up.'

'Tell Richard to say you are not at home.'

'Yes; and everybody will understand why. And for what am I to deny myself in that way to the best and oldest friend I have? If any such orders are to be given, let him give them and then see what will come of it.'

Mrs Trevelyan had described Colonel Osborne truly as far as words went, in saying that he had known her since she was a baby, and that he was an older man than her father. Colonel Osborne's age exceeded her father's by about a month, and as he was now past fifty, he might be considered perhaps, in that respect, to be a safe friend for a young married woman. But he was in every respect a man very different from Sir Marmaduke. Sir Marmaduke, blessed and at the same time burdened as he was with a wife and eight daughters, and condemned as he had been to pass a large portion of his life within the tropics, had become at fifty what many people call quite a middle-aged man. That is to say, he was one from whom the effervescence and elasticity and salt of youth had altogether passed away. He was fat and slow, thinking much of his wife and eight daughters, thinking much also of his dinner. Now Colonel Osborne was a bachelor, with no burdens but those imposed upon him by his position as a member of Parliament, a man of fortune to whom the world had been very easy. It was not therefore said so decidedly of him as of Sir Marmaduke, that he was a middle-aged man, although he had probably already lived more than two-thirds of his life. And he was a good-looking man of his age, bald indeed at the top of his head, and with a considerable sprinkling of grey hair through his bushy beard; but upright in his carriage, active, and quick in his step, who dressed well, and was clearly determined to make the most he could of what remained to him of the advantages of youth. Colonel Osborne was always so dressed that no one ever observed the nature of his garments, being no doubt well aware that no man after twenty-five can afford to call special attention to his coat, his hat, his cravat, or his trousers; but nevertheless the matter was one to which he paid much attention, and he was by no means lax in ascertaining what his tailor did for him. He always rode a pretty horse, and mounted his groom on one at any rate as pretty. He was known to have an excellent stud down in the shires, and had the reputation of going well with hounds. Poor Sir Marmaduke could not have ridden a hunt to save either his government or his credit. When, therefore, Mrs Trevelyan declared to her sister that Colonel Osborne was a man whom she was entitled to regard with semi-parental feelings of veneration because he was older than her father, she made a comparison which was more true in the letter than in the spirit. And when she asserted that Colonel Osborne had known her since she was a baby, she fell again into the same mistake. Colonel Osborne had indeed known her when she was a baby, and had in old days been the very intimate friend of her father; but of herself he had seen little or nothing since those baby days, till he had met her just as she was about to become Mrs Trevelyan; and though it was natural that so old a friend should come to her and congratulate her and renew his friendship, nevertheless it was not true that he made his appearance in her husband's house in the guise of the useful old family friend, who gives silver cups to the children and kisses the little girls for the sake of the old affection which he has borne for the parents. We all know the appearance of that old gentleman, how pleasant and dear a fellow he is, how welcome is his face within the gate, how free he makes with our wine, generally abusing it, how he tells our eldest daughter to light his candle for him, how he gave silver cups when the girls were born, and now bestows tea-services as they get married—a most useful, safe, and charming fellow, not a year younger-looking or more nimble than ourselves, without whom life would be very blank. We all know that man; but such a man was not Colonel Osborne in the house of Mr Trevelyan's young bride.

Emily Rowley, when she was brought home from the Mandarin Islands to be the wife of Louis Trevelyan, was a very handsome young woman, tall, with a bust rather full for her age, with dark eyes eyes that looked to be dark because her eye-brows and eye-lashes were nearly black, but which were in truth so varying in colour that you could not tell their hue. Her brown hair was very dark and very soft; and the tint of her complexion was brown also, though the colour of her cheeks was often so bright as to induce her enemies to say falsely of her that she painted them. And she was very strong, as are some girls who come from the tropics, and whom a tropical climate has suited. She could sit on her horse the whole day long, and would never be weary with dancing at the Government House balls. When Colonel Osborne was introduced to her as the baby whom he had known, he thought it would be very pleasant to be intimate with so pleasant a friend, meaning no harm indeed, as but few men do mean harm on such occasions, but still, not regarding the beautiful young woman whom he had seen as one of a generation succeeding to that of his own, to whom it would be his duty to make himself useful on account of the old friendship which he bore to her father.

It was, moreover, well known in London though not known at all to Mrs Trevelyan that this ancient Lothario had before this made himself troublesome in more than one family. He was fond of intimacies with married ladies, and perhaps was not averse to the excitement of marital hostility. It must be remembered, however, that the hostility to which allusion is here made was not the hostility of the pistol or the horsewhip nor indeed was it generally the hostility of a word of spoken anger. A young husband may dislike the too-friendly bearing of a friend, and may yet abstain from that outrage on his own dignity and on his wife, which is conveyed by a word of suspicion. Louis Trevelyan having taken a strong dislike to Colonel Osborne, and having failed to make his wife understand that this dislike should have induced her to throw cold water upon the Colonel's friendship, had allowed himself to speak a word which probably he would have willingly recalled as soon as spoken. But words spoken cannot be recalled, and many a man and many a woman who has spoken a word at once regretted, are far too proud to express that regret. So it was with Louis Trevelyan when he told his wife that he did not wish Colonel Osborne to come so often to his house. He had said it with a flashing eye and an angry tone; and though she had seen the eye flash before, and was familiar with the angry tone, she had never before felt herself to be insulted by her husband. As soon as the word had been spoken Trevelyan had left the room and had gone down among his books. But when he was alone he knew that he had insulted his wife. He was quite aware that he should have spoken to her gently, and have explained to her, with his arm round her waist, that it would be better for both of them that this friend's friendship should be limited. There is so much in a turn of the eye and in the tone given to a word when such things have to be said, so much more of importance than in the words themselves. As Trevelyan thought of this, and remembered what his manner had been, how much anger he had expressed, how far he had been from having his arm round his wife's waist as he spoke to her, he almost made up his mind to go upstairs and to apologise. But he was one to whose nature the giving of any apology was repulsive. He could not bear to have to own himself to have been wrong. And then his wife had been most provoking in her manner to him. When he had endeavoured to make her understand his wishes by certain disparaging hints which he had thrown out as to Colonel Osborne, saying that he was a dangerous man, one who did not show his true character, a snake in the grass, a man without settled principles, and such like, his wife had taken up the cudgels for her friend, and had openly declared that she did not believe a word of the things that were alleged against him. 'But still for all that it is true,' the husband had said. 'I have no doubt that you think so,' the wife had replied. 'Men do believe evil of one another, very often. But you must excuse me if I say that I think you are mistaken. I have known Colonel Osborne much longer than you have done, Louis, and papa has always had the highest opinion of him.' Then Mr Trevelyan had become very angry, and had spoken those words which he could not recall. As he walked to and fro among his books downstairs, he almost felt that he ought to beg his wife's pardon. He knew his wife well enough to be sure that she would not forgive him unless he did so. He would do so, he thought, but not exactly now. A moment would come in which it might be easier than at present. He would be able to assure her when he went up to dress for dinner, that he had meant no harm. They were going out to dine at the house of a lady of rank, the Countess Dowager of Milborough, a lady standing high in the world's esteem, of whom his wife stood a little in awe; and he calculated that this feeling, if it did not make his task easy would yet take from it some of its difficulty. Emily would be, not exactly cowed, by the prospect of Lady Milborough's dinner, but perhaps a little reduced from her usual self-assertion. He would say a word to her when he was dressing, assuring her that he had not intended to animadvert in the slightest degree upon her own conduct.

Luncheon was served, and the two ladies went down into the dining-room. Mr Trevelyan did not appear. There was nothing in itself singular in that, as he was accustomed to declare that luncheon was a meal too much in the day, and that a man should eat nothing beyond a biscuit between breakfast and dinner. But he would sometimes come in and eat his biscuit standing on the hearth-rug, and drink what he would call half a quarter of a glass of sherry. It would probably have been well that he should have done so now; but he remained in his library behind the dining-room, and when his wife and his sister-in-law had gone upstairs, he became anxious to learn whether, Colonel Osborne would come on that day, and, if so, whether he would be admitted. He had been told that Nora Rowley was to be called for by another lady, a Mrs Fairfax, to go out and look at pictures. His wife had declined to join Mrs Fairfax's party, having declared that, as she was going to dine out, she would not leave her baby all the afternoon. Louis Trevelyan, though he strove to apply his mind to an article which he was writing for a scientific quarterly review, could not keep himself from anxiety as to this expected visit from Colonel Osborne. He was not in the least jealous. He swore to himself fifty times over that any such feeling on his part would be a monstrous injury to his wife. Nevertheless he knew that he would be gratified if on that special day Colonel Osborne should be informed that his wife was not at home. Whether the man were admitted or not, he would beg his wife's pardon; but he could, he thought, do so with more thorough efficacy and affection if she should have shown a disposition to comply with his wishes on this day.

'Do say a word to Richard,' said Nora to her sister in a whisper as they were going upstairs after luncheon.

'I will not,' said Mrs Trevelyan.

'May I do it?'

'Certainly not, Nora. I should feel that I were demeaning myself were I to allow what was said to me in such a manner to have any effect upon me.'

'I think you are so wrong, Emily. I do indeed.'

'You must allow me to be the best judge what to do in my own house, and with my own husband.'

'Oh, yes; certainly.'

'If he gives me any command I will obey it. Or if he had expressed his wish in any other words I would have complied. But to be told that he would rather not have Colonel Osborne here! If you had seen his manner and heard his words, you would not have been surprised that I should feel it as I do. It was a gross insult and it was not the first.'

As she spoke the fire flashed from her eye, and the bright red colour of her cheek told a tale of her anger which her sister well knew how to read. Then there was a knock at the door, and they both knew that Colonel Osborne was there. Louis

Trevelyan, sitting in his library, also knew of whose coming that knock gave notice.

CHAPTER II. COLONEL OSBORNE

It has been already said that Colonel Osborne was a bachelor, a man of fortune, a member of Parliament, and one who carried his half century of years lightly on his shoulders. It will only be necessary to say further of him that he was a man popular with those among whom he lived, as a politician, as a sportsman, and as a member of society. He could speak well in the House, though he spoke but seldom, and it was generally thought of him that he might have been something considerable, had it not suited him better to be nothing at all. He was supposed to be a Conservative, and generally voted with the conservative party; but he could boast that he was altogether independent, and on an occasion would take the trouble of proving himself to be so. He was in possession of excellent health; had all that the world could give; was fond of books, pictures, architecture, and china; had various tastes, and the means of indulging them, and was one of those few men on whom it seems that every pleasant thing has been lavished. There was that little slur on his good name to which allusion has been made; but those who knew Colonel Osborne best were generally willing to declare that no harm was intended, and that the evils which arose were always to be attributed to mistaken jealousy. He had, his friends said, a free and pleasant way with women which women like, a pleasant way of free friendship; that there was no more, and that the harm which had come had always come from false suspicion. But there were certain ladies about the town—good, motherly, discreet women—who hated the name of Colonel Osborne, who would not admit him within their doors, who would not bow to him in other people's houses, who would always speak of him as a serpent, a hyena, a kite, or a shark. Old Lady Milborough was one of these, a daughter of a friend of hers having once admitted the serpent to her intimacy.

'Augustus Poole was wise enough to take his wife abroad,' said old Lady Milborough, discussing about this time with a gossip of hers the danger of Mrs Trevelyan's position, 'or there would have been a breakup there; and yet there never was a better girl in the world than Jane Marriott.'

The reader may be quite certain that Colonel Osborne had no premeditated evil intention when he allowed himself to become the intimate friend of his old friend's daughter. There was nothing fiendish in his nature. He was not a man who boasted of his conquests. He was not a ravening wolf going about seeking whom he might devour, and determined to devour whatever might come in his way; but he liked that which was pleasant; and of all pleasant things the company of a pretty clever woman was to him the pleasantest. At this exact period of his life no woman was so pleasantly pretty to him, and so agreeably clever, as Mrs Trevelyan.

When Louis Trevelyan heard on the stairs the step of the dangerous man, he got up from his chair as though he too would have gone into the drawing-room, and it would perhaps have been well had he done so. Could he have done this, and kept his temper with the man, he would have paved the way for an easy reconciliation with his wife. But when he reached the door of his room, and had placed his hand upon the lock, he withdrew again. He told himself he withdrew because he would not allow himself to be jealous; but in truth he did so because he knew he could not have brought himself to be civil to the man he hated. So he sat down, and took up his pen, and began to cudgel his brain about the scientific article. He was intent on raising a dispute with some learned pundit about the waves of sound, but he could think of no other sound than that of the light steps of Colonel Osborne as he had gone upstairs. He put down his pen, and clenched his fist, and allowed a black frown to settle upon his brow. 'What right had the man to come there, unasked by him, and disturb his happiness? And then this poor wife of his, who knew so little of English life, who had lived in the Mandarin Islands almost since she had been a child, who had lived in one colony or another almost since she had been born, who had had so few of those advantages for which he should have looked in marrying a wife, how was the poor girl to conduct herself properly when subjected to the arts and practised villanies of this viper? And yet the poor girl was so stiff in her temper, had picked up such a trick of obstinacy in those tropical regions, that Louis Trevelyan felt that he did not know how to manage her. He too had heard how Jane Marriott had been carried off to Naples after she had become Mrs Poole. Must he too carry off his wife to Naples in order to place her out of the reach of this hyena? It was terrible to him to think that he must pack up everything and run away from such a one as Colonel Osborne. And even were he to consent to do this, how could he explain it all to that very wife for whose sake he would do it? If she got a hint of the reason she would, he did not doubt, refuse to go. As he thought of it, and as that visit upstairs prolonged itself, he almost thought it would be best for him to be round with her! We all know what a husband means when he resolves to be round with his wife. He began to think that he would not apologise at all for the words he had spoken but would speak them again somewhat more sharply than before. She would be very wrathful with him; there would be a silent enduring indignation, which, as he understood well, would be infinitely worse than any torrent of words. But was he, a man, to abstain from doing that which he believed to be his duty because he was afraid of his wife's anger? Should he be deterred from saying that which he conceived it would be right that he should say, because she was stiff-necked? No. He would not apologise, but would tell her again that it was necessary, both for his happiness and for hers, that all intimacy with Colonel Osborne should be discontinued.

He was brought to this strongly marital resolution by the length of the man's present visit; by that and by the fact that, during the latter portion of it, his wife was alone with Colonel Osborne. Nora had been there when the man came, but Mrs Fairfax had called, not getting out of her carriage, and Nora had been constrained to go down to her. She had hesitated a moment, and Colonel Osborne had observed and partly understood the hesitation. When he saw it, had he been perfectly well-minded in the matter, he would have gone too. But he probably told himself that Nora Rowley was a fool, and that in such matters it was quite enough for a man to know that he did not intend any harm.

'You had better go down, Nora,' said Mrs Trevelyan; 'Mrs Fairfax will be ever so angry if you keep her waiting.'

Then Nora had gone and the two were alone together. Nora had gone, and Trevelyan had heard her as she was going and knew that Colonel Osborne was alone with his wife.

'If you can manage that it will be so nice,' said Mrs Trevelyan, continuing the conversation.

'My dear Emily,' he said, 'you must not talk of my managing it, or you will spoil it all.'

He had called them both Emily and Nora when Sir Marmaduke and Lady Rowley were with them before the marriage, and, taking the liberty of a very old family friend, had continued the practice. Mrs Trevelyan was quite aware that she had been so called by him in the presence of her husband and that her husband had not objected. But that was now some months ago, before baby was born; and she was aware also that he had not called her so latterly in presence of her husband. She thoroughly wished that she knew how to ask him not to do so again; but the matter was very difficult, as she could not make such a request without betraying some fear on her husband's part. The subject which they were now discussing was too important to her to allow her to dwell upon this trouble at the moment, and so she permitted him to go on with his speech.

'If I were to manage it, as you call it, which I can't do at all, it would be a gross job.'

'That's all nonsense to us, Colonel Osborne. Ladies always like political jobs, and think that they and they only make politics bearable. But this would not be a job at all. Papa could do it better than anybody else. Think how long he has been at it!'

The matter in discussion was the chance of an order being sent out to Sir Marmaduke to come home from his islands at the public expense, to give evidence, respecting colonial government in general, to a committee of the House of

Commons which was about to sit on the subject. The committee had been voted, and two governors were to be brought home for the purpose of giving evidence. What arrangement could be so pleasant to a governor living in the Mandarin Islands, who had had a holiday lately, and who could but ill afford to take any holidays at his own expense? Colonel Osborne was on this committee, and, moreover, was on good terms at the Colonial Office. There were men in office who would be glad to do Colonel Osborne a service, and then if this were a job, it would be so very little of a job! Perhaps Sir Marmaduke might not be the very best man for the purpose. Perhaps the government of the Mandarins did not afford the best specimen of that colonial lore which it was the business of the committee to master. But then two governors were to come, and it might be as well to have one of the best sort, and one of the second best. No one supposed that excellent old Sir Marmaduke was a paragon of a governor, but then he had an infinity of experience! For over twenty years he had been from island to island, and had at least steered clear of great scrapes.

'We'll try it, at any rate,' said the Colonel.

'Do, Colonel Osborne. Mamma would come with him, of course?'

'We should leave him to manage all that. It's not very likely that he would leave Lady Rowley behind.'

'He never has. I know he thinks more of mamma than he ever does of himself. Fancy having them here in the autumn! I suppose if he came for the end of the session, they wouldn't send him back quite at once?'

'I rather fancy that our foreign and colonial servants know how to stretch a point when they find themselves in England.'

'Of course they do, Colonel Osborne; and why shouldn't they? Think of all that they have to endure out in those horrible places. How would you like to live in the Mandarins?'

'I should prefer London, certainly.'

'Of course you would; and you mustn't begrudge papa a month or two when he comes. I never cared about your being in parliament before, but I shall think so much of you now if you can manage to get papa home.'

There could be nothing more innocent than this—nothing more innocent at any rate as regarded any offence against Mr Trevelyan. But just then there came a word which a little startled Mrs Trevelyan, and made her feel afraid that she was doing wrong.

'I must make one stipulation with you, Emily,' said the Colonel.

'What is that?'

'You must not tell your husband.'

'Oh, dear! and why not?'

'I am sure you are sharp enough to see why you should not. A word of this repeated at any club would put an end at once to your project, and would be very damaging to me. And, beyond that, I wouldn't wish him to know that I had meddled with it at all. I am very chary of having my name connected with anything of the kind; and, upon my word, I wouldn't do it for any living human being but yourself. You'll promise me, Emily?'

She gave the promise, but there were two things in the matter, as it stood at present, which she did not at all like. She was very averse to having any secret from her husband with Colonel Osborne; and she was not at all pleased at being told that he was doing for her a favour that he would not have done for any other living human being. Had he said so to her yesterday, before those offensive words had been spoken by her husband, she would not have thought much about it. She would have connected the man's friendship for herself with his very old friendship for her father, and she would have regarded the assurance as made to the Rowleys in general, and not to herself in particular. But now, after what had occurred, it pained her to be told by Colonel Osborne that he would make, specially on her behalf, a sacrifice of his political pride which he would make for no other person living. And then, as he had called her by her Christian name, as he had exacted the promise, there had been a tone of affection in his voice that she had almost felt to be too warm. But she gave the promise; and when he pressed her hand at parting, she pressed his again, in token of gratitude for the kindness to be done to her father and mother.

Immediately afterwards Colonel Osborne went away, and Mrs Trevelyan was left alone in her drawing-room. She knew that her husband was still downstairs, and listened for a moment to hear whether he would now come up to her. And he, too, had heard the Colonel's step as he went, and for a few moments had doubted whether or no he would at once go to his wife. Though he believed himself to be a man very firm of purpose, his mind had oscillated backwards and forwards within the last quarter of an hour between those two purposes of being round with his wife, and of begging her pardon for the words which he had already spoken. He believed that he would best do his duty by that plan of being round with her; but then it would be so much pleasanter at any rate, so much easier, to beg her pardon. But of one thing he was quite certain, he must by some means exclude Colonel Osborne from his house. He could not live and continue to endure the feelings which he had suffered while sitting downstairs at his desk, with the knowledge that Colonel Osborne was closeted with his wife upstairs. It might be that there was nothing in it. That his wife was innocent he was quite sure. But nevertheless, he was himself so much affected by some feeling which pervaded him in reference to this man, that all his energy was destroyed., and his powers of mind and body were paralysed. He could not, and would not, stand it. Rather than that, he would follow Mr Poole, and take his wife to Naples. So resolving, he put his hat on his head and walked out of the house. He would have the advantage of the afternoon's consideration before he took either the one step or the other.

As soon as he was gone Emily Trevelyan went upstairs to her baby. She would not stir as long as there had been a chance of his coming to her. She very much wished that he would come, and had made up her mind, in spite of the fierceness of her assertion to her sister, to accept any slightest hint at an apology which her husband might offer to her. To this state of mind she was brought by the consciousness of having a secret from him, and by a sense not of impropriety on her own part, but of conduct which some people might have called improper in her mode of parting from the man against whom her husband had warned her. The warmth of that hand-pressing, and the affectionate tone in which her name had been pronounced, and the promise made to her, softened her heart towards her husband. Had he gone to her now and said a word to her in gentleness all might have been made right. But he did not go to her.

'If he chooses to be cross and sulky, he may be cross and sulky,' said Mrs Trevelyan to herself as she went up to her baby.

'Has Louis been with you?' Nora asked, as soon as Mrs Fairfax had brought her home.

'I have not seen him since you left me,' said Mrs Trevelyan.

'I suppose he went out before Colonel Osborne?'

'No, indeed. He waited till Colonel Osborne had gone, and then he went himself; but he did not come near me. It is for him to judge of his own conduct, but I must say that I think he is very foolish.'

This the young wife said in a tone which clearly indicated that she had judged her husband's conduct, and had found it to be very foolish indeed.

'Do you think that papa and mamma will really come?' said Nora, changing the subject of conversation.

'How can I tell? How am I to know? After all that has passed I am afraid to say a word lest I should be accused of doing wrong. But remember this, Nora, you are not to speak of it to any one.'

'You will tell Louis?'

'No; I will tell no one.'

'Dear, dear Emily; pray do not keep anything secret from him.'

'What do you mean by secret? There isn't any secret. Only in such matters as that about politics no gentleman likes to have his name talked about!'

A look of great distress came upon Nora's face as she heard this. To her it seemed to be very bad that there should be a secret between her sister and Colonel Osborne to be kept from her brother-in-law.

'I suppose you will suspect me next?' said Mrs Trevelyan, angrily.

'Emily, how can you say anything so cruel?'

'You look as if you did.'

'I only mean that I think it would be wiser to tell all this to Louis.'

'How can I tell him Colonel Osborne's private business, when Colonel Osborne has desired me not to do so. For whose sake is Colonel Osborne doing this? For papa's and mamma's! I suppose Louis won't be jealous, because I want to have papa and mamma home. It would not be a bit less unreasonable than the other.'

CHAPTER III. LADY MILBOROUGH'S DINNER PARTY

Louis Trevelyan went down to his club in Pall Mall, the Acrobats, and there heard a rumour that added to his anger against Colonel Osborne. The Acrobats was a very distinguished club, into which it was now difficult for a young man to find his way, and almost impossible for a man who was no longer young, and therefore known to many. It had been founded some twenty years since with the idea of promoting muscular exercise and gymnastic amusements; but the promoters had become fat and lethargic, and the Acrobats spent their time mostly in playing whist, and in ordering and eating their dinners. There were supposed to be, in some out-of-the-way part of the building, certain poles and sticks and parallel bars with which feats of activity might be practised, but no one ever asked for them now-a-days, and a man, when he became an Acrobat, did so with a view either to the whist or the cook, or possibly to the social excellences of the club. Louis Trevelyan was an Acrobat as was also Colonel Osborne.

'So old Rowley is coming home,' said one distinguished Acrobat to another in Trevelyan's hearing.

'How the deuce is he managing that? He was here a year ago?'

'Osborne is getting it done. He is to come as a witness for this committee. It must be no end of a lounge for him. It doesn't count as leave, and he has every shilling paid for him, down to his cab-fares when he goes out to dinner. There's nothing like having a friend at Court.'

Such was the secrecy of Colonel Osborne's secret! He had been so chary of having his name mentioned in connection with a political job, that he had found it necessary to impose on his young friend the burden of a secret from her husband, and yet the husband heard the whole story told openly at his club on the same day! There was nothing in the story to anger Trevelyan had he not immediately felt that there must be some plan in the matter between his wife and Colonel Osborne, of which he had been kept ignorant. Hitherto, indeed, his wife, as the reader knows, could not have told him. He had not seen her since the matter had been discussed between her and her friend. But he was angry because he first learned at his club that which he thought he ought to have learned at home. As soon as he reached his house he went at once to his wife's room, but her maid was with her, and nothing could be said at that moment. He then dressed himself, intending to go to Emily as soon as the girl had left her; but the girl remained—was, as he believed, kept in the room purposely by his wife, so that he should have no moment of private conversation. He went downstairs, therefore, and found Nora standing by the drawing-room fire.

'So you are dressed first today?' he said. 'I thought your turn always came last.'

'Emily sent Jenny to me first today because she thought you would be home, and she didn't go up to dress till the last minute.'

This was intended well by Nora, but it did not have the desired effect. Trevelyan, who had no command over his own features, frowned, and showed that he was displeased. He hesitated a moment, thinking whether he would ask Nora any question as to this report about her father and mother; but, before he had spoken, his wife was in the room.

'We are all late, I fear,' said Emily.

'You, at any rate, are the last,' said her husband.

'About half a minute,' said the wife.

Then they got into the hired brougham which was standing at the door.

Trevelyan, in the sweet days of his early confidence with his wife, had offered to keep a carriage for her, explaining to her that the luxury, though costly, would not be beyond his reach. But she had persuaded him against the carriage, and there had come to be an agreement that instead of the carriage there should always be an autumn tour. 'One learns something from going about; but one learns nothing from keeping a carriage,' Emily had said. Those had been happy days, in which it had been intended that everything should always be rose-coloured. Now he was meditating whether, in lieu of that autumn tour, it would not be necessary to take his wife away to Naples altogether, so that she might be removed from the influence of, of, of, of—no, not even to himself would he think of Colonel Osborne as his wife's lover. The idea was too horrible! And yet, how dreadful was it that he should have, for any reason, to withdraw her from the influence of any man!

Lady Milborough lived ever so far away, in Eccleston Square, but Trevelyan did not say a single word to either of his companions during the journey. He was cross and vexed, and was conscious that they knew that he was cross and vexed. Mrs Trevelyan and her sister talked to each other the whole way, but they did so in that tone which clearly indicates that the conversation is made up, not for any interest attached to the questions asked or the answers given, but because it is expedient that there should not be silence. Nora said something about Marshall and Snellgrove and tried to make believe that she was very anxious for her sister's answer. And Emily said something about the opera at Covent Garden, which was intended to show that her mind was quite at ease. But both of them failed altogether, and knew that they failed. Once or twice Trevelyan thought that he would say a word in token, as it were, of repentance. Like the naughty child who knew that he was naughty, he was trying to be good. But he could not do it. The fiend was too strong within him. She must have known that there was a proposition for her father's return through Colonel Osborne's influence. As that man at the club had heard it, how could she not have known it? When they got out at Lady Milborough's door he had spoken to neither of them.

There was a large dull party, made up mostly of old people. Lady Milborough and Trevelyan's mother had been bosom friends, and Lady Milborough had on this account taken upon herself to be much interested in Trevelyan's wife. But Louis Trevelyan himself, in discussing Lady Milborough with Emily, had rather turned his mother's old friend into ridicule, and Emily had, of course, followed her husband's mode of thinking. Lady Milborough had once or twice given her some advice on small matters, telling her that this or that air would be good for her baby, and explaining that a mother during a certain interesting portion of her life, should refresh herself with a certain kind of malt liquor. Of all counsel on such domestic subjects Mrs Trevelyan was impatient, as indeed it was her nature to be in all matters, and consequently, authorized as she had been by her husband's manner of speaking of his mother's friend, she had taken a habit of quizzing Lady Milborough behind her back, and almost of continuing the practice before the old lady's face. Lady Milborough, who was the most affectionate old soul alive, and good-tempered with her friends to a fault, had never resented this, but had come to fear that Mrs Trevelyan was perhaps a little flighty. She had never as yet allowed herself to say anything worse of her young friend's wife than that. And she would always add that that kind of thing would cure itself as the nursery became full. It must be understood therefore that Mrs Trevelyan was not anticipating much pleasure from Lady Milborough's party, and that she had accepted the invitation as a matter of duty.

There was present among the guests a certain Honourable Charles Glascock, the eldest son of Lord Peterborough, who made the affair more interesting to Nora than it was to her sister. It had been whispered into Nora's ears, by more than one person and among others by Lady Milborough, whose own daughters were all married, that she might if she thought fit become the Honourable Mrs Charles Glascock. Now, whether she might think fit, or whether she might not, the presence of the gentleman under such circumstances, as far as she was concerned, gave an interest to the evening. And as Lady Milborough took care that Mr Glascock should take Nora down to dinner, the interest was very great. Mr Glascock was a good-looking man, just under forty, in Parliament, heir to a peerage, and known to be well off in respect to income. Lady Milborough and Mrs Trevelyan had told Nora Rowley that should encouragement in that direction come in her way, she ought to allow herself to fall in love with Mr Glascock. A certain amount of encouragement had come in her way, but she had not as yet allowed herself to fall in love with Mr Glascock.

It seemed to her that Mr Glascock was quite conscious of the advantages of his own position, and that his powers of talking about other matters than those with which he was immediately connected were limited. She did believe that he had in truth paid her the compliment of falling in love with her, and this is a compliment to which few girls are indifferent. Nora might perhaps have tried to fall in love with Mr Glascock, had she not been forced to make comparisons between him and another. This other one had not fallen in love with her, as she well knew; and she certainly had not fallen in love with him. But still the comparison was forced upon her, and it did not result in favour of Mr Glascock. On the present occasion Mr Glascock as he sat next to her almost proposed to her.

'You have never seen Monkhams?' he said. Monkhams was his father's seat, a very grand place in Worcestershire. Of course he knew very well that she had never seen Monkhams. How should she have seen it?

'I have never been in that part of England at all,' she replied.

'I should so like to show you Monkhams. The oaks there are the finest in the kingdom. Do you like oaks?'

'Who does not like oaks? But we have none in the islands, and nobody has ever seen so few as I have.'

'I'll show you Monkhams some day. Shall I? Indeed I hope that some day I may really show you Monkhams.'

Now when an unmarried man talks to a young lady of really showing her the house in which it will be his destiny to live, he can hardly mean other than to invite her to live there with him. It must at least be his purpose to signify that, if duly encouraged, he will so invite her. But Nora Rowley did not give Mr Glascock much encouragement on this occasion.

'I'm afraid it is not likely that anything will ever take me into that part of the country,' she said. There was something perhaps in her tone which checked Mr Glascock, so that he did not then press the invitation.

When the ladies were upstairs in the drawing-room, Lady Milborough contrived to seat herself on a couch intended for two persons only, close to Mrs Trevelyan. Emily, thinking that she might perhaps hear some advice about Guinness's stout, prepared herself to be saucy. But the matter in hand was graver than that. Lady Milborough's mind was uneasy about Colonel Osborne.

'My dear,' said she, 'was not your father very intimate with that Colonel Osborne?'

'He is very intimate with him, Lady Milborough.'

'Ah, yes; I thought I had heard so. That makes it of course natural that you should know him.'

'We have known him all our lives,' said Emily, forgetting probably that out of the twenty-three years and some months which she had hitherto lived, there had been a consecutive period of more than twenty years in which she had never seen this man whom she had known all her life.

'That makes a difference, of course; and I don't mean to say anything against him.'

'I hope not, Lady Milborough, because we are all especially fond of him.' This was said with so much of purpose, that poor, dear old Lady Milborough was stopped in her good work. She knew well the terrible strait to which Augustus Poole had been brought with his wife, although nobody supposed that Poole's wife had ever entertained a wrong thought in her pretty little heart. Nevertheless he had been compelled to break up his establishment, and take his wife to Naples, because this horrid Colonel would make himself at home in Mrs Poole's drawing-room in Knightsbridge. Augustus Poole, with courage enough to take any man by the beard, had taking by the beard been possible, had found it impossible to dislodge the Colonel. He could not do so without making a row which would have been disgraceful to himself and injurious to his wife; and therefore he had taken Mrs Poole to Naples. Lady Milborough knew the whole story, and thought that she foresaw that the same thing was about to happen in the drawing-room in Curzon Street. When she attempted to say a word to the wife, she found herself stopped. She could not go on in that quarter after the reception with which the beginning of her word had been met. But perhaps she might succeed better with the husband. After all, her friendship was with the Trevelyan side, and not with the Rowleys.

'My dear Louis,' she said, 'I want to speak a word to you. Come here.' And then she led him into a distant corner, Mrs Trevelyan watching her all the while, and guessing why her husband was thus carried away. 'I just want to give you a little hint, which I am sure I believe is quite unnecessary,' continued Lady Milborough. Then she paused, but Trevelyan would not speak. She looked into his face, and saw that it was black. But the man was the only child of her dearest friend, and she persevered. 'Do you know I don't quite like that Colonel Osborne coming so much to your house.' The face before her became still blacker, but still the man said nothing. 'I dare say it is a prejudice on my part, but I have always disliked him. I think he is a dangerous friend—what I call a snake in the grass. And though Emily's high good sense, and love for you, and general feelings on such a subject, are just what a husband must desire—Indeed, I am quite sure that the possibility of anything wrong has never entered into her head. But it is the very purity of her innocence which makes the danger. He is a bad man, and I would just say a word to her, if I were you, to make her understand that his coming to her of a morning is not desirable. Upon my word, I believe there is nothing he likes so much as going about and making mischief between men and their wives.'

Thus she delivered herself; and Louis Trevelyan, though he was sore and angry, could not but feel that she had taken the part of a friend. All that she had said had been true; all that she had said to him he had said to himself more than once. He too hated the man. He believed him to be a snake in the grass. But it was intolerably bitter to him that he should be warned about his wife's conduct by any living human being; that he, to whom the world had been so full of good fortune, that he, who had in truth taught himself to think that he deserved so much good fortune, should be made the subject of care on behalf of his friend, because of danger between himself and his wife! On the spur of the moment he did not know what answer to make. 'He is not a man whom I like myself,' he said.

'Just be careful, Louis, that is all,' said Lady Milborough, and then she was gone.

To be cautioned about his wife's conduct cannot be pleasant to any man, and it was very unpleasant to Louis Trevelyan. He, too, had been asked a question about Sir Marmaduke's expected visit to England after the ladies had left the room. All the town had heard of it except himself. He hardly spoke another word that evening till the brougham was announced; and his wife had observed his silence. When they were seated in the carriage, he together with his wife and Nora Rowley, he immediately asked a question about Sir Marmaduke. 'Emily,' he said, 'is there any truth in a report I hear that your father is coming home?' No answer was made, and for a moment or two there was silence. 'You must have heard of it, then?' he said. 'Perhaps you can tell me, Nora, as Emily will not reply. Have you heard anything of your father's coming?'

'Yes; I have heard of it,' said Nora slowly.

'And why have I not been told?'

'It was to be kept a secret,' said Mrs Trevelyan boldly.

'A secret from me; and everybody else knows it! And why was it to be a secret?'

'Colonel Osborne did not wish that it should be known,' said Mrs Trevelyan.

'And what has Colonel Osborne to do between you and your father in any matter with which I may not be made acquainted? I will have nothing more between you and Colonel Osborne. You shall not see Colonel Osborne. Do you hear me?'

'Yes, I hear you, Louis.'

'And do you mean to obey me? By G—, you shall obey me. Remember this, that I lay my positive order upon you, that you shall not see Colonel Osborne again. You do not know it, perhaps, but you are already forfeiting your reputation as an honest woman, and bringing disgrace upon me by your familiarity with Colonel Osborne.'

'Oh, Louis, do not say that!' said Nora.

'You had better let him speak it all at once,' said Emily.

'I have said what I have got to say. It is now only necessary that you should give me your solemn assurance that you will obey me.'

'If you have said all that you have to say, perhaps you will listen to me,' said his wife.

'I will listen to nothing till you have given me your promise.' 'Then I certainly shall not give it you.'

'Dear Emily, pray, pray do what he tells you,' said Nora.

'She has yet to learn that it is her duty to do as I tell her,' said Trevelyan. 'And because she is obstinate, and will not learn from those who know better than herself what a woman may do, and what she may not, she will ruin herself, and destroy my happiness.'

'I know that you have destroyed my happiness by your unreasonable jealousy,' said the wife. 'Have you considered what I must feel in having such words addressed to me by my husband? If I am fit to be told that I must promise not to see any man living, I cannot be fit to be any man's wife.' Then she burst out into an hysterical fit of tears, and in this condition she got out of the carriage, entered her house, and hurried up to her own room.

'Indeed, she has not been to blame,' said Nora to Trevelyan on the staircase.

'Why has there been a secret kept from me between her and this man; and that too, after I had cautioned her against being intimate with him? I am sorry that she should suffer; but it is better that she should suffer a little now, than that we should both suffer much by-and-by.'

Nora endeavoured to explain to him the truth about the committee, and Colonel Osborne's promised influence, and the reason why there was to be a secret. But she was too much in a hurry to get to her sister to make the matter plain, and he was too much angered to listen to her. He shook his head when she spoke of Colonel Osborne's dislike to have his name mentioned in connection with the matter. 'All the world knows it,' he said with scornful laughter.

It was in vain that Nora tried to explain to him that though all the world might know it, Emily herself had only heard of the proposition as a thing quite unsettled, as to which nothing at present should be spoken openly. It was in vain to endeavour to make peace on that night. Nora hurried up to her sister, and found that the hysterical tears had again given place to anger. She would not see her husband, unless he would beg her pardon; and he would not see her unless she would give the promise he demanded. And the husband and wife did not see each other again on that night.

CHAPTER IV. HUGH STANBURY

It has been already stated that Nora Rowley was not quite so well disposed as perhaps she ought to have been to fall in love with the Honourable Charles Glascock, there having come upon her the habit of comparing him with another gentleman whenever this duty of falling in love with Mr Glascock was exacted from her. That other gentleman was one with whom she knew that it was quite out of the question that she should fall in love, because he had not a shilling in the world; and the other gentleman was equally aware that it was not open to him to fall in love with Nora Rowley for the same reason. In regard to such matters Nora Rowley had been properly brought up, having been made to understand by the best and most cautious of mothers, that in that matter of falling in love it was absolutely necessary that bread and cheese should be considered. 'Romance is a very pretty thing,' Lady Rowley had been wont to say to her daughters, 'and I don't think life would be worth having without a little of it. I should be very sorry to think that either of my girls would marry a man only because he had money. But you can't even be romantic without something to eat and drink.' Nora thoroughly understood all this, and being well aware that her fortune in the world, if it ever was to be made at all, could only be made by marriage, had laid down for herself certain hard lines lines intended to be as fast as they were hard. Let what might come to her in the way of likings and dislikings, let the temptation to her be ever so strong, she would never allow her heart to rest on a man who, if he should ask her to be his wife, would not have the means of supporting her. There were many, she knew, who would condemn such a resolution as cold, selfish, and heartless. She heard people saying so daily. She read in books that it ought to be so regarded. But she declared to herself that she would respect the judgment neither of the people nor of the books. To be poor alone, to have to live without a husband, to look forward to a life in which there would be nothing of a career, almost nothing to do, to await the vacuity of an existence in which she would be useful to no one, was a destiny which she could teach herself to endure, because it might probably be forced upon her by necessity. Were her father to die there would hardly be bread for that female flock to eat. As it was, she was eating the bread of a man in whose house she was no more than a visitor. The lot of a woman; as she often told herself, was wretched, unfortunate, almost degrading. For a woman such as herself there was no path open to her energy, other than that of getting a husband. Nora Rowley thought of all this till she was almost sick of the prospect of her life—especially sick of it when she was told with much authority by the Lady Milboroughs of her acquaintance, that it was her bounden duty to fall in love with Mr Glascock. As to falling in love with Mr Glascock, she had not as yet quite made up her mind. There was so much to be said on that side of the question, if such falling in love could only be made possible. But she had quite made up her mind that she would never fall in love with a poor man. In spite, however, of all that, she felt herself compelled to make comparisons between Mr Glascock and one Mr Hugh Stanbury, a gentleman who had not a shilling.

Mr Hugh Stanbury had been at college the most intimate friend of Louis Trevelyan, and at Oxford had been, in spite of Trevelyan's successes, a bigger man than his friend. Stanbury had not taken so high a degree as Trevelyan, indeed had not gone out in honours at all. He had done little for the credit of his college, and had never put himself in the way of wrapping himself up for life in the scanty lambswool of a fellowship. But he had won for himself reputation as a clever speaker, as a man who had learned much that college tutors do not profess to teach, as a hard-headed, ready-witted fellow, who, having the world as an oyster before him, which it was necessary that he should open, would certainly find either a knife or a sword with which to open it.

Immediately on leaving college he had come to town, and had entered himself at Lincoln's Inn. Now, at the time of our story, he was a barrister of four years' standing, but had never yet made a guinea. He had never made a guinea by his work as a barrister, and was beginning to doubt of himself whether he ever would do so. Not, as he knew well, that guineas are generally made with ease by barristers of four years' standing, but because, as he said to his friends, he did not see his way to the knack of it. He did not know an attorney in the world, and could not conceive how any attorney should ever be induced to apply to him for legal aid. He had done his work of learning his trade about as well as other young men, but had had no means of distinguishing himself within his reach. He went the Western Circuit because his aunt, old Miss Stanbury, lived at Exeter, but, as he declared of himself, had he had another aunt living at York, he would have had nothing whatsoever to guide him in his choice. He sat idle in the courts, and hated himself for so sitting. So it had been with him for two years without any consolation or additional burden from other employment than that of his profession. After that, by some chance, he had become acquainted with the editor of the Daily Record, and by degrees had taken to the writing of articles. He had been told by all his friends, and especially by Trevelyan, that if he did this, he might as well sell his gown and wig. He declared, in reply, that he had no objection to sell his gown and wig. He did not see how he should ever make more money out of them than he would do by such sale. But for the articles which he wrote, he received instant payment, a process which he found to be most consolatory, most comfortable, and, as he said to Trevelyan, as warm to him as a blanket in winter.

Trevelyan, who was a year younger than Stanbury, had taken upon himself to be very angry. He professed that he did not think much of the trade of a journalist, and told Stanbury that he was sinking from the highest to almost the lowest business by which an educated man and a gentleman could earn his bread. Stanbury had simply replied that he saw some bread on the one side, but none on the other; and that bread from some side was indispensable to him. Then there had come to be that famous war between Great Britain and the republic of Patagonia, and Hugh Stanbury had been sent out as a special correspondent by the editor and proprietor of the *Daily Record*. His letters had been much read, and had called up a great deal of newspaper pugnacity. He had made important statements which had been flatly denied, and found to be utterly false; which again had been warmly reasserted and proved to be most remarkably true to the letter. In this way the correspondence, and he as its author, became so much talked about that, on his return to England, he did actually sell his gown and, wig and declare to his friends and to Trevelyan among the number that he intended to look to journalism for his future career.

He had been often at the house in Curzon Street in the earliest happy days of his friend's marriage, and had thus become acquainted—intimately acquainted—with Nora Rowley. And now again, since his return from Patagonia, that acquaintance had been renewed. Quite lately, since the actual sale of that wig and gown had been effected, he had not been there so frequently as before, because Trevelyan had expressed his indignation almost too openly.

'That such a man as you should be so faint-hearted,' Trevelyan had said, 'is a thing that I can not understand.'

'Is a man faint-hearted when he finds it improbable that he shall be able to leap his horse over a house.'

'What you had to do, had been done by hundreds before you.'

'What I had to do has never yet been done by any man,' replied Stanbury. 'I had to live upon nothing till the lucky hour should strike.'

'I think you have been cowardly,' said Trevelyan.

Even this had made no quarrel between the two men; but Stanbury had expressed himself annoyed by his friend's language, and partly on that account, and partly perhaps on another, had stayed away from Curzon Street. As Nora Rowley had made comparisons about him, so had he made comparisons about her. He had owned to himself that had it been possible that he should marry, he would willingly entrust his happiness to Miss Rowley. And he had thought once or twice that

Trevelyan had wished that such an arrangement might be made at some future day. Trevelyan had always been much more sanguine in expecting success for his friend at the Bar than Stanbury had been for himself. It might well be that such a man as Trevelyan might think that a clever rising barrister would be an excellent husband for his sister-in-law, but that a man who earned a precarious living as a writer for a penny paper would be by no means so desirable a connection. Stanbury, as he thought of this, declared to himself that he would not care two straws for Trevelyan in the matter, if he could see his way without other impediments. But the other impediments were there in such strength and numbers as to make him feel that it could not have been intended by Fate that he should take to himself a wife. Although those letters of his to the Daily Record had been so pre-eminently successful, he had never yet been able to earn by writing above twenty-five or thirty pounds a month. If that might be continued to him he could live upon it himself; but, even with his moderate views, it would not suffice for himself and family.

He had told Trevelyan that while living as an expectant barrister he had no means of subsistence. In this, as Trevelyan knew, he was not strictly correct. There was an allowance of 100 pounds a year coming to him from the aunt whose residence at Exeter had induced him to devote himself to the Western Circuit. His father had been a clergyman with a small living in Devonshire, and had now been dead some fifteen years. His mother and two sisters were still living in a small cottage in his late father's parish, on the interest of the money arising from a life insurance. Some pittance from sixty to seventy pounds a year was all they had among them. But there was a rich aunt, Miss Stanbury, to whom had come considerable wealth in a manner most romantic—the little tale shall be told before this larger tale is completed—and this aunt had undertaken to educate and place out in the world her nephew Hugh. So Hugh had been sent to Harrow, and then to Oxford, where he had much displeased his aunt by not accomplishing great things, and then had been set down to make his fortune as a barrister in London, with an allowance of 100 pounds a year, his aunt having paid, moreover, certain fees for entrance, tuition, and the like. The very hour in which Miss Stanbury learned that her nephew was writing for a penny newspaper she sent off a dispatch to tell him that he must give up her or the penny paper. He replied by saying that he felt himself called upon to earn his bread in the only line from which, as it seemed to him, bread would be forthcoming. By return of post he got another letter to say that he might draw for the quarter then becoming due, but that that would be the last. And it was the last.

Stanbury made an ineffectual effort to induce his aunt to make over the allowance or at least a part of it to his mother and sisters, but the old lady paid no attention whatever to the request. She never had given, and at that moment did not intend to give, a shilling to the widow and daughters of her brother. Nor did she intend, or had she ever intended, to leave a shilling of her money to Hugh Stanbury, as she had very often told him. The money was, at her death, to go back to the people from whom it had come to her.

When Nora Rowley made those comparisons between Mr Hugh Stanbury and Mr Charles Glascock, they were always wound up very much in favour of the briefless barrister. It was not that he was the handsomer man, for he was by no means handsome, nor was he the bigger man, for Mr Glascock was six feet tall; nor was he better dressed, for Stanbury was untidy rather than otherwise in his outward person. Nor had he any air of fashion or special grace to recommend him, for he was undoubtedly an awkward-mannered man. But there was a glance of sunshine in his eye, and a sweetness in the curl of his mouth when he smiled, which made Nora feel that it would have been all up with her had she not made so very strong a law for her own guidance. Stanbury was a man about five feet ten, with shoulders more than broad in proportion, stout limbed, rather awkward of his gait, with large feet and hands, with soft wavy light hair, with light grey eyes, with a broad, but by no means ugly, nose. His mouth and lips were large, and he rarely showed his teeth. He wore no other beard than whiskers, which he was apt to cut away through heaviness of his hand in shaving, till Nora longed to bid him be more careful. 'He doesn't care what sort of a guy he makes of himself, she once said to her sister, almost angrily. 'He is a plain man, and he knows it,' Emily had replied. Mr Trevelyan was doubtless a handsome man, and it was almost on Nora's tongue to say something ill-natured on the subject. Hugh Stanbury was reputed to be somewhat hot in spirit and manner. He would be very sage in argument, pounding down his ideas on politics, religion, or social life with his fist as well as his voice. He was quick, perhaps, at making antipathies, and quick, too, in making friendships; impressionable, demonstrative, eager, rapid in his movements sometimes to the great detriment of his shins and knuckles; and he possessed the sweetest temper that was ever given to a man for the blessing of a woman. This was the man between whom and Mr Glascock Nora Rowley found it to be impossible not to make comparisons.

On the very day after Lady Milborough's dinner party Stanbury overtook Trevelyan in the street, and asked his friend where he was going eastward. Trevelyan was on his way to call upon his lawyer, and said so. But he did not say why he was going to his lawyer. He had sent to his wife by Nora that morning to know whether she would make to him the promise he required. The only answer which Nora could draw from her sister was a counter question, demanding whether he would ask her pardon for the injury he had done her. Nora had been most eager, most anxious, most conciliatory as a messenger; but no good had come of these messages, and Trevelyan had gone forth to tell all his trouble to his family lawyer. Old Mr Bideawhile had been his father's ancient and esteemed friend, and he could tell things to Mr Bideawhile which he could not bring himself to tell to any other living man; and he could generally condescend to accept Mr Bideawhile's advice, knowing that his father before him had been guided by the same.

'But you are out of your way for Lincoln's Inn Fields,' said Stanbury.

'I have to call at Twining's. And where are you going?'

'I have been three times round St. James's Park to collect my thoughts,' said Stanbury, 'and now I'm on my way to the Daily R., 250, Fleet Street. It is my custom of an afternoon. I am prepared to instruct the British public of tomorrow on any subject, as per order, from the downfall of a European compact to the price of a London mutton chop.'

'I suppose there is nothing more to be said about it,' said Trevelyan, after a pause.

'Not another word. How should there be? Aunt Jemima has already drawn tight the purse strings, and it would soon be the casual ward in earnest if it were not for the *Daily R*. God bless the *Daily R*. Only think what a thing it is to have all subjects open to one, from the destinies of France to the profit proper to a butcher.'

'If you like it!'

'I do like it. It may not be altogether honest. I don't know what is. But it's a deal honester than defending thieves and bamboozling juries. How is your wife?'

'She's pretty well, thank you.'

Stanbury knew at once from the tone of his friend's voice that there was something wrong.

'And Louis the less?' he said, asking after Trevelyan's child. 'He's all right.'

'And Miss Rowley? When one begins one's inquiries one is bound to go through the whole family.'

'Miss Rowley is pretty well,' said Trevelyan.

Previously to this, Trevelyan when speaking of his sister-in-law to Stanbury, had always called her Nora, and had been wont to speak of her as though she were almost as much the friend of one of them as of the other. The change of tone on this occasion was in truth occasioned by the sadness of the man's thoughts in reference to his wife, but Stanbury attributed it to another cause. 'He need not be afraid of me,' he said to himself, 'and at least he should not show me that he is.' Then they parted, Trevelyan going into Twining's bank, and Stanbury passing on towards the office of the Daily R.

Stanbury had in truth been altogether mistaken as to the state of his friend's mind on that morning. Trevelyan, although he had, according to his custom, put in a word in condemnation of the newspaper line of life, was at the moment thinking whether he would not tell all his trouble to Hugh Stanbury. He knew that he should not find anywhere, not even in Mr Bideawhile, a more friendly or more trustworthy listener. When Nora Rowley's name had been mentioned, he had not thought of her. He had simply repeated the name with the usual answer. He was at the moment cautioning himself against a confidence which after all might not be necessary, and which on this occasion was not made. When one is in trouble it is a great ease to tell one's trouble to a friend; but then one should always wash one's dirty linen at home. The latter consideration prevailed, and Trevelyan allowed his friend to go on without burdening him with the story of that domestic quarrel. Nor did he on that occasion tell it to Mr Bideawhile; for Mr Bideawhile was not found at his chambers.

CHAPTER V. SHEWING HOW THE QUARREL PROGRESSED

Trevelyan got back to his own house at about three, and on going into the library, found on his table a letter to him addressed in his wife's handwriting. He opened it quickly, hoping to find that promise which he had demanded, and resolving that if it were made he would at once become affectionate, yielding, and gentle to his wife. But there was not a word written by his wife within the envelope. It contained simply another letter, already opened, addressed to her. This letter had been brought up to her during her husband's absence from the house, and was as follows:

Acrobats,
Thursday.

DEAR EMILY,

I have just come from the Colonial Office. It is all settled, and Sir M. has been sent for. Of course, you will tell T. now. Yours,   F.O.

The letter was, of course, from Colonel Osborne, and Mrs Trevelyan, when she received it, had had great doubts whether she would enclose it to her husband opened or unopened. She had hitherto refused to make the promise which her husband exacted, but nevertheless, she was minded to obey him; Had he included in his demand any requirement that she should receive no letter from Colonel Osborne, she would not have opened this one. But nothing had been said about letters, and she would not shew herself to be afraid. So she read the note, and then sent it down to be put on Mr Trevelyan's table in an envelope addressed to him.

'If he is not altogether blinded, it will show him how cruelly he has wronged me,' said she to her sister. She was sitting at the time with her boy in her lap, telling herself that the child's features were in all respects the very same as his father's, and that, come what come might, the child should always be taught by her to love and respect his father. And then there came a horrible thought. What if the child should be taken away from her? If this quarrel, out of which she saw no present mode of escape, were to lead to a separation between her and her husband, would not the law, and the judges, and the courts, and all the Lady Milboroughs of their joint acquaintance into the bargain, say that the child should go with his father? The judges, and the courts, and the Lady Milboroughs would, of course, say that she was the sinner. And what could she do without her boy? Would not any humility, any grovelling in the dust be better for her than that? 'It is a very poor thing to be a woman,' she said to her sister.

'It is perhaps better than being a dog,' said Nora; 'but, of course, we can't compare ourselves to men.'

'It would be better to be a dog. One wouldn't be made to suffer so much. When a puppy is taken away from its mother, she is bad enough for a few days, but she gets over it in a week.' There was a pause then for a few moments. Nora knew well which way ran the current of her sister's thoughts, and had nothing at the present moment which she could say on that subject.

'It is very hard for a woman to know what to do,' continued Emily, 'but if she is to marry, I think she had better marry a fool. After all, a fool generally knows that he is a fool, and will trust some one, though he may not trust his wife.'

'I will never wittingly marry a fool,' said Nora.

'You will marry Mr Glascock, of course. I don't say that he is a fool; but I do not think he has that kind of strength which shows itself in perversity.'

'If he asked me, I should not have him, and he will never ask me.'

'He will ask you, and, of course, you'll take him. Why not? You can't be otherwise than a woman. And you must marry. And this man is a gentleman, and will be a peer. There is nothing on earth against him, except that he does not set the Thames on fire. Louis intends to set the Thames on fire some day, and see what comes of it.'

'All the same, I shall not marry Mr Glascock. A woman can die, at any rate,' said Nora.

'No, she can't. A woman must be decent; and to die of want is very indecent. She can't die, and she mustn't be in want, and she oughtn't to be a burden. I suppose it was thought necessary that every man should have two to choose from; and therefore there are so many more of us than the world wants. I wonder whether you'd mind taking that downstairs to his table? I don't like to send it by the servant; and I don't want to go myself.'

Then Nora had taken the letter down, and left it where Louis Trevelyan would be sure to find it.

He did find it, and was sorely disappointed when he perceived that it contained no word from his wife to himself. He opened Colonel Osborne's note, and read it, and became, as he did so, almost more angry than before. Who was this man that he should dare to address another man's wife as 'Dear Emily'? At the moment

Trevelyan remembered well enough that he had heard the man so call his wife, that it had been done openly in his presence, and had not given him a thought. But Lady Rowley and Sir Marmaduke had then been present also; and that man on that occasion had been the old friend of the old father, and not the would-be young friend of the young daughter. Trevelyan could hardly reason about it, but felt that whereas the one was not improper, the other was grossly impertinent and even wicked. And then, again, his wife, his Emily, was to show to him, to her husband, or was not to show to him, the letter which she received from this man, the letter in which she was addressed as 'Dear Emily,' according to this man's judgment and wish, and not according to his judgment and wish—not according to the judgment and wish of him who was her husband, her lord, and her master! 'Of course, you will tell T. now.' This was intolerable to him. It made him feel that he was to be regarded as second, and this man to be regarded as first. And then he began to recapitulate all the good things he had done for his wife, and all the causes which he had given her for gratitude. Had he not taken her to his bosom, and bestowed upon her the half of all that he had, simply for herself, asking for nothing more than her love? He had possessed money, position, a name all that makes life worth having. He had found her in a remote corner of the world, with no fortune, with no advantages of family or social standing, so circumstanced that any friend would have warned him against such a marriage; but he had given her his heart, and his hand, and his house, and had asked for nothing in return but that he should be all in all to her, that he should be her one god upon earth. And he had done more even than this. 'Bring your sister,' he had said. 'The house shall be big enough for her also, and she shall be my sister as well as yours.' Who had ever done more for a woman, or shown a more absolute confidence? And now what was the return he received? She was not contented with her one god upon earth, but must make to herself other gods—another god, and that too out of a lump of the basest clay to be found around her. He thought that he could remember to have heard it said in early days, long before he himself had had an idea of marrying, that no man should look for a wife from among the tropics, that women educated amidst the languors of those sunny climes rarely came to possess those high ideas of conjugal duty and feminine truth which a man should regard as the first requisites of a good wife. As he thought of all this, he almost regretted that he had ever visited the Mandarins, or ever heard the name of Sir Marmaduke Rowley.

He should have nourished no such thoughts in his heart. He had, indeed, been generous to his wife and to his wife's family; but we may almost say that the man who is really generous in such matters is unconscious of his own generosity. The giver who gives the most, gives, and does not know that he gives. And had not she given too? In that matter of giving between a man and his wife, if each gives all, the two are equal, let the things given be what they may! King Cophetua did nothing for his beggar maid, unless she were to him, after he had married her, as royal a queen as though he had taken her from the oldest stock of reigning families then extant. Trevelyan knew all this himself, had said so to himself a score of times, though not probably in spoken words or formed sentences. But, that all was equal between himself and the wife of his bosom, had been a thing ascertained by him as a certainty. There was no debt of gratitude from her to him which he did not acknowledge to exist also as from him to her. But yet, in his anger, he could not keep himself from thinking of the gifts he had showered upon her. And he had been, was, would ever be, if she would only allow it, so true to her! He had selected no other friend to take her place in his councils! There was no 'dear Mary' or 'dear Augusta' with whom he had secrets to be kept from his wife. When there arose with him any question of interest such as was this of the return of Sir Marmaduke to her, he would show it in all its bearings to his wife. He had his secrets too, but his secrets had all been made secrets for her also. There was not a woman in the world in whose company he took special delight in her absence.

And if there had been, how much less would have been her ground of complaint? Let a man have any such friendships, what friendships he may, he does not disgrace his wife. He felt himself to be so true of heart that he desired no such friendships; but for a man indulging in such friendships there might be excuse. Even though a man be false, a woman is not shamed and brought unto the dust before all the world. But the slightest rumour on a woman's name is a load of infamy on her husband's shoulders. It was not enough for Cæsar that his wife should be true; it was necessary to Cæsar that she should not even be suspected. Trevelyan told himself that he suspected his wife of no sin. God forbid that it should ever come to that, both for his sake and for hers; and, above all, for the sake of that boy who was so dear to them both! But there would be the vile whispers, and dirty slanders would be dropped from envious tongues into envious ears, and minds prone to evil would think evil of him and of his. Had not Lady Milborough already cautioned him? Oh, that he should have lived to have been cautioned about his wife, that he should be told that eyes outside had looked into the sacred shrine of his heart and seen that things there were fatally amiss! And yet Lady Milborough was quite right. Had he not in his hand at this moment a document that proved her to be right? 'Dear Emily'! He took this note and crushed it in his fist and then pulled it into fragments.

But what should he do? There was, first of all considerations, the duty which he owed to his wife, and the love which he bore her. That she was ignorant and innocent he was sure; but then she was so contumacious that he hardly knew how to take a step in the direction of guarding her from the effects of her ignorance, and maintaining for her the advantages of her innocence. He was her master, and she must know that he was her master. But how was he to proceed when she refused to obey the plainest and most necessary command which he laid upon her? Let a man be ever so much his wife's master, he cannot maintain his masterdom by any power which the law places in his hands. He had asked his wife for a promise of obedience, and she would not give it to him! What was he to do next? He could, no doubt, at least he thought so, keep the man from her presence. He could order the servant not to admit the man, and the servant would, doubtless, obey him. But to what a condition would he then have been brought! Would not the world then be over for him over for him as the husband of a wife whom he could not love unless he respected her? Better that there should be no such world, than call in the aid of a servant to guard the conduct of his wife!

As he thought of it all it seemed to him that if she would not obey him, and give him this promise, they must be separated. He would not live with her, he would not give her the privileges of his wife, if she refused to render to him the obedience which was his privilege. The more he thought of it, the more convinced he was that he ought not to yield to her. Let her once yield to him, and then his tenderness should begin, and there should be no limit to it. But he would not see her till she had yielded. He would not see her; and if he should find that she did see Colonel Osborne, then he would tell her that she could no longer dwell under the same roof with him.

His resolution on these points was very strong, and yet there came over him a feeling that it was his duty to be gentle. There was a feeling also that that privilege of receiving obedience, which was so indubitably his own, could only be maintained by certain wise practices on his part in which gentleness must predominate. Wives are bound to obey their husbands, but obedience cannot be exacted from wives, as it may from servants, by aid of law and with penalties, or as from a horse, by punishments, and manger curtailments. A man should be master in his own house, but he should make his mastery palatable, equitable, smooth, soft to the touch, a thing almost unfelt. How was he to do all this now, when he had already given an order to which obedience had been refused unless under certain stipulations an agreement with which would be degradation to him? He had pointed out to his wife her duty, and she had said she would do her duty as pointed out, on condition that he would beg her pardon for having pointed it out! This he could not and would not do. Let the heavens fall, and the falling of the heavens in this case was a separation between him and his wife, but he would not consent to such injustice as that!

But what was he to do at this moment especially with reference to that note which he had destroyed. At last he resolved to write to his wife, and he consequently did write and send to her the following letter:

May 4.

DEAREST EMILY,

If Colonel Osborne should write to you again, it will be better that you should not open his letter. As you know his handwriting you will have no difficulty in so arranging. Should any further letter come from Colonel Osborne addressed to you, you had better put it under cover to me, and take no notice of it yourself.

I shall dine at the club today. We were to have gone to Mrs Peacock's in the evening. You had better write a line to say that we shall not be there. I am very sorry that Nora should lose her evening. Pray think very carefully over what I have asked of you. My request to you is, that you shall give me a promise that you will not willingly see Colonel Osborne again. Of course you will understand that this is not supposed to extend to accidental meetings, as to which, should they occur, and they would be sure to occur, you would find that they would be wholly unnoticed by me.

But I must request that you will comply with my wish in this matter. If you will send for me I will go to you instantly, and after one word from you to the desired effect, you will find that there will be no recurrence by me to a subject so hateful. As I have done, and am doing what I think to be right, I cannot stultify myself by saying that I think I have been wrong.

Yours always, dearest Emily,
With the most thorough love,   LOUIS TREVELYAN.

This letter he himself put on his wife's dressing-room table, and then he went out to his club.

CHAPTER VI. SHEWING HOW RECONCILIATION WAS MADE

'Look at that,' said Mrs Trevelyan, when her sister came into her room about an hour before dinnertime. Nora read the letter, and then asked her sister what she meant to do. 'I have written to Mrs Peacock. I don't know what else I can do. It is very hard upon you that you should have been kept at home. But I don't suppose Mr Glascock would have been at Mrs Peacock's.'

'And what else will you do, Emily?'

'Nothing, simply live deserted and forlorn till he shall choose to find his wits again. There is nothing else that a woman can do. If he chooses to dine at his club every day I can't help it. We must put off all the engagements, and that will be hard upon you.'

'Don't talk about me. It is too terrible to think that there should be such a quarrel.'

'What can I do? Have I been wrong?'

'Simply do what he tells you, whether it is wrong or right. If it's right, it ought to be done, and if it's wrong, it will not be your fault.'

'That's very easily said, and it sounds logical; but you must know it's unreasonable.'

'I don't care about reason. He is your husband, and if he wishes it, you should do it. And what will be the harm? You don't mean to see Colonel Osborne any more. You have already said that he's not to be admitted.'

'I have said that nobody is to be admitted. Louis has driven me to that. How can I look the servant in the face and tell him that any special gentleman is not to be admitted to see me? Oh dear! oh dear! have I done anything to deserve it? Was ever so monstrous an accusation made against any woman! If it were not for my boy, I would defy him to do his worst.'

On the day following Nora again became a messenger between the husband and wife, and before dinner-time a reconciliation had been effected. Of course the wife gave way at last; and of course she gave way so cunningly that the husband received none of the gratification which he had expected in her surrender. 'Tell him to come,' Nora had urged. 'Of course he can come if he pleases,' Emily had replied. Then Nora had told Louis to come, and Louis had demanded whether, if he did so, the promise which he exacted would be given. It is to be feared that Nora perverted the truth a little; but if ever such perversion may be forgiven, forgiveness was due to her. If they could only be brought together, she was sure that there would be a reconciliation. They were brought together, and there was a reconciliation.

'Dearest Emily, I am so glad to come to you,' said the husband, walking up to his wife in their bed-room, and taking her in his arms.

'I have been very unhappy, Louis, for the last two days,' said she, very gravely returning his kiss, but returning it somewhat coldly.

'We have both been unhappy, I am sure,' said he. Then he paused that the promise might be made to him. He had certainly understood that it was to be made without reserve as an act on her part which she had fully consented to perform. But she stood silent, with one hand on the dressing table, looking away from him, very beautiful, and dignified too, in her manner; but not, as far as he could judge, either repentant or submissive. 'Nora said that you would make me the promise which I ask from you.'

'I cannot think, Louis, how you can want such a promise from me.'

'I think it right to ask it; I do indeed.'

'Can you imagine that I shall ever willingly see this gentleman again after what has occurred? It will be for you to tell the servant. I do not know how I can do that. But, as a matter of course, I will encourage no person to come to your house of whom you disapprove. It would be exactly the same of any man or of any woman.' 'That is all that I ask.'

'I am surprised that you should have thought it necessary to make any formal request in the matter. Your word was quite sufficient. That you should find cause of complaint in Colonel Osborne's coming here is of course a different thing.'

Quite a different thing,' said he.

I cannot pretend to understand either your motives or your fears. I do not understand them. My own self-respect prevents me from supposing it to be possible that you have attributed an evil thought to me.'

Indeed, indeed, I never have,' said the husband.

'That I can assure you I regard as a matter of course,' said the wife.

'But you know, Emily, the way in which the world talks.'

'The world! And do you regard the world, Louis?'

'Lady Milborough, I believe, spoke to yourself.'

'Lady Milborough! No, she did not speak to me. She began to do so, but I was careful to silence her at once. From you, Louis, I am bound to hear whatever you may choose to say to me; but I will not hear from any other lips a single word that may be injurious to your honour.' This she said very quietly, with much dignity, and he felt that he had better not answer her. She had given him the promise which he had demanded, and he began to fear that if he pushed the matter further she might go back even from that amount of submission. So he kissed her again, and had the boy brought into the room, and by the time that he went to dress for dinner he was able, at any rate, to seem to be well pleased.

'Richard,' he said to the servant, as soon as he was downstairs, 'when Colonel Osborne calls again, say' that your mistress is not at home.' He gave the order in the most indifferent tone of voice which he could assume; but as he gave it he felt thoroughly ashamed of it. Richard, who, with the other servants, had of course known that there had been a quarrel between his master and mistress for the last two days, no doubt understood all about it.

While they were sitting at dinner on the next day, a Saturday, there came another note from Colonel Osborne. The servant brought it to his mistress, and she, when she had looked at it, put it down by her plate. Trevelyan knew immediately from whom the letter had come, and understood how impossible it was for his wife to give it up in the servant's presence. The letter lay there till the man was out of the room, and then she handed it to Nora. 'Will you give that to Louis?' she said. 'It comes from the man whom he supposes to be my lover.'

'Emily!' said he, jumping from his seat, 'how can you allow words so horrible and so untrue to fall from your mouth?' 'If it be not so, why am I to be placed in such a position as this? The servant knows, of course, from whom the letter comes, and sees that I have been forbidden to open it.' Then the man returned to the room, and the remainder of the dinner passed off almost in silence. It was their custom when they dined without company to leave the dining-room together, but on this evening Trevelyan remained for a few minutes that he might read Colonel Osborne's letter, He waited, standing on the rug with his face to the fire-place, till he was quite alone, and then he opened it. It ran as follows:

'Dear Emily,' Trevelyan, as he read this, cursed Colonel Osborne between his teeth.

House of Commons,
Saturday.

Dear Emily,

I called this afternoon, but you were out. I am afraid you will be disappointed by what I have to tell you, but you should rather be glad of it. They say at the C.O. that Sir Marmaduke would not receive their letter if sent now till the middle of

June, and that he could not be in London, let him do what he would, till the end of July. They hope to have the session over by that time, and therefore the committee is to be put off till next session. They mean to have Lord Bowles home from Canada, and they think that Bowles would like to be here in the winter. Sir Marmaduke will be summoned for February next, and will of course stretch his stay over the hot months. All this will, on the whole, be for the best. Lady Rowley could hardly have packed up her things and come away at a day's notice, whatever your father might have done. I'll call tomorrow at luncheon time.

Yours always,

F. O.

There was nothing objectionable in this letter excepting always the 'Dear Emily'; nothing which it was not imperative on Colonel Osborne to communicate to the person to whom it was addressed. Trevelyan must now go upstairs and tell the contents of the letter to his wife. But he felt that he had created for himself a terrible trouble. He must tell his wife what was in the letter, but the very telling of it would be a renewing of the soreness of his wound. And then what was to be done in reference to the threatened visit for the Sunday morning? Trevelyan knew very well that were his wife denied at that hour, Colonel Osborne would understand the whole matter. He had doubtless in his anger intended that Colonel Osborne should understand the whole matter; but he was calmer now than he had been then, and almost wished that the command given by him had not been so definite and imperious. He remained with his arm on the mantel-piece, thinking of it, for some ten minutes, and then went up into the drawing-room. 'Emily,' he said, walking up to the table at which she was sitting, 'you had better read that letter.'

'I would so much rather not,' she replied haughtily.

'Then Nora can read it. It concerns you both equally.'

Nora, with hesitating hand, took the letter and read it. 'They are not to come after all,' said she, 'till next February.'

'And why not?' asked Mrs Trevelyan.

'Something about the session. I don't quite understand.'

'Lord Bowles is to come from Canada,' said Louis, 'and they think he would prefer being here in the winter. I dare say he would.'

'But what has that to do with papa?'

'I suppose they must both be here together,' said Nora.

'I call that very hard indeed,' said Mrs Trevelyan.

'I can't agree with you there,' said her husband. 'His coming at all is so much of a favour that it is almost a job.'

'I don't see that it is a job at all,' said Mrs Trevelyan. 'Somebody is wanted, and nobody can know more of the service than papa does. But as the other man is a lord I suppose papa must give way. Does he say anything about mamma, Nora?'

'You had better read the letter yourself,' said Trevelyan, who was desirous that his wife should know of the threatened visit.

'No, Louis, I shall not do that. You must not blow hot and cold too. Till the other day I should have thought that Colonel Osborne's letters were as innocent as an old newspaper. As you have supposed them to be poisoned I will have nothing to do with them.'

This speech made him very angry. It seemed that his wife, who had yielded to him, was determined to take out the value of her submission in the most disagreeable words which she could utter. Nora now closed the letter and handed it back to her brother-in-law. He laid it down on the table beside him, and sat for a while with his eyes fixed upon his book. At last he spoke again. 'Colonel Osborne says that he will call tomorrow at luncheon time. You can admit him, if you please, and thank him for the trouble he has taken in this matter.'

'I shall not remain in the room if he be admitted,' said Mrs Trevelyan.

There was silence again for some minutes, and the cloud upon Trevelyan's brow became blacker than before. Then he rose from his chair and walked round to the sofa on which his wife was sitting. 'I presume,' said he, 'that your wishes and mine in this matter must be the same.'

'I cannot tell what your wishes are,' she replied. 'I never was more in the dark on any subject in my life. My wishes at present are confined to a desire to save you as far as may be possible from the shame which must be attached to your own suspicions.'

'I have never had any suspicions.'

'A husband without suspicions does not intercept his wife's letters. A husband without suspicions does not call in the aid of his servants to guard his wife. A husband without suspicions.'

'Emily,' exclaimed Nora Rowley, 'how can you say such things on purpose to provoke him?'

'Yes; on purpose to provoke me,' said Trevelyan.

'And have I not been provoked? Have I not been injured? You say now that you have not suspected me, and yet in what condition do I find myself? Because an old woman has chosen to talk scandal about me, I am placed in a position in my own house which is disgraceful to you and insupportable to myself. This man has been in the habit of coming here on Sundays, and will, of course, know that we are at home. You must manage it as you please. If you choose to receive him, I will go upstairs.'

'Why can't you let him come in and go away, just as usual?' said Nora.

'Because Louis has made me promise that I will never willingly be in his company again,' said Mrs Trevelyan. 'I would have given the world to avoid a promise so disgraceful to me; but it was exacted, and it shall be kept.' Having so spoken, she swept out of the room, and went upstairs to the nursery. Trevelyan sat for an hour with his book before him, reading or pretending to read, but his wife did not come downstairs. Then Nora went up to her, and he descended to his solitude below. So far he had hardly gained much by the enforced obedience of his wife.

On the next morning the three went to church together; as they were walking home Trevelyan's heart was filled with returning gentleness towards his wife. He could not bear to be at wrath with her after the church service which they had just heard together. But he was softer-hearted than was she, and knowing this, was almost afraid to say anything that would again bring forth from her expressions of scorn. As soon as they were alone within the house he took her by the hand and led her apart. 'Let all this be,' said he, 'as though it had never been.'

'That will hardly be possible, Louis,' she answered. 'I cannot forget that I have been cautioned.'

'But cannot you bring yourself to believe that I have meant it all for your good?'

'I have never doubted it, Louis never for a moment. But it has hurt me to find that you should think that such caution was needed for my good.'

It was almost on his tongue to beg her pardon, to acknowledge that he had made a mistake, and to implore her to forget that he had ever made an objection to Colonel Osborne's visit. He remembered at this moment the painful odiousness of that 'Dear Emily;' but he had to reconcile himself even to that, telling himself that, after all, Colonel Osborne was an old man, a man older even than his wife's father. If she would only have met him with gentleness, he would have withdrawn his command, and have acknowledged that he had been wrong. But she was hard, dignified, obedient, and resentful. 'It will, I think,' he said, 'be better for both of us that he should be asked in to lunch today.'

'You must judge of that,' said Emily. 'Perhaps, upon the whole, it will be best. I can only say that I will not be present. I will lunch upstairs with baby, and you can make what excuse for me you please.' This was all very bad, but it was in this way that things were allowed to arrange themselves. Richard was told that Colonel Osborne was coming to lunch, and when he came something was muttered to him about Mrs Trevelyan being not quite well. It was Nora who told the innocent fib, and though she did not tell it well, she did her very best. She felt that her brother-in-law was very wretched, and she was most anxious to relieve him. Colonel Osborne did not stay long, and then Nora went upstairs to her sister.

Louis Trevelyan felt that he had disgraced himself. He had meant to have been strong, and he had, as he knew, been very weak. He had meant to have acted in a high-minded, honest, manly manner; but circumstances had been so untoward with him, that on looking at his own conduct, it seemed to him to have been mean, and almost false and cowardly. As the order for the exclusion of this hated man from his house had been given, he should at any rate have stuck to the order. At the moment of his vacillation he had simply intended to make things easy for his wife; but she had taken advantage of his vacillation, and had now clearly conquered him. Perhaps he respected her more than he had done when he was resolving, three or four days since, that he would be the master in his own house; but it may be feared that the tenderness of his love for her had been impaired.

Late in the afternoon his wife and sister-in-law came down dressed for walking, and, finding Trevelyan in the library, they asked him to join them; it was a custom with them to walk in the park on a Sunday afternoon, and he at once assented, and went out with them. Emily, who had had her triumph, was very gracious. There should not be a word more said by her about Colonel Osborne. She would avoid that gentleman, never receiving him in Curzon Street, and having as little to say to him as possible elsewhere; but she would not throw his name in her husband's teeth, or make any reference to the injury which had so manifestly been done to her. Unless Louis should be indiscreet, it should be as though it had been forgotten. As they walked by Chesterfield House and Stanhope Street into the park, she began to discuss the sermon they had heard that morning, and when she found that that subject was not alluring, she spoke of a dinner to which they were to go at Mrs Fairfax's house. Louis Trevelyan was quite aware that he was being treated as a naughty boy, who was to be forgiven.

They went across Hyde Park into Kensington Gardens, and still the same thing was going on. Nora found it to be almost impossible to say a word. Trevelyan answered his wife's questions, but was otherwise silent. Emily worked very hard at her mission of forgiveness, and hardly ceased in her efforts at conciliatory conversation. Women can work so much harder in this way than men find it possible to do! She never flagged, but continued to be fluent, conciliatory, and intolerably wearisome. On a sudden they came across two men together, who, as they all knew, were barely acquainted with each other. These were Colonel Osborne and Hugh Stanbury. 'I am glad to find you are able to be out,' said the Colonel.

'Thanks; yes. I think my seclusion just now was almost as much due to baby as to anything else. Mr Stanbury, how is it we never see you now?'

'It is the *D.R.*, Mrs Trevelyan nothing else. The *D.R.* is a most grateful mistress, but somewhat exacting. I am allowed a couple of hours on Sundays, but otherwise my time is wholly passed in Fleet Street.'

'How very unpleasant.'

'Well; yes. The unpleasantness of this world consists chiefly in the fact that when a man wants wages, he must earn them. The Christian philosophers have a theory about it. Don't they call it the primeval fall, original sin, and that kind of thing?'

'Mr Stanbury, I won't have irreligion. I hope that doesn't come from writing for the newspapers.'

'Certainly not with me, Mrs Trevelyan. I have never been put on to take that branch yet. Scruby does that with us, and does it excellently. It was he who touched up the Ritualists, and then the Commission, and then the Low Church bishops, till he didn't leave one of them a leg to stand upon.'

'What is it, then, that the *Daily Record* upholds?'

'It upholds the *Daily Record*. Believe in that and you will surely be saved.' Then he turned to Miss Rowley, and they two were soon walking on together, each manifestly interested in what the other was saying, though there was no word of tenderness spoken between them.

Colonel Osborne was now between Mr and Mrs Trevelyan. She would have avoided the position had it been possible for her to do so. While they were falling into their present places, she had made a little mute appeal to her husband to take her away from the spot, to give her his arm and return with her, to save her in some way from remaining in company with the man to whose company for her he had objected; but he took no such step. It had seemed to him that he could take no such step without showing his hostility to Colonel Osborne.

They walked on along the broad path together, and the Colonel was between them.

'I hope you think it satisfactory about Sir Rowley,' he said.

'Beggars must not be choosers, you know, Colonel Osborne. I felt a little disappointed when I found that we were not to see them till February next.'

'They will stay longer then, you know, than they could now.'

'I have no doubt when the time comes we shall all believe it to be better.'

'I suppose you think, Emily, that a little pudding today is better than much tomorrow.'

Colonel Osborne certainly had a caressing, would-be affectionate mode of talking to women, which, unless it were reciprocated and enjoyed, was likely to make itself disagreeable. No possible words could have been more innocent than those he had now spoken; but he had turned his face down close to her face, and had almost whispered them. And then, too, he had again called her by her Christian name. Trevelyan had not heard the words. He had walked on, making the distance between him and the other man greater than was necessary, anxious to show to his wife that he had no jealousy at such a meeting as this. But his wife was determined that she would put an end to this state of things, let the cost be what it might. She did not say a word to Colonel Osborne, but addressed herself at once to her husband. 'Louis,' she said, 'will you give me your arm? We will go back, if you please.' Then she took her husband's arm and turned herself and him abruptly away from their companion.

The thing was done in such a manner that it was impossible that Colonel Osborne should not perceive that he had been left in anger. When Trevelyan and his wife had gone back a few yards, he was obliged to return for Nora. He did so, and then rejoined his wife.

'It was quite unnecessary, Emily,' he said, 'that you should behave like that.'

'Your suspicions,' she said, 'have made it almost impossible for me to behave with propriety.'

'You have told him everything now,' said Trevelyan.

'And it was requisite that he should be told,' said his wife. Then they walked home without interchanging another word. When they reached their house, Emily at once went up to her own room, and Trevelyan to his. They parted as though they had no common interest which was worthy of a moment's conversation. And she by her step, and gait, and every movement of her body showed to him that she was not his wife now in any sense that could bring to him a feeling of domestic happiness. Her compliance with his command was of no use to him unless she could be brought to comply in spirit. Unless she would be soft to him he could not be happy. He walked about his room uneasily for half-an-hour, trying to shake off his sorrow, and then he went up to her room. 'Emily,' he said, 'for God's sake let all this pass away.'

'What is to pass away?'

'This feeling of rancour between you and me. What is the world to us unless we can love one another? At any rate it will be nothing to me.'

'Do you doubt my love?' said she.

'No; certainly not.'

'Nor I yours. Without love, Louis, you and I can not be happy. But love alone will not make us so. There must be trust, and there must also be forbearance. My feeling of annoyance will pass away in time; and till it does, I will shew it as little as may be possible.'

He felt that he had nothing more to say, and then he left her; but he had gained nothing by the interview. She was still hard and cold, and still assumed a tone which seemed to imply that she had manifestly been the injured person.

Colonel Osborne, when he was left alone, stood for a few moments on the spot, and then with a whistle, a shake of the head, and a little low chuckle of laughter, rejoined the crowd.

CHAPTER VII. MISS JEMIMA STANBURY, OF EXETER

Miss Jemima Stanbury, the aunt of our friend Hugh, was a maiden lady, very much respected, indeed, in the city of Exeter. It is to be hoped that no readers of these pages will be so un-English as to be unable to appreciate the difference between county society and town society, the society, that is, of a provincial town, or so ignorant as not to know also that there may be persons so privileged, that although they live distinctly within a provincial town, there is accorded to them, as though by brevet rank, all the merit of living in the county. In reference to persons so privileged, it is considered that they have been made free from the contamination of contiguous bricks and mortar by certain inner gifts, probably of birth, occasionally of profession, possibly of merit. It is very rarely, indeed, that money alone will bestow this acknowledged rank; and in Exeter, which by the stringency and excellence of its well-defined rules on such matters, may perhaps be said to take the lead of all English provincial towns, money alone has never availed. Good blood, especially if it be blood good in Devonshire, is rarely rejected. Clergymen are allowed within the pale though by no means as certainly as used to be the case; and, indeed, in these days of literates, clergymen have to pass harder examinations than those ever imposed upon them by bishops' chaplains, before they are admitted *ad eundem* among the chosen ones of the city of Exeter. The wives and daughters of the old prebendaries see well to that. And, as has been said, special merit may prevail. Sir Peter Mancrudy, the great Exeter physician, has won his way in, not at all by being Sir Peter, which has stood in his way rather than otherwise, but by the acknowledged excellence of his book about saltzes. Sir Peter Mancrudy is supposed to have quite a metropolitan, almost a European reputation and therefore is acknowledged to belong to the county set, although he never dines out at any house beyond the limits of the city. Now, let it be known that no inhabitant of Exeter ever achieved a clearer right to be regarded as 'county,' in opposition to 'town,' than had Miss Jemima Stanbury. There was not a tradesman in Exeter who was not aware of it, and who did not touch his hat to her accordingly. The men who drove the flies, when summoned to take her out at night, would bring oats with them, knowing how probable it was that they might have to travel far. A distinct apology was made if she was asked to drink tea with people who were simply 'town'. The Noels of Doddescombe Leigh, the Cliffords of Budleigh Salterton, the Powels of Haldon, the Cheritons of Alphington—all county persons, but very frequently in the city—were greeted by her, and greeted her, on terms of equality. Her most intimate friend was old Mrs MacHugh, the widow of the last dean but two, who could not have stood higher had she been the widow of the last bishop. And then, although Miss Stanbury was intimate with the Frenches of Heavitree, with the Wrights of Northernhay, with the Apjohns of Helion Villa, a really magnificent house, two miles out of the city on the Crediton Road, and with the Crumbies of Cronstadt House, Saint Ide's, who would have been county people, if living in the country made the difference, although she was intimate with all these families, her manner to them was not the same, nor was it expected to be the same, as with those of her own acknowledged set. These things are understood in Exeter so well!

Miss Stanbury belonged to the county set, but she lived in a large brick house, standing in the Close, almost behind the Cathedral. Indeed it was so close to the eastern end of the edifice that a carriage could not be brought quite up to her door. It was a large brick house, very old, with a door in the middle, and five steps ascending to it between high iron rails. On each side of the door there were two windows on the ground floor, and above that there were three tiers of five windows each, and the house was double throughout, having as many windows looking out behind into a gloomy courtyard. But the glory of the house consisted in this, that there was a garden attached to it, a garden with very high walls, over which the boughs of trees might be seen, giving to the otherwise gloomy abode a touch of freshness in the summer, and a look of space in the winter, which no doubt added something to the reputation even of Miss Stanbury. The fact for it was a fact that there was no gloomier or less attractive spot in the whole city than Miss Stanbury's garden, when seen inside, did not militate against this advantage. There were but half-a-dozen trees, and a few square yards of grass that was never green, and a damp ungravelled path on which no one ever walked. Seen from the inside the garden was not much; but, from the outside, it gave a distinct character to the house, and produced an unexpressed acknowledgment that the owner of it ought to belong to the county set.

The house and all that was in it belonged to Miss Stanbury herself, as did also many other houses in the neighbourhood. She was the owner of the 'Cock and Bottle,' a very decent second class inn on the other side of the Close, an inn supposed to have clerical tendencies, which made it quite suitable for a close. The choristers took their beer there, and the landlord was a retired verger. Nearly the whole of one side of a dark passage leading out of the Close towards the High Street belonged to her; and though the passage be narrow and the houses dark, the locality is known to be good for trade. And she owned two large houses in the High Street, and a great warehouse at St. Thomas's, and had been bought out of land by the Railway at St. David's much to her own dissatisfaction, as she was wont to express herself, but, undoubtedly, at a very high price. It will be understood therefore, that Miss Stanbury was wealthy, and that she was bound to the city in which she lived by peculiar ties.

But Miss Stanbury had not been born to this wealth, nor can she be said to have inherited from her forefathers any of these high privileges which had been awarded to her. She had achieved them by the romance of her life and the manner in which she had carried herself amidst its vicissitudes. Her father had been vicar of Nuncombe Putney, a parish lying twenty miles west of Exeter, among the moors. And on her father's death, her brother, also now dead, had become vicar of the same parish—her brother, whose only son, Hugh. Stanbury, we already know, working for the 'D. R.' up in London. When Miss Stanbury was twenty-one she became engaged to a certain Mr Brooke Burgess, the eldest son of a banker in Exeter or, it might, perhaps, be better said, a banker himself; for at the time Mr Brooke Burgess was in the firm. It need not here be told how various misfortunes arose, how Mr Burgess quarrelled with the Stanbury family, how Jemima quarrelled with her own family, how, when her father died, she went out from Nuncombe Putney parsonage, and lived on the smallest pittance in a city lodging, how her lover was untrue to her and did not marry her, and how at last he died and left her every shilling that he possessed.

The Devonshire people, at the time, had been much divided as to the merits of the Stanbury quarrel. There were many who said that the brother could not have acted otherwise than he did; and that Miss Stanbury, though by force of character and force of circumstances she had weathered the storm, had in truth been very indiscreet. The results, however, were as have been described. At the period of which we treat, Miss Stanbury was a very rich lady, living by herself in Exeter, admitted, without question, to be one of the county set, and still at variance with her brother's family. Except to Hugh, she had never spoken a word to one of them since her brother's death. When the money came into her hands, she at that time being over forty, and her nephew being then just ten years old, she had undertaken to educate him, and to start him in the world. We know how she had kept her word, and how and why she had withdrawn herself from any further responsibility in the matter.

And in regard to this business of starting the young man she had been careful to let it be known that she would do no more than start him. In the formal document, by means of which she had made the proposal to her brother, she had been careful to let it be understood that simple education was all that she intended to bestow upon him 'and that only,' she had added, 'in the event of my surviving till his education be completed.' And to Hugh himself she had declared that any allowance which she made him after he was called to the Bar, was only made in order to give him room for his foot, a spot of ground from whence to make his first leap. We know how he made that leap, infinitely to the disgust of his aunt, who, when he refused obedience to her in the matter of withdrawing from the Daily Record, immediately withdrew from him, not only her patronage and assistance, but even her friendship and acquaintance. This was the letter which she wrote to him:

> The Close,
> Exeter,
> April 15, 186—.

I don't think that writing radical stuff for a penny newspaper is a respectable occupation for a gentleman, and I will have nothing to do with it. If you choose to do such work, I cannot help it; but it was not for such that I sent you to Harrow and Oxford, nor yet up to London and paid 100 pounds a year to Mr Lambert. I think you are treating me badly, but that is nothing to your bad treatment of yourself. You need not trouble yourself to answer this, unless you are prepared to say that you will not write any more stuff for that penny newspaper. Only I wish to be understood. I will have no connection that I can help, and no acquaintance at all, with radical scribblers and incendiaries.   JEMIMA STANBURY.

Hugh Stanbury had answered this; thanking his aunt for past favours, and explaining to her or striving to do so that he felt it to be his duty to earn his bread, as a means of earning it had come within his reach. He might as well have spared himself the trouble. She simply wrote a few words across his own letter in red ink: 'The bread of unworthiness should never be earned or eaten;' and then' sent the letter back under a blank envelope to her nephew.

She was a thorough Tory of the old school. Had Hugh taken to writing for a newspaper that had cost sixpence, or even threepence for its copies, she might perhaps have forgiven him. At any rate the offence would not have been so flagrant. And had the paper been conservative instead of liberal, she would have had some qualms of conscience before she gave him up. But to live by writing for a newspaper! and for a penny newspaper!! and for a penny radical newspaper!!! It was more than she could endure. Of what nature were the articles which he contributed it was impossible that she should have any idea, for no consideration would have induced her to look at a penny newspaper, or to admit it within her doors. She herself took in the John Bull and the Herald, and daily groaned deeply at the way in which those once great organs of true British public feeling were becoming demoralised and perverted. Had any reduction been made in the price of either of them, she would at once have stopped her subscription. In the matter of politics she had long since come to think that every thing good was over. She hated the name of Reform so much that she could not bring herself to believe in Mr Disraeli and his bill. For many years she had believed in Lord Derby. She would fain believe in him still if she could. It was the great desire of her heart to have some one in whom she believed. In the bishop of her diocese she did believe, and annually sent him some little comforting present from her own hand. And in two or three of the clergymen around her she believed, finding in them a flavour of the unascetic godliness of ancient days which was gratifying to her palate. But in politics there was hardly a name remaining to which she could fix her faith and declare that there should be her guide. For awhile she, thought she would cling to Mr Lowe; but, when she made inquiry, she found that there was no base there of really well-formed conservative granite. The three gentlemen who had dissevered themselves from Mr Disraeli when Mr Disraeli was passing his Reform bill, were doubtless very good in their way; but they were not big enough to fill her heart. She tried to make herself happy with General Peel, but General Peel was after all no more than a shade to her. But the untruth of others never made her untrue, and she still talked of the excellence of George III and the glories of the subsequent reign. She had a bust of Lord Eldon before which she was accustomed to stand with hands closed and to weep or to think that she wept.

She was a little woman, now nearly sixty years of age, with bright grey eyes, and a strong Roman nose, and thin lips, and a sharp-cut chin. She wore a head-gear that almost amounted to a mob-cap, and beneath it her grey hair was always frizzled with the greatest care. Her dress was invariably of black silk, and she had five gowns: one for church, one for evening parties, one for driving out, and one for evenings at home and one for mornings. The dress, when new, always went to church. Nothing, as she was wont to say, was too good for the Lord's house. In the days of crinolines she had protested that she had never worn one—a protest, however, which was hardly true; and now, in these later days, her hatred was especially developed in reference to the head-dresses of young women. 'Chignon' was a word which she had never been heard to pronounce. She would talk of 'those bandboxes which the sluts wear behind their noddles;' for Miss Stanbury allowed herself the use of much strong language. She was very punctilious in all her habits, breakfasting ever at half-past eight, and dining always at six. Half-past five had been her time, till the bishop, who, on an occasion, was to be her guest, once signified to her that such an hour cut up the day and interfered with clerical work. Her lunch was always of bread and cheese, and they who lunched with her either eat that or the bread without the cheese. An afternoon 'tea' was a thing horrible to her imagination. Tea and buttered toast at half-past eight in the evening was the great luxury of her life. She was as strong as a horse, and had never hitherto known a day's illness. As a consequence of this, she did not believe in the illness of other people, especially not in the illness of women. She did not like a girl who could not drink a glass of beer with her bread and cheese in the middle of the day, and she thought that a glass of port after dinner was good for everybody. Indeed, she had a thorough belief in port wine, thinking that it would go far to cure most miseries. But she could not put up with the idea that a woman, young or old, should want the stimulus of a glass of sherry to support her at any odd time of the day. Hot concoctions of strong drink at Christmas she would allow to everybody, and was very strong in recommending such comforts to ladies blessed, or about to be blessed, with babies. She took the sacrament every month, and gave away exactly a tenth of her income to the poor. She believed that there was a special holiness in a tithe of a thing, and attributed the commencement of the downfall of the Church of England to rent charges, and the commutation of clergymen's incomes. Since Judas, there had never been, to her thinking, a traitor so base, or an apostate so sinful, as Colenso; and yet, of the nature of Colenso's teaching she was as ignorant as the towers of the cathedral opposite to her.

She believed in Exeter, thinking that there was no other provincial town in England in which a maiden lady could live safely and decently. London to her was an abode of sin; and though, as we have seen, she delighted to call herself one of the county set, she did not love the fields and lanes. And in Exeter the only place for a lady was the Close. Southernhay and Northernhay might be very well, and there was, doubtless a respectable neighbourhood on the Heavitree side of the town; but for the new streets, and especially for the suburban villas, she had no endurance. She liked to deal at dear shops; but would leave any shop, either dear or cheap, in regard to which a printed advertisement should reach her eye. She paid all her bills at the end of each six months, and almost took a delight in high prices. She would rejoice that bread should be cheap, and grieve that meat should be dear, because of the poor; but in regard to other matters no reduction in the cost of an article ever pleased her. She had houses as to which she was told by her agent that the rents should be raised; but she would not raise them. She had others which it was difficult to let without lowering the rents, but she would not lower them. All change was to her hateful and unnecessary.

She kept three maid-servants, and a man came in every day to clean the knives and boots. Service with her was well requited, and much labour was never exacted. But it was not every young woman who could live with her. A rigidity as to hours, as to religious exercises, and as to dress, was exacted, under which many poor girls altogether broke down; but they who could stand this rigidity came to know that their places were very valuable. No one belonging to them need want for aught, when once the good opinion of Miss Stanbury had been earned. When once she believed in her servant there was nobody like that servant. There was not a man in Exeter could clean a boot except Giles Hickbody and if not in Exeter, then where else? And her own maid Martha, who had lived with her now for twenty years, and who had come with her to the brick house when she first inhabited it, was such a woman that no other servant anywhere was fit to hold a candle to her. But then Martha had great gifts, was never ill, and really liked having sermons read to her.

Such was Miss Stanbury, who had now discarded her nephew Hugh. She had never been tenderly affectionate to Hugh, or she would hardly have asked him to live in

London on a hundred a year. She had never really been kind to him since he was a boy, for although she had paid for him, she had been almost penurious in her manner of doing so, and had repeatedly-given him to understand, that in the event of her death not a shilling would be left to him. Indeed, as to that matter of bequeathing her money, it was understood that it was her purpose to let it all go back to the Burgess family. With the Burgess family she had kept up no sustained connection, it being quite understood that she was never to be asked to meet the only one of them now left in Exeter. Nor was it as yet known to any one in what manner the money was to go back, how it was to be divided, or who were to be the recipients. But she had declared that it should go back, explaining that she had conceived it to be a duty to let her own relations know that they would not inherit her wealth at her death.

About a week after she had sent back poor Hugh's letter with the endorsement on it as to unworthy bread, she summoned Martha to the back parlour in which she was accustomed to write her letters. It was one of the theories of her life that different rooms should be used only for the purposes for which they were intended. She never allowed pens and ink up into the bed-rooms, and had she ever heard that any guest in her house was reading in bed, she would have made an instant personal attack upon that guest, whether male or female, which would have surprised that guest. Poor Hugh would have got on better with her had he not been discovered once smoking in the garden. Nor would she have writing materials in the drawing-room or dining-room. There was a chamber behind the dining-room in which there was an inkbottle, and if there was a letter to be written, let the writer go there and write it. In the writing of many letters, however, she put no confidence, and regarded penny postage as one of the strongest evidences of the coming ruin.

'Martha,' she said, 'I want to speak to you. Sit down. I think I am going to do something.' Martha sat down, but did not speak a word. There had been no question asked of her, and the time for speaking had not come. 'I am writing to Mrs Stanbury, at Nuncombe Putney; and what do you think I am saying to her?'

Now the question had been asked, and it was Martha's duty to reply.

'Writing to Mrs Stanbury, ma'am?'

'Yes, to Mrs Stanbury.'

'It ain't possible for me to say, ma'am, unless it's to put Mr Hugh from going on with the newspapers.'

'When. my nephew won't be controlled by me, I shan't go elsewhere to look for control over him; you may be sure of that, Martha. And remember, Martha, I don't want to have his name mentioned again in the house. You will tell them all so, if you please.'

'He was a very nice gentleman, ma'am.'

'Martha, I won't have it; and there's an end of it. I won't have it. Perhaps I know what goes to the making of a nice gentleman as well as you do.'

'Mr Hugh, ma'am.'

'I won't have it, Martha. And when I say so, let there be an end of it.' As she said this, she got up from her chair, and shook her head, and took a turn about the room. 'If I'm not mistress here, I'm nobody.'

'Of course you're mistress here, ma'am.'

'And if I don't know what's fit to be done, and what's not fit, I'm too old to learn; and, what's more, I won't be taught. I'm not going to have my house crammed with radical incendiary stuff, printed with ink that stinks, on paper made out of straw. If I can't live without penny literature, at any rate I'll die without it. Now listen to me.'

'Yes, ma'am.'

'I have asked Mrs Stanbury to send one of the girls over here.'

'To live, ma'am?' Martha's tone as she asked the question, showed how deeply she felt its importance.

'Yes, Martha; to live.'

'You'll never like it, ma'am.'

'I don't suppose I shall.'

'You'll never get on with it, ma'am; never. The young lady'll be out of the house in a week; or if she ain't, somebody else will.'

'You mean yourself.'

'I'm only a servant, ma'am, and it don't signify about me.'

'You're a fool.'

'That's true, ma'am, I don't doubt.'

'I've sent for her, and we must do the best we can. Perhaps she won't come.'

'She'll come fast enough,' said Martha. 'But whether she'll stay, that's a different thing. I don't see how it's possible she's to stay. I'm told they're feckless, idle young ladies. She'll be so soft, ma'am, and you.'

'Well; what of me?'

'You'll be so hard, ma'am!'

'I'm not a bit harder than you, Martha; nor yet so hard. I'll do my duty, or at least I'll try. Now you know all about it, and you may go away. There's the letter, and I mean to go out and post it myself.'

CHAPTER VIII. 'I KNOW IT WILL DO'

Miss Stanbury carried her letter all the way to the chief post-office in the city, having no faith whatever in those little subsidiary receiving houses which are established in different parts of the city. As for the iron pillar boxes which had been erected of late years for the receipt of letters, one of which—a most hateful thing to her—stood almost close to her own hall door, she had not the faintest belief that any letter put into one of them would ever reach its destination. She could not understand why people should not walk with their letters to a respectable post-office instead of chucking them into an iron stump as she called it out in the middle of the street with nobody to look after it. Positive orders had been given that no letter from her house should ever be put into the iron post. Her epistle to her sister-in-law, of whom she never spoke otherwise than as Mrs Stanbury, was as follows:

The Close,
Exeter,
22nd April, 186—

My Dear Sister Stanbury,

Your son, Hugh, has taken to courses of which I do not approve, and therefore I have put an end to my connection with him. I shall be happy to entertain your daughter Dorothy in my house if you and she approve of such a plan. Should you agree to this, she will be welcome to receive you or her sister, not her brother, in my house any Wednesday morning between half-past nine and half-past twelve. I will endeavour to make my house pleasant to her and useful, and will make her an allowance of 25 pounds per annum for her clothes as long as she may remain with me. I shall expect her to be regular at meals, to be constant in going to church, and not to read modern novels.

I intend the arrangement to be permanent, but of course I must retain the power of closing it if, and when, I shall see fit. Its permanence must be contingent on my life. I have no power of providing for any one after my death,

Yours truly,   Jemima Stanbury.

I hope the young lady does not have any false hair about her.

When this note was received at Nuncombe Putney the amazement which it occasioned was extreme. Mrs Stanbury, the widow of the late vicar, lived in a little morsel of a cottage on the outskirts of the village, with her two daughters, Priscilla and Dorothy. Their whole income, out of which it was necessary that they should pay rent for their cottage, was less than 70 pounds per annum. During the last few months a five-pound note now and again had found its way to Nuncombe Putney out of the coffers of the 'D. R.'; but the ladies there were most unwilling to be so relieved, thinking that their brother's career was of infinitely more importance than their comforts or even than their living. They were very poor, but they were accustomed to poverty. The elder sister was older than Hugh, but Dorothy, the younger, to whom this strange invitation was now made, was two years younger than her brother, and was now nearly twenty-six. How they had lived, and dressed themselves, and had continued to be called ladies by the inhabitants of the village was, and is, and will be a mystery to those who have had the spending of much larger incomes, but have still been always poor. But they had lived, had gone to church every Sunday in decent apparel, and had kept up friendly relations with the family of the present vicar, and with one or two other neighbours.

When the letter had been read first by the mother, and then aloud, and then by each of them separately, in the little sitting-room in the cottage, there was silence among them for neither of them desired to be the first to express an opinion. Nothing could be more natural than the proposed arrangement, had it not been made unnatural by a quarrel existing nearly throughout the whole life of the person most nearly concerned. Priscilla, the elder daughter, was the one of the family who was generally the ruler, and she at last expressed an opinion adverse to the arrangement. 'My dear, you would never be able to bear it,' said Priscilla.

'I suppose not,' said Mrs Stanbury, plaintively.

'I could try,' said Dorothy.

'My dear, you don't know that woman,' said Priscilla.

'Of course I don't know her,' said Dorothy.

'She has always been very good to Hugh,' said Mrs Stanbury.

'I don't think she has been good to him at all,' said Priscilla.

'But think what a saving it would be,' said Dorothy. 'And I could send home half of what Aunt Stanbury says she would give me.'

'You must not think of that,' said Priscilla, 'because she expects you to be dressed.'

'I should like to try,' she said, before the morning was over 'if you and mamma don't think it would be wrong.'

The conference that day ended in a written request to Aunt Stanbury that a week might be allowed for consideration, the letter being written by Priscilla, but signed with her mother's name, and with a very long epistle to Hugh, in which each of the ladies took a part, and in which advice and decision were demanded. It was very evident to Hugh that his mother and Dorothy were for compliance, and that Priscilla was for refusal. But he never doubted for a moment. 'Of course she will go,' he said in his answer to Priscilla; 'and she must understand that Aunt Stanbury is a most excellent woman, as true as the sun, thoroughly honest, with no fault but this, that she likes her own way. Of course Dolly can go back again if she finds the house too hard for her.' Then he sent another five-pound note, observing that Dolly's journey to Exeter would cost money, and that her wardrobe would want some improvement.

'I'm very glad that it isn't me,' said Priscilla, who, however, did not attempt to oppose the decision of the man of the family. Dorothy was greatly gratified by the excitement of the proposed change in her life, and the following letter, the product of the wisdom of the family, was written by Mrs Stanbury.

Nuncombe Putney,
1st May, 186—

MY DEAR SISTER STANBURY,

We are all very thankful for the kindness of your offer, which my daughter Dorothy will accept with feelings of affectionate gratitude. I think you will find her docile, good-tempered, and amiable; but a mother, of course, speaks well of her own child. She will endeavour to comply with your wishes in all things reasonable. She; of course, understands that should the arrangement not suit, she will come back home on the expression of your wish that it should be so. And she will, of course, do the same, if she should find that living in Exeter does not suit herself.' (This sentence was inserted at the instance of Priscilla, after much urgent expostulation.) 'Dorothy will be ready to go to you on any day you may fix after the 7th of this month.

Believe me to remain,
Your affectionate sister-in-law,   P. STANBURY.

'She's going to come,' said Miss Stanbury to Martha, holding the letter in her hand.

'I never doubted her coming, ma'am,' said Martha.

'And I mean her to stay, unless it's her own fault. She'll have the small room upstairs, looking out front, next to mine. And you must go and fetch her.'

'Go and fetch her, ma'am?'

'Yes. If you won't, I must.'

'She ain't a child, ma'am. She's twenty-five years old, and surely she can come to Exeter by herself, with a railroad all the way from Lessboro'.'

'There's no place a young woman is insulted in so bad as those railway carriages, and I won't have her come by herself. If she is to live with me, she shall begin decently at any rate.'

Martha argued the matter, but was of course beaten, and on the day fixed started early in the morning for Nuncombe Putney, and returned in the afternoon to the Close with her charge. By the time that she had reached the house she had in some degree reconciled herself to the dangerous step that her mistress had taken, partly by perceiving that in face Dorothy Stanbury was very like her brother Hugh, and partly, perhaps, by finding that the young woman's manner to herself was both gentle and sprightly. She knew well that gentleness alone, without some back-bone of strength under it, would not long succeed with Miss Stanbury. 'As far as I can judge, ma'am, she's a sweet young lady,' said Martha, when she reported her arrival to her mistress, who had retired upstairs to her own room, in order that she might thus hear a word of tidings from her lieutenant, before she showed herself on the field of action.

'Sweet! I hate your sweets,' said Miss Stanbury. 'Then why did you send for her, ma'am?'

'Because I was an old fool. But I must go down and receive her, I suppose.'

Then Miss Stanbury went down, almost trembling as she went The matter to her was one of vital importance She was going to change the whole tenor of her life for the sake as she told herself of doing her duty by a relative whom she did not even know But we may fairly suppose that there had in truth been a feeling beyond that, which taught her to desire to have some one near her to whom she might not only do her duty as guardian, but whom she might also love. She had tried this with her nephew; but her nephew had been too strong for her, too far from her, too unlike to herself. When he came to see her he had smoked a short pipe, which had been shocking to her, and he had spoken of Reform, and Trades' Unions, and meetings in the parks, as though they had not been Devil's ordinances. And he was very shy of going to church, utterly refusing to be taken there twice on the same Sunday. And he had told his aunt that owing to a peculiar and unfortunate weakness in his constitution he could not listen to the reading of sermons. And then she was almost certain that he had once kissed one of the maids! She had found it impossible to manage him in any way; and when he positively declared himself as permanently devoted to the degrading iniquities of penny newspapers, she had thought it best to cast him off altogether. Now, thus late in life, she was going to make another venture, to try an altogether new mode of living in order, as she said to herself, that she might be of some use to somebody but, no doubt, with a further unexpressed hope in her bosom, that the solitude of her life might be relieved by the companionship of some one whom she might love. She had arrayed herself in a clean cap and her evening gown, and she went downstairs looking sternly, with a fully-developed idea that she must initiate her new duties by assuming a mastery at once. But inwardly she trembled, and was intensely anxious as to the first appearance of her niece. Of course there would be a little morsel of a bonnet. She hated those vile patches dirty dirty flat daubs of millinery as she called them, but they had become too general for her to refuse admittance for such a thing within her doors. But a chignon, a bandbox behind the noddle, she would not endure. And then there were other details of feminine gear, which shall not be specified, as to which she was painfully anxious, almost forgetting in her anxiety that the dress of this young woman whom she was about to see must have ever been regulated by the closest possible economy.

The first thing she saw on entering the room was a dark straw hat, a straw hat with a strong penthouse flap to it, and her heart was immediately softened.

'My dear,' she said, 'I am glad to see you.'

Dorothy, who, on her part, was trembling also, whose position was one to justify most intense anxiety, murmured some reply.

'Take off your hat,' said the aunt, 'and let me give you a kiss.'

The hat was taken off and the kiss was given. There was certainly no chignon there. Dorothy Stanbury was light haired, with almost flaxen ringlets, worn after the old-fashioned way which we used to think so pretty when we were young. She had very soft grey eyes, which ever seemed to beseech you to do something when they looked at you, and her mouth was a beseeching mouth. There are women who, even amidst their strongest efforts at giving assistance to others, always look as though they were asking aid themselves, and such a one was Dorothy Stanbury. Her complexion was pale, but there was always present in it a tint of pink running here and there, changing with every word she spoke, changing indeed with every pulse of her heart. Nothing ever was softer than her cheek; but her hands were thin and hard, and almost fibrous with the working of the thread upon them. She was rather tall than otherwise, but that extreme look of feminine dependence which always accompanied her, took away something even from the appearance of her height.

'These are all real, at any rate,' said her aunt, taking hold of the curls, 'and won't be hurt by a little cold water.'

Dorothy smiled but said nothing, and was then taken up to her bed-room. Indeed, when the aunt and niece sat down to dinner together Dorothy had hardly spoken. But Miss Stanbury had spoken, and things upon the whole had gone very well.

'I hope you like roast chicken, my dear?' said Miss Stanbury.

'Oh, thank you.'

'And bread sauce? Jane, I do hope the bread sauce is hot.'

If the reader thinks that Miss Stanbury was indifferent to considerations of the table, the reader is altogether ignorant of Miss Stanbury's character. When Miss Stanbury gave her niece the liver-wing, and picked out from the attendant sausages one that had been well browned and properly broken in the frying, she meant to do a real kindness.

'And now, my dear, there are mashed potatoes and bread sauce. As for green vegetables, I don't know what has become of them. They tell me I may have green peas from France at a shilling a quart; but if I can't have English green peas, I won't have any.'

Miss Stanbury was standing up as she said this, as she always did on such occasions, liking to have a full mastery over the dish.

'I hope you like it, my dear?'

'Everything is so very nice.'

'That's right. I like to see a young woman with an appetite. Remember that God sends the good things for us to eat; and as long as we don't take more than our share, and give away something to those who haven't a fair share of their own, I for one think it quite right to enjoy my victuals. Jane, this bread sauce isn't hot. It never is hot. Don't tell me; I know what hot is!'

Dorothy thought that her aunt was very angry; but Jane knew Miss Stanbury better, and bore the scolding without shaking in her shoes.

'And now, my dear, you must take a glass of port wine. It will do you good after your journey.'

Dorothy attempted to explain that she never did drink any wine, but her aunt talked down her scruples at once.

'One glass of port wine never did anybody any harm, and as there is port wine, it must be intended that somebody should drink it.'

Miss Stanbury, as she sipped hers out very slowly, seemed to enjoy it very much. Although May had come, there was a fire in the grate, and she sat with her toes on the fender, and her silk dress folded up above her knees. She sat quite silent in this position for a quarter of an hour, every now and then raising her glass to her lips. Dorothy sat silent also. To her, in the newness of her condition, speech was impossible.

'I think it will do,' said Miss Stanbury at last.

As Dorothy had no idea what would do, she could make no reply to this.

'I'm sure it will do,' said Miss Stanbury, after another short interval. 'You're as like my poor sister as two eggs. You don't have headaches, do you?'

Dorothy said that she was not ordinarily affected in that way.

'When girls have headaches it comes from tight-lacing, and not walking enough, and carrying all manner of nasty smells about with them. I know what headaches mean. How is a woman not to have a headache, when she carries a thing on the back of her poll as big as a gardener's wheel-barrow? Come, it's a fine evening, and we'll go out and look at the towers. You've never even seen them yet, I suppose?'

So they went out, and finding the verger at the Cathedral door, he being a great friend of Miss Stanbury, they walked up and down the aisles, and Dorothy was instructed as to what would be expected from her in regard to the outward forms of religion. She was to go to the Cathedral service on the morning of every week-day, and on Sundays in the afternoon. On Sunday mornings she was to attend the little church of St. Margaret. On Sunday evenings it was the practice of Miss Stanbury to read a sermon in the dining-room to all of whom her household consisted. Did Dorothy like daily services? Dorothy, who was more patient than her brother, and whose life had been much less energetic, said that she had no objection to going to church every day when there was not too much to do.

'There never need be too much to do to attend the Lord's house,' said Miss Stanbury, somewhat angrily.

'Only if you've got to make the beds,' said Dorothy.

'My dear, I beg your pardon,' said Miss Stanbury. 'I beg your pardon, heartily. I'm a thoughtless old woman, I know. Never mind. Now, we'll go in.'

Later in the evening, when she gave her niece a candlestick to go to bed, she repeated what she had said before.

'It'll do very well, my dear. I'm sure it'll do. But if you read in bed either night or morning, I'll never forgive you.'

This last caution was uttered with so much energy, that Dorothy gave a little jump as she promised obedience.

CHAPTER IX. SHEWING HOW THE QUARREL PROGRESSED AGAIN

On one Sunday morning, when the month of May was nearly over, Hugh Stanbury met Colonel Osborne in Curzon Street, not many yards from Trevelyan's door. Colonel Osborne had just come from the house, and Stanbury was going to it. Hugh had not spoken to Osborne since the day, now a fortnight since, on which both of them had witnessed the scene in the park; but on that occasion they had been left together, and it had been impossible for them not to say a few words about their mutual friends. Osborne had expressed his sorrow that there should be any misunderstanding, and had called Trevelyan a 'confounded fool.' Stanbury had suggested that there was something in it which they two probably did not understand, and that matters would be sure to come all right. 'The truth is Trevelyan bullies her,' said Osborne; 'and if he goes on with that he'll be sure to get the worst of it.' Now on this present occasion Stanbury asked whether he would find the ladies at home. 'Yes, they are both there,' said Osborne. 'Trevelyan has just gone out in a huff. She'll never be able to go on living with him. Anybody can see that with half an eye.' Then he had passed on, and Hugh Stanbury knocked at the door.

He was shown up into the drawing-room, and found both the sisters there; but he could see that Mrs Trevelyan had been in tears. The avowed purpose of his visit—that is, the purpose which he had avowed to himself—was to talk about his sister Dorothy. He had told Miss Rowley, while walking in the park with her, how Dorothy had been invited over to Exeter by her aunt, and how he had counselled his sister to accept the invitation. Nora had expressed herself very interested as to Dorothy's fate, and had said how much she wished that she knew Dorothy. We all understand how sweet it is, when two such persons as Hugh Stanbury and Nora Rowley cannot speak of their love for each other, to say these tender things in regard to some one else. Nora had been quite anxious to know how Dorothy had been received by that old conservative warrior, as Hugh Stanbury had called his aunt, and Hugh had now come to Curzon Street with a letter from Dorothy in his pocket. But when he saw that there had been some cause for trouble, he hardly knew how to introduce his subject.

'Trevelyan is not at home?' he asked.

'No,' said Emily, with her face turned away. 'He went out and left us a quarter of an hour since. Did you meet Colonel Osborne?'

'I was speaking to him in the street not a moment since.' As he answered he could see that Nora was making some sign to her sister. Nora was most anxious that Emily should not speak of what had just occurred, but her signs were all thrown away. 'Somebody must tell him,' said Mrs Trevelyan, 'and I don't know who can do so better than so old a friend as Mr Stanbury.'

'Tell what, and to whom?' he asked.

'No, no, no,' said Nora.

'Then I must tell him myself,' said she, 'that is all. As for standing this kind of life, it is out of the question. I should either destroy myself or go mad.'

'If I could do any good I should be so happy,' said Stanbury.

'Nobody can do any good between a man and wife,' said Nora.

Then Mrs Trevelyan began to tell her story, putting aside, with an impatient motion of her hands, the efforts which her sister made to stop her. She was very angry, and as she told it, standing up, all trace of sobbing soon disappeared from her voice. 'The fact is,' she said, 'he does not know his own mind, or what to fear or what not to fear. He told me that I was never to see Colonel Osborne again.'

'What is the use, Emily, of your repeating that to Mr Stanbury?'

'Why should I not repeat it? Colonel Osborne is papa's oldest friend, and mine too. He is a man I like very much, who is a real friend to me. As he is old enough to be my father, one would have thought that my husband could have found no objection.'

'I don't know much about his age,' said Stanbury.

'It does make a difference. It must make a difference. I should not think of becoming so intimate with a younger man. But, however, when my husband told me that I was to see him no more, though the insult nearly killed me, I determined to obey him. An order was given that Colonel Osborne should not be admitted. You may imagine how painful it was; but it was given, and I was prepared to bear it.'

'But he had been lunching with you on that Sunday.'

'Yes; that is just it. As soon as it was given Louis would rescind it, because he was ashamed of what he had done. He was so jealous that he did not want me to see the man; and yet he was so afraid that it should be known that he ordered me to see him. He ordered him into the house at last, and I—I went away upstairs.'

'That was on the Sunday that we met you in the park?' asked Stanbury.

'What is the use of going back to all that?' said Nora.

'Then I met him by chance in the park,' continued Mrs Trevelyan, 'and because he said a word which I knew would anger my husband, I left him abruptly. Since that my husband has begged that things might go on as they were before. He could not bear that Colonel Osborne himself should think that he was jealous. Well; I gave way, and the man has been here as before. And now there has been a scene which has been disgraceful to us all. I cannot stand it, and I won't. If he does not behave himself with more manliness I will leave him.'

'But what can I do?'

'Nothing, Mr Stanbury,' said Nora.

'Yes; you can do this. You can go to him from me, and can tell him that I have chosen you as a messenger because you are his friend. You can tell him that I am willing to obey him in anything. If he chooses, I will consent that Colonel Osborne shall be asked never to come into my presence again. It will be very absurd; but if he chooses, I will consent. Or I will let things go on as they are, and continue to receive my father's old friend when he comes. But if I do, I will not put up with an imputation on my conduct because he does not like the way in which the gentleman thinks fit to address me. I take upon myself to say that if any man alive spoke to me as he ought not to speak, I should know how to resent it myself. But I cannot fly into a passion with an old gentleman for calling me by my Christian name, when he has done so habitually for years.'

From all this it will appear that the great godsend of a rich marriage, with all manner of attendant comforts, which had come in the way of the Rowley family as they were living at the Mandarins, had not turned out to be an unmixed blessing. In the matter of the quarrel, as it had hitherto progressed, the husband had perhaps been more in the wrong than his wife; but the wife, in spite of all her promises of perfect obedience, had proved herself to be a woman very hard to manage. Had she been earnest in her desire to please her lord and master in this matter of Colonel Osborne's visits, to please him even after he had so vacillated in his own behests, she might probably have so received the man as to have quelled all feeling of jealousy in her husband's bosom. But instead of doing so she had told herself that as she was innocent, and as her innocence had been acknowledged, and as she had been specially instructed to receive this man whom she had before been specially instructed not to receive, she would now fall back exactly into her old manner with him. She had told Colonel Osborne never to allude to that meeting in the park, and to ask no creature as to what had occasioned her conduct on that Sunday; thus having a mystery with him, which of course he understood as well as she did. And then she had again taken to writing notes to him and receiving notes from him—none of which she showed to her husband. She was more intimate with him than ever, and yet she hardly ever mentioned his name to her husband. Trevelyan, acknowledging to himself that he had done no good by his former interference, feeling that he had put himself in the wrong on that occasion, and that his wife had got the better of him, had borne with all this with soreness and a moody savageness of general conduct, but still without further words of anger with reference to the man himself. But now, on this Sunday, when his wife had been closeted with Colonel Osborne in the back drawing-room, leaving him with his sister-in-law, his temper had become too hot for him, and he had suddenly left the house, declaring that he would not walk with the two women on that day. 'Why not, Louis?' his wife had said, coming up to him. 'Never mind why not, but I shall not,' he had answered; and then he left the room.

'What is the matter with him?' Colonel Osborne had asked.

'It is impossible to say what is the matter with him,' Mrs Trevelyan had replied. After that she had at once gone upstairs to her child, telling herself that she was doing all that the strictest propriety could require in leaving the man's society as soon as her husband was gone. Then there was an awkward minute or two between Nora and Colonel Osborne, and he took his leave.

Stanbury at last promised that he would see Trevelyan, repeating, however, very frequently that often used assertion, that no task is so hopeless as that of interfering between a man and his wife. Nevertheless he promised, and undertook to look for Trevelyan at the Acrobats on that afternoon. At last he got a moment in which to produce the letter from his sister, and was able to turn the conversation for a few minutes to his own affairs. Dorothy's letter was read and discussed by both the ladies with much zeal. 'It is quite a strange world to me,' said Dorothy, 'but I am beginning to find myself more at my ease than I was at first. Aunt Stanbury is very good-natured, and when I know what she wants, I think I shall be able to please her. What you said of her disposition is not so bad to me, as of course a girl in my position does not expect to have her own way.'

'Why shouldn't she have her share of her own way as well as anybody else?' said Mrs Trevelyan.

'Poor Dorothy would never want to have her own way,' said Hugh.

'She ought to want it,' said Mrs Trevelyan.

'She has spirit enough to turn if she's trodden on,' said Hugh.

'That's more than what most women have,' said Mrs Trevelyan.

Then he went on with the letter. 'She is very generous, and has given me £6 5s in advance of my allowance. When I said I would send part of it home to mamma, she seemed to be angry, and said that she wanted me always to look nice about my clothes. She told me afterwards to do as I pleased, and that I might try my own way for the first quarter. So I was frightened, and only sent thirty shillings. We went out the other evening to drink tea with Mrs MacHugh, an old lady whose husband was once dean. I had to go, and it was all very nice. There were a great many clergymen there, but many of them were young men.' 'Poor Dorothy,' exclaimed Nora. 'One of them was the minor canon who chants the service every morning. He is a bachelor.' 'Then there is a hope for her,' said Nora, 'and he always talks a little as though he were singing the Litany.' 'That's very bad,' said Nora; 'fancy having a husband to sing the Litany to you always.' 'Better that, perhaps, than having him always singing something else,' said Mrs Trevelyan.

It was decided between them that Dorothy's state might on the whole be considered as flourishing, but that Hugh was bound as a brother to go down to Exeter and look after her. He explained, however, that he was expressly debarred from calling on his sister, even between the hours of half-past nine and half-past twelve on Wednesday mornings, and that he could not see her at all unless he did so surreptitiously.

'If I were you I would see my sister in spite of all the old viragos in Exeter,' said Mrs Trevelyan. 'I have no idea of anybody taking so much upon themselves.'

'You must remember, Mrs Trevelyan, that she has taken upon herself much also in the way of kindness, in doing what perhaps I ought to call charity. I wonder what I should have been doing now if it were not for my Aunt Stanbury.'

He took his leave, and went at once from Curzon Street to Trevelyan's club, and found that Trevelyan had not been there as yet. In another hour he called again, and was about to give it up, when he met the man whom he was seeking on the steps.

'I was looking for you,' he said.

'Well, here I am.'

It was impossible not to see in the look of Trevelyan's face, and not to hear in the tone of his voice, that he was, at the moment, in an angry and unhappy frame of mind. He did not move as though he were willing to accompany his friend, and seemed almost to know beforehand that the approaching interview was to be an unpleasant one.

'I want to speak to you, and perhaps you wouldn't mind taking a turn with me,' said Stanbury.

But Trevelyan objected to this, and led the way into the club waiting-room. A club waiting-room is always a gloomy, unpromising place for a confidential conversation, and so Stanbury felt it to be on the present occasion. But he had no alternative. There they were together, and he must do as he had promised.

Trevelyan kept on his hat and did not sit down, and looked very gloomy. Stanbury having to commence without any assistance from outward auxiliaries, almost forgot what it was that he had promised to do.

'I have just come from Curzon Street,' he said.

'Well!'

'At least I was there about two hours ago.'

'It doesn't matter, I suppose, whether it was two hours or two minutes,' said Trevelyan.

'Not in the least. The fact is this; I happened to come upon the two girls there, when they were very unhappy, and your wife asked me to come and say a word or two to you.'

'Was Colonel Osborne there?'

'No; I had met him in the street a minute or two before.'

'Well, now; look here, Stanbury. If you'll take my advice, you'll keep your hands out of this. It is not but that I regard you as being as good a friend as I have in the world; but, to own the truth, I cannot put up with interference between myself and my wife.'

'Of course you understand that I only come as a messenger.'

'You had better not be a messenger in such a cause. If she has anything to say she can say it to myself.'

'Am I to understand that you will not listen to me?'

'I had rather not.'

'I think you are wrong,' said Stanbury.

'In that matter you must allow me to judge for myself. I can easily understand that a young woman like her, especially with her sister to back her, should induce such a one as you to take her part.'

'I am taking nobody's part. You wrong your wife, and you especially wrong Miss Rowley.'

'If you please, Stanbury, we will say nothing more about it.' This Trevelyan said holding the door of the room half open in his hand, so that the other was obliged to pass out through it.

'Good evening,' said Stanbury, with much anger.

'Good evening,' said Trevelyan, with an assumption of indifference.

Stanbury went away in absolute wrath, though the trouble which he had had in the interview was much less than he had anticipated, and the result quite as favourable. He had known that no good would come of his visit. And yet he was now full of anger against Trevelyan, and had become a partisan in the matter which was exactly that which he had resolutely determined that he would not become. 'I believe that no woman on earth could live with him,' he said to himself as he walked away. 'It was always the same with him—a desire for mastery, which he did not know how to use when he had obtained it. If it were Nora, instead of the other sister, he would break her sweet heart within a month.'

Trevelyan dined at his club, and hardly spoke a word to any one during the evening. At about eleven he started to walk home, but went by no means straight thither, taking a long turn through St. James's Park, and by Pimlico. It was necessary that he should make up his mind as to what he would do. He had sternly refused the interference of a friend, and he must be prepared to act on his own responsibility. He knew well that he could not begin again with his wife on the next day as though nothing had happened. Stanbury's visit to him, if it had done nothing else, had made this impossible. He determined that he would not go to her room to-night, but would see her as early as possible in the morning and would then talk to her with all the wisdom of which he was master.

How many husbands have come to the same resolution; and how few of them have found the words of wisdom to be efficacious!

CHAPTER X. HARD WORDS

It is to be feared that men in general do not regret as they should do any temporary ill-feeling, or irritating jealousy between husbands and wives, of which they themselves have been the cause. The author is not speaking now of actual love-makings, of intrigues and devilish villany, either perpetrated or imagined; but rather of those passing gusts of short-lived and unfounded suspicion to which, as to other accidents, very well-regulated families may occasionally be liable. When such suspicion rises in the bosom of a wife, some woman intervening or being believed to intervene between her and the man who is her own, that woman who has intervened or been supposed to intervene, will either glory in her position or bewail it bitterly, according to the circumstances of the case. We will charitably suppose that, in a great majority of such instances, she will bewail it. But when such painful jealous doubts annoy the husband, the man who is in the way will almost always feel himself justified in extracting a slightly pleasurable sensation from the transaction. He will say to himself probably, unconsciously indeed, and with no formed words, that the husband is an ass, an ass if he be in a twitter either for that which he has kept or for that which he has been unable to keep, that the lady has shewn a good deal of appreciation, and that he himself is is is quite a Captain Bold of Halifax! All the while he will not have the slightest intention of wronging the husband's honour, and will have received no greater favour from the intimacy accorded to him than the privilege of running on one day to Marshall and Snellgrove's, the haberdashers, and on another to Handcocks', the jewellers. If he be allowed to buy a present or two, or to pay a few shillings here or there, he has achieved much. Terrible things now and again do occur, even here in England; but women, with us, are slow to burn their household gods. It happens, however, occasionally, as we are all aware, that the outward garments of a domestic deity will be a little scorched; and when this occurs, the man who is the interloper will generally find a gentle consolation in his position, let its interest be ever so flaccid and unreal, and its troubles in running about, and the like, ever so considerable and time-destructive.

It was so certainly with Colonel Osborne when he became aware that his intimacy with Mrs Trevelyan had caused her husband uneasiness. He was not especially a vicious man, and had now, as we know, reached a time of life when such vice as that in question might be supposed to have lost its charm for him. A gentleman over fifty, popular in London, with a seat in Parliament, fond of good dinners, and possessed of everything which the world has to give, could hardly have wished to run away with his neighbour's wife, or to have destroyed the happiness of his old friend's daughter. Such wickedness had never come into his head; but he had a certain pleasure in being the confidential friend of a very pretty woman; and when he heard that that pretty woman's husband was jealous, the pleasure was enhanced rather than otherwise. On that Sunday, as he had left the house in Curzon Street, he had told Stanbury that Trevelyan had just gone off in a huff, which was true enough, and he had walked from thence down Clarges Street, and across Piccadilly to St. James's Street, with a jauntier step than usual, because he was aware that he himself had been the occasion of that trouble. This was very wrong; but there is reason to believe that many such men as Colonel Osborne, who are bachelors at fifty, are equally malicious.

He thought a good deal about it on that evening, and was still thinking about it on the following morning. He had promised to go up to Curzon Street on the Monday really on some most trivial mission, on a matter of business which no man could have taken in hand whose time was of the slightest value to himself or any one else. But now that mission assumed an importance in his eyes, and seemed to require either a special observance or a special excuse. There was no real reason why he should not have stayed away from Curzon Street for the next fortnight; and had he done so he need have made no excuse to Mrs Trevelyan when he met her. But the opportunity for a little excitement was not to be missed, and instead of going he wrote to her the following note:

Albany,
Monday.

Dear Emily,

What was it all about yesterday? I was to have come up with the words of that opera, but perhaps it will be better to send it. If it be not wicked, do tell me whether I am to consider myself as a banished man. I thought that our little meetings were so innocent and so pleasant! The green-eyed monster is of all monsters the most monstrous and the most unreasonable. Pray let me have a line, if it be not forbidden.

Yours always heartily,   F. O.

Putting aside all joking, I beg you to remember that I consider myself always entitled to be regarded by you as your most sincere friend.

When this was brought to Mrs Trevelyan, about twelve o'clock in the day, she had already undergone the infliction of those words of wisdom which her husband had prepared for her, and which were threatened at the close of the last chapter. Her husband had come up to her while she was yet in her bed-room, and had striven hard to prevail against her. But his success had been very doubtful. In regard to the number of words, Mrs Trevelyan certainly had had the best of it. As far as any understanding one of another was concerned, the conversation had been useless. She believed herself to be injured and aggrieved, and would continue so to assert, let him implore her to listen to him as loudly as he might. 'Yes I will listen, and I will obey you,' she had said, 'but I will not endure such insults without telling you that I feel them.' Then he had left her fully conscious that he had failed, and went forth out of his house into the City, to his club, to wander about the streets, not knowing what he had best do to bring back that state of tranquillity at home which he felt to be so desirable.

Mrs Trevelyan was alone when Colonel Osborne's note was brought to her, and was at that moment struggling with herself in anger against her husband. If he laid any command upon her, she would execute it; but she would never cease to tell him that he had ill-used her. She would din it into his ears, let him come to her as often as he might with his wise words. Wise words!

What was the use of wise words when a man was such a fool in nature? And as for Colonel Osborne she would see him if he came to her three times a day, unless her husband gave some clearly intelligible order to the contrary. She was fortifying her mind with this resolution when Colonel Osborne's letter was brought to her. She asked whether any servant was waiting for an answer. No the servant, who had left it, had gone at once. She read the note, and sat working, with it before her, for a quarter of an hour; and then walked over to her desk and answered it.

My Dear Colonel Osborne,

It will be best to say nothing whatever about the occurrence of yesterday; and if possible, not to think of it. As far as I am concerned, I wish for no change except that people should be more reasonable. You can call of course whenever you please; and I am very grateful for your expression of friendship.

Yours most sincerely,

                                                                    Emily Trevelyan.

Thanks for the words of the opera.

When she had written this, being determined that all should be open and above board, she put a penny stamp on the envelope, and desired that the letter should be posted. But she destroyed that which she had received from Colonel Osborne. In all things she would act as she would have done if her husband had not been so foolish, and there could have been no reason why she should have kept so unimportant a communication.

In the course of the day Trevelyan passed through the hall to the room which he himself was accustomed to occupy behind the parlour, and as he did so saw the note lying ready to be posted, took it up, and read the address.

He held it for a moment in his hand, then replaced it on the hall table, and passed on. When he reached his own table he sat down hurriedly, and took up in his hand some Review that was lying ready for him to read. But he was quite unable to fix his mind on the words before him. He had spoken to his wife on that morning in the strongest language he could use as to the unseemliness of her intimacy with Colonel Osborne; and then, the first thing she had done when his back was turned was to write to this very Colonel Osborne, and tell him, no doubt, what had occurred between her and her husband. He sat thinking of it all for many minutes. He would probably have declared himself that he had thought of it for an hour as he sat there. Then he got up, went upstairs and walked slowly into the drawing-room. There he found his wife sitting with her sister. 'Nora,' he said, 'I want to speak to Emily. Will you forgive me, if I ask you to leave us for a few minutes?' Nora, with an anxious look at Emily, got up and left the room.

'Why do you send her away?' said Mrs Trevelyan.

'Because I wish to be alone with you for a few minutes. Since what I said to you this morning, you have written to Colonel Osborne.'

'Yes I have. I do not know how you have found it out; but I suppose you keep a watch on me.'

'I keep no watch on you. As I came into the house, I saw your letter lying in the hall.'

'Very well. You could have read it if you pleased.'

'Emily, this matter is becoming very serious, and I strongly advise you to be on your guard in what you say. I will bear much for you, and much for our boy; but I will not bear to have my name made a reproach.'

'Sir, if you think your name is shamed by me, we had better part,' said Mrs Trevelyan, rising from her chair, and confronting him with a look before which his own almost quailed.

'It may be that we had better part,' he said, slowly. 'But in the first place I wish you to tell me what were the contents of that letter.'

'If it was there when you came in, no doubt it is there still. Go and look at it.'

'That is no answer to me. I have desired you to tell me what are its contents.'

'I shall not tell you. I will not demean myself by repeating anything so insignificant in my own justification. If you suspect me of writing what I should not write, you will suspect me also of lying to conceal it.'

'Have you heard from Colonel Osborne this morning?'

'I have.'

'And where is his letter?'

'I have destroyed it.'

Again he paused, trying to think what he had better do, trying to be calm. And she stood still opposite to him, confronting him with the scorn of her bright angry eyes. Of course, he was not calm. He was the very reverse of calm. 'And you refuse to tell me what you wrote,' he said.

'The letter is there,' she answered, pointing away towards the door. 'If you want to play the spy, go and look at it for yourself.'

'Do you call me a spy?'

'And what have you called me? Because you are a husband, is the privilege of vituperation to be all on your side?'

'It is impossible that I should put up with this,' he said 'quite impossible. This would kill me. Anything is better than this. My present orders to you are not to see Colonel Osborne, not to write to him or have any communication with him, and to put under cover to me, unopened, any letter that may come from him. I shall expect your implicit obedience to these orders.'

'Well go on.'

'Have I your promise?'

'No no. You have no promise. I will make no promise exacted from me in so disgraceful a manner.'

'You refuse to obey me?'

'I will refuse nothing, and will promise nothing.'

'Then we must part—that is all. I will take care that you shall hear from me before tomorrow morning.'

So saying, he left the room, and, passing through the hall, saw that the letter had been taken away.

CHAPTER XI. LADY MILBOROUGH AS AMBASSADOR

'Of course, I know you are right,' said Nora to her sister 'right as far as Colonel Osborne is concerned; but nevertheless you ought to give way.'

'And be trampled upon?' said Mrs Trevelyan.

'Yes; and be trampled upon, if he should trample on you, which, however, he is the last man in the world to do.'

'And to endure any insult and any names? You yourself you would be a Griselda, I suppose.'

'I don't want to talk about myself,' said Nora, 'nor about Griselda. But I know that, however unreasonable it may seem, you had better give way to him now and tell him what there was in the note to Colonel Osborne.'

'Never! He has ordered me not to see him or to write to him, or to open his letters having, mind you, ordered just the reverse a day or two before; and I will obey him. Absurd as it is, I will obey him. But as for submitting to him, and letting him suppose that I think he is right— never! I should be lying to him then, and I will never lie to him. He has said that we must part, and I suppose it will be better so. How can a woman live with a man that suspects her? He cannot take my baby from me.'

There were many such conversations as the above between the two sisters before Mrs Trevelyan received from her husband the communication with which she had been threatened. And Nora, acting on her own judgment in the matter, made an attempt to see Mr Trevelyan, writing to him a pretty little note, and beseeching him to be kind to her. But he declined to see her, and the two women sat at home, with the baby between them, holding such pleasant conversations as that above narrated. When such tempests occur in a family, a woman will generally suffer the least during the thick of the tempest. While the hurricane is at the fiercest, she will be sustained by the most thorough conviction that the right is on her side, that she is aggrieved, that there is nothing for her to acknowledge, and no position that she need surrender. Whereas her husband will desire a compromise, even amidst the violence of the storm. But afterwards, when the wind has lulled, but while the heavens around are still all black and murky, then the woman's sufferings begin. When passion gives way to thought and memory, she feels the loneliness of her position, the loneliness, and the possible degradation. It is all very well for a man to talk about his name and his honour; but it is the woman's honour and the woman's name that are, in truth, placed in jeopardy. Let the woman do what she will, the man can, in truth, show his face in the world and, after awhile, does show his face. But the woman may be compelled to veil hers, either by her own fault, or by his. Mrs Trevelyan was now told that she was to be separated from her husband, and she did not, at any rate, believe that she had done any harm. But, if such separation did come, where could she live, what could she do, what position in the world would she possess? Would not her face be, in truth, veiled as effectually as though she had disgraced herself and her husband?

And then there was that terrible question about the child. Mrs Trevelyan had said a dozen times to her sister that her husband could not take the boy away from her. Nora, however, had never assented to this, partly from a conviction of her own ignorance, not knowing what might be the power of a husband in such a matter, and partly thinking that any argument would be good and fair by which she could induce her sister to avoid a catastrophe so terrible as that which was now threatened.

'I suppose he could take him, if he chose,' she said at last.

'I don't believe he is wicked like that,' said Mrs Trevelyan. 'He would not wish to kill me.'

'But he will say that he loves baby as well as you do.'

'He will never take my child from me. He could never be so bad as that.'

'And you will never be so bad as to leave him,' said Nora after a pause. 'I will not believe that it can come to that. You know that he is good at heart, that nobody on earth loves you as he does.'

So they went on for two days, and on the evening the second day there came a letter from Trevelyan to his wife. They had neither of them seen him, although he had been in and out of the house. And on the afternoon of the Sunday a new grievance, a very terrible grievance, was added to those which Mrs Trevelyan was made to bear. Her husband had told one of the servants in the house that Colonel Osborne was not to be admitted. And the servant to whom he had given this order was the cook. There is no reason why a cook should be less trustworthy in such a matter than any other servant; and in Mr Trevelyan's household there was a reason why she should be more so as she, and she alone, was what we generally call an old family domestic. She had lived with her master's mother, and had known her master when he was a boy. Looking about him, therefore, for someone in his house to whom he could speak, feeling that he was bound to convey the order through some medium, he called to him the ancient cook, and imparted to her so much of his trouble as was necessary to make the order intelligible. This he did with various ill-worded assurances to Mrs Prodgers that there really was nothing amiss. But when Mrs Trevelyan heard what had been done, which she did from Mrs Prodgers herself, Mrs Prodgers having been desired by her master to make the communication, she declared to her sister that everything was now over. She could never again live with a husband who had disgraced his wife by desiring her own cook to keep a guard upon her. Had the footman been instructed not to admit Colonel Osborne there would have been in such instruction some apparent adherence to the recognised usages of society. If you do not desire either your friend or your enemy to be received into your house, you communicate your desire to the person who has charge of the door. But the cook!

'And now, Nora, if it were you, do you mean to say that you would remain with him?' asked Mrs Trevelyan.

Nora simply replied that anything under any circumstances would be better than a separation.

On the morning of the third day there came the following letter:

Wednesday, June 1, 12 midnight.

DEAREST EMILY,

You will readily believe me when I say that I never in my life was so wretched as I have been during the last two days. That you and I should be in the same house together and not able to speak to each other is in itself a misery, but this is terribly enhanced by the dread lest this state of things should be made to continue.

I want you to understand that I do not in the least suspect you of having as yet done anything wrong or having even said anything injurious either to my position as your husband, or to your position as my wife. But I cannot but perceive that you are allowing yourself to be entrapped into an intimacy with Colonel Osborne which, if it be not checked, will be destructive to my happiness and your own. After what had passed before, you cannot have thought it right to receive letters from him which I was not to see, or to write letters to him of which I was not to know the contents. It must be manifest to you that such conduct on your part is wrong as judged by any of the rules by which a wife's conduct can be measured. And yet you have refused even to say that this shall be discontinued! I need hardly explain to you that if you persist in this refusal you and I cannot continue to live together as man and wife. All my hopes and prospects in life will be blighted by such a separation. I have not as yet been able to think what I should do in such wretched circumstances. And for you, as also for Nora, such a catastrophe would be most lamentable. Do, therefore, think of it well, and write me such a letter as may bring me back to your side.

There is only one friend in the world to whom I could endure to talk of this great grief, and I have been to her and told her everything. You will know that I mean Lady Milborough. After much difficult conversation I have persuaded her to see you, and she will call in Curzon Street to-morrow about twelve. There can be no kinder-hearted, or more gentle woman in the world than Lady Milborough; nor did any one ever have a warmer friend than both you and I have in her. Let me implore you then to listen to her, and be guided by her advice.

Pray believe, dearest Emily, that I am now, as ever, your most affectionate husband, and that I have no wish so strong as that we should not be compelled to part.

Louis Trevelyan.

This epistle was, in many respects, a very injudicious composition. Trevelyan should have trusted either to the eloquence of his own written words, or to that of the ambassador whom he was about to despatch; but by sending both he weakened both. And then there were certain words in the letter which were odious to Mrs Trevelyan, and must have been odious to any young wife. He had said that he did not 'as yet' suspect her of having done anything wrong. And then, when he endeavoured to explain to her that a separation would be very injurious to herself, he had coupled her sister with her, thus seeming to imply that the injury to be avoided was of a material kind. She had better do what he told her, as, otherwise, she and her sister would not have a roof over their head! That was the nature of the threat which his words were supposed to convey.

The matter had become so serious, that Mrs Trevelyan, haughty and stiff-necked as she was, did not dare to abstain from showing the letter to her sister. She had no other counsellor, at any rate, till Lady Milborough came, and the weight of the battle was too great for her own unaided spirit. The letter had been written late at night, as was shown by the precision of the date, and had been brought to her early in the morning. At first she had determined to say nothing about it to Nora, but she was not strong enough to maintain such a purpose. She felt that she needed the poor consolation of discussing her wretchedness. She first declared that she would not see Lady Milborough. 'I hate her, and she knows that I hate her, and she ought not to have thought of coming,' said Mrs Trevelyan.

But she was at last beaten out of this purpose by Nora's argument, that all the world would be against her if she refused to see her husband's old friend. And then, though the letter was an odious letter, as she declared a dozen times, she took some little comfort in the fact that not a word was said in it about the baby. She thought that if she could take her child with her into any separation, she could endure it, and her husband would ultimately be conquered.

'Yes; I'll see her,' she said, as they finished the discussion. 'As he chooses to send her, I suppose I had better see her. But I don't think he does much to mend matters when he sends the woman whom he knows I dislike more than any other in all London.'

Exactly at twelve o'clock Lady Milborough's carriage was at the door. Trevelyan was in the house at the time and heard the knock at the door. During those two or three days of absolute wretchedness, he spent most of his hours under the same roof with his wife and sister-in-law, though he spoke to neither of them. He had had his doubts as to the reception of Lady Milborough, and was, to tell the truth, listening with most anxious ear, when her Ladyship was announced. His wife, however, was not so bitterly contumacious as to refuse admittance to his friend, and he heard the rustle of the ponderous silk as the old woman was shown upstairs. When Lady Milborough reached the drawing-room, Mrs Trevelyan was alone.

'I had better see her by myself,' she had said to her sister.

Nora had then left her, with one word of prayer that she would be as little defiant as possible.

'That must depend,' Emily had said, with a little shake of her head.

There had been a suggestion that the child should be with her, but the mother herself had rejected this.

'It would be stagey,' she had said, 'and clap-trap. There is nothing I hate so much as that.'

She was sitting, therefore, quite alone, and as stiff as a man in armour, when Lady Milborough was shown up to her.

And Lady Milborough herself was not at all comfortable as she commenced the interview. She had prepared many wise words to be spoken, but was not so little ignorant of the character of the woman with whom she had to deal, as to suppose that the wise words would get themselves spoken without interruption. She had known from the first that Mrs Trevelyan would have much to say for herself, and the feeling that it would be so became stronger than ever as she entered the room. The ordinary feelings between the two ladies were cold and constrained, and then there was silence for a few moments when the Countess had taken her seat. Mrs Trevelyan had quite determined that the enemy should fire the first shot.

'This is a very sad state of things,' said the Countess.

'Yes, indeed, Lady Milborough.'

'The saddest in the world and so unnecessary is it not?'

'Very unnecessary, indeed, as I think.'

'Yes, my dear, yes. But, of course, we must remember.'

Then Lady Milborough could not clearly bring to her mind what it was that she had to remember.

'The fact is, my dear, that all this kind of thing is too monstrous to be thought of. Goodness, gracious, me; two young people like you and Louis, who thoroughly love each other, and who have got a baby, to think of being separated! Of course it is out of the question.'

'You cannot suppose, Lady Milborough, that I want to be separated from my husband?'

'Of course not. How should it be possible? The very idea is too shocking to be thought of. I declare I haven't slept since Louis was talking to me about it. But, my dear, you must remember, you know, that a husband has a right to expect some sort of submission from his wife.'

'He has a right to expect obedience, Lady Milborough.'

'Of course; that is all one wants.'

'And I will obey Mr Trevelyan in anything reasonable.'

'But, my dear, who is to say what is reasonable? That, you see, is always the difficulty. You must allow that your husband is the person who ought to decide that.'

'Has he told you that I have refused to obey him, Lady Milborough?'

The Countess paused a moment before she replied. 'Well, yes; I think he has,' she said. 'He asked you to do something about a letter, a letter to that Colonel Osborne, who is a man, my dear, really to be very much afraid of; a man who has done a great deal of harm, and you declined. Now in a matter of that kind of course the husband—'

'Lady Milborough, I must ask you to listen to me. You have listened to Mr Trevelyan, and I must ask you to listen to me. I am sorry to trouble you, but as you have come here about this unpleasant business, you must forgive me if I insist upon it.'

'Of course I will listen to you, my dear.'

'I have never refused to obey my husband, and I do not refuse now. The gentleman of whom you have been speaking is an old friend of my father's, and has become my friend. Nevertheless, had Mr Trevelyan given me any plain order about him, I should have obeyed him. A wife does not feel that her chances of happiness are increased when she finds that her husband suspects her of being too intimate with another man. It is a thing very hard to bear. But I would have endeavoured to bear it, knowing how important it is for both our sakes, and more especially for our child. I would have made excuses, and would have endeavoured to think that this horrid feeling on his part is nothing more than a short delusion.'

'But, my dear—'

'I must ask you to hear me out, Lady Milborough. But when he tells me first that I am not to meet the man, and so instructs the servants; then tells me that I am to meet him, and go on just as I was going before, and then again tells me that I am not to see him, and again instructs the servants and, above all, the cook that Colonel Osborne is not to come into the house, then obedience becomes rather difficult.'

'Just say now that you will do what he wants, and then all will be right.'

'I will not say so to you, Lady Milborough. It is not to you that I ought to say it. But as he has chosen to send you here, I will explain to you that I have never disobeyed him. When I was free, in accordance with Mr Trevelyan's wishes, to have what intercourse I pleased with Colonel Osborne, I received a note from that gentleman on a most trivial matter. I answered it as trivially. My husband saw my letter, closed, and questioned me about it. I told him that the letter was still there, and that if he chose to be a spy upon my actions he could open it and read it.'

'My dear, how could you bring yourself to use the word spy to your husband?'

'How could he bring himself to accuse me as he did? If he cares for me let him come and beg my pardon for the insult he has offered me.'

'Oh, Mrs Trevelyan!'

'Yes; that seems very wrong to you, who have not had to bear it. It is very easy for a stranger to take a husband's part, and help to put down a poor woman who has been ill used. I have done nothing wrong, nothing to be ashamed of; and I will not say that I have. I never have spoken a word to Colonel Osborne that all the world might not hear.'

'Nobody has accused you, my dear.'

'Yes; he has accused me, and you have accused me, and you will make all the world accuse me. He may put me out of his house if he likes, but he shall not make me say I have been wrong, when I know I have been right. He cannot take my child from me.'

'But he will.'

'No,' shouted Mrs Trevelyan, jumping up from her chair, 'no; he shall never do that. I will cling to him so that he cannot separate us. He will never be so wicked, such a monster as that. I would go about the world saying what a monster he had been to me.' The passion of the interview was becoming too great for Lady Milborough's power of moderating it, and she was beginning to feel herself to be in a difficulty. 'Lady Milborough,' continued Mrs Trevelyan, 'tell him from me that I will bear anything but that. That I will not bear.'

'Dear Mrs Trevelyan, do not let us talk about it.'

'Who wants to talk about it? Why do you come here and threaten me with a thing so horrible? I do not believe you. He would not dare to separate me and my child.'

'But you have only to say that you will submit yourself to him.'

'I have submitted myself to him, and I will submit no further. What does he want? Why does he send you here? He does not know what he wants. He has made himself miserable by an absurd idea, and he wants everybody to tell him that he has been right. He has been very wrong; and if he desires to be wise now, he will come back to his home, and say nothing further about it. He will gain nothing by sending messengers here.'

Lady Milborough, who had undertaken a most disagreeable task from the purest motives of old friendship, did not like being called a messenger; but the woman before her was so strong in her words, so eager, and so passionate, that she did not know how to resent the injury. And there was coming over her an idea, of which she herself was hardly conscious, that after all, perhaps, the husband was not in the right. She had come there with the general idea that wives, and especially young wives, should be submissive. She had naturally taken the husband's part; and having a preconceived dislike to Colonel Osborne, she had been willing enough to think that precautionary measures were necessary in reference to so eminent, and notorious, and experienced a Lothario. She had never altogether loved Mrs Trevelyan, and had always been a little in dread of her. But she had thought that the authority with which she would be invested on this occasion, the manifest right on her side, and the undeniable truth of her grand argument, that a wife should obey, would carry her, if not easily, still successfully through all difficulties. It was probably the case that Lady Milborough when preparing for her visit, had anticipated a triumph. But when she had been closeted for an hour with Mrs Trevelyan, she found that she was not triumphant. She was told that she was a messenger, and an unwelcome messenger; and she began to feel that she did not know how she was to take herself away.

'I am sure I have done everything for the best,' she said, getting up from her chair.

'The best will be to send him back, and make him feel the truth.'

'The best for you, my dear, will be to consider well what should be the duty of a wife.'

'I have considered, Lady Milborough. It cannot be a wife's duty to acknowledge that she has been wrong in such a matter as this.'

Then Lady Milborough made her curtsey and got herself away in some manner that was sufficiently awkward, and Mrs Trevelyan curtseyed also as she rang the bell; and, though she was sore and wretched, and, in truth, sadly frightened, she was not awkward. In that encounter, so far as it had gone, she had been the victor.

As soon as she was alone and the carriage had been driven well away from the door, Mrs Trevelyan left the drawing-room and went up to the nursery. As she entered she clothed her face with her sweetest smile. 'How is his own mother's dearest, dearest, darling duck' she said, putting out her arms and taking the boy from the nurse. The child was at this time about ten months old, and was a strong, hearty, happy infant, always laughing when he was awake and always sleeping when he did not laugh, because his little limbs were free from pain and his little stomach was not annoyed by internal troubles. He kicked, and crowed, and sputtered, when his mother took him, and put up his little fingers to clutch her hair, and was to her as a young god upon the earth. Nothing in the world had ever been created so beautiful, so joyous, so satisfactory, so divine! And they told her that this apple of her eye was to be taken away from her! No that must be impossible. 'I will take him into my own room, nurse, for a little while—you have had him all the morning,' she said; as though the 'having baby' was a privilege over which there might almost be a quarrel. Then she took her boy away with her, and when she was alone with him, went through such a service in baby-worship as most mothers will understand. Divide these two! No; nobody should do that. Sooner than that, she, the mother, would consent to be no more than a servant in her husband's house. Was not her baby all the world to her?

On the evening of that day the husband and wife had an interview together in the library, which, unfortunately, was as unsatisfactory as Lady Milborough's visit. The cause of the failure of them all lay probably in this, that there was no decided point which, if conceded, would have brought about a reconciliation. Trevelyan asked for general submission, which he regarded as his right, and which in the existing circumstances he thought it necessary to claim, and though Mrs Trevelyan did not refuse to be submissive she would make no promise on the subject. But the truth was that each desired that the other should acknowledge a fault, and that neither of them would make that acknowledgment. Emily Trevelyan felt acutely that she had been ill-used, not only by her husband's suspicion, but by the manner in which he had talked of his suspicion to others, to Lady Milborough and the cook, and she was quite convinced that she was right herself, because he had been so vacillating in his conduct about Colonel Osborne. But Trevelyan was equally sure that justice was on his side. Emily must have known his real wishes about Colonel Osborne; but when she had found that he had rescinded his verbal orders about the admission of the man to the house, which he had done to save himself and her from slander and gossip, she had taken advantage of this and had thrown herself more entirely than ever into the intimacy of which he disapproved!

When they met, each was so sore that no approach to terms was made by them.

'If I am to be treated in that way, I would rather not live with you,' said the wife. 'It is impossible to live with a husband who is jealous.'

'All I ask of you is that you shall promise me to have no further communication with this man.'

'I will make no promise that implies my own disgrace.'

'Then we must part; and if that be so, this house will be given up. You may live where you please in the country, not in London; but I shall take steps that Colonel Osborne does not see you.'

'I will not remain in the room with you to be insulted thus,' said Mrs Trevelyan. And she did not remain, but left the chamber, slamming the door after her as she went.

'It will be better that she should go,' said Trevelyan, when he found himself alone. And so it came to pass that that blessing of a rich marriage, which had as it were fallen upon them at the Mandarins from out of heaven, had become, after an interval of but two short years, anything but an unmixed blessing.

CHAPTER XII. MISS STANBURY'S GENEROSITY

On one Wednesday morning early in June, great preparations were being made at the brick house in the Close at Exeter for an event which can hardly be said to have required any preparation at all. Mrs Stanbury and her elder daughter were coming into Exeter from Nuncombe Putney to visit Dorothy. The reader may perhaps remember that when Miss Stanbury's invitation was sent to her niece, she was pleased to promise that such visits should be permitted on a Wednesday morning. Such a visit was now to be made, and old Miss Stanbury was quite moved by the occasion. 'I shall not see them, you know, Martha,' she had said, on the afternoon of the preceding day.

'I suppose not, ma'am.'

'Certainly not. Why should I? It would do no good.'

'It is not for me to say, ma'am, of course.'

'No, Martha, it is not. And I am sure that I am right. It's no good going back and undoing in ten minutes what twenty years have done. She's a poor harmless creature, I believe.'

'The most harmless in the world, ma'am.'

'But she was as bad as poison to me when she was young, and what's the good of trying to change it now? If I was to tell her that I loved her, I should only be lying.'

'Then, ma'am, I would not say it.'

'And I don't mean. But you'll take in some wine and cake, you know.'

'I don't think they'll care for wine and cake.'

'Will you do as I tell you? What matters whether they care for it or not. They need not take it. It will look better for Miss Dorothy. If Dorothy is to remain here I shall choose that she should be respected.' And so the question of the cake and wine had been decided overnight. But when the morning came Miss Stanbury was still in a twitter. Half-past ten had been the hour fixed for the visit, in consequence of there being a train in from Lessboro', due at the Exeter station at ten. As Miss Stanbury breakfasted always at half-past eight, there was no need of hurry on account of the expected visit. But, nevertheless, she was in a fuss all the morning; and spoke of the coming period as one in which she must necessarily put herself into solitary confinement.

'Perhaps your mamma will be cold,' she said, 'and will expect a fire.'

'Oh, dear, no, Aunt Stanbury.'

'It could be lighted of course. It is a pity they should come just so as to prevent you from going to morning service; is it not?'

'I could go with you, aunt, and be back very nearly in time. They won't mind waiting a quarter of an hour.'

'What; and have them here all alone! I wouldn't think of such a thing. I shall go up-stairs. You had better come to me when they are gone. Don't hurry them. I don't want you to hurry them at all; and if you require anything, Martha will wait upon you. I have told the girls to keep out of the way. They are so giddy, there's no knowing what they might be after. Besides they've got their work to mind.'

All this was very terrible to poor Dorothy, who had not as yet quite recovered from the original fear with which her aunt had inspired her— so terrible that she was almost sorry that her mother and sister were coming to her. When the knock was heard at the door, precisely as the cathedral clock was striking half-past ten, to secure which punctuality, and thereby not to offend the owner of the mansion, Mrs Stanbury and Priscilla had been walking about the Close for the last ten minutes Miss Stanbury was still in the parlour.

'There they are!' she exclaimed, jumping up. 'They haven't given a body much time to run away, have they, my dear? Half a minute, Martha just half a minute!' Then she gathered up her things as though she had been ill-treated in being driven to make so sudden a retreat, and Martha, as soon as the last hem of her mistress's dress had become invisible on the stairs, opened the front door for the visitors.

'Do you mean to say you like it?' said Priscilla, when they had been there about a quarter of an hour.

'H—u—sh,' whispered Mrs Stanbury.

'I don't suppose she's listening at the door,' said Priscilla.

'Indeed, she's not,' said Dorothy. 'There can't be a truer, honester woman, than Aunt Stanbury.'

'But is she kind to you, Dolly?' asked the mother.

'Very kind; too kind. Only I don't understand her quite, and then she gets angry with me. I know she thinks I'm a fool, and that's the worst of it.'

'Then, if I were you, I would come home,' said Priscilla.

'She'll never forgive you if you do,' said Mrs Stanbury.

'And who need care about her forgiveness?' said Priscilla.

'I don't mean to go home yet, at any rate,' said Dorothy. Then there was a knock at the door, and Martha entered with the cake and wine. 'Miss Stanbury's compliments, ladies, and she hopes you'll take a glass of sherry.' Whereupon she filled out the glasses and carried them round.

'Pray give my compliments and thanks to my sister Stanbury,' said Dorothy's mother. But Priscilla put down the glass of wine without touching it, and looked her sternest at the maid.

Altogether, the visit was not very successful, and poor Dorothy almost felt that if she chose to remain in the Close she must lose her mother and sister, and that without really making a friend of her aunt. There had as yet been no quarrel, nothing that had been plainly recognised as disagreeable; but there had not as yet come to be any sympathy, or assured signs of comfortable love. Miss Stanbury had declared more than once that it would do, but had not succeeded in showing in what the success consisted. When she was told that the two ladies were gone, she desired that Dorothy might be sent to her, and immediately began to make anxious inquiries.

'Well, my dear, and what do they think of it?'

'I don't know, aunt, that they think very much.'

'And what do they say about it?'

'They didn't say very much, aunt. I was very glad to see mamma and Priscilla. Perhaps I ought to tell you that mamma gave me back the money I sent her.'

'What did she do that for?' asked Miss Stanbury very sharply.

'Because she says that Hugh sends her now what she wants.' Miss Stanbury, when she heard this, looked very sour. 'I thought it best to tell you, you know.'

'It will never come to any good, got in that way, never.'

'But, Aunt Stanbury, isn't it good of him to send it?'

'I don't know. I suppose it's better than drinking, and smoking, and gambling. But I dare say he gets enough for that too. When a man, born and bred like a gentleman, condescends to let out his talents and education for such purposes, I dare say they are willing enough to pay him. The devil always does pay high wages. But that only makes it so much the worse. One almost comes to doubt whether any one ought to learn to write at all, when it is used for such vile purposes. I've said what I've got to say, and I don't mean to say anything more. What's the use? But it has been hard upon me very. It was my money did it, and I feel I've misused it. It's a disgrace to me which I don't deserve.'

For a couple of minutes Dorothy remained quite silent, and Miss Stanbury did not herself say anything further. Nor during that time did she observe her niece, or she would probably have seen that the subject was not to be dropped. Dorothy, though she was silent, was not calm, and was preparing herself for a crusade in her brother's defence.

'Aunt Stanbury, he's my brother, you know.'

'Of course he's your brother. I wish he were not.'

'I think him the best brother in the world and the best son.'

'Why does he sell himself to write sedition?'

'He doesn't sell himself to write sedition. I don't see why it should be sedition, or anything wicked, because it's sold for a penny.'

'If you are going to cram him down my throat, Dorothy, you and I had better part.'

'I don't want to say anything about him, only you ought not to abuse him before me.'

By this time Dorothy was beginning to sob, but Miss Stanbury's countenance was still very grim and very stern. 'He's coming home to Nuncombe Putney, and I want to see see him,' continued Dorothy.

'Hugh Stanbury coming to Exeter! He won't come here.'

'Then I'd rather go home, Aunt Stanbury.'

'Very well, very well,' said Miss Stanbury, and she got up and left the room.

Dorothy was in dismay, and began to think that there was nothing for her to do but to pack up her clothes and prepare for her departure. She was very sorry for what had occurred, being fully alive to the importance of the aid not only to herself, but to her mother and sister, which was afforded by the present arrangement, and she felt very angry with herself, in that she had already driven her aunt to quarrel with her. But she had found it to be impossible to hear her own brother abused without saying a word on his behalf. She did not see her aunt again till dinner-time, and then there was hardly a word uttered. Once or twice Dorothy made a little effort to speak, but these attempts failed utterly. The old woman would hardly reply even by a monosyllable, but simply muttered something, or shook her head when she was addressed. Jane, who waited at table, was very demure and silent, and Martha, who once came into the room during the meal, merely whispered a word into Miss Stanbury's ear. When the cloth was removed, and two glasses of port had been poured out by Miss Stanbury herself, Dorothy felt that she could endure this treatment no longer. How was it possible that she could drink wine under such circumstances?

'Not for me, Aunt Stanbury,' said she, with a deploring tone.

'Why not?'

'I couldn't drink it today.'

'Why didn't you say so before it was poured out? And why not today? Come, drink it. Do as I bid you.' And she stood over her niece, as a tragedy queen in a play with a bowl of poison. Dorothy took it and sipped it from mere force of obedience. 'You make as many bones about a glass of port wine as though it were senna and salts,' said Miss Stanbury. 'Now I've got something to say to you.' By this time the servant was gone, and the two were seated alone together in the parlour. Dorothy, who had not as yet swallowed above half her wine, at once put the glass down. There was an importance in her aunt's tone which frightened her, and made her feel that some evil was coming. And yet, as she had made up her mind that she must return home, there was no further evil that she need dread. 'You didn't write any of those horrid articles?' said Miss Stanbury.

'No, aunt; I didn't write them. I shouldn't know how.'

'And I hope you'll never learn. They say women are to vote, and become doctors, and if so, there's no knowing what devil's tricks they mayn't do. But it isn't your fault about that filthy newspaper. How he can let himself down to write stuff that is to be printed on straw is what I can't understand.'

'I don't see how it can make a difference as he writes it.'

'It would make a great deal of difference to me. And I'm told that what they call ink comes off on your fingers like lamp-black. I never touched one, thank God; but they tell me so. All the same; it isn't your fault.'

'I've nothing to do with it, Aunt Stanbury.'

'Of course you've not. And as he is your brother it wouldn't be natural that you should like to throw him off. And, my dear, I like you for taking his part. Only you needn't have been so fierce with an old woman.'

'Indeed indeed I didn't mean to be fierce, Aunt Stanbury.'

'I never was taken up so short in my life. But we won't mind that. There; he shall come and see you. I suppose he won't insist on leaving any of his nastiness about.'

'But is he to come here, Aunt Stanbury?'

'He may if he pleases.'

'Oh, Aunt Stanbury!'

'When he was here last he generally had a pipe in his mouth, and I dare say he never puts it down at all now. Those things grow upon young people so fast. But if he could leave it on the door-step just while he's here I should be obliged to him.'

'But, dear aunt, couldn't I see him in the street?'

'Out in the street! No, my dear. All the world is not to know that he's your brother; and he is dressed in such a rapscallion manner that the people would think you were talking to a house-breaker.' Dorothy's face became again red as she heard this, and the angry words were very nearly spoken. 'The last time I saw him,' continued Miss Stanbury, 'he had on a short, rough jacket, with enormous buttons, and one of those flipperty-flopperty things on his head, that the butcher-boys wear. And, oh, the smell of tobacco! As he had been up in London I suppose he thought Exeter was no better than a village, and he might do just as he pleased. But he knew that if I'm particular about anything, it is about a gentleman's hat in the streets. And he wanted me me to walk with him across to Mrs MacHugh's! We should have been hooted about the Close like a pair of mad dogs and so I told him.'

'All the young men seem to dress like that now, Aunt Stanbury.'

'No, they don't. Mr Gibson doesn't dress like that.'

'But he's a clergyman, Aunt Stanbury.'

'Perhaps I'm an old fool. I dare say I am, and of course that's what you mean. At any rate I'm too old to change, and I don't mean to try. I like to see a difference between a gentleman and a house-breaker. For the matter of that I'm told that there is a difference, and that the house-breakers all look like gentlemen now. It may be proper to make us all stand on our heads, with our legs sticking up in the air; but I for one don't like being topsy-turvy, and I won't try it. When is he to reach Exeter?'

'He is coming on Tuesday next, by the last train.'

'Then you can't see him that night. That's out of the question. No doubt he'll sleep at the Nag's Head, as that's the lowest radical public-house in the city. Martha shall try to find him. She knows more about his doings than I do. If he chooses to come here the following morning before he goes down to Nuncombe Putney, well and good. I shall wait up till Martha comes back from the train on Tuesday night, and hear.' Dorothy was of course full of gratitude and thanks; but yet she felt almost disappointed by the result of her aunt's clemency on the matter. She had desired to take her brother's part, and it had seemed to her as though she had done so in a very lukewarm manner. She had listened to an immense number of accusations against him, and had been unable to reply to them because she had been conquered by the promise of a visit. And now it was out of the question that she should speak of going. Her aunt had given way to her, and of course had conquered her.

Late on the Tuesday evening, after ten o'clock, Hugh Stanbury was walking round the Close with his aunt's old servant. He had not put up at that dreadfully radical establishment of which Miss Stanbury was so much afraid, but had taken a bedroom at the Railway Inn. From there he had walked up to the Close with Martha, and now was having a few last words with her before he would allow her to return to the house.

'I suppose she'd as soon see the devil as see me,' said Hugh.

'If you speak in that way, Mr Hugh, I won't listen to you.'

'And yet I did everything I could to please her; and I don't think any boy ever loved an old woman better than I did her.'

'That was while she used to send you cakes, and ham, and jam to school, Mr Hugh.'

'Of course it was, and while she sent me flannel waistcoats to Oxford. But when I didn't care any longer for cakes or flannel then she got tired of me. It is much better as it is, if she'll only be good to Dorothy.'

'She never was bad to any body, Mr Hugh. But I don't think an old lady like her ever takes to a woman as she does to a young man, if only he'll let her have a little more of her own way than you would. It's my belief that you might have had it all for your own some day, if you'd done as you ought.'

'That's nonsense, Martha. She means to leave it all to the Burgesses. I've heard her say so.'

'Say so; yes. People don't always do what they say. If you'd managed rightly you might have it all and so you might now.'

'I'll tell you what, old girl; I shan't try. Live for the next twenty years under her apron strings, that I may have the chance at the end of it of cutting some poor devil out of his money! Do you know the meaning of making a score off your own bat, Martha?'

'No, I don't; and if it's anything you're like to do, I don't think I should be the better for learning by all accounts. And now if you please, I'll go in.'

'Good night, Martha. My love to them both, and say I'll be there tomorrow exactly at half-past nine. You'd better take it. It won't turn to slate-stone. It hasn't come from the old gentleman.'

'I don't want anything of that kind, Mr Hugh indeed I don't.'

'Nonsense. If you don't take it you'll offend me. I believe you think I'm not much better than a schoolboy still.'

'I don't think you're half so good, Mr Hugh,' said the old servant, sticking the sovereign which Hugh had given her in under her glove as she spoke.

On the next morning that other visit was made at the brick house, and Miss Stanbury was again in a fuss. On this occasion, however, she was in a much better humour than before, and was full of little jokes as to the nature of the visitation. Of course, she was not to see her nephew herself, and no message was to be delivered from her, and none was to be given to her from him. But an accurate report was to be made to her as to his appearance, and Dorothy was to be enabled to answer a variety of questions respecting him after he was gone. 'Of course, I don't want to know anything about his money,' Miss Stanbury said, 'only I should like to know how much these people can afford to pay for their penny trash.' On this occasion she had left the room and gone up-stairs before the knock came at the door, but she managed, by peeping over the balcony, to catch a glimpse of the 'flipperty-flopperty' hat which her nephew certainly had with him on this occasion.

Hugh Stanbury had great news for his sister. The cottage in which Mrs Stanbury lived at Nuncombe Putney, was the tiniest little dwelling in which a lady and her two daughters ever sheltered themselves. There was, indeed, a sitting-room, two bed-rooms, and a kitchen; but they were all so diminutive in size that the cottage was little more than a cabin. But there was a house in the village, not large indeed, but eminently respectable, three stories high, covered with ivy, having a garden behind it, and generally called the Clock House, because there had once been a clock upon it. This house had been lately vacated, and Hugh informed his sister that he was thinking of taking it for his mother's accommodation. Now, the late occupants of the Clock House, at Nuncombe Putney, had been people with five or six hundred a-year. Had other matters been in accordance, the house would almost have entitled them to consider themselves as county people. A gardener had always been kept there and a cow!

'The Clock House for mamma!'

'Well, yes. Don't say a word about it as yet to Aunt Stanbury, as she'll think that I've sold myself altogether to the old gentleman.'

'But, Hugh, how can mamma live there?'

'The fact is, Dorothy, there is a secret. I can't tell you quite yet. Of course, you'll know it, and everybody will know it, if the thing comes about. But as you won't talk, I will tell you what most concerns ourselves.'

'And am I to go back?'

'Certainly not if you will take my advice. Stick to your aunt. You don't want to smoke pipes, and wear Tom-and-Jerry hats, and write for the penny newspapers.'

Now Hugh Stanbury's secret was this, that Louis Trevelyan's wife and sister-in-law were to leave the house in Curzon Street, and come and live at Nuncombe Putney, with Mrs Stanbury and Priscilla. Such, at least, was the plan to be carried out, if Hugh Stanbury should be successful in his present negotiations.

CHAPTER XIII. THE HONOURABLE MR GLASCOCK

By the end of July Mrs Trevelyan with her sister was established in the Clock House, at Nuncombe Putney, under the protection of Hugh's mother; but before the reader is made acquainted with any of the circumstances of their life there, a few words must be said of an occurrence which took place before those two ladies left Curzon Street.

As to the quarrel between Trevelyan and his wife, things went from bad to worse. Lady Milborough continued to interfere, writing letters to Emily which were full of good sense, but which, as Emily said herself, never really touched the point of dispute. 'Am I, who am altogether unconscious of having done anything amiss, to confess that I have been in the wrong? If it were about a small matter, I would not mind, for the sake of peace. But when it concerns my conduct in reference to another man I would rather die first,' That had been Mrs Trevelyan's line of thought and argument in the matter; but then old Lady Milborough in her letters spoke only of the duty of obedience as promised at the altar. 'But I didn't promise to tell a lie,' said Mrs Trevelyan. And there were interviews between Lady Milborough and Trevelyan, and interviews between Lady Milborough and Nora Rowley. The poor dear old dowager was exceedingly busy and full of groans, prescribing Naples, prescribing a course of extra prayers, prescribing a general course of letting bygones be bygones to which, however, Trevelyan would by no means assent without some assurance, which he might regard as a guarantee, prescribing retirement to a small town in the west of France, if Naples would not suffice; but she could effect nothing.

Mrs Trevelyan, indeed, did a thing which was sure of itself to render any steps taken for a reconciliation ineffectual. In the midst of all this turmoil while she and her husband were still living in the same house, but apart because of their absurd quarrel respecting Colonel Osborne, she wrote another letter to that gentleman. The argument by which she justified this to herself, and to her sister after it was done, was the real propriety of her own conduct throughout her whole intimacy with Colonel Osborne. 'But that is just what Louis doesn't want you to do,' Nora had said, filled with anger and dismay. 'Then let Louis give me an order to that effect, and behave to me like a husband, and I will obey him,' Emily had answered. And she had gone on to plead that in her present condition she was under no orders from her husband. She was left to judge for herself, and judging for herself she knew, as she said, that it best that she should write to Colonel Osborne. Unfortunately there was no ground for hoping that Colonel Osborne was ignorant of this insane jealousy on the part of her husband. It was better, therefore, she said, that she should write to him whom on the occasion she took care to name to her sister as 'papa's old friend' and explain to him what she would wish him to do, and what not to do. Colonel Osborne answered the letter very quickly, throwing much more of demonstrative affection than he should have done into his 'Dear Emily' and his 'Dearest Friend.' Of course Mrs Trevelyan had burned this answer, and of course Mr Trevelyan had been told of the correspondence. His wife, indeed, had been especially careful that there should be nothing secret about the matter that it should be so known in the house that Mr Trevelyan should be sure to hear of it. And he had heard of it, and been driven almost mad by it. He had flown off to Lady Milborough, and had reduced his old friend to despair by declaring that, after all, he began to fear that his wife was was was infatuated by that d scoundrel. Lady Milborough forgave the language, but protested that he was wrong in his suspicion. 'To continue to correspond with him after what I have said to her!' exclaimed Trevelyan. 'Take her to Naples at once,' said Lady Milborough, 'at once!' 'And have him after me?' said Trevelyan. Lady Milborough had no answer ready, and not having thought of this looked very blank. 'I should find it harder to deal with her there even than here,' continued Trevelyan. Then it was that Lady Milborough spoke of the small town in the west of France, urging as her reason that such a man as Colonel Osborne would certainly not follow them there; but Trevelyan had become indignant at this, declaring that if his wife's good name could be preserved in no other manner than that, it would not be worth preserving at all. Then Lady Milborough had begun to cry, and had continued crying for a very long time. She was very unhappy as unhappy as her nature would allow her to be. She would have made almost any sacrifice to bring the two young people together, would have willingly given her time, her money, her labour in the cause, would probably herself have gone to the little town in the west of France, had her going been of any service. But, nevertheless, after her own fashion, she extracted no small enjoyment out of the circumstances of this miserable quarrel. The Lady Milboroughs of the day hate the Colonel Osbornes from the very bottoms of their warm hearts and pure souls; but they respect the Colonel Osbornes almost as much as they hate them, and find it to be an inestimable privilege to be brought into some contact with these roaring lions.

But there arose to dear Lady Milborough a great trouble out of this quarrel, irrespective of the absolute horror of the separation of a young husband from his young wife. And the excess of her trouble on this head was great proof of the real goodness of her heart. For, in this matter, the welfare of Trevelyan himself was not concerned but rather that of the Rowley family. Now the Rowleys had not given Lady Milborough any special reason for loving them. When she had first heard that her dear young friend Louis was going to marry a girl from the Mandarins, she had been almost in despair. It was her opinion that had he properly understood his own position, he would have promoted his welfare by falling in love with the daughter of some English country gentleman or some English peer, to which honour, with his advantages, Lady Milborough thought that he might have aspired. Nevertheless, when the girl from the Mandarins had been brought home as Mrs Trevelyan, Lady Milborough had received her with open arms—had received even the sister-in-law with arms partly open. Had either of them shown any tendency to regard her as a mother, she would have showered motherly cares upon them. For Lady Milborough was like an old hen, in her capacity for taking many under her wings. The two sisters had hardly done more than bear with her, Nora, indeed, bearing with her more graciously than Mrs Trevelyan; and in return, even for this, the old dowager was full of motherly regard. Now she knew well that Mr Glascock was over head and ears in love with Nora Rowley. It only wanted the slightest management and the easiest discretion to bring him on his knees, with an offer of his hand. And, then, how much that hand contained, how much, indeed, as compared with that other hand, which was to be given in return, and which was to speak the truth completely empty! Mr Glascock was the heir to a peer, was the heir to a rich peer, was the heir to a very, very old peer. He was in Parliament. The world spoke well of him. He was not, so to say, by any means an old man himself. He was good-tempered, reasonable, easily led, and yet by no means despicable. On all subjects connected with land, he held an opinion that was very much respected, and was supposed to be a thoroughly good specimen of an upper-class Englishman. Here was a suitor! But it was not to be supposed that such a man as Mr Glascock would be so violently in love as to propose to a girl whose nearest known friend and female relation was misbehaving herself?

Only they who have closely watched the natural uneasinesses of human hens can understand how great was Lady Milborough's anxiety on this occasion. Marriage to her was a thing always delightful to contemplate. Though she had never been sordidly a matchmaker, the course of the world around her had taught her to regard men as fish to be caught, and girls as the anglers who ought to catch them. Or, rather, could her mind have been accurately analysed, it would have been found that the girl was regarded as half-angler and half-bait. Any girl that angled visibly with her own hook, with a manifestly expressed desire to catch a fish, was odious to her. And she was very gentle-hearted in regard to the fishes, thinking that every fish in the river should have the hook and bait presented to him in the mildest, pleasantest form. But still, when the trout was well in the basket, her joy was great; and then came across her unlaborious mind some half-formed idea that a great ordinance of nature was being accomplished in the teeth of difficulties. For as she well knew there is a difficulty in the catching of fish.

Lady Milborough, in her kind anxiety on Nora's behalf that the fish should be landed before Nora might be swept away in her sister's ruin hardly knew what step she might safely take. Mrs Trevelyan would not see her again having already declared that any further interview would be painful and useless. She had spoken to Trevelyan, but Trevelyan had declared that he could do nothing. What was there that he could have done? He could not, as he said, overlook the gross improprieties of his wife's conduct, because his wife's sister had, or might possibly have, a lover. And then as to speaking to Mr Glascock himself nobody knew better than Lady Milborough how very apt fish are to be frightened.

But at last Lady Milborough did speak to Mr Glascock making no allusion whatever to the hook prepared for himself, but saying a word or two as to the affairs of that other fish, whose circumstances, as he floundered about in the bucket of matrimony, were not as happy as they might have been. The care, the discretion, nay, the wisdom with which she did this were most excellent. She had become aware that Mr Glascock had already heard of the unfortunate affair in Curzon Street. Indeed, every one who knew the Trevelyans had heard of it, and a great many who did not know them. No harm, therefore, could be done by mentioning the circumstance. Lady Milborough did mention it, explaining that the only person really in fault was that odious destroyer of the peace of families, Colonel Osborne, of whom Lady Milborough, on that occasion, said some very severe things indeed. Poor dear Mrs Trevelyan was foolish, obstinate, and self-reliant but as innocent as the babe unborn. That things would come right before long no one who knew the affair—and she knew it from beginning to end—could for a moment doubt. The real victim would be that sweetest of all girls, Nora Rowley. Mr Glascock innocently asked why Nora Rowley should be a victim. 'Don't you understand, Mr Glascock, how the most remote connection with a thing of that kind tarnishes a young woman's standing in the world?' Mr Glascock was almost angry with the well-pleased Countess as he declared that he could not see that Miss Rowley's standing was at all tarnished; and old Lady Milborough, when he got up and left her, felt that she had done a good morning's work. If Nora could have known it all, Nora ought to have been very grateful, for Mr Glascock got into a cab in Eccleston Square and had himself driven direct to Curzon Street. He himself believed that he was at that moment only doing the thing which he had for some time past resolved that he would do; but we perhaps may be justified in thinking that the actual resolution was first fixed by the discretion of Lady Milborough's communication. At any rate he arrived in Curzon Street with his mind fully resolved, and had spent the minutes in the cab considering how he had better perform the business in hand.

He was at once shown into the drawing-room, where he found the two sisters, and Mrs Trevelyan, as soon as she saw him, understood the purpose of his coming. There was an air of determination about him, a manifest intention of doing something, an absence of that vagueness which almost always flavours a morning visit. This was so strongly marked that Mrs Trevelyan felt that she would have been almost justified in getting up and declaring that, as this visit was paid to her sister, she would retire. But, any such declaration on her part was unnecessary, as Mr Glascock had not been in the room three minutes before he asked her to go. By some clever device of his own, he got her into the back room and whispered to her that he wanted to say a few words in private to her sister.

'Oh, certainly,' said Mrs Trevelyan, smiling.

'I dare say you may guess what they are,' said he. 'I don't know what chance I may have?'

'I can tell you nothing about that,' she replied, 'as I know nothing. But you have my good wishes.'

And then she went.

It may be presumed that gradually some idea of Mr Glascock's intention had made its way into Nora's mind by the time that she found herself alone with that gentleman. Why else had he brought into the room with him that manifest air of a purpose? Why else had he taken the very strong step of sending the lady of the house out of her own drawing-room? Nora, beginning to understand this, put herself into an attitude of defence. She had never told herself that she would refuse Mr Glascock. She had never acknowledged to herself that there was another man whom she liked better than she liked Mr Glascock. But had she ever encouraged any wish for such an interview, her feelings at this moment would have been very different from what they were. As it was, she would have given much to postpone it, so that she might have asked herself questions, and have discovered whether she could reconcile herself to do that which, no doubt, all her friends would commend her for doing. Of course, it was clear enough to the mind of the girl that she had her fortune to make, and that her beauty and youth were the capital on which she had to found it. She had not lived so far from all taint of corruption as to feel any actual horror at the idea of a girl giving herself to a man not because the man had already, by his own capacities in that direction, forced her heart from her but because he was one likely to be at all points a good husband. Had all this affair concerned any other girl, any friend of her own, and had she known all the circumstances of the case, she would have had no hesitation in recommending that other girl to marry Mr Glascock. A girl thrown out upon the world without a shilling must make her hay while the sun shines. But, nevertheless, there was something within her bosom which made her long for a better thing than this. She had dreamed, if she had not thought, of being able to worship a man; but she could hardly worship Mr Glascock. She had dreamed, if she had not thought, of leaning upon a man all through life with her whole weight, as though that man had been specially made to be her staff, her prop, her support, her wall of comfort and protection. She knew that if she were to marry Mr Glascock and become Lady Peterborough, in due course she must stand a good deal by her own strength, and live without that comfortable leaning. Nevertheless, when she found herself alone with the man, she by no means knew whether she would refuse him or not. But she knew that she must pluck up courage for an important moment, and she collected herself, braced her muscles, as it were, for a fight, and threw her mind into an attitude of contest.

Mr Glascock, as soon as the door was shut behind Mrs Trevelyan's back, took a chair and placed it close beside the head of the sofa on which Nora was sitting. 'Miss Rowley,' he said, 'you and I have known each other now for some months, and I hope you have learned to regard me as a friend.'

'Oh, yes, indeed,' said Nora, with some spirit.

'It has seemed to me that we have met as friends, and I can most truly say for myself, that I have taken the greatest possible pleasure in your acquaintance. It is not only that I admire you very much,' he looked straight before him as he said this, and moved about the point of the stick which he was holding in both his hands 'it is not only that, perhaps not chiefly that, though I do admire you very much; but the truth is, that I like everything about you.'

Nora smiled, but she said nothing. It was better, she thought, to let him tell his story; but his mode of telling it was not without its efficacy. It was not the simple praise which made its way with her but a certain tone in the words which seemed to convince her that they were true. If he had really found her, or fancied her to be what he said, there was a manliness in his telling her so in the plainest words that pleased her much.

'I know,' continued he, 'that this is a very bald way of telling, of pleading my cause; but I don't know whether a bald way may not be the best, if it can only make itself understood to be true. Of course, Miss Rowley, you know what I mean. As I said before, you have all those things which not only make me love you, but which make me like you also. If you think that you can love me, say so; and, as long as I live, I will do my best to make you happy as my wife.'

There was a clearness of expression in this, and a downright surrender of himself, which so flattered her and so fluttered her that she was almost reduced to the giving of herself up because she could not reply to such an appeal in language less courteous than that of agreement. After a moment or two she found herself remaining silent, with a growing feeling that silence would be taken as conveying consent. There floated quickly across her brain an idea of the hardness of a woman's lot, in that she should be called upon to decide her future fate for life in half a minute. He had had weeks to think of this, weeks in which it would have been almost unmaidenly in her so to think of it as to have made up her mind to accept the man. Had she so made up her mind, and had he not come to her, where would she have been then? But he had come to her. There he was, still poking about with his stick, waiting for her, and she must answer him. And he was the eldest son of a peer, an enormous match for her, very proper in all respects; such a man, that if she should accept him, everybody around her would regard her fortune in life as miraculously successful. He was not such a man that anyone would point at her and say 'there; see another of them who has sold herself for money and a title!' Mr Glascock was not an Apollo, not an admirable Crichton; but he was a man whom any girl might have learned to love. Now he had asked her to be his wife, and it was necessary that she should answer him. He sat there waiting for her very patiently, still poking about the point of his stick.

Did she really love him? Though she was so pressed by consideration of time, she did find a moment in which to ask herself the question. With a quick turn of an eye she glanced at him, to see what he was like. Up to this moment, though she knew him well, she could have given no details of his personal appearance. He was a better-looking man than Hugh Stanbury, so she told herself with a passing thought; but he lacked, he lacked; what was it that he lacked? Was it youth, or spirit, or strength; or was it some outward sign of an inward gift of mind? Was it that he was heavy while Hugh was light? Was it that she could find no fire in his eye, while Hugh's eyes were full of flashing? Or was it that for her, especially for her, Hugh was the appointed staff and appropriate wall of protection? Be all that as it might, she knew at the moment that she did love, not this man, but that other who was writing articles for the Daily Record. She must refuse the offer that was so brilliant, and give up the idea of reigning as queen at Monkhams.

'Oh, Mr Glascock,' she said, 'I ought to answer you more quickly.'

'No, dearest; not more quickly than suits you. Nothing ever in this world can be more important both to you and to me. If you want more time to think of it, take more time.'

'No, Mr Glascock; I do not. I don't know why I should have paused. Is not the truth best?'

'Yes certainly the truth is best.'

'I do not love you. Pray, pray understand me.'

'I understand it too well, Miss Rowley.' The stick was still going, and the eyes more intently, fixed than ever on something opposite.

'I do like you; I like you very much. And I am so grateful! I cannot understand why such a man as you should want to make me your wife.'

'Because I love you better than all the others; simply that. That reason, and that only, justifies a man in wanting to marry a girl.' What a good fellow he was, and how flattering were his words! Did he not deserve what he wanted, even though it could not be given without a sacrifice? But yet she did not love him. As she looked at him again she could not there recognise her staff. And she looked at him she was more than ever convinced that that other staff ought to be her staff. 'May I come again after a month, say?' he asked, when there had been another short period of silence.

'No, no. Why should you trouble yourself? I am not worth it.'

'It is for me to judge of that, Miss Rowley.'

'All the same, I know that I am not worth it. And I could not tell you to do that.'

'Then I will wait, and come again without your telling me.'

'Oh, Mr Glascock, I did not mean that; indeed I did not. Pray do not think that. Take what I say as final. I like you more than I can say; and I feel a gratitude to you that I cannot express, which I shall never forget. I have never known any one who has seemed to be so good as you. But It is just what I said before.' And then she fairly burst into tears.

'Miss Rowley,' he said, very slowly, 'pray do not think that I want to ask any question which it might embarrass you to answer. But my happiness is so greatly at stake; and, if you will allow me to say so, your happiness, too, is so greatly concerned, that it is most important that we should not come to a conclusion too quickly. If I thought that your heart were vacant I would wait patiently. I have been thinking of you as my possible wife for weeks past, for months past. Of course you have not had such thoughts about me.' As he said this she almost loved him for his considerate goodness. 'It has sometimes seemed to me odd that girls should love men in such a hurry. If your heart be free, I will wait. And if you esteem me, you can see, and try whether you cannot learn to love me.'

'I do esteem you.'

'It depends on that question, then?' he said, slowly.

She sat silent for fully a minute, with her hands clasped; and then she answered him in a whisper. 'I do not know,' she said.

He also was silent for a while before he spoke again. He ceased to poke with his stick, and got up from his chair, and stood a little apart from her, not looking at her even yet.

'I see,' he said at last. 'I understand. Well, Miss Rowley, I quite perceive that I cannot press my suit any further now. But I shall not despair altogether. I know this, that if I might possibly succeed, I should be a very happy man. Good-bye, Miss Rowley.'

She took his offered hand and pressed it so warmly, that had he not been manly and big-hearted, he would have taken such pressure as a sign that she wished him to ask her again. But such was his nature.

'God bless you,' he said, 'and make you happy, whatever you may choose to do.'

Then he left her, and she heard him walk down the stairs with heavy slow steps, and she thought that she could perceive from the sound that he was sad at heart, but that he was resolved not to show his sadness outwardly.

When she was alone she began to think in earnest of what she had done. If the reader were told that she regretted the decision which she had been forced to make so rapidly, a wrong impression would be given of the condition of her thoughts. But there came upon her suddenly a strange capacity for counting up and making a mental inventory of all that might have been hers. She knew—and where is the girl so placed that does not know?—that it is a great thing to be an English peeress. Now, as she stood there thinking of it all, she was Nora Rowley without a shilling in the world, and without a prospect of a shilling. She had often heard her mother speak fearful words of future possible days, when colonial governing should no longer be within the capacity of Sir Marmaduke. She had been taught from a very early age that all the material prosperity of her life must depend on matrimony. She could never be comfortably disposed of in the world, unless some fitting man who possessed those things of which she was so bare, should wish to make her his wife. Now there had come a man so thoroughly fitting, so marvellously endowed, that no worldly blessing would have been wanting. Mr Glascock had more than once spoken to her of the glories of Monkhams. She thought of Monkhams now more than she had ever thought of the place before. It would have been a great privilege to be the mistress of an old time-honoured mansion, to call oaks and elms her own, to know that acres of gardens were submitted to her caprices, to look at herds of cows and oxen, and be aware that they lowed on her own pastures. And to have been the mother of a future peer of England, to have the nursing, and sweet custody and very making of a future senator would not that have been much? And the man himself who would have been her husband was such a one that any woman might have trusted herself to him with perfect confidence. Now that he was gone she almost fancied that she did love him. Then she thought of Hugh Stanbury, sitting as he had described himself, in a little dark closet at the office of the 'D. R.,' in a very old inky shooting-coat, with a tarnished square-cut cloth cap upon his head, with a short pipe in his mouth, writing at midnight for the next morning's impression, this or that article according to the order of his master, 'the tallow-chandler'; for the editor of the *Daily Record* was a gentleman whose father happened to be a grocer in the City, and Hugh had been accustomed thus to describe the family trade. And she might certainly have had the peer, and the acres of garden, and the big house, and the senatorial honours; whereas the tallowchandler's journeyman had never been so outspoken. She told herself from moment to moment that she had done right; that she would do the same a dozen times, if a dozen times the experiment could be repeated; but still, still, there was the remembrance of all that she had lost. How would her mother look at her, her anxious, heavily-laden mother, when the story should be told of all that had been offered to her and all that had been refused?

As she was thinking of this Mrs Trevelyan came into the room. Nora felt that though she might dread to meet her mother, she could be bold enough on such an occasion before her sister. Emily had not done so well with her own affairs, as to enable her to preach with advantage about marriage.

'He has gone?' said Mrs Trevelyan, as she opened the door.

'Yes, he has gone.'

'Well? Do not pretend, Nora, that you will not tell me.'

'There is nothing worth the telling, Emily.'

'What do you mean? I am sure he has proposed. He told me in so many words that it was his intention.'

'Whatever has happened, dear, you may be quite sure that I shall never be Mrs Glascock.'

'Then you have refused him because of Hugh Stanbury!'

'I have refused him, Emily, because I did not love him. Pray let that be enough.'

Then she walked out of the room with something of stateliness in her gait as might become a girl who had had it in her power to be the future Lady Peterborough; but as soon as she reached the sacredness of her own chamber, she gave way to an agony of tears. It would, indeed, be much to be a Lady Peterborough. And she had, in truth, refused it all because of Hugh Stanbury! Was Hugh Stanbury worth so great a sacrifice?

CHAPTER XIV. THE CLOCK HOUSE AT NUNCOMBE PUTNEY

It was not till a fortnight had passed after the transaction recorded in the last chapter, that Mrs Trevelyan and Nora Rowley first heard the proposition that they should go to live at Nuncombe Putney. From bad to worse the quarrel between the husband and the wife had gone on, till Trevelyan had at last told his friend Lady Milborough that he had made up his mind that they must live apart. She is so self-willed and perhaps I am the same,' he had said, 'that it is impossible that we should live together.' Lady Milborough had implored and called to witness all testimonies, profane and sacred, against such a step—had almost gone down on her knees. Go to Naples; why not Naples? Or to the quiet town in the west of France, which was so dull that a wicked roaring lion, fond of cities and gambling, and eating and drinking, could not live in such a place! Oh, why not go to the quiet town in the west of France? Was not anything better than this flying in the face of God and man? Perhaps Trevelyan did not himself like the idea of the quiet dull French town. Perhaps he thought that the flying in the face of God and man was all done by his wife, not by him; and that it was right that his wife should feel the consequences. After many such entreaties, many such arguments, it was at last decided that the house in Curzon Street should be given up, and that he and his wife live apart.

'And what about Nora Rowley?' asked Lady Milborough, who had become aware by this time of Nora's insane folly in having refused Mr Glascock.

'She will go with her sister, I suppose.'

'And who will maintain her? Dear, dear, dear! It does seem as though some young people were bent upon cutting their own throats, and all their family's.'

Poor Lady Milborough just at this time went as near to disliking the Rowleys as was compatible with her nature. It was not possible to her to hate anybody. She thought that she hated the Colonel Osbornes; but even that was a mistake. She was very angry, however, with both Mrs Trevelyan and her sister, and was disposed to speak of them as though they had been born to create trouble and vexation.

Trevelyan had not given any direct answer to that question about Nora Rowley's maintenance, but he was quite prepared to bear all necessary expense in that direction, at any rate till Sir Marmaduke should have arrived. At first there had been an idea that the two sisters should go to the house of their aunt, Mrs Outhouse. Mrs Outhouse was the wife as the reader may perhaps remember of a clergyman living in the east of London. St. Diddulph's-in-the-East was very much in the east indeed. It was a parish outside the City, lying near the river, very populous, very poor, very low in character, and very uncomfortable. There was a rectory-house, queerly situated at the end of a little blind lane, with a gate of its own, and a so-called garden about twenty yards square. But the rectory of St. Diddulph's cannot be said to have been a comfortable abode. The neighbourhood was certainly not alluring. Of visiting society within a distance of three or four miles there was none but what was afforded by the families of other East-end clergymen. And then Mr Outhouse himself was a somewhat singular man. He was very religious, devoted to his work, most kind to the poor; but he was unfortunately a strongly-biased man, and at the same time very obstinate withal. He had never allied himself very cordially with his wife's brother, Sir Marmaduke, allowing himself to be carried away by a prejudice that people living at the West-end, who frequented clubs and were connected in any way with fashion, could not be appropriate companions for himself. The very title which Sir Marmaduke had acquired was repulsive to him, and had induced him to tell his wife more than once that Sir this or Sir that could not be fitting associates for a poor East-end clergyman. Then his wife's niece had married a man of fashion, a man supposed at St. Diddulph's to be very closely allied to fashion; and Mr Outhouse had never been induced even to dine in the house in Curzon Street. When, therefore, he heard that Mr and Mrs Trevelyan were to be separated within two years of their marriage, it could not be expected that he should be very eager to lend to the two sisters the use of his rectory.

There had been interviews between Mr Outhouse and Trevelyan, and between Mrs Outhouse and her niece; and then there was an interview between Mr Outhouse and Emily, in which it was decided that Mrs Trevelyan would not go to the parsonage of St. Diddulph's. She had been very outspoken to her uncle, declaring that she by no means intended to carry herself as a disgraced woman. Mr Outhouse had quoted St. Paul to her; 'Wives, obey your husbands.' Then she had got up and had spoken very angrily. 'I look for support from you,' she said, 'as the man who is the nearest to me, till my father shall come.' 'But I cannot support you in what is wrong,' said the clergyman. Then Mrs Trevelyan had left the room, and would not see her uncle again.

She carried things altogether with a high hand at this time. When old Mr Bideawhile called upon her, her husband's ancient family lawyer, she told that gentleman that if it was her husband's will that they should live apart, it must be so. She could not force him to remain with her. She could not compel him to keep up the house in Curzon Street. She had certain rights, she believed. She spoke then, she said, of pecuniary rights not of those other rights which her husband was determined, and was no doubt able, to ignore. She did not really know what those pecuniary rights might be, nor was she careful to learn their exact extent. She would thank Mr Bideawhile to see that things were properly arranged. But of this her husband, and Mr Bideawhile, might be quite sure; she would take nothing as a favour. She would not go to her uncle's house. She declined to tell Mr Bideawhile why she had so decided; but she had decided. She was ready to listen to any suggestion that her husband might make as to her residence, but she must claim to have some choice in the matter. As to her sister, of course she intended to give Nora a home as long as such a home might be wanted. It would be very sad for Nora, but in existing circumstances such an arrangement would be expedient. She would not go into details as to expense. Her husband was driving her away from him, and it was for him to say what proportion of his income he would choose to give for her maintenance for hers and for that of the child. She was not desirous of anything beyond the means of decent living, but of course she must for the present find a home for her sister as well as for herself. When speaking of her baby she had striven hard so to speak that Mr Bideawhile should find no trace of doubt in the tones of her voice. And yet she had been full of doubt full of fear. As Mr Bideawhile had uttered nothing antagonistic to her wishes in this matter had seemed to agree that wherever the mother went thither the child would go also Mrs Trevelyan had considered herself to be successful in this interview.

The idea of a residence at Nuncombe Putney had occurred first to Trevelyan himself, and he had spoken of it to Hugh Stanbury. There had been some difficulty in this, because he had snubbed Stanbury grievously when his friend had attempted to do some work of gentle interference between him and his wife; and when he began the conversation, he took the trouble of stating, in the first instance, that the separation was a thing fixed so that nothing might be urged on that subject. 'It is to be. You will understand that,' he said; 'and if you think that your mother would agree to the arrangement, it would be satisfactory to me, and might, I think, be made pleasant to her. Of course, your mother would be made to understand that the only fault with which my wife is charged is that of indomitable disobedience to my wishes.'

'Incompatibility of temper,' suggested Stanbury.

'You may call it that if you please; though I must say for myself that I do not think that I have displayed any temper to which a woman has a right to object. Then he had gone on to explain what he was prepared to do about money. He would pay, through Stanbury's hands, so much for maintenance and so much for house rent, on the understanding that the money was not to go into his wife's hands. 'I shall prefer,' he said, 'to make myself, on her behalf, what disbursements may be necessary. I will take care that she receives a proper sum quarterly through Mr

Bideawhile for her own clothes and for those of our poor boy.' Then Stanbury had told him of the Clock House, and there had been an agreement made between them; an agreement which was then, of course, subject to the approval of the ladies at Nuncombe Putney. When the suggestion was made to Mrs Trevelyan with a proposition that the Clock House should be taken for one year, and that for that year, at least, her boy should remain with her she assented to it. She did so with all the calmness that she was able to assume; but, in truth, almost everything seemed to have been gained, when she found that she was not to be separated from her baby. 'I have no objection to living in Devonshire if Mr Trevelyan wishes it,' she said, in her most stately manner; 'and certainly no objection to living with Mr Stanbury's mother.' Then Mr Bideawhile explained to her that Nuncombe Putney was not a large town was, in fact, a very small and a very remote village. 'That will make no difference whatsoever as far as I am concerned,' she answered; 'and as for my sister, she must put up with it till my father and my mother are here. I believe the scenery at Nuncombe Putney is very pretty.' 'Lovely!' said Mr Bideawhile, who had a general idea that Devonshire is supposed to be a picturesque county. 'With such a life before me as I must lead,' continued Mrs Trevelyan, 'an ugly neighbourhood, one that would itself have had no interest for a stranger, would certainly have been an additional sorrow.' So it had been settled, and by the end of July, Mrs Trevelyan, with her sister and baby, was established at the Clock House, under the protection of Mrs Stanbury. Mrs Trevelyan had brought down her own maid and her own nurse, and had found that the arrangements made by her husband had, in truth, been liberal. The house in Curzon Street had been given up, the furniture had been sent to a warehouse, and Mr Trevelyan had gone into lodgings. 'There never were two young people so insane since the world began,' said Lady Milborough to her old friend, Mrs Fairfax, when the thing was done.

'They will be together again before next April,' Mrs Fairfax had replied. But Mrs Fairfax was a jolly dame who made the best of everything. Lady Milborough raised her hands in despair and shook her head. 'I don't suppose, though, that Mr Glascock will go to Devonshire after his lady love,' said Mrs Fairfax. Lady Milborough again raised her hands, and again shook her head.

Mrs Stanbury had given an easy assent when her son proposed to her this new mode of life, but Priscilla had had her doubts. Like all women, she thought that when a man was to be separated from his wife, the woman must he in the wrong. And though it must be doubtless comfortable to go from the cottage to the Clock House, it would, she said, with much prudence, be very uncomfortable to go back from the Clock House to the cottage. Hugh replied very cavalierly generously, that is, rashly, and somewhat impetuously that he would guarantee them against any such degradation.

'We don't want to be a burden upon you, my dear,' said the mother.

'You would be a great burden on me,' he replied, 'if you were living uncomfortably while I am able to make you comfortable.'

Mrs Stanbury was soon won over by Mrs Trevelyan, by Nora, and especially by the baby; and even Priscilla, after a week or two, began to feel that she liked their company. Priscilla was a young woman who read a great deal, and even had some gifts of understanding what she read. She borrowed books from the clergyman, and paid a penny a week to the landlady of the Stag and Antlers for the hire during half a day of the weekly newspaper. But now there came a box of books from Exeter, and a daily paper from London, and to improve all this both the new corners were able to talk with her about the things she read. She soon declared to her mother that she liked Miss Rowley much the best of the two. Mrs Trevelyan was too fond of having her own way. She began to understand, she would say to her mother, that a man might find it difficult to live with Mrs Trevelyan. 'She hardly ever yields about anything,' said Priscilla. As Miss Priscilla Stanbury was also very fond of having her own way, it was not surprising that she should object to that quality in this lady, who had come to live under the same roof with her.

The country about Nuncombe Putney is perhaps as pretty as any in England. It is beyond the river Teign, between that and Dartmoor, and is so lovely in all its variations of rivers, rivulets, broken ground, hills and dales, old broken, battered, time-worn timber, green knolls, rich pastures, and heathy common, that the wonder is that English lovers of scenery know so little of it. At the Stag and Antlers old Mrs Crocket, than whom no old woman in the public line was ever more generous, more peppery, or more kind, kept two clean bed-rooms, and could cook a leg of Dartmoor mutton and make an apple pie against any woman in Devonshire. 'Drat your fish!' she would say, when some self-indulgent and exacting traveller would wish for more than these accustomed viands. 'Cock you up with dainties! If you can't eat your victuals without fish, you must go to Exeter. And then you'll get it stinking may-hap.' Now Priscilla Stanbury and Mrs Crocket were great friends, and there had been times of deep want, in which Mrs Crocket's friendship had been very serviceable to the ladies at the cottage. The three young women had been to the inn one morning to ask after a conveyance from Nuncombe Putney to Princetown, and had found that a four-wheeled open carriage with an old horse and a very young driver could be hired there. 'We have never dreamed of such a thing,' Priscilla Stanbury had said, 'and the only time I was at Prince-town I walked there and back.' So they had called at the 'Stag and Antlers,' and Mrs Crocket had told them her mind upon several matters.

'What a dear old woman!' said Nora, as they came away, having made their bargain for the open carriage.

'I think she takes quite enough upon herself, you know,' said Mrs Trevelyan.

'She is a dear old woman,' said Priscilla, not attending at all to the last words that had been spoken. 'She is one of the best friends I have in the world. If I were to say the best out of my own family, perhaps I should not be wrong.'

'But she uses such very odd language for a woman,' said Mrs Trevelyan. Now Mrs Crocket had certainly 'dratted' and 'darned' the boy, who wouldn't come as fast as she had wished, and had laughed at Mrs Trevelyan very contemptuously, when that lady had suggested that the urchin, who was at last brought forth, might not be a safe charioteer down some of the hills.

'I suppose I'm used to it,' said Priscilla. 'At any rate I know I like it. And I like her.'

'I dare say she's a good sort of woman,' said Mrs Trevelyan, 'only—'

'I am not saying anything about her being a good woman now,' said Priscilla, interrupting the other with some vehemence, 'but only that she is my friend.'

'I liked her of all things,' said Nora. 'Has she lived here always?'

'Yes; all her life. The house belonged to her father and to her grandfather before her, and I think she says she has never slept out of it a dozen times in her life. Her husband is dead, and her daughters are married away, and she has the great grief and trouble of a ne'er-do-well son. He's away now, and she's all alone.' Then after a pause, she continued; 'I dare say it seems odd to you, Mrs Trevelyan, that we should speak of the innkeeper as a dear friend; but you must remember that we have been poor among the poorest and are so indeed now. We only came into our present house to receive you. That is where we used to live,' and she pointed to the tiny cottage, which now that it was dismantled and desolate, looked to be doubly poor. 'There have been times when we should have gone to bed very hungry if it had not been for Mrs Crocket.'

Later in the day Mrs Trevelyan, finding Priscilla alone, had apologized for what she had said about the old woman. 'I was very thoughtless and forgetful, but I hope you will not be angry with me. I will be ever so fond of her if you will forgive me.'

'Very well,' said Priscilla, smiling; 'on those conditions I will forgive you.' And from that time there sprang up something like a feeling of friendship between Priscilla and Mrs Trevelyan. Nevertheless Priscilla was still of opinion that the Clock House arrangement was dangerous, and should never have been made; and Mrs Stanbury, always timid of her own nature, began to fear that it must be so, as soon as she was removed from the influence of her son. She did not see much even of the few neighbours who lived around her, but she fancied that people looked at her in church as though she had done that which she ought not to have done, in taking herself to a big and comfortable house for the sake of lending her protection to a lady who was separated from her husband. It was not that she believed that

Mrs Trevelyan had been wrong; but that, knowing herself to be weak, she fancied that she and her daughter would be enveloped in the danger and suspicion which could not but attach themselves to the lady's condition, instead of raising the lady out of the cloud as would have been the case had she herself been strong. Mrs Trevelyan, who was sharpsighted and clear-witted, soon saw that it was so, and spoke to Priscilla on the subject before she had been a fortnight in the house. 'I am afraid your mother does not like our being here,' she said.

'How am I to answer that?' Priscilla replied.

'Just tell the truth.'

'The truth is so uncivil. At first I did not like it. I disliked it very much.'

'Why did you give way?'

'I didn't give way. Hugh talked my mother over. Mamma does what I tell her, except when Hugh tells her something else. I was afraid, because, down here, knowing nothing of the world, I didn't wish that we, little people, should be mixed up in the quarrels and disagreements of those who are so much bigger.'

'I don't know who it is that is big in this matter.'

'You are big at any rate by comparison. But now it must go on. The house has been taken, and my fears are over as regards you. What you observe in mamma is only the effect, not yet quite worn out, of what I said before you came. You may be quite sure of this that we neither of us believe a word against you. Your position is a very unfortunate one; but if it can be remedied by your staying here with us, pray stay with us.'

'It cannot be remedied,' said Emily; 'but we could not be anywhere more comfortable than we are here.'

CHAPTER XV. WHAT THEY SAID ABOUT IT IN THE CLOSE

When Miss Stanbury, in the Close at Exeter, was first told of the arrangement that had been made at Nuncombe Putney, she said some very hard words as to the thing that had been done. She was quite sure that Mrs Trevelyan was no better than she should be. Ladies who were separated from their husbands never were any better than they should be. And what was to be thought of any woman, who, when separated from her husband, would put herself under the protection of such a Paladin as Hugh Stanbury. She heard the tidings of course from Dorothy, and spoke her mind even to Dorothy plainly enough; but it was to Martha that she expressed herself with her fullest vehemence.

'We always knew,' she said, 'that my brother had married an addle-pated, silly woman, one of the most unsuited to be the mistress of a clergyman's house that ever a man set eyes on; but I didn't think she'd allow herself to be led into such a stupid thing as this.'

'I don't suppose the lady has done anything amiss any more than combing her husband's hair, and the like of that,' said Martha.

'Don't tell me! Why, by their own story, she has got a lover.'

'But he ain't to come after her down here, I suppose. And as for lovers, ma'am, I'm told that the most of 'em have 'em up in London. But it don't mean much, only just idle talking and gallivanting.'

'When women can't keep themselves from idle talking with strange gentlemen, they are very far gone on the road to the devil. That's my notion. And that was everybody's notion a few years ago. But now, what with divorce bills, and woman's rights, and penny papers, and false hair, and married women being just like giggling girls, and giggling girls knowing just as much as married women, when a woman has been married a year or two she begins to think whether she mayn't have more fun for her money by living apart from her husband.'

'Miss Dorothy says—'

'Oh, bother what Miss Dorothy says! Miss Dorothy only knows what it has suited that scamp, her brother, to tell her. I understand this woman has come away because of a lover; and if that's so, my sister-in-law is very wrong to receive her.

The temptation of the Clock House has been too much for her. It's not my doing; that's all.'

That evening Miss Stanbury and Dorothy went out to tea at the house of Mrs MacHugh, and there the matter was very much discussed. The family of the Trevelyans was known by name in these parts, and the fact of Mrs Trevelyan having been sent to live in a Devonshire village, with Devonshire ladies who had a relation in Exeter so well esteemed as Miss Stanbury of the Close, were circumstances of themselves sufficient to ensure a considerable amount of prestige at the city tea-table for the tidings of this unfortunate family quarrel. Some reticence was of course necessary because of the presence of Miss Stanbury and of Dorothy. To Miss Stanbury herself Mrs MacHugh and Mrs Crumbie, of Cronstadt House, did not scruple to express themselves very plainly, and to whisper a question as to what was to be done should the lover make his appearance at Nuncombe Putney; but they who spoke of the matter before Dorothy, were at first more charitable, or, at least, more forbearing. Mr Gibson, who was one of the minor canons, and the two Miss Frenches from Heavitree, who had the reputation of hunting unmarried clergymen in couples, seemed to have heard all about it. When Mrs MacHugh and Miss Stanbury, with Mr and Mrs Crumbie, had seated themselves at their whist-table, the younger people were able to express their opinions without danger of interruption or of rebuke. It was known to all Exeter by this time, that Dorothy Stanbury's mother had gone to the Clock House, and that she had done so in order that Mrs Trevelyan might have a home. But it was not yet known whether anybody had called upon them. There was Mrs Merton, the wife of the present parson of Nuncombe, who had known the Stanburys for the last twenty years; and there was Mrs Ellison of Lessboro', who lived only four miles from Nuncombe, and who kept a pony-carriage. It would be a great thing to know how these ladies had behaved in so difficult and embarrassing a position. Mrs Trevelyan and her sister had now been at Nuncombe Putney for more than a fortnight, and something in that matter of calling must have been done or have been left undone. In answer to an ingeniously-framed question asked by Camilla French, Dorothy at once set the matter at rest. 'Mrs Merton,' said Camilla French, 'must find it a great thing to have two new ladies come to the village, especially now that she has lost you, Miss Stanbury?'

'Mamma tells me,' said Dorothy, 'that Mrs Trevelyan and Miss Rowley do not mean to know anybody. They have given it out quite plainly, so that there should be no mistake.'

'Dear, dear!' said Camilla French.

'I dare say it's for the best,' said Arabella French, who was the elder, and who looked very meek and soft. Miss French almost always looked meek and soft.

'I'm afraid it will make it very dull for your mother not seeing her old friends,' said Mr Gibson.

'Mamma won't feel that at all,' said Dorothy.

'Mrs Stanbury, I suppose, will see her own friends at her own house just the same,' said Camilla.

'There would be great difficulty in that, when there is a lady who is to remain unknown,' said Arabella. 'Don't you think so, Mr Gibson?' Mr Gibson replied that perhaps there might be a difficulty, but he wasn't sure. The difficulty, he thought, might be got over if the ladies did not always occupy the same room.

'You have never seen Mrs Trevelyan, have you, Miss Stanbury?' asked Camilla.

'Never.'

'She is not an old family friend, then or anything of that sort?'

'Oh, dear, no.'

'Because,' said Arabella, 'it is so odd how different people get together sometimes.' Then Dorothy explained that Mr Trevelyan and her brother Hugh had long been friends.

'Oh! of Mr Trevelyan,' said Camilla. 'Then it is he that has sent his wife to Nuncombe, not she that has come there?'

'I suppose there has been some agreement,' said Dorothy.

'Just so; just so,' said Arabella, the meek. 'I should like to see her. They say that she is very beautiful; don't they?'

'My brother says that she is handsome.'

'Exceedingly lovely, I'm told,' said Camilla. 'I should like to see her shouldn't you, Mr Gibson?'

'I always like to see a pretty woman,' said Mr Gibson, with a polite bow, which the sisters shared between them.

'I suppose she'll go to church,' said Camilla.

'Very likely not,' said Arabella. 'Ladies of that sort very often don't go to church. I dare say you'll find that she'll never stir out of the place at all, and that not a soul in Nuncombe will ever see her except the gardener. It is such a thing for a woman to be separated from her husband! Don't you think so, Mr Gibson?'

'Of course it is,' said he, with a shake of his head, which was intended to imply that the censure of the church must of course attend any sundering of those whom the church had bound together; but which implied also by the absence from it of any intense clerical severity, that as the separated wife was allowed to live with so very respectable a lady as Mrs Stanbury, there must probably be some mitigating circumstances attending this special separation.

'I wonder what he is like?' said Camilla, after a pause.

'Who?' asked Arabella.

'The gentleman,' said Camilla.

'What gentleman?' demanded Arabella.

'I don't mean Mr Trevelyan,' said Camilla.

'I don't believe there really is eh is there?' said Mr Gibson, very timidly.

'Oh, dear, yes,' said Arabella.

'I'm afraid there's something of the kind,' said Camilla. 'I've heard that there is, and I've heard his name.' Then she whispered very closely into the ear of Mr Gibson the words, 'Colonel Osborne,' as though her lips were far too pure to mention aloud any sound so full of iniquity.

'Indeed!' said Mr Gibson.

'But he's quite an old man,' said Dorothy, 'and knew her father intimately before she was born. And, as far as I can understand, her husband does not suspect her in the least. And it's only because there's a misunderstanding between them, and not at all because of the gentleman.'

'Oh!' exclaimed Camilla.

'Ah!' exclaimed Arabella.

'That would make a difference,' said Mr Gibson.

'But for a married woman to have her name mentioned at all with a gentleman it is so bad; is it not, Mr Gibson?' And then Arabella also had her whisper into the clergyman's ear very closely. 'I'm afraid there's not a doubt about the Colonel. I'm afraid not. I am indeed.'

'Two by honours and the odd, and it's my deal,' said Miss Stanbury, briskly, and the sharp click with which she put the markers down upon the table was heard all through the room. 'I don't want anybody to tell me,' she said, 'that when a young woman is parted from her husband, the chances are ten to one that she has been very foolish.'

'But what's a woman to do, if her husband beats her?' said Mrs Crumbie.

'Beat him again,' said Mrs MacHugh.

'And the husband will be sure to have the worst of it,' said Mr Crumbie. 'Well, I declare, if you haven't turned up an honour again, Miss Stanbury!'

'It was your wife that cut it to me, Mr Crumbie.' Then they were again at once immersed in the play, and the name neither of Trevelyan nor Osborne was heard till Miss Stanbury was marking her double under the candlestick; but during all the pauses in the game the conversation went back to the same topic, and when the rubber was over they who had been playing it lost themselves for ten minutes in the allurements of the interesting subject. It was so singular a coincidence that the lady should have gone to Nuncombe Putney of all villages in England, and to the house of Mrs Stanbury of all ladies in England. And then was she innocent, or was she guilty; and if guilty, in what degree? That she had been allowed to bring her baby with her was considered to be a great point in her favour. Mr Crumbie's opinion was that it was 'only a few words'. Mrs Crumbie was afraid that she had been a little light. Mrs MacHugh said that there was never fire without smoke. And Miss Stanbury, as she took her departure, declared that the young women of the present day didn't know what they were after. 'They think that the world should be all frolic and dancing, and they have no more idea of doing their duty and earning their bread than a boy home for the holidays has of doing lessons.'

Then, as she went home with Dorothy across the Close, she spoke a word which she intended to be very serious. 'I don't mean to say anything against your mother for what she has done as yet. Somebody must take the woman in, and perhaps it was natural. But if that Colonel what's-his-name makes his way down to Nuncombe Putney, your mother must send her packing, if she has any respect either for herself or for Priscilla.'

CHAPTER XVI. DARTMOOR

The well-weighed decision of Miss Stanbury respecting the Stanbury Trevelyan arrangement at Nuncombe Putney had been communicated to Dorothy as the two walked home at night across the Close from Mrs MacHugh's house, and it was accepted by Dorothy as being wise and proper. It amounted to this. If Mrs Trevelyan should behave herself with propriety in her retirement at the Clock House, no further blame in the matter should be attributed to Mrs Stanbury for receiving her at any rate in Dorothy's hearing. The existing scheme, whether wise or foolish, should be regarded as an accepted scheme. But if Mrs Trevelyan should be indiscreet if, for instance, Colonel Osborne should show himself at Nuncombe Putney then, for the sake of the family, Miss Stanbury would speak out, and would speak out very loudly. All this Dorothy understood, and she could perceive that her aunt had strong suspicion that there would be indiscretion.

'I never knew one like her,' said Miss Stanbury, 'who, when she'd got away from one man, didn't want to have another dangling after her.'

A week had hardly passed after the party at Mrs MacHugh's, and Mrs Trevelyan had hardly been three weeks at Nuncombe Putney, before the tidings which Miss Stanbury almost expected reached her ears.

'The Colonel's been at the Clock House, ma'am,' said Martha.

Now, it was quite understood in the Close by this time that 'the Colonel' meant Colonel Osborne.

'No!'

'I'm told he has though, ma'am, for sure and certain.'

'Who says so?'

'Giles Hickbody was down at Lessboro', and see'd him hisself a portly, middle-aged man; not one of your young scampish-like lovers.'

'That's the man.'

'Oh, yes. He went over to Nuncombe Putney, as sure as anything hired Mrs Clegg's chaise and pair, and asked for Mrs Trevelyan's house as open as anything. When

Giles asked in the yard, they told him as how that was the married lady's young man.'

'I'd like to be at his tail, so I would, with a mop-handle,' said Miss Stanbury, whose hatred for those sins by which the comfort and respectability of the world are destroyed, was not only sincere, but intense. 'Well; and what then?'

'He came back and slept at Mrs Clegg's that night at least, that was what he said he should do.'

Miss Stanbury, however, was not so precipitate or uncharitable as to act strongly upon information such as this. Before she even said a word to Dorothy, she made further inquiry. She made very minute inquiry, writing even to her very old and intimate friend Mrs Ellison, of Lessboro' writing to that lady a most cautious and guarded letter. At last it became a fact proved to her mind that Colonel Osborne had been at the Clock House, had been received there, and had remained there for hours had been allowed access to Mrs Trevelyan, and had slept the night at the inn at Lessboro'. The thing was so terrible to Miss Stanbury's mind, that even false hair, Dr Colenso, and penny newspapers did not account for it.

'I shall begin to believe that the Evil One has been allowed to come among us in person because of our sins,' she said to Martha and she meant it.

In the meantime, Mrs Trevelyan, as may be remembered, had hired Mrs Crocket's open carriage, and the three young women, Mrs Trevelyan, Nora, and Priscilla, made a little excursion to Princetown, somewhat after the fashion of a picnic. At Princetown, in the middle of Dartmoor, about nine miles from Nuncombe Putney, is the prison establishment at which are kept convicts undergoing penal servitude. It is regarded by all the country round with great interest, chiefly because the prisoners now and again escape, and then there comes a period of interesting excitement until the escaped felon shall have been again taken. How can you tell where he may be, or whether it may not suit him to find his rest in your own cupboard, or under your own bed? And then, as escape without notice will of course be the felon's object, to attain that he will probably cut your throat, and the throat of everybody belonging to you. All which considerations give an interest to Princetown, and excite in the hearts of the Devonians of these parts a strong affection for the Dartmoor prison. Of those who visit Princetown comparatively few effect an entrance within the walls of the gaol. They look at the gloomy place with a mysterious interest, feeling something akin to envy for the prisoners who have enjoyed the privilege of solving the mysteries of prison life, and who know how men feel when they have their hair cut short, and are free from moral responsibility for their own conduct, and are moved about in gangs, and treated like wild beasts.

But the journey to Princetown, from whatever side it is approached, has the charm of wild and beautiful scenery. The spot itself is ugly enough; but you can go not thither without breathing the sweetest, freshest air, and encountering that delightful sense of romance which moorland scenery always produces. The idea of our three friends was to see the Moor rather than the prison, to learn something of the country around, and to enjoy the excitement of eating a sandwich sitting on a hillock, in exchange for the ordinary comforts of a good dinner with chairs and tables. A bottle of sherry and water and a paper of sandwiches contained their whole banquet; for ladies, though they like good things at picnics, and, indeed, at other times, almost as well as men like them, very seldom prepare dainties for themselves alone. Men are wiser and more thoughtful, and are careful to have the good things, even if they are to be enjoyed without companionship.

Mrs Crocket's boy, though he was only about three feet high, was a miracle of skill and discretion. He used the machine, as the patent drag is called, in going down the hills with the utmost care. He never forced the beast beyond a walk if there was the slightest rise in the ground; and as there was always a rise, the journey was slow. But the three ladies enjoyed it thoroughly, and Mrs Trevelyan was in better spirits than she herself had thought to be possible for her in her present condition. Most of us have recognised the fact that a dram of spirits will create, that a so-called nip of brandy will create hilarity, or, at least, alacrity, and that a glass of sherry will often 'pick up' and set in order the prostrate animal and mental faculties of the drinker. But we are not sufficiently alive to the fact that copious draughts of fresh air—of air fresh and unaccustomed—will have precisely the same effect. We do know that now and again it is very essential to 'change the air'; but we generally consider that to do that with any chance of advantage, it is necessary to go far afield; and we think also that such change of the air is only needful when sickness of the body has come upon us, or when it threatens to come. We are seldom aware that we may imbibe long potations of pleasure and healthy excitement without perhaps going out of our own county; that such potations are within a day's journey of most of us; and that they are to be had for half-a-crown a head, all expenses told. Mrs Trevelyan probably did not know that the cloud was lifted off her mind, and the load of her sorrow made light to her, by the special vigour of the air of the Moor; but she did know that she was enjoying herself, and that the world was pleasanter to her than it had been for months past.

When they had sat upon their hillocks, and eaten their sandwiches regretting that the basket of provisions had not been bigger and had drunk their sherry and water out of the little horn mug which Mrs Crocket had lent them, Nora started off across the moorland alone. The horse had been left to be fed in Princetown, and they had walked back to a bush under which they had rashly left their basket of provender concealed. It happened, however, that on that day there was no escaped felon about to watch what they had done, and the food and the drink had been found secure. Nora had gone off, and as her sister and Priscilla sat leaning against their hillocks with their backs to the road, she could be seen standing now on one little eminence and now on another, thinking, doubtless, as she stood on the one how good it would be to be Lady Peterborough, and, as she stood on the other, how much better to be Mrs Hugh Stanbury. Only before she could be Mrs Hugh Stanbury it would be necessary that Mr Hugh Stanbury should share her opinion and necessary also that he should be able to maintain a wife. 'I should never do to be a very poor man's wife,' she said to herself; and remembered as she said it, that in reference to the prospect of her being Lady Peterborough, the man who was to be Lord Peterborough was at any rate ready to make her his wife, and on that side there were none of those difficulties about house, and money, and position which stood in the way of the Hugh-Stanbury side of the question. She was not, she thought, fit to be the wife of a very poor man; but she conceived of herself that she would do very well as a future Lady Peterborough in the drawing-rooms of Monkhams. She was so far vain as to fancy that she could look, and speak, and move, and have her being after the fashion which is approved for the Lady Peterboroughs of the world. It was not clear to her that Nature had not expressly intended her to be a Lady Peterborough; whereas, as far as she could see, Nature had not intended her to be a Mrs Hugh Stanbury, with a precarious income of perhaps ten guineas a week when journalism was doing well. So she moved on to another little eminence to think of it there. It was clear to her that if she should accept Mr Glascock she would sell herself, and not give herself away; and she had told herself scores of times before this, that a young woman should give herself away, and not sell herself— should either give herself away, or keep herself to herself, as circumstances might go. She had been quite sure that she would never sell herself. But this was a lesson which she had taught herself when she was very young, before she had come to understand the world and its hard necessities. Nothing, she now told herself, could be worse than to hang like a millstone round the neck of a poor man. It might be a very good thing to give herself away for love but it would not be a good thing to be the means of ruining the man she loved, even if that man were willing to be so ruined. And then she thought that she could also love that other man a little—could love him sufficiently for comfortable domestic purposes. And it would undoubtedly be very pleasant to have all the troubles of her life settled for her. If she were Mrs Glascock, known to the world as the future Lady Peterborough, would it not be within her power to bring her sister and her sister's husband again together? The tribute of the Monkhams authority and influence to her sister's side of the question would be most salutary. She tried to make herself believe that in this way she would be doing a good deed. Upon the whole, she thought that if Mr Glascock should give her another chance she would accept him. And he had distinctly promised that he would give her another chance. It might be that this unfortunate quarrel in the Trevelyan family would deter him. People do not wish to ally themselves with family quarrels. But if the chance came in her way she would accept it. She had made up her mind to that, when she turned round from off the last knoll on which she had stood, to return to her sister and Priscilla Stanbury.

They two had sat still under the shade of a thorn bush, looking at Nora as she was wandering about, and talking together more freely than they had ever done before on the circumstances that had brought them together. 'How pretty she looks,' Priscilla had said, as Nora was standing with her figure clearly marked by the light.

'Yes; she is very pretty, and has been much admired. This terrible affair of mine is a cruel blow to her.'

'You mean that it is bad for her to come and live here without society.'

'Not exactly that though of course it would be better for her to go out. And I don't know how a girl is ever to get settled in the world unless she goes out. But it is always an injury to be connected in any way with a woman who is separated from her husband. It must be bad for you.'

'It won't hurt me,' said Priscilla. 'Nothing of that kind can hurt me.'

'I mean that people say such ill-natured things.'

'I stand alone, and can take care of myself,' said Priscilla. 'I defy the evil tongues of all the world to hurt me. My personal cares are limited to an old gown and bread and cheese. I like a pair of gloves to go to church with, but that is only the remnant of a prejudice. The world has so very little to give me, that I am pretty nearly sure that it will take nothing away.'

'And you are contented?'

'Well, no; I can't say that I am contented. I hardly think that anybody ought to be contented. Should my mother die and Dorothy remain with my aunt, or get married, I should be utterly alone in the world. Providence, or whatever you call it, has made me a lady after a fashion, so that I can't live with the ploughmen's wives, and at the same time has so used me in other respects, that I can't live with anybody else.'

'Why should not you get married, as well as Dorothy?'

'Who would have me? And if I had a husband I should want a good one, a man with a head on his shoulders, and a heart. Even if I were young and good-looking, or rich, I doubt whether I could please myself. As it is, I am as likely to be taken bodily to heaven, as to become any man's wife.'

'I suppose most women think so of themselves at some time, and yet they are married.'

'I am not fit to marry. I am often cross, and I like my own way, and I have a distaste for men. I never in my life saw a man whom I wished even to make my intimate friend. I should think any man an idiot who to make soft speeches to me, and I should tell him so.'

'Ah; you might find it different when he went on with it.'

'But I think,' said Priscilla, 'that when a woman is married there is nothing to which she should not submit on behalf of her husband.'

'You mean that for me.'

'Of course I mean it for you. How should I not be thinking of you, living as you are under the same roof with us? And I am thinking of Louey.' Louey was the baby. 'What are you to do when after a year or two his father shall send for him to have him under his own care?'

'Nothing shall separate me from my child,' said Mrs Trevelyan eagerly.

'That is easily said; but I suppose the power of doing as he pleased would be with him.'

'Why should it be with him? I do not at all know that it would be with him. I have not left his house. It is he that has turned me out.'

'There can, I think, be very little doubt what you should do,' said Priscilla, after a pause, during which she had got up from her seat under the thorn bush.

'What should I do?' asked Mrs Trevelyan.

'Go back to him.'

'I will to-morrow if he will write and ask me. Nay; how could I help myself? I am his creature, and must go or come as he bids me. I am here only because he has sent me.'

'You should write and ask him to take you.'

'Ask him to forgive me because he has ill-treated me?'

'Never mind about that,' said Priscilla, standing over her companion, who was still lying under the bush. 'All that is twopenny-halfpenny pride, which should be thrown to the winds. The more right you have been hitherto the better you can afford to go on being right. What is it that we all live upon but self-esteem? When we want praise it is only because praise enables us to think well of ourselves. Every one to himself is the centre and pivot of all the world.'

'It's a very poor world that goes round upon my pivot,' said Mrs Trevelyan.

'I don't know how this quarrel came up,' exclaimed Priscilla, 'and I don't care to know. But it seems a trumpery quarrel as to who should beg each other's pardon first, and all that kind of thing. Sheer and simple nonsense! Ask him to let it all be forgotten. I suppose he loves you?'

'How can I know? He did once.'

'And you love him?'

'Yes. I love him certainly.'

'I don't see how you can have a doubt. Here is Jack with the carriage, and if we don't mind he'll pass us by without seeing us.'

Then Mrs Trevelyan got up, and when they had succeeded in diverting Jack's attention for a moment from the horse, they called to Nora, who was still moving about from one knoll to another, and who showed no desire to abandon the contemplations in which she had been engaged.

It had been mid-day before they left home in the morning, and they were due to be at home in time for tea, which is an epoch in the day generally allowed to be more elastic than some others. When Mrs Stanbury lived in the cottage her hour for tea had been six; this had been stretched to half-past seven when she received Mrs Trevelyan at the Clock House; and it was half-past eight before Jack landed them at their door. It was manifest to them all as they entered the house that there was an air of mystery in the face of the girl who had opened the door for them. She did not speak, however, till they were all within the passage. Then she uttered a few words very solemnly. 'There be a gentleman come,' she said.

'A gentleman!' said Mrs Trevelyan, thinking in the first moment of her husband, and in the second of Colonel Osborne.

'He be for you, miss,' said the girl, bobbing her head at Nora.

Upon hearing this Nora sank speechless into the chair which stood in the passage.

CHAPTER XVII. A GENTLEMAN COMES TO NUNCOMBE PUTNEY

It soon became known to them all as they remained clustered in the hall that Mr Glascock was in the house. Mrs Stanbury came out to them and informed them that he had been at Nuncombe Putney for the last hours, and that he had asked for Mrs Trevelyan when he called. It became evident as the affairs of the evening went on, that Mrs Stanbury had for a few minutes been thrown into a terrible state of amazement, thinking that 'the Colonel' had appeared. The strange gentleman, however, having obtained admittance, explained who he was, saying that he was very desirous of seeing Mrs Trevelyan and Miss Rowley. It may be presumed that a glimmer of light did make its way into Mrs Stanbury's mind on the subject; but up to the moment at which the three travellers arrived, she had been in doubt on the subject. Mr Glascock had declared that he would take a walk, and in the course of the afternoon had expressed high approval of Mrs Crocket's culinary skill. When Mrs Crocket heard that she had entertained the son of a lord, she was very loud in her praise of the manner in which he had eaten two mutton chops and called for a third. He had thought it no disgrace to apply himself to the second half of an apple pie, and had professed himself to be an ardent admirer of Devonshire cream. 'It's them counter-skippers as turns up their little noses at the victuals as is set before them,' said Mrs Crocket.

After his dinner Mr Glascock had returned to the Clock House, and had been sitting there for an hour with Mrs Stanbury, not much to her delight or to his, when the carriage was driven up to the door.

'He is to go back to Lessboro' to-night,' said Mrs Stanbury in a whisper.

'Of course you must see him before he goes,' said Mrs Trevelyan to her sister. There had, as was natural, been very much said between the two sisters about Mr Glascock. Nora had abstained from asserting in any decided way that she disliked the man, and had always absolutely refused to allow Hugh Stanbury's name to be mixed up with the question. 'Whatever might be her own thoughts about Hugh Stanbury she had kept them even from her sister. 'When her sister had told her that she had refused Mr Glascock because of Hugh, she had shown herself to be indignant, and had since that said one or two fine things as to her capacity to refuse a brilliant offer simply because the man who made it was indifferent to her. Mrs Trevelyan had learned from her that her Suitor had declared his intention to persevere; and here was perseverance with a vengeance! 'Of course you must see him at once,' said Mrs Trevelyan. Nora for a few seconds had remained silent, and then had run up to her room. Her sister followed her instantly.

'What is the meaning of it all?' said Priscilla to her mother.

'I suppose he is in love with Miss Rowley,' said Mrs Stanbury.

'But who is he?'

Then Mrs Stanbury told all that she knew, She had seen from his card that he was an Honourable Mr Glascock. She had collected from what he had said that he was an old friend of the two ladies. Her conviction was strong in Mr Glascock's favour thinking, as she expressed herself, that everything was right and proper but she could hardly explain why she thought so.

'I do wish that they had never come,' said Priscilla, who could not rid herself of an idea that there must be danger in having to do with women who had men running after them.

'Of course I'll see him,' said Nora to her sister. 'I have not refused to see him. Why do you scold me?'

'I have not scolded you, Nora; but I do want you to how immensely important this is.'

'Of course it is important.'

'And so much the more so because of my misfortunes! Think how good he must be, how strong must be his attachment, when he comes down here after you in this way.'

'But I have to think of my own feelings.'

'You know you like him. You have told me so. And only fancy what mamma will feel! Such a position! And the man so excellent! Everybody says that he hasn't a fault in any way.'

'I hate people without faults.'

'Oh, Nora, Nora, that is foolish! There, there; you must go down. Pray pray do not let any absurd fancy stand in your way, and destroy everything. It will never come again, Nora. And, only think; it is all now your own if you will only whisper one word.'

'Ah! one word and that a falsehood!'

'No no. Say you will try to love him, and that will enough. And you do love him?'

'Do I?'

'Yes, you do. It is only the opposition of your nature that makes you fight against him. Will you go now?'

'Let me be for two minutes by myself,' said Nora, 'and then I'll come down. Tell him that I'm coming.' Mrs Trevelyan stooped over her, kissed her, and then left her.

Nora, as soon as she was alone, stood upright in the middle of the room and held her hands up to her forehead. She had been far from thinking, when she was considering the matter easily among the hillocks, that the necessity for an absolute decision would come upon her so instantaneously. She had told herself only this morning that it would be wise to accept the man, if he should ever ask a second time and he had come already. He had been waiting for her in the village while she had been thinking whether he would ever come across her path again. She thought that it would have been easier for her now to have gone down with a 'yes' in her mouth, if her sister had not pressed her so hard to say that 'yes,' The very pressure from her sister seemed to imply that such pressure ought to be resisted. Why should there have been pressure, unless there were reasons against her marrying him? And yet, if she chose to take him, who would have a right to complain of her? Hugh Stanbury had never spoken to her a word that would justify her in even supposing that he would consider himself to be ill-used. All others of her friends would certainly rejoice, would applaud her, pat her on the back, cover her with caresses, and tell her that she had been born under a happy star. And she did like the man. Nay she thought she loved him. She withdrew her hands from her brow, assured herself that her lot in life was cast, and with hurrying fingers attempted to smooth her hair and to arrange her ribbons before the glass. She would go to the encounter boldly and accept him honestly. It was her duty to do so. What might she not do for brothers and sisters as the wife of Lord Peterborough of Monkhams? She saw that that arrangement before the glass could be of no service, and she stepped quickly to the door. If he did not like her as she was, he need not ask her. Her mind was made up, and she would do it. But as she went down the stairs to the room in which she knew that he was waiting for her, there came over her a cold feeling of self-accusation almost of disgrace. 'I do not care,' she said. 'I know that I'm right.' She opened the door quickly, that there might be no further doubt, and found that she was alone with him.

'Miss Rowley,' he said, 'I am afraid you will think that I am persecuting you.'

'I have no right to think that,' she answered.

'I'll tell you why I have come. My dear father, who has always been my best friend, is very ill. He is at Naples, and I must go to him. He is very old, you know over eighty; and will never live to come back to England. From what I hear, I think it probable that I may remain with him till everything is over.'

'I did not know that he was so old as that.'

'They say that he can hardly live above a month or two. He will never see my wife if I can have a wife; but I should like to tell him, if it were possible that—'

'I understand you, Mr Glascock.'

'I told you that I should come to you again, and as I may possibly linger at Naples all the winter, I could not go without seeing you. Miss Rowley, may I hope that you can love me?'

She did not answer him a word, but stood looking away from him with her hands clasped together. Had he asked her whether she would be his wife, it is possible that the answer which she had prepared would have been spoken. But he had put the question in another form. Did she love him? If she could only bring herself to say that she could love him, she might be lady of Monkhams before the next summer had come round.

'Nora,' he said, 'do you think that you can love me?'

'No,' she said, and there was something almost of fierceness in the tone of her voice as she answered him.

'And must that be your final answer to me?'

'Mr Glascock, what can I say?' she replied. 'I will tell you the honest truth—I will tell you everything. I came into this room determined to accept you. But you are so good, and so kind, and so upright, that I cannot tell you a falsehood. I do not love you. I ought not to take what you offer me. If I did, it would be because you are rich, and a lord; and not because I love you. I love some one else. There pray, pray do not tell of me; but I do.' Then she flung away from him and hid her face in a corner of the sofa out of the light.

Her lover stood silent, not knowing how to go on with the conversation, not knowing how to bring it to an end. After what she had now said to him it was impossible that he should press her further. It was almost impossible that he should wish to do so. When a lady is frank enough to declare that her heart is not her own to give, a man can hardly wish to make further prayer for the gift. 'If so,' he said, 'of course I have nothing to hope.'

She was sobbing, and could not answer him. She was half repentant, partly proud of what she had done half repentant in that she had lost what had seemed to her to be so good, and full of remorse in that she had so unnecessarily told her secret.

'Perhaps,' said he, 'I ought to assure you that what you have told me shall never be repeated by my lips.'

She thanked him for this by a motion of her head and hand, not by words and then he was gone. How he managed to bid adieu to Mrs Stanbury and her sister, or whether he saw them as he left the house, she never knew. In her corner of the sofa, weeping in the dark, partly proud and partly repentant, she remained till her sister came to her. 'Emily,' she said, jumping up, 'say nothing about it; not a word. It is of no use. The thing is done and over, and let it altogether be forgotten.'

'It is done and over, certainly,' said Mrs Trevelyan.

'Exactly; and I suppose a girl may do what she likes with herself in that way. If I choose to decline to take anything that is pleasant, and nice, and comfortable, nobody has a right to scold me. And I won't be scolded.'

'But, my child, who is scolding you?'

'You mean to scold me. But it is of no use. The man has gone, and there is an end of it. Nothing that you can say or I can think will bring him back again. I don't want anybody to tell me that it would be better to be Lady Peterborough, with everything that the world has to give, than to live here without a soul to speak to, and to have to go back to those horrible islands next year. You can't think that I am very comfortable.'

'But what did you say to him, Nora?'

'What did I say to him? What could I say to him? Why didn't he ask me to be his wife without saying anything about love? He asked me if I loved him. Of course I don't love him. I would have said I did, but it stuck in my throat. I am willing enough, I believe, to sell myself to the devil, but I don't know how to do it. Never mind. It's done, and now I'll go to bed.'

She did go to bed, and Mrs Trevelyan explained to the two ladies as much as was necessary of what had occurred. When Mrs Stanbury came to understand that the gentleman who had been closeted with her would, probably, in a few months be a lord himself, that he was a very rich man, a member of Parliament, and one of those who are decidedly born with gold spoons in their mouths, and understood also that Nora Rowley had refused him, she was lost in amazement. Mr Glascock was about forty years of age, and appeared to Nora Rowley, who was nearly twenty years his junior, to be almost an old man. But to Mrs Stanbury, who was over sixty, Mr Glascock seemed to be quite in the flower of his age. The bald place at the top of his head simply showed that he had passed his boyhood, and the grey hairs at the back of his whiskers were no more than outward signs of manly discretion. She could not understand why any girl should refuse such an offer, unless the man were himself bad in morals, or in temper. But Mrs Trevelyan had told her while Nora and Mr Glascock were closeted together, that he was believed by them all to be good and gentle. Nevertheless she felt a considerable increase of respect for a young lady who had refused the eldest son of a lord. Priscilla, when she heard what had occurred, expressed to her mother a moderated approval. According to her views a girl would much more often be right to refuse an offer of marriage than to accept it, let him who made the offer be who he might. And the fact of the man having been sent away with a refusal somewhat softened Priscilla's anger at his coming there at all.

'I suppose he is a goose,' said she to her mother, 'and I hope there won't be any more of this kind running after them while they are with us.'

Nora, when she was alone, wept till her heart was almost broken. It was done, and the man was gone, and the thing was over. She had quite sufficient knowledge of the world to realise perfectly the difference between such a position as that which had been offered to her, and the position which in all probability she would now be called upon to fill. She had had her chance, and Fortune had placed great things at her disposal. It must said of her also that the great things which Fortune had offered to her were treasures very valuable in her eyes. Whether it be right and wise to covet or to desire wealth and rank, there was no doubt but that she coveted them. She had been instructed to believe in them, and she did believe in them. In some mysterious manner of which she herself knew nothing, taught by some preceptor the nobility of whose lessons she had not recognised though she had accepted them, she had learned other things also: to revere truth and love, and to be ambitious as regarded herself of conferring the gift of her whole heart upon some one whom she could worship as a hero. She had spoken the simple truth when she had told her sister that she had been willing to sell herself to the devil, but that she had failed in her attempt to execute the contract. But now as she lay weeping on her bed, tearing herself with remorse, picturing to herself in the most vivid colours all that she had thrown away, telling herself of all that she might have done and all she might have been, had she not allowed the insane folly of a moment to get the better of her, she received little or no comfort from the reflection that she had been true to her better instincts. She had told the man that she had refused him because she loved Hugh Stanbury at least, as far as she could remember what had passed, she had so told him. And how mean it was of her to allow herself to be actuated by an insane passion for a man who had never spoken to her of love, and how silly of her afterwards to confess it! Of what service could such a passion be to her life? Even were it returned, she could not marry such a one as Hugh Stanbury. She knew enough of herself to be quite sure that were he to ask her to do so tomorrow, she would refuse him. Better go and be scorched, and bored to death, and buried at the Mandarins, than attempt to regulate a poor household which, as soon as she made one of its number, would be on the sure road to ruin! For a moment there came upon her, not a thought, hardly an idea, something of a waking dream that she would write to Mr Glascock and withdraw all that she had said. Were she to do so he would probably despise her, and tell her that he despised her but there might be a chance. It was possible that such a declaration would bring him back to her and did it not bring him back to her she would only be where she was, a poor lost, shipwrecked creature, who had flung herself upon the rocks and thrown away her only chance of a prosperous voyage across the ocean of life; her only chance, for she was not like other girls, who at any rate remain on the scene of action, and may refit their spars and still win their way. For there were to be no more seasons in London, no more living in Curzon Street, no renewed power of entering the ball-rooms and crowded staircases in which high-born wealthy lovers can be conquered. A great prospect had been given to her, and she had flung it aside! That letter of retractation was, however, quite out of the question. The reader must not suppose that she had ever thought that she could write it. She thought of nothing but of coming misery and remorse. In her wretchedness she fancied that she had absolutely disclosed to the man who loved her the name of him whom she had been mad enough to say that she loved. But what did it matter? Let it be as it might, she was destroyed.

The next morning she came down to breakfast pale as a ghost; and they who saw her knew at once that she had done that which had made her a wretched woman.

CHAPTER XVIII. THE STANBURY CORRESPONDENCE

Half an hour after the proper time, when the others had finished their tea and bread and butter, Nora Rowley came down among them pale as a ghost. Her sister had gone to her while she was dressing, but she had declared that she would prefer to be alone. She would be down directly, she had said, and had completed her toilet without even the assistance of her maid. She drank her cup of tea and pretended to eat her toast; and then sat herself down, very wretchedly, to think of it all again. It had been all within her grasp all of which she had ever dreamed! And now it was gone! Each of her three companions strove from time to time to draw her into conversation, but she seemed to be resolute in her refusal. At first, till her utter prostration had become a fact plainly recognised by them all, she made some little attempt at an answer when a direct question was asked of her; but after a while she only shook her head, and was silent, giving way to absolute despair.

Late in the evening she went out into the garden, and Priscilla followed her. It was now the end of July, and the summer was in its glory. The ladies, during the day, would remain in the drawing-room with the windows open and the blinds down, and would sit in the evening reading and working, or perhaps pretending to read and work, under the shade of a cedar which stood upon the lawn. No retirement could possibly be more secluded than was that of the garden of the Clock House. No stranger could see into it, or hear sounds from out of it. Though it was not extensive, it was so well furnished with those charming garden shrubs which, in congenial soils, become large trees, that one party of wanderers might seem to be lost from another amidst its walls. On this evening Mrs Stanbury and Mrs Trevelyan had gone out as usual, but Priscilla had remained with Nora Rowley. After a while Nora also got up and went through the window all alone. Priscilla, having waited for a few minutes, followed her; and caught her in a long green walk that led round the bottom of the orchard.

'What makes you so wretched?' she said.

'Why do you say I am wretched?'

'Because it's so visible. How is one to go on living with you all day and not notice it?'

'I wish you wouldn't notice it. I don't think it kind of you to notice it. If I wanted to talk of it, I would say so.'

'It is better generally to speak of a trouble than to keep it to oneself,' said Priscilla.

'All the same, I would prefer not to speak of mine,' said Nora.

Then they parted, one going one way and one the other, and Priscilla was certainly angry at the reception which had been given to the sympathy which she had proffered. The next day passed almost without a word spoken between the two. Mrs Stanbury had not ventured as yet to mention to her guest the subject of the rejected lover, and had not even said much on the subject to Mrs Trevelyan. Between the two sisters there had been, of course, some discussion on the matter. It was impossible that it should be allowed to pass without it; but such discussions always resulted in an assertion on the part of Nora that she would not be scolded. Mrs Trevelyan was very tender with her, and made no attempt to scold her—tried, at last, simply to console her; but Nora was so continually at work scolding herself, that every word spoken to her on the subject of Mr Glascock's visit seemed to her to carry with it a rebuke.

But on the second day she herself accosted Priscilla Stanbury. 'Come into the garden,' she said, when they two were for a moment alone together; 'I want to speak to you.' Priscilla, without answering, folded up her work and put on her hat. 'Come down to the green walk,' said Nora. 'I was savage to you last night, and I want to beg your pardon.'

'You were savage,' said Priscilla, smiling, 'and you shall have my pardon. Who would not pardon you any offence, if you asked it?'

'I am so miserable!' she said.

'But why?'

'I don't know. I can't tell. And it is of no use talking about it now, for it is all over. But I ought not to have been cross to you, and I am very sorry.'

'That does not signify a straw; only so far, that when I have been cross, and have begged a person's pardon, which I don't do as often as I ought, I always feel that it begets kindness. If I could help you in your trouble I would.'

'You can't fetch him back again.'

'You mean Mr Glascock. Shall I go and try?'

Nora smiled and shook her head. 'I wonder what he would say if you asked him. But if he came, I should do the same thing.'

'I do not in the least know what you have done, my dear. I only see that you mope about, and are more down in the mouth than any one ought to be, unless some great trouble has come.'

'A great trouble has come.'

'I suppose you have had your choice either to accept your lover or to reject him.'

'No; I have not had my choice.'

'It seems to me that no one has dictated to you; or, at least, that you have obeyed no dictation.'

'Of course, I can't explain it to you. It is impossible that I should.'

'If you mean that you regret what you have done because you have been false to the man, I can sympathise with you. No one has ever a right to be false, and if you are repenting a falsehood, I will willingly help you to eat your ashes and to wear your sackcloth. But if you are repenting a truth—'

'I am.'

'Then you must eat your ashes by yourself, for me; and I do not think that you will ever be able to digest them.'

'I do not want anybody to help me,' said Nora proudly.

'Nobody can help you, if I understand the matter rightly. You have got to get the better of your own covetousness and evil desires, and you are in the fair way to get the better of them if you have already refused to be this man's wife because you could not bring yourself to commit the sin of marrying him when you did not love him. I suppose that is about the truth of it; and indeed, indeed, I do sympathise with you. If you have done that, though it is no more than the plainest duty, I will love you for it. One finds so few people that will do any duty that taxes their self-indulgence.'

'But he did not ask me to marry him.'

'Then I do not understand anything about it.'

'He asked me to love him.'

'But he meant you to be his wife?'

'Oh yes he meant that of course.'

'And what did you say?' asked Priscilla.

'That I didn't love him,' replied Nora.

'And that was the truth?'

'Yes it was the truth.'

'And what do you regret? that you didn't tell him a lie?'

'No not that,' said Nora slowly.

'What then? You cannot regret that you have not basely deceived a man who has treated you with a loving generosity?' They walked on silent for a few yards, and then Priscilla repeated her question. 'You cannot mean that you are sorry that you did not persuade yourself to do evil?'

'I don't want to go back to the islands, and to lose myself there, and to be nobody; that is what I mean. And I might have been so much! Could one step from the very highest rung of the ladder to the very lowest and not feel it?'

'But you have gone up the ladder if you only knew it,' said Priscilla. 'There was a choice given to you between the foulest mire of the clay of the world, and the sunlight of the very God. You have chosen the sunlight, and you are crying after the clay! I cannot pity you; but I can esteem you, and love you, and believe in you. And I do. You'll 'get yourself right at last, and there's my hand on it, if you'll take it.' Nora took the hand that was offered to her, held it in her own for some seconds, and then walked back to the house and up to her own room in silence.

The post used to come into Nuncombe Putney at about eight in the morning, carried thither by a wooden-legged man who rode a donkey. There is a general understanding that the wooden-legged men in country parishes should be employed as postmen, owing to the great steadiness of demeanour which a wooden leg is generally found to produce. It may be that such men are slower in their operations than would be biped postmen; but as all private employers of labour demand labourers with two legs, it is well that the lame and halt should find a refuge in the less exacting service of the government. The one-legged man who rode his donkey into Nuncombe Putney would reach his post-office not above half an hour after his proper time; but he was very slow in stumping round the village, and seldom reached the Clock House much before ten. On a certain morning two or three days after the conversation just recorded it was past ten when he brought two letters to the door, one for Mrs Trevelyan, and one for Mrs Stanbury. The ladies had finished their breakfast, and were seated together at an open window. As was usual, the letters were given into Priscilla's hands, and the newspaper which accompanied them into those of Mrs Trevelyan, its undoubted owner. When her letter was handed to her, she looked at the address closely and then walked away with it into her own room.

'I think it's from Louis,' said Nora, as soon as the door was closed. 'If so, he is telling her to come back.'

'Mamma, this is for you,' said Priscilla. 'It is from Aunt Stanbury. I know her handwriting.'

'From your aunt? What can she be writing about? There is something wrong with Dorothy.' Mrs Stanbury held the letter but did not open it. 'You had better read it, my dear. If she is ill, pray let her come home.'

But the letter spoke of nothing amiss as regarded Dorothy, and did not indeed even mention Dorothy's name. Luckily Priscilla read the letter in silence, for it was an angry letter. 'What is it, Priscilla? Why don't you tell me? Is anything wrong?' said Mrs Stanbury.

'Nothing is wrong, mamma except that my aunt is a silly woman.'

'Goodness me! what is it?'

'It is a family matter,' said Nora smiling, 'and I will go.

'What can it be?' demanded Mrs Stanbury again as soon as Nora had left the room.

'You shall hear what it can be. I will read it to you,' said Priscilla. 'It seems to me that of all the women that ever lived my Aunt Stanbury is the most prejudiced, the most unjust, and the most given to evil thinking of her neighbours. This is what she has thought fit to write to you, mamma.' Then Priscilla read her aunt's letter, which was as follows:

The Close,
Exeter,
July 31, 186—.

Dear Sister Stanbury,

I am informed that the lady who is living with you because she could not continue to live under the same roof with her lawful husband, has received a visit at your house from a gentleman who was named as her lover before she left her own. I am given to understand that it was because of this gentleman's visits to her in London, and because she would not give up seeing him, that her husband would not live with her any longer.

'But the man has never been here at all,' said Mrs Stanbury, in dismay.

'Of course he has not been here. But let me go on.'

'I have got nothing to do with your visitors,' continued the letter, 'and I should not interfere but for the credit of the family. There ought to be somebody to explain to you that much of the abominable disgrace of the whole proceeding will rest upon you, if you permit such goings on in your house. I suppose it is your house. At any rate you are regarded as the mistress of the establishment, and it is for you to tell the lady that she must go elsewhere. I do hope that you have done so, or at least that you will do so now. It is intolerable that the widow of my brother a clergyman should harbour a lady who is separated from her husband and who receives visits from a gentleman who is reputed to be her lover. I wonder much that your eldest daughter should countenance such a proceeding.

Yours truly,   JEMIMA STANBURY.'

Mrs Stanbury, when the letter had been read to her, held up both her hands in despair. 'Dear, dear,' she exclaimed. 'Oh, dear!'

'She had such pleasure in writing it,' said Priscilla, 'that one ought hardly to begrudge it her.' The blackest spot in the character of Priscilla Stanbury was her hatred for her aunt in Exeter. She knew that her aunt had high qualities, and yet she hated her aunt. She was well aware that her aunt was regarded as a shining light by very many good people in the county, and yet she hated her aunt. She could not but acknowledge that her aunt had been generous to her brother, and was now very generous to her sister, and yet she hated her aunt. It was now a triumph to her that her aunt had fallen into so terrible a quagmire, and she was by no means disposed to let the sinning old woman easily out of it.

'It is as pretty a specimen,' she said, 'as I ever knew of malice and eaves-dropping combined.'

'Don't use such hard words, my dear.'

'Look at her words to us,' said Priscilla. 'What business has she to talk to you about the credit of the family and abominable disgrace? You have held your head up in poverty, while she has been rolling in money.'

'She has been very good to Hugh and now to Dorothy.'

'If I were Dorothy I would have none of her goodness. She likes some one to trample on some one of the name to patronise. She shan't trample on you and me, mamma.'

Then there was a discussion as to what should be done; or rather a discourse in which Priscilla explained what she thought fit to do. Nothing, she decided, should be said to Mrs Trevelyan on the subject; but an answer should be sent to Aunt Stanbury. Priscilla herself would write this answer, and herself would sign it. There was some difference of opinion on this point, as Mrs Stanbury thought that if she might be allowed to put her name to it, even though Priscilla should write it, the wording of it would be made, in some degree, mild to suit her own character. But her daughter was imperative, and she gave way.

'It shall be mild enough in words,' said Priscilla, 'and very short.'

Then she wrote her letter as follows:

Nuncombe Putney,
August 1, 186—.

DEAR AUNT STANBURY,

You have found a mare's nest. The gentleman you speak of has never been here at all, and the people who bring you news have probably hoaxed you. I don't think that mamma has ever disgraced the family, and you can have no reason for thinking that she ever will. You should, at any rate, be sure of what you are saying before you make such cruel accusations,

Yours truly,

PRISCILLA STANBURY.

P.S. Another gentleman did call here not to see Mrs Trevelyan; but I suppose mamma's house need not be closed against all visitors.

Poor Dorothy had passed evil hours from the moment in which her aunt had so far certified herself as to Colonel Osborne's visit to Nuncombe as to make her feel it to be incumbent on her to interfere. After much consideration Miss Stanbury had told her niece the dreadful news, and had told also what she intended to do. Dorothy, who was in truth horrified at the iniquity of the fact which was related, and who never dreamed of doubting the truth of her aunt's information, hardly knew how to interpose. 'I am sure mamma won't let there be anything wrong,' she had said.

'And you don't call this wrong?' said Miss Stanbury, in a tone of indignation.

'But perhaps mamma will tell them to go.'

'I hope she will. I hope she has. But he was allowed to be there for hours. And now three days have passed and there is no sign of anything being done. He came and went and may come again when he pleases.' Still Dorothy pleaded. 'I shall do my duty,' said Miss Stanbury.

'I am quite sure mamma will do nothing wrong,' said Dorothy. But the letter was written and sent, and the answer to the letter reached the house in the Close in due time.

When Miss. Stanbury had read and re-read the very short reply which her niece had written, she became at first pale with dismay, and then red with renewed vigour and obstinacy. She had made herself, as she thought, quite certain of her facts before she had acted on her information. There was some equivocation, some most unworthy deceit in Priscilla's letter. Or could it be possible that she herself had been mistaken? Another gentleman had been there not, however, with the object of seeing Mrs Trevelyan! So said Priscilla. But she had made herself sure that the man in question was a man from London, a middle-aged, man from London, who had specially asked for Mrs Trevelyan, and who had at once been known to Mrs Clegg, at the Lessboro' inn, to be Mrs Trevelyan's lover. Miss Stanbury was very unhappy, and at last sent for Giles Hickbody. Giles Hickbody had never pretended to know the name. He had seen the man and had described him, 'Quite a swell, ma'am; and a Lon'oner, and one as'd be up to anything; but not a young 'un; no, not just a young 'un, zartainly.' He was cross-examined again now, and said that all he knew about the man's name was that there was a handle to it. This was ended by Miss Stanbury sending him down to Lessboro' to learn the very name of the gentleman, and by his coming back with that of the Honourable George Glascock written on a piece of paper. 'They says now as he was arter the other young 'ooman,' said Giles Hickbody. Then was the confusion of Miss Stanbury complete.

It was late when Giles returned from Lessboro', and nothing could be done that night. It was too late to write a letter for the next morning's post. Miss Stanbury, who was as proud of her own discrimination as she was just and true, felt that a day of humiliation had indeed come for her. She hated Priscilla almost as vigorously as Priscilla hated her. To Priscilla she would not write to own her fault; but it was incumbent on her to confess it to Mrs Stanbury. It was incumbent on her also to confess it to Dorothy. All that night she did not sleep, and the next morning she went about abashed, wretched, hardly mistress of her own maids. She must confess it also to Martha, and Martha would be very stern to her. Martha had poob-poohed the whole story of the lover, seeming to think that there could be no reasonable objection to a lover past fifty.

'Dorothy,' she said at last, about noon, 'I have been over hasty about your mother and this man. I am sorry for it, and must beg everybody's pardon.'

'I knew mamma would do nothing wrong,' said Dorothy.

'To do wrong is human, and she, I suppose, is not more free than others; but in this matter I was misinformed. I shall write and beg her pardon; and now I beg your pardon.'

'Not mine, Aunt Stanbury.'

'Yes, yours and your mother's, and the lady's also for against her has the fault been most grievous. I shall write to your mother and express my contrition.' She put off the evil hour of writing as long as she could, but before dinner the painful letter had been written, and carried by herself to the post. It was as follows:

The Close,
August 9, 186—.

DEAR SISTER STANBURY,

I have now learned that the information was false on which my former letter was based. I am heartily sorry for any annoyance I may have given you. I can only inform you that my intentions were good and upright. Nevertheless, I humbly beg your pardon.

Yours truly,

JEMIMA STANBURY.

Mrs Stanbury, when she received this, was inclined to let the matter drop. That her sister-in-law should express such abject contrition was to her such a lowering of the great ones of the earth, that the apology conveyed to her more pain than pleasure. She could not hinder herself from sympathising with all that her sister-in-law had felt when she had found herself called upon to humiliate herself. But it was not so with Priscilla. Mrs Stanbury did not observe that her daughter's name was scrupulously avoided in the apology; but Priscilla observed it. She would not let the matter drop, without an attempt at the last word. She therefore wrote back again as follows:

Nuncombe Putney,
August 4, 186—.

DEAR AUNT STANBURY,

I am glad you have satisfied yourself about the gentleman who has so much disquieted you. I do not know that the whole affair would be worth a moment's consideration, were it not that mamma and I, living as we do so secluded a life, are peculiarly apt to feel any attack upon our good name which is pretty nearly all that is left to us. If ever there were women who should be free from attack, at any rate from those of their own family, we are such women. We never interfere with you, or with anybody; and I think you might abstain from harassing us by accusations.

Pray do not write to mamma in such a strain again, unless you are quite sure of your ground.

Yours truly,

PRISCILLA STANBURY.

'Impudent vixen!' said Miss Stanbury to Martha, when she had read the letter. 'Ill-conditioned, impudent vixen!'

'She was provoked, miss,' said Martha.

'Well; yes; yes and I suppose it is right that you should tell me of it. I dare say it is part of what I ought to bear for being an old fool, and too cautious about my own flesh and blood. I will bear it. There. I was wrong, and I will say that I have been justly punished. There there!'

How very much would Miss Stanbury's tone have been changed had she known that at that very moment Colonel Osborne was eating his breakfast at Mrs Crocket's inn, in Nuncombe Putney!

CHAPTER XIX. BOZZLE, THE EX-POLICEMAN

When Mr Trevelyan had gone through the miserable task of breaking up his establishment in Curzon Street, and had seen all his furniture packed, including his books, his pictures, and his pet Italian ornaments, it was necessary that he should go and live somewhere. He was very wretched at this time so wretched that life was a burden to him. He was a man who loved his wife, to whom his child was very dear; and he was one too to whom the ordinary comforts of domestic life were attractive and necessary. There are men to whom release from the constraint imposed by family ties will be, at any rate for a time, felt as a release. But he was not such a man. There was no delight to him in being able to dine at his club, and being free to go whither he pleased in the evening. As it was, it pleased him to go nowhere in the evenings; and his mornings were equally blank to him. He went so often to Mr Bideawhile, that the poor old lawyer became quite tired of the Trevelyan family quarrel. Even Lady Milborough, with all her power of sympathising, began to feel that she would almost prefer on any morning that her dear young friend, Louis Trevelyan, should not be announced. Nevertheless, she always saw him when he came, and administered comfort according to her light. Of course he would have his wife back before long. That was the only consolation she was able to offer; and she offered it so often that he began gradually to feel that something might be done towards bringing about so desirable an event. After what had occurred they could not live again in Curzon Street nor even in London for awhile; but Naples was open to them. Lady Milborough said so much to him of the advantages which always came in such circumstances from going to Naples, that he began to regard such a trip as almost the natural conclusion of his adventure. But then there came that very difficult question what step should be first taken? Lady Milborough proposed that he should go boldly down to Nuncombe Putney, and make the arrangement. 'She will only be too glad to jump into your arms,' said Lady Milborough. Trevelyan thought that if he went to Nuncombe Putney, his wife might perhaps jump into his arms; but what would come after that? How would he stand then in reference to his authority? Would she own that she had been wrong? Would she promise to behave better in future? He did not believe that she was yet sufficiently broken in spirit to make any such promise. And he told himself again and again that it would be absurd in him to allow her to return to him without such subjection, after all that he had gone through in defence of his marital rights. If he were to write to her a long letter, argumentative, affectionate, exhaustive, it might be better. He was inclined to believe of himself that he was good at writing long, affectionate, argumentative, and exhaustive letters. But he would not do even this as yet. He had broken up his house, and scattered all his domestic gods to the winds, because she had behaved badly to him; and the thing done was too important to allow of redress being found so easily.

So he lived on, a wretched life in London. He could hardly endure to show himself at his club, fearing that every one would be talking of him as the man who was separated from his wife, perhaps as the man of whose wife Colonel Osborne was the dear friend. No doubt for a day or two there had been much of such conversation; but it had died away from the club long before his consciousness had become callous. At first he had gone into a lodging in Mayfair; but this had been but for a day or two. After that he had taken a set of furnished chambers in Lincoln's Inn, immediately under those in which Stanbury lived; and thus it came to pass that he and Stanbury were very much thrown together. As Trevelyan would always talk of his wife this was rather a bore; but our friend bore with it, and would even continue to instruct the world through the columns of the *D. R.* while Trevelyan was descanting on the peculiar cruelty of his own position.

'I wish to be just, and even generous; and I do love her with all my heart,' he said one afternoon, when Hugh was very hard at work.

'It is all very well for gentlemen to call themselves reformers,' Hugh was writing, 'but have these gentlemen ever realised to themselves the meaning of that word? We think that they have never done so as long as—' 'Of course you love her,' said Hugh, with his eyes still on the paper, still leaning on his pen, but finding by the cessation of sound that Trevelyan had paused, and therefore knowing that it was necessary that he should speak.

'As much as ever,' said Trevelyan, with energy.

'As long as they follow such a leader, in such a cause, into whichever lobby he may choose to take them'—'Exactly so, exactly,' said Stanbury; 'just as much as ever.'

'You are not listening to a word,' said Trevelyan.

'I haven't missed a single expression you have used,' said Stanbury. 'But a fellow has to do two things at a time when he's on the daily press.'

'I beg your pardon for interrupting you,' said Trevelyan, angrily, getting up, taking his hat, and stalking off to the house of Lady Milborough. In this way he became rather a bore to his friends. He could not divest his mind of the injury which had accrued to him from his wife's conduct, nor could he help talking of the grief with which his mind was laden. And he was troubled with sore suspicions, which, as far as they concerned his wife, had certainly not been merited. It had seemed to him that she had persisted in her intimacy with Colonel Osborne in a manner that was not compatible with that wife-like indifference which he regarded as her duty. Why had she written to him and received letters from him when her husband had plainly told her that any such communication was objectionable? She had done so, and as far as Trevelyan could remember her words, had plainly declared that she would continue to do so. He had sent her away, into the most remote retirement he could find for her; but the post was open to her. He had heard much of Mrs Stanbury, and Priscilla, from his friend Hugh, and thoroughly believed that his wife was in respectable hands. But what was to prevent Colonel Osborne from going after her if he chose to do so? And if he did so choose, Mrs Stanbury could not prevent their meeting. He was racked with jealousy, and yet he did not cease to declare to himself that he knew his wife too well to believe that she would sin. He could not rid himself of his jealousy, but he tried with all his might to make the man whom he hated the object of it, rather than the woman whom he loved.

He hated Colonel Osborne with all his heart. It was a regret to him that the days of duelling were over; so that he could not shoot the man. And yet, had duelling been possible to him, Colonel Osborne had done nothing that would have justified him in calling his enemy out or would even have enabled him to do so with any chance of inducing his enemy to fight. Circumstances, he thought, were cruel to him beyond compare, in that he should have been made to suffer so great torment without having any of the satisfaction of revenge. Even Lady Milborough, with all her horror as to the Colonel, could not tell him that the Colonel was amenable to any punishment. He was advised that he must take his wife away and live at Naples because of this man, that he must banish himself entirely if he chose to repossess himself of his wife and child; and yet nothing could be done to the unprincipled rascal by whom all his wrong and sufferings were occasioned! Thinking it very possible that Colonel Osborne would follow his wife, he had a watch set upon the Colonel. He had found a retired policeman, a most discreet man, as he was assured who, for a consideration, undertook the management of interesting jobs of this kind. The man was one Bozzle, who had not lived without a certain reputation in the police courts. In these days of his madness, therefore, he took Mr Bozzle into his pay; and after a while he got a letter from Bozzle with the Exeter post-mark. Colonel Osborne had left London with a ticket for Lessboro'. Bozzle also had taken a place by the same train for that small town. The letter was written in the railway carriage, and, as Bozzle explained, would be posted by him as he passed through Exeter. A further communication should be made by the next day's post, in a letter which Mr Bozzle proposed to address to Z. A., Post-office, Waterloo Place.

On receiving this first letter, Trevelyan was in an agony of doubt, as well as misery. What should he do? Should he go to Lady Milborough, or to Stanbury; or should he at once follow Colonel Osborne and Mr Bozzle to Lessboro'. It ended in his resolving at last to wait for the letter which was to be addressed to Z. A. But he spent an interval of horrible suspense, and of insane rage. Let the laws say what they might, he would have the man's blood, if he found that the man had even attempted to wrong him. Then, at last, the second letter reached him. Colonel Osborne and Mr Bozzle had each of them spent the day in the neighbourhood of Lessboro', not exactly in each other's company, but very near to each other. 'The Colonel' had ordered a gig, on the day after his arrival at Lessboro', for the village of Cockchaffington; and, for all Mr Bozzle knew, the Colonel had gone to Cockchaffington. Mr Bozzle was ultimately inclined to think that the Colonel had really spent his day in going to Cockchaffington. Mr Bozzle himself, knowing the wiles of such men as Colonel Osborne, and thinking at first that that journey to Cockchaffington might only be a deep ruse, had walked over to Nuncombe Putney. There he had had a pint of beer and some bread and cheese at Mrs Crocket's house, and had asked various questions, to which he did not receive very satisfactory answers. But he inspected the Clock House very minutely, and came to a decided opinion as to the point at which it would be attacked, if burglary were the object of the assailants. And he observed the iron gates, and the steps, and the shape of the trees, and the old pigeon-house-looking fabric in which the clock used to be placed. There was no knowing when information might be wanted, or what information might not be of use. But he made himself tolerably sure that Colonel Osborne did not visit Nuncombe Putney on that day; and then he walked back to Lessboro'. Having done this, he applied himself to the little memorandum book in which he kept the records of these interesting duties, and entered a claim against his employer for a conveyance to Nuncombe Putney and back, including driver and ostler; and then he wrote his letter. After that he had a hot supper, with three glasses of brandy and water, and went to bed with a thorough conviction that he had earned his bread on that day.

The letter to Z. A. did not give all these particulars, but it did explain that Colonel Osborne had gone off apparently, to Cockchaffington, and that he Bozzle had himself visited Nuncombe Putney. 'The hawk hasn't been nigh the dovecot as yet,' said Mr Bozzle in his letter, meaning to be both mysterious and facetious.

It would be difficult to say whether the wit or the mystery disgusted Trevelyan the most. He had felt that he was defiling himself with dirt when he first went to Mr Bozzle. He knew that he was having recourse to means that were base and low which could not be other than base or low, let the circumstances be what they might. But Mr Bozzle's conversation had not been quite so bad as Mr Bozzle's letters; as it may have been that Mr Bozzle's successful activity was more insupportable than his futile attempts. But, nevertheless, something must be done. It could not be that Colonel Osborne should have gone down to the close neighbourhood of Nuncombe Putney without the intention of seeing the lady whom his obtrusive pertinacity had driven to that seclusion. It was terrible to Trevelyan that Colonel Osborne should be there, and not the less terrible because such a one as Mr Bozzle was watching the Colonel on his behalf. Should he go to Nuncombe Putney himself? And if so, when he got to Nuncombe Putney what should he do there? At last, in his suspense and his grief, he resolved that he would tell the whole to Hugh Stanbury.

'Do you mean,' said Hugh, 'that you have put a policeman on his track?'

'The man was a policeman once.'

'What we call a private detective. I can't say I think you were right.'

'But you see that it was necessary,' said Trevelyan.

'I can't say that it was necessary. To speak out, I can't understand that a wife should be worth watching who requires watching.'

'Is a man to do nothing then? And even now it is not my wife whom I doubt.'

'As for Colonel Osborne, if he chooses to go to Lessboro', why shouldn't he? Nothing that you can do, or that Bozzle can do, can prevent him. He has a perfect right to go to Lessboro'.'

'But he has not a right to go to my wife.'

'And if your wife refuses to see him; or having seen him—for a man may force his way in anywhere with a little trouble—if she sends him away with a flea in his ear, as I believe she would?'

'She is so frightfully indiscreet.'

'I don't see what Bozzle can do.'

'He has found out at any rate that Osborne is there,' said Trevelyan. 'I am not more fond of dealing with such fellows than you are yourself. But I think it is my duty to know what is going on. What ought I to do now?'

'I should do nothing except dismiss Bozzle.'

'You know that that is nonsense, Stanbury.'

'Whatever I did I should dismiss Bozzle.' Stanbury was now quite in earnest, and, as he repeated his suggestion for the dismissal of the policeman, pushed his writing things away from him. 'If you ask my opinion, you know, I must tell you what I think. I should get rid of Bozzle as a beginning. If you will only think of it, how can your wife come back to you if she learns that you have set a detective to watch her?'

'But I haven't set the man to watch her.'

'Colonel Osborne is nothing to you, except as he is concerned with her. This man is now down in her neighbourhood; and, if she learns that, how can she help feeling it as a deep insult? Of course the man watches her as a cat watches a mouse.'

'But what am I to do? I can't write to the man and tell him to come away. Osborne is down there, and I must do something. Will you go down to Nuncombe Putney yourself, and let me know the truth?'

After much debating of the subject, Hugh Stansbury said that he would himself go down to Nuncombe Putney alone. There were difficulties about the D. R.; but he would go to the office of the newspaper and overcome them. How far the presence of Nora Rowley at his mother's house may have assisted in bringing him to undertake the journey, perhaps need not be accurately stated. He acknowledged to himself that the claims of friendship were strong upon him; and that as he had loudly disapproved of the Bozzle arrangement, he ought to lend a hand to some other scheme of action.

Moreover, having professed his conviction that no improper visiting could possibly take place under his mother's roof, he felt bound to shew that he was not afraid to trust to that conviction himself. He declared that he would be ready to proceed to Nuncombe Putney tomorrow but only on condition that he might have plenary power to dismiss Bozzle.

'There can be no reason why you should take any notice of the man,' said Trevelyan.

'How can I help noticing him when I find him prowling about the place? Of course I shall know who he is.'

'I don't see that you need know anything about him.'

'My dear Trevelyan, you cannot have two ambassadors engaged in the same service without communication with each other. And any communication with Mr Bozzle, except that of sending him back to London, I will not have.' The controversy was ended by the writing of a letter from Trevelyan to Bozzle, which was confided to Stanbury, in which the ex-policeman was thanked for his activity and requested to return to London for the present 'As we are now aware that Colonel Osborne is in the neighbourhood,' said the letter, 'my friend Mr Stanbury will know what to do.'

As soon as this was settled Stanbury went to the office of the *D. R.* and made arrangement as to his work for three days. Jones could do the article on the Irish Church upon a pinch like this, although he had not given much study to the subject as yet; and Puddlethwaite, who was great in City matters, would try his hand on the present state of society in Rome, a subject on which it was essential that the *D. R.* should express itself at once. Having settled these little troubles Stanbury returned to his friend, and in the evening they dined together at a tavern.

'And now, Trevelyan, let me know fairly what it is that you wish,' said Stanbury.

'I wish to have my wife back again.'

'Simply that. If she will agree to come back, you will make no difficulty.'

'No; not quite simply that. I shall desire that she shall be guided by my wishes as to any intimacies she may form.'

'That is all very well; but is she to give any undertaking? Do you intend to exact any promise from her? It is my opinion that she will be willing enough to come back, and that when she is with you there will be no further cause for quarrelling. But I don't think she will bind herself by any exacted promise; and certainly not through a third person.'

'Then say nothing about it. Let her write a letter to me proposing to come and she shall come.'

'Very well. So far I understand. And now what about Colonel Osborne? You don't want me to quarrel with him I suppose?'

'I should like to keep that for myself,' said Trevelyan, grimly.

'If you will take my advice you will not trouble yourself about him,' said Stanbury. 'But as far as I am concerned, I am not to meddle or make with him? Of course,' continued Stanbury, after a pause, 'if I find that he is intruding himself in my mother's house, I shall tell him that he must not come there.'

'But if you find him installed in your mother's house as a visitor how then?'

'I do not regard that as possible.'

'I don't mean living there,' said Trevelyan, 'but coming backwards and forwards going on in habits of intimacy with with ?' His voice trembled so as he asked these questions, that he could not pronounce the word which was to complete them.

'With Mrs Trevelyan, you mean.'

'Yes; with my wife. I don't say that it is so; but it may be so. You will be bound to tell me the truth.'

'I will certainly tell you the truth.'

'And the whole truth.'

'Yes; the whole truth.'

'Should it be so I will never see her again never. And as for him—but never mind.' Then there was another short period of silence, during which Stanbury smoked his pipe and sipped his whisky toddy. 'You must see,' continued Trevelyan, 'that it is absolutely necessary that I should do something. It is all very well for you to say that you do not like detectives. Neither do I like them. But what was I to do? When you condemn me you hardly realise the difficulties of my position.'

'It is the deuce of a nuisance certainly,' said Stansbury, through the cloud of smoke, thinking now not at all of Mrs Trevelyan, but of Mrs Trevelyan's sister.

'It makes a man almost feel that he had better not marry at all,' said Trevelyan.

'I don't see that. Of course there may come troubles. The tiles may fall on your head, you know, as you walk through the streets. As far as I can see, women go straight enough nineteen times out of twenty. But they don't like being what I call looked after.'

'And did I look after my wife more than I ought?'

'I don't mean that; but if I were married, which I never shall be, for I shall never attain to the respectability of a fixed income, I fancy I shouldn't look after my wife at all. It seems to me that women hate to be told about their duties.'

'But if you saw your wife, quite innocently, falling into an improper intimacy, taking up with people she ought not to know, doing that in ignorance, which could not but compromise yourself, wouldn't you speak a word then?'

'Oh! I might just say, in an off-hand way, that Jones was a rascal, or a liar, or a fool, or anything of that sort. But I would never caution her against Jones. By George, I believe a woman can stand anything better than that.'

'You have never tried it, my friend.'

'And I don't suppose I ever shall. As for me, I believe Aunt Stanbury was right when she said that I was a radical vagabond. I dare say I shall never try the thing myself, and therefore it's very easy to have a theory. But! must be off. Good night, old fellow. I'll do the best I can; and, at any rate, I'll let you know the truth.'

There had been a question during the day as to whether Stanbury should let his sister know by letter that he was expected; but it had been decided that he should appear at Nuncombe without any previous notification of his arrival. Trevelyan had thought that this was very necessary, and when Stanbury had urged that such a measure seemed to imply suspicion, he had declared that in no other way could the truth be obtained. He, Trevelyan, simply wanted to know the facts as they were occurring. It was a fact that Colonel Osborne was down in the neighbourhood of

Nuncombe Putney. That, at least, had been ascertained. It might very possibly be the case that he would be refused admittance to the Clock House, that all the ladies there would combine to keep him out. But, so Trevelyan urged, the truth on this point was desired. It was essentially necessary to his happiness that he should know what was being done.

'Your mother and sister,' said he, 'cannot be afraid of your coming suddenly among them.'

Stanbury, so urged, had found it necessary to yield, but yet he had felt that he himself was almost acting like a detective policeman, in purposely falling down upon them without a word of announcement. Had chance circumstances made it necessary that he should go in such a manner he would have thought nothing of it. It would simply have been a pleasant joke to him.

As he went down by the train on the following day, he almost felt ashamed of the part which he had been called upon to perform.

CHAPTER XX. SHEWING HOW COLONEL OSBORNE WENT TO COCKCHAFFINGTON

Together with Miss Stanbury's first letter to her sister-in-law a letter had also been delivered to Mrs Trevelyan. Nora Rowley, as her sister had left the room with this in her hand, had expressed her opinion that it had come from Trevelyan; but it had in truth been written by Colonel Osborne. And when that second letter from Miss Stanbury had been received at the Clock House, that in which she in plain terms begged pardon for the accusation conveyed in her first letter, Colonel Osborne had started on his deceitful little journey to Cockchaffington, and Mr Bozzle, the ex-policeman who had him in hand, had already asked his way to Nuncombe Putney.

When Colonel Osborne learned that Louis Trevelyan had broken up his establishment in Curzon Street, and had sent his wife away into a barbarous retirement in Dartmoor, for such was the nature of the information on the subject which was spread among Trevelyan's friends in London, and when he was made aware also that all this was done on his account because he was so closely intimate with Trevelyan's wife, and because Trevelyan's wife was, and persisted in continuing to be, so closely intimate with him his vanity was gratified. Although it might be true and no doubt was true that he said much to his friends and to himself of the deep sorrow which he felt that such a trouble should befall his old friend and his old friend's daughter; nevertheless, as he curled his grey whiskers before the glass, and made the most of such remnant of hair as was left on the top of his head, as he looked to the padding of his coat, and completed a study of the wrinkles beneath his eyes, so that in conversation they might be as little apparent as possible, he felt more of pleasure than of pain in regard to the whole affair. It was very sad that it should be so, but it was human. Had it been in his power to set the whole matter right by a word, he would probably have spoken that word; but as this was not possible, as Trevelyan had in his opinion made a gross fool of himself, as Emily Trevelyan was very nice, and not the less nice in that she certainly was fond of himself, as great tyranny had been used towards her, and as he himself had still the plea of old family friendship to protect his conscience—to protect his conscience unless he went so far as to make that plea an additional sting to his conscience—he thought that, as a man, he must follow up the matter. Here was a young, and fashionable, and very pretty woman banished to the wilds of Dartmoor for his sake. And, as far as he could understand, she would not have been so banished had she consented to say that she would give up her acquaintance with him. In such circumstances as these was it possible that he should do nothing? Various ideas ran through his head. He began to think that if Trevelyan were out of the way, he might might perhaps be almost tempted to make this woman his wife. She was so nice that he almost thought that he might be rash enough for that, although he knew well the satisfaction of being a bachelor; but as the thought suggested itself to him, he was well aware that he was thinking of a thing quite distant from him. The reader is not to suppose that Colonel Osborne meditated any making-away with the husband. Our colonel was certainly not the man for a murder. Nor did he even think of running away with his friend's daughter. Though he told himself that he could dispose of his wrinkles satisfactorily, still he knew himself and his powers sufficiently to be aware that he was no longer fit to be the hero of such a romance as that. He acknowledged to himself that there was much labour to be gone through in running away with another man's wife; and that the results, in respect to personal comfort, are not always happy. But what if Mrs Trevelyan were to divorce herself from her husband on the score of her husband's cruelty? Various horrors were related as to the man's treatment of his wife. By some it was said that she was in the prison on Dartmoor or, if not actually in the prison, an arrangement which the prison discipline might perhaps make difficult, that she was in the custody of one of the prison warders who possessed a prim cottage and a grim wife, just outside the prison walls. Colonel Osborne did not himself believe even so much as this, but he did believe that Mrs Trevelyan had been banished to some inhospitable region, to some dreary comfortless abode, of which, as the wife of a man of fortune, she would have great ground to complain. So thinking, he did not probably declare to himself that a divorce should be obtained, and that, in such event, he would marry the lady, but ideas came across his mind in that direction. Trevelyan was a cruel Bluebeard; Emily, as he was studious to call Mrs Trevelyan, was a dear injured saint. And as for himself, though he acknowledged to himself that the lumbago pinched him now and again, so that he could not rise from his chair with all the alacrity of youth, yet, when he walked along Pall Mall with his coat properly buttoned, he could not but observe that a great many young women looked at him with admiring eyes.

It was thus with no settled scheme that the Colonel went to work, and made inquiries, and ascertained Mrs Trevelyan's address in Devonshire. When he learned it, he thought that he had done much; though, in truth, there had been no secrecy in the matter. Scores of people knew Mrs Trevelyan's address besides the newsvendor who supplied her paper, from whose boy Colonel Osborne's servant obtained the information. But when the information had been obtained, it was expedient that it should be used; and therefore Colonel Osborne wrote the following letter:

Acrobats Club,
July 31, 186—

DEAR EMILY,

Twice the Colonel wrote DEAREST EMILY, and twice he tore the sheet on which the words were written. He longed to be ardent, but still it was so necessary to be prudent! He was not quite sure of the lady. Women sometimes tell their husbands, even when they have quarrelled with them. And, although ardent expressions in writing to pretty women are pleasant to male writers, it is not pleasant for a gentleman to be asked what on earth he means by that sort of thing at his tune of life. The Colonel gave half an hour to the consideration, and then began the letter, DEAR EMILY. If prudence be the soul of valour, may it not be considered also the very mainspring, or, perhaps, the pivot of love?

DEAR EMILY

I need hardly tell you with what dismay I have heard of all that has taken place in Curzon Street. I fear that you must have suffered much, and that you are suffering now. It is an inexpressible relief to me to hear that you have your child with you, and Nora. But, nevertheless, to have your home taken away from you, to be sent out of London, to be banished from all society! And for what? The manner in which the minds of some men work is quite incomprehensible.

As for myself, I feel that I have lost the company of a friend whom indeed I can very ill spare. I have a thousand things to say to you, and among them one or two which I feel that I must say that I ought to say. As it happens, an old schoolfellow of mine is Vicar of Cockchaffington, a village which I find by the map is very near to Nuncombe Putney. I saw him in town last spring, and he then asked me to pay him a visit. There is something in his church which people go to see, and though I don't understand churches much, I shall go and see it. I shall run down on Wednesday, and shall sleep at the inn at Lessboro'. I see that Lessboro' is a market town, and I suppose there is an inn. I shall go over to my friend on the Thursday, but shall return to Lessboro'. Though a man be ever so eager to see a church doorway, he need not sleep at the parsonage. On the following day, I will get over to Nuncombe Putney, and I hope that you will see me. Considering my long friendship with you, and my great attachment to your father and mother, I do not think that the strictest martinet would tell you that you need hesitate in the matter.

I have seen Mr Trevelyan twice at the club, but he has not spoken to me. Under such circumstances I could not of course speak to him. Indeed, I may say that my feelings towards him just at present are of such a nature as to preclude me from doing so with any appearance of cordiality.

Dear Emily,
Believe me now, as always, your affectionate friend,   FREDERIC OSBORNE.

When he read that letter over to himself a second time he felt quite sure that he had not committed himself. Even if his friend were to send the letter to her husband, it could not do him any harm. He was aware that he might have dilated more on the old friendship between himself and Sir Marmaduke, but he experienced a certain distaste to the mention of things appertaining to years long past. It did not quite suit him in his present frame of mind to speak of his regard in those quasi-paternal terms which he would have used had it satisfied him to represent himself simply as her father's friend. His language therefore had been a little doubtful, so that the lady might, if she were so minded, look upon him in that tender light in which her husband had certainly chosen to regard him.

When the letter was handed to Mrs Trevelyan, she at once took it with her up to her own room, so that she might be alone when she read it. The handwriting was quite familiar to her, and she did not choose that even her sister should see it. She had told herself twenty times over that, while living at Nuncombe Putney, she was not living under the guardianship of Mrs Stanbury. She would consent to live under the guardianship of no one, as her husband did not choose to remain with her and protect her. She had done no wrong, and she would submit to no other authority, than that of her legal lord and master. Nor, according to her views of her own position, was it in his power to depute that authority to others. He had caused the separation, and now she must be the sole judge of her own actions. In itself, a correspondence between her and her father's old friend was in no degree criminal or even faulty. There was no reason, moral, social, or religious, why an old man, over fifty, who had known her all her life, should not write to her. But yet she could not say aloud before Mrs Stanbury, and Priscilla, and her sister, that she had received a letter from Colonel Osborne. She felt that the colour had come to her cheek, and that she could not even walk out of the room as though the letter had been a matter of indifference to her.

And would it have been a matter of indifference had there been nobody there to see her? Mrs Trevelyan was certainly not in love with Colonel Osborne. She was not more so now than she had been when her father's friend, purposely dressed for the occasion, had kissed her in the vestry of the church in which she was married, and had given her a blessing, which was then intended to be semi-paternal as from an old man to a young woman. She was not in love with him never would be, never could be in love with him. Reader, you may believe in her so far as that. But where is the woman, who, when she is neglected, thrown over, and suspected by the man that she loves, will not feel the desire of some sympathy, some solicitude, some show of regard from another man? This woman's life, too, had not hitherto been of such a nature that the tranquillity of the Clock House at Nuncombe Putney afforded to her all that she desired. She had been there now a month, and was almost sick from the want of excitement. And she was full of wrath against her husband. Why had he sent her there to break her heart in, a disgraceful retirement, when she had never wronged him? From morning to night she had no employment, no amusement, nothing to satisfy her cravings. Why was she to be doomed to such an existence? She had declared that as long as she could have her boy with her, she would be happy. She was allowed to have her boy; but she was anything but happy. When she received Colonel Osborne's letter, while she held it in her hand still unopened, she never for a moment thought that that could make her happy. But there was in it something of excitement. And she painted the man to herself in brighter colours now than she had ever given to him in her former portraits. He cared for her. He was gracious to her. He appreciated her talents, her beauty, and her conduct. He knew that she deserved a treatment very different from that accorded to her by her husband. Why should she reject the sympathy of her father's oldest friend, because her husband was madly jealous about an old man? Her husband had chosen to send her away, and to leave her, so that she must act on her own judgment. Acting on her own judgment, she read Colonel Osborne's letter from first to last. She knew that he was wrong to speak of coming to Nuncombe Putney; but yet she thought that she would see him. She had a dim perception that she was standing on the edge of a precipice, on broken ground which might fall under her without a moment's warning, and yet she would not retreat from the danger. Though Colonel Osborne was wrong, very wrong in coming to see her, yet she liked him for coming. Though she would be half afraid to tell her news to Mrs Stanbury, and more than half afraid to tell Priscilla, yet she liked the excitement of the fear. Nora would scold her; but Nora's scolding she thought she could answer. And then it was not the fact that Colonel Osborne was coming down to Devonshire to see her. He was coming as far as Lessboro' to see his friend at Cockchaffington. And when at Lessboro', was it likely that he should leave the neighbourhood without seeing the daughter of his old ally? And why should he do so?

Was he to be unnatural in his conduct, uncivil, and unfriendly, because Mr Trevelyan had been foolish, suspicious, and insane?

So arguing with herself, she answered Colonel Osborne's letter before she had spoken on the subject to any one in the house and this was her answer:

The Clock House,
Nuncombe Putney,
Monday.

My Dear Colonel Osborne,

I must leave it to your own judgment to decide whether you will come to Nuncombe Putney or not. There are reasons which would seem to make it expedient that you should stay away even though circumstances are bringing you into the immediate neighbourhood. But of these reasons I will leave you to be the judge. I will never let it be said that I myself have had cause to dread the visit of any old friend. Nevertheless, if you stay away, I shall understand why you do so.

Personally, I shall be glad to see you as I have always been. It seems odd to me that I cannot write in warmer tones to my father's and mother's oldest friend. Of course, you will understand that though I shall readily see you if you call, I cannot ask you to stay. In the first place, I am not now living in my own house. I am staying with Mrs Stanbury, and the place is called the Clock House.

Yours very sincerely,

EMILY TREVELYAN.

Soon after she had written it, Nora came into her room, and at once asked concerning the letter which she had seen delivered to her sister that morning.

'It was from Colonel Osborne,' said Mrs Trevelyan.

'From Colonel Osborne! How very wrong!'

'I don't see that it is wrong at all. Because Louis is foolish and mad, that cannot make another man wrong for doing the most ordinary thing in the world.'

'I had hoped it had been from Louis,' said Nora.

'Oh dear, no. He is by no means so considerate. I do not suppose I shall hear from him, till he chooses to give some fresh order about myself or my child. He will hardly trouble himself to write to me, unless he take up some new freak to show me that he is my master.'

'And what does Colonel Osborne say?'

'He is coming here.'

'Coming here?' almost shouted Nora.

'Yes; absolutely here. Does it sound to you as if Lucifer himself were about to show his face. The fact is he happens to have a friend in the neighbourhood whom he has long promised to visit; and as he must be at Lessboro', he does not choose to go away without the compliment of a call. It will be as much to you as to me.'

'I don't want to see him in the least,' said Nora.

'There is his letter. As you seem to be so suspicious you had better read it.'

Then Nora read it.

'And there is a copy of my answer,' said Mrs Trevelyan. 'I shall keep both, because I know so well what ill-natured things people will say.'

'Dear Emily, do not send it,' said Nora.

'Indeed I shall. I will not be frightened by bugbears And I will not be driven to confess to any man on earth that I am afraid to see him. Why should I be afraid of Colonel Osborne? I will not submit to acknowledge that there can be any danger in Colonel Osborne. Were I to do so I should be repeating the insult against myself. If my husband wished to guide me in such matters why did he not stay with me?'

Then she went out into the village and posted the letter. Nora meanwhile was thinking whether she would call in the assistance of Priscilla Stanbury; but she did not like to take any such a step in opposition to her sister.

CHAPTER XXI. SHEWING HOW COLONEL OSBORNE WENT TO NUNCOMBE PUTNEY

Colonel Osborne was expected at Nuncombe Putney on the Friday, and, it was Thursday evening before either Mrs Stanbury or Priscilla was told of his coming. Emily had argued the matter with Nora, declaring that she would make the communication herself, and that she would make it when she pleased, and how she pleased. 'If Mrs Stanbury thinks,' said she, 'that I am going to be treated as a prisoner, or that I will not judge myself as to whom I may see, or whom I may not see, she is very much mistaken.' Nora felt that were she to give information to those ladies in opposition to her sister's wishes, she would express suspicion on her own part by doing so; and she was silent. On that same Thursday Priscilla had written her last defiant letter to her aunt, that letter in which she had cautioned her aunt to make no further accusation without being sure of her facts. To Priscilla's imagination that coming of Lucifer in person, of which Mrs Trevelyan had spoken, would hardly have been worse than the coming of Colonel Osborne. When, therefore, Mrs Trevelyan declared the fact on the Thursday evening, vainly endeavouring to speak of the threatened visit in an ordinary voice, and as of an ordinary circumstance, it was as though a thunderbolt had fallen upon them.

'Colonel Osborne coming here!' said Priscilla, mindful of the Stanbury correspondence mindful of the evil tongues of the world.

'And why not?' demanded Mrs Trevelyan, who had heard nothing of the Stanbury correspondence.

'Oh dear, oh dear!' ejaculated Mrs Stanbury, who, of course, was aware of all that had passed between the Clock House and the house in the Close, though the letters had been written by her daughter.

Nora was determined to stand up for her sister, whatever might be the circumstances of the case. 'I wish Colonel Osborne were not coming,' said she, 'because it makes a foolish fuss; but I cannot understand how anybody can suppose it to be wrong that Emily should see papa's very oldest friend in the world.'

'But why is he coming?' demanded Priscilla.

'Because he wants to see an acquaintance at Cockchaffington;' said Mrs Trevelyan; 'and there is a wonderful church-door there.'

'A church-fiddlestick!' said Priscilla.

The matter was debated throughout all the evening. At one time there was a great quarrel between the ladies, and then there was a reconciliation. The point on which Mrs Trevelyan stood with the greatest firmness was this that it did not become her, as a married woman 'whose conduct had always been good and who was more careful as to that than she was even of her name, to be ashamed to meet any man. 'Why should I not see Colonel Osborne, or Colonel anybody else who might call here with the same justification for calling which his old friendship gives him?' Priscilla endeavoured to explain to her that her husband's known wishes ought to hinder her from doing so. 'My husband should have remained with me, to express his wishes,' Mrs Trevelyan replied.

Neither could Mrs Stanbury nor could Priscilla bring herself to say that the man should not be admitted into the house. In the course of the debate, in the heat of her anger, Mrs Trevelyan declared that were any such threat held out to her, she would leave the house and see Colonel Osborne in the Street, or at the inn.

'No, Emily; no,' said Nora.

'But I will. I will not submit to be treated as a guilty woman, or as a prisoner. They may say what they like, but I won't be shut up.'

'No one has tried to shut you up,' said Priscilla.

'You are afraid of that old woman at Exeter,' said Mrs Trevelyan; for by this time the facts of the Stanbury correspondence had all been elicited in general conversation; 'and yet you know how uncharitable and malicious she is.'

'We are not afraid of her,' said Priscilla. 'We are afraid of nothing but of doing wrong.'

'And will it be wrong to let an old gentleman come into the house,' said Nora, 'who is nearly sixty, and who has known us ever since we were born?'

'If he is nearly sixty, Priscilla,' said Mrs Stanbury, 'that does seem to make a difference.' Mrs Stanbury herself was only just sixty, and she felt herself to be quite an old woman.

'They may be devils at eighty,' said Priscilla.

'Colonel Osborne is not a devil at all,' said Nora.

'But mamma is so foolish,' said Priscilla. 'The man's age does not matter in the least.'

'I beg your pardon, my dear,' said Mrs Stanbury, very humbly.

At that time the quarrel was raging, but afterwards came the reconciliation. Had it not been for the Stanbury correspondence the fact of Colonel Osborne's threatened visit would have been admitted as a thing necessary, as a disagreeable necessity; but how was the visit to be admitted and passed over in the teeth of that correspondence? Priscilla felt very keenly the peculiar cruelty of her position. Of course, Aunt Stanbury would hear of the visit. Indeed, any secrecy in the matter was not compatible with Priscilla's ideas of honesty. Her aunt had apologised humbly for having said that Colonel Osborne had been at Nuncombe. That apology, doubtless, had been due. Colonel Osborne had not been at Nuncombe when the accusation had been made, and the accusation had been unjust and false. But his coming had been spoken of by Priscilla in her own letters as an occurrence which was quite out of the question. Her anger against her aunt had been for saying that the man had come, not for objecting to such a visit. And now the man was coming, and Aunt Stanbury would know all about it. How great, how terrible, how crushing would be Aunt Stanbury's triumph!

'I must write and tell her,' said Priscilla.

'I am sure I shall not object,' said Mrs Trevelyan. 'And Hugh must be told,' said Mrs Stanbury.

'You may tell all the world, if you like,' said Mrs Trevelyan.

In this way it was settled among them that Colonel Osborne was to be received. On the next morning, Friday morning, Colonel Osborne, doubtless having heard something of Mrs Crocket from his friend at Cockchaffington, was up early, and had himself driven over to Nuncombe Putney before breakfast. The ever-watchful Bozzle was, of course, at his heels or rather, not at his heels on the first two miles of the journey; for Bozzle, with painful zeal, had made himself aware of all the facts, and had started on the Nuncombe Putney road half an hour before the Colonel's fly was in motion. And when the fly passed him he was lying discreetly hidden behind an old oak. The driver, however, had caught a glimpse of him as he was topping a hill, and having seen him about on the previous day, and perceiving that he was dressed in a decent coat and trousers, and that, nevertheless, he was not a gentleman, began to suspect that he was somebody. There was a great deal said afterwards about Bozzle in Mrs Clegg's yard at Lessboro'; but the Lessboro' mind was never able to satisfy itself altogether respecting Bozzle and his mission. As to Colonel Osborne and his mission, the Lessboro' mind did satisfy itself with much certainty. The horse was hardly taken from out of Colonel Osborne's fly in Mrs Crocket's yard when Bozzle stepped into the village by a path which he had already discovered, and soon busied himself among the tombs in the churchyard. Now, one corner of the churchyard was immediately opposite to the iron gate leading into the Clock House. 'Drat 'un,' said the wooden-legged postman, still sitting on his donkey, to Mrs Crocket's ostler, 'if there be'ant the chap as was here yesterday when I was a starting, and I zeed 'un in Lezbro' Street thick very morning.' 'He be'ant arter no good, that 'un,' said the ostler. After that a close watch was kept upon the watcher.

In the meantime, Colonel Osborne had ordered his breakfast at the Stag and Antlers, and had asked questions as to the position of the Clock House. He was altogether ignorant of Mr Bozzle, although Mr Bozzle had been on his track now for two days and two nights. He had determined, as he came on to Nuncombe Putney, that he would not be shame-faced about his visit to Mrs Trevelyan. It is possible that he was not so keen in the matter as he had. Been when he planned his journey in London; and, it may be, that he really tried to make himself believe that he had come all the way to the confines of Dartmoor to see the porch of Cockchaffington Church. The session in London was over, and it was necessary for such a man as Colonel Osborne that he should do something with himself before he went down to the Scotch grouse. He had long desired to see something of the most picturesque county in England; and now, as he sat eating his breakfast in Mrs Crocket's parlour, he almost looked upon his dear Emily as a subsidiary attraction. 'Oh, that's the Clock House,' he said to Mrs Crocket. 'No, I have not the pleasure of knowing Mrs Stanbury; very respectable lady, so I have heard; widow of a clergyman; ah, yes; son up in London; I know him, always writing books, is he? Very clever, I dare say. But there's a lady indeed, two ladies whom I do know. Mrs Trevelyan is there, I think and Miss Rowley.'

'You be'ant Muster Trevelyan, be you?' said Mrs Crocket, looking at him very hard.

'No, I'm not Mr Trevelyan.'

'Nor yet "the Colonel" they doo be talking about?'

'Well, yes, I am a colonel. I don't know why anybody should talk about me. I'll just step out now, however, and see my friends.'

'It's madam's lover,' said Mrs Crocket to herself, 'as sure as eggs is eggs.' As she said so, Colonel Osborne boldly walked across the village and pulled the bell at the iron gate, while Bozzle, crouching among the tombs, saw the handle in his hand. 'There he is,' said Priscilla. Everybody in the Clock House had known that the fly, which they had seen, had brought 'the Colonel' into Nuncombe Putney. Everybody had known that he had breakfasted at the Stag and Antlers. And everybody now knew that he was at the gate, ringing the bell. 'Into the drawing room,' said Mrs Stanbury, with a fearful, tremulous whisper to the girl who went across the little garden in front to open the iron gate. The girl felt as though Apollyon were there, and as though she were called upon to admit Apollyon. Mrs Stanbury having uttered her whisper, hurried way upstairs. Priscilla held her ground in the parlour, determined to be near the scene of action if there might be need. And it must be acknowledged that she peeped from behind the curtain, anxious to catch a glimpse of the terrible man, whose coming to Nuncombe Putney she regarded as so severe a misfortune.

The plan of the campaign had all been arranged. Mrs Trevelyan and Nora together received Colonel Osborne in the drawing-room. It was understood that Nora was to remain there during the whole visit. 'It is horrible to think that such a precaution should be necessary,' Mrs Trevelyan had said, 'but perhaps it may be best. There is no knowing what the malice of people may not invent.'

'My dear girls,' said the Colonel, 'I am delighted to see you,' and he gave a hand to each.

'We are not very cheerful here,' said Mrs Trevelyan, 'as you may imagine.'

'But the scenery is beautiful,' said Nora, 'and the people we are living with are very kind and nice.'

'I am very glad of that,' said the Colonel. Then there was a pause, and it seemed, for a moment, that none of them knew how to begin a general conversation. Colonel Osborne was quite sure, by this time, that he had come down to Devonshire with the express object of seeing the door of the church at Cockchaffington, and Mrs Trevelyan was beginning to think that he certainly had not come to see her. 'Have you heard from your father since you have been here?' asked the Colonel.

Then there was an explanation about Sir Marmaduke and Lady Rowley. Mr Trevelyan's name was not mentioned; but Mrs Trevelyan stated that she had explained to her mother all the painful circumstances of her present life. Sir Marmaduke, as Colonel Osborne was aware, was expected to be in England in the spring, and Lady Rowley would, of course, come with him. Nora thought that they might probably now come before that time; but Mrs Trevelyan declared that it was out of the question that they should do so. She was sure that her father could not leave the islands except when he did so in obedience to official orders. The expense of doing so would be ruinous to him. And what good would he do? In this way there was a great deal of family conversation, in which Colonel Osborne was able to take a part; but not a word was said about Mr Trevelyan.

Nor did 'the Colonel' find an opportunity of expressing a spark of that sentiment, for the purpose of expressing which he had made this journey to Devonshire. It is not pleasant to make love in the presence of a third person, even when that love is all fair and above board; but it is quite impracticable to do so to a married lady, when that married lady's sister is present. No more futile visit than this of Colonel

Osborne's to the Clock House was ever made. And yet, though not a word was spoken to which Mr Trevelyan himself could have taken the slightest exception, the visit, futile as it was, could not but do an enormous deal of harm. Mrs Crocket had already guessed that the fine gentleman down from London was the lover of the married lady at the Clock House, who was separated from her husband. The wooden-legged postman and the ostler were not long in connecting the man among the tombstones with the visitor to the house. Trevelyan, as we are aware, already knew that Colonel Osborne was in the neighbourhood. And poor Priscilla Stanbury was now exposed to the terrible necessity of owning the truth to her aunt. 'The Colonel,' when he had sat an hour with his young friends, took his leave; and, as he walked back to Mrs Crocket's, and ordered that his fly might be got ready for him, his mind was heavy with the disagreeable feeling that he had made an ass of himself. The whole affair had been a failure; and though he might be able to pass off the porch at Cockchaffington among his friends, he could not but be aware himself that he had spent his time, his trouble, and his money for nothing. He became aware, as he returned to Lessboro', that had he intended to make any pleasant use whatever of his position in reference to Mrs Trevelyan, the tone of his letter and his whole mode of proceeding should have been less patriarchal. And he should have contrived a meeting without the presence of Nora Rowley.

As soon as he had left them, Mrs Trevelyan went to her own room, and Nora at once rejoined Priscilla.

'Is he gone?' asked Priscilla.

'Oh, yes he has gone.'

'What would I have given that he had never come!'

'And yet,' said Nora, 'what harm has he done? I wish he had not come, because, of course, people will talk! But nothing was more natural than that he should come over to see us when he was so near us.'

'Nora!'

'What do you mean?'

'You don't believe all that? In the neighbourhood! I believe he came on purpose to see your sister, and I think that it was a dastardly and most ungentleman-like thing to do.'

'I am quite sure you are wrong, then altogether wrong,' said Nora.

'Very well. We must have our own opinions. I am glad you can be so charitable. But he should not have come here to this house, even though imperative business had brought him into the very village. But men in their vanity never think of the injury they may do to a woman's name. Now I must go and write to my aunt. I am not going to have it said hereafter that I deceived her. And then I shall write to Hugh. Oh dear; oh dear!'

'I am afraid we are a great trouble to you.'

'I will not deceive you, because I like you. This is a great trouble to me. I have meant to be so prudent, and with all my prudence I have not been able to keep clear of rocks. And I have been so indignant with Aunt Stanbury! Now I must go and eat humble-pie.'

Then she ate humble pie after the following fashion:

The Clock House,
Friday, August 5.

Dear Aunt Stanbury,

After what has passed between us, I think it right to tell you that Colonel Osborne has been at Nuncombe Putney, and that he called at the Clock House this morning. We did not see him. But Mrs Trevelyan and Miss Rowley, together, did see him. He remained here perhaps an hour.

'I should not have thought it necessary to mention this to you, the matter being one in which you are not concerned, were it not for our former correspondence. When I last wrote, I had no idea that he was coming nor had mamma. And when you first wrote, he was not even expected by Mrs Trevelyan. The man you wrote about, was another gentleman as I told you before. All this is most disagreeable, and tiresome and would be quite nonsensical, but that circumstances seem to make it necessary.

As for Colonel Osborne, I wish he had not been here; but his coming would do no harm only that it will be talked about.

I think you will understand how it is that I feel myself constrained to write to you. I do hope that you will spare mamma, who is disturbed and harassed when she gets angry letters. If you have anything to say to myself, I don't mind it.

Yours truly,   Priscilla Stanbury.

She wrote also to her brother Hugh; but Hugh himself reached Nuncombe Putney before the letter reached him.

Mr Bozzle watched the Colonel out of the house, and watched him out of the village. When the Colonel was fairly started, Mr Bozzle walked back to Lessboro'.

CHAPTER XXII. SHEWING HOW MISS STANBURY BEHAVED TO HER TWO NIECES

The triumph of Miss Stanbury when she received her niece's letter was very great—so great that in its first flush she could not restrain herself exhibiting it to Dorothy. 'Well well what do you think, Dolly?'

'About what, aunt? I don't know who the letter is from.'

'Nobody writes to me now so constant as your sister Priscilla. The letter is from Priscilla. Colonel Osborne has been at the Clock House, after all. I knew that he would be there. I knew it! I knew it!'

Dorothy, when she heard this, was dumbfounded. She had rested her defence of her mother and sister on the impossibility of any such visit being admitted. According to her lights the coming of Colonel Osborne, after all that had been said, would be like the coming of Lucifer himself. The Colonel was, to her imagination, a horrible roaring lion. She had no idea that the erratic manoeuvres of such a beast might be milder and more innocent than the wooing of any turtle-dove. She would have asked whether the roaring lion had gone away again, and, if so, whether he had taken his prey with him, were it not that she was too much frightened at the moment to ask any question. That her mother and sister should have been wilfully concerned in such iniquity was quite incredible to her, but yet she did not know how to defend them. 'But are you quite sure of it, Aunt Stanbury? May there not be another mistake?'

'No mistake this time, I think, my dear. Any way, Priscilla says that he is there.' Now in this there was a mistake. Priscilla had said nothing of the kind.

'You don't mean that he is staying at the Clock House, Aunt Stanbury?'

'I don't know where he is now. I'm not his keeper. And, I'm glad to say, I'm not the lady's keeper either. Ah, me! It's a bad business. You can't touch pitch and not be defiled, my dear. If your mother wanted the Clock House, I would sooner have taken it for her myself than that all this should have happened for the family's sake.'

But Miss Stanbury, when she was alone, and when she had read her niece's three letters again and again, began to understand something of Priscilla's honesty, and began also to perceive that there might have been a great difficulty respecting the for which neither her niece nor her sister-in-law could fairly be held to be ...ble. It was perhaps the plainest characteristic of all the Stanburys that they ...ever wilfully dishonest. Ignorant, prejudiced, and passionate they might be. ...r anger Miss Stanbury, of Exeter, could be almost malicious; and her niece at ...combe Putney was very like her aunt. Each could say most cruel things, most ...ust things, when actuated by a mistaken consciousness of perfect right on her ...wn side. But neither of them could lie even by silence. Let an error be brought ...ome to either of them so as to be acknowledged at home and the error would be assuredly confessed aloud. And, indeed, with differences in the shades, Hugh and Dorothy were of the same nature. They were possessed of sweeter tempers than their aunt and sister, but they were filled with the same eager readiness to believe themselves to be right and to own themselves to others to be wrong, when they had been constrained to make such confession to themselves. The chances of life, and something probably of inner nature, had made Dorothy mild and obedient; whereas, in regard to Hugh, the circumstances of his life and disposition had made him obstinate and self-reliant. But in all was to be found the same belief in self which amounted almost to conceit, the same warmth of affection, and the same love of justice.

When Miss Stanbury had again perused the correspondence, and had come to see, dimly, how things had gone at Nuncombe Putney, when the conviction came upon her mind that Priscilla had entertained a horror as to the coming of this Colonel equal to that which she herself had felt when her imagination painted to her all that her niece had suffered, her heart was softened somewhat. She had declared to Dorothy that pitch, if touched, would certainly defile; and she had, at first, intended to send the same opinion, couched in very forcible words, to her correspondents at the Clock House. They should not continue to go astray for want of being told that they were going astray. It must be acknowledged, too, that there was a certain amount of ignoble wrath in the bosom of Miss Stanbury because her sister-in-law had taken the Clock House. She had never been told, and had not even condescended to ask Dorothy, whether the house was taken and paid for by her nephew on behalf of his mother, or whether it was paid for by Mr Trevelyan on behalf of his wife. In the latter case, Mrs Stanbury would, she thought, be little more than an upper servant, or keeper as she expressed it to herself. Such an arrangement appeared to her to be quite disgraceful in a Stanbury; but yet she believed that such must be the existing arrangement, as she could not bring herself to conceive that Hugh Stanbury could keep such an establishment over his mother's head out of money earned by writing for a penny newspaper. There would be a triumph of democracy in this which would vanquish her altogether. She had, therefore, been anxious enough to trample on Priscilla and upon all the affairs of the Clock House; but yet she had been unable to ignore the nobility of Priscilla's truth, and having acknowledged it to herself she found herself compelled to acknowledge it aloud. She sat down to think in silence, and it was not till she had fortified herself by her first draught of beer, and till she had finished her first portion of bread and cheese, that she spoke. 'I have written to your sister herself, this time,' she said. 'I don't know that I ever wrote a line to her before in my life.'

'Poor Priscilla!' Dorothy did not mean to be severe on her aunt, either in regard to the letters which had not been written, or to the one letter which now had been written. But Dorothy pitied her sister, whom she felt to be in trouble.

'Well; I don't know about her being so poor. Priscilla, I'll be bound, thinks as well of herself as any of us do.'

'She'd cut her fingers off before she'd mean to do wrong,' said Dorothy.

'But what does that come to? What's the good of that? It isn't meaning to do right that will save us. For aught I know, the Radicals may mean to do right. Mr Beales means to do right perhaps.'

'But, aunt if everybody did the best they could?'

'Tush, my dear! you are getting beyond your depth. There are such things still, thank God! as spiritual pastors and masters. Entrust yourself to them. Do what they think right.' Now if aught were known in Exeter of Miss Stanbury, this was known that if any clergyman volunteered to give to her, unasked and uninvited, counsel, either ghostly or bodily, that clergyman would be sent from her presence with a wigging which he would not soon forget. The thing had been tried more than once, and the wigging had been complete. There was no more attentive listener in church than Miss Stanbury; and she would, now and again, appeal to a clergyman on some knotty point. But for the ordinary authority of spiritual pastors and masters she shewed more of abstract reverence than of practical obedience.

'I'm sure Priscilla does the best she can,' said Dorothy, going back to the old subject.

'Ah well yes. What I want to say about Priscilla is this. It is a thousand pities she is so obstinate, so pigheaded, so certain that she can manage everything for herself better than anybody else can for her.' Miss Stanbury was striving to say something good of her niece, but found the task to be difficult and distasteful to her.

'She has managed for mamma ever so many years; and since she took it we have hardly ever been in debt,' said Dorothy.

'She'll do all that, I don't doubt. I don't suppose she cares much for ribbons and false hair for herself.'

'Who? Priscilla! The idea of Priscilla with false hair!'

'I dare say not, I dare say not. I do not think she'd spend her mother's money on things of that kind.'

'Aunt Stanbury, you don't know her.'

'Ah; very well. Perhaps I don't. But, come, my dear, you are very hard upon me, and very anxious to take your sister's part. And what is it all about? I've just written to her as civil a letter as one woman ever wrote to another. And if I had chosen, I could have—could have—h—m—m.' Miss Stanbury, as she hesitated for words in which to complete her sentence, revelled in the strength of the vituperation which she could have poured upon her niece's head, had she chosen to write her last letter about Colonel Osborne in her severe strain.

'If you have written kindly to her, I am so much obliged to you,' said Dorothy.

'The truth is, Priscilla has meant to be right. Meaning won't go for much when the account is taken, unless the meaning comes from a proper source. But the poor girl has done as well as she has known how. I believe it is Hugh's fault more than anybody else's.' This accusation was not pleasant to Dorothy, but she was too intent just now on Priscilla's case to defend her brother, 'That man never ought to have been there; and that woman never ought to have been there. There cannot be a doubt about that. If Priscilla were sitting there opposite to me, she would own as much. I am sure she would.' Miss Stanbury was quite right if she meant to assert that Priscilla had owned as much to herself. 'And because I think so, I am willing to forgive her part in the matter. To me, personally, she has always been rude—most uncourteous and, and, and unlike a younger woman to an older one, and an aunt, and all that. I suppose it is because she hates me.'

'Oh, no, Aunt Stanbury!'

'My dear, I suppose it is. Why else should she treat me in such a way? But I do believe of her that she would rather eat an honest, dry crust, than dishonest cake and ale.'

'She would rather starve than pick up a crumb that was dishonest,' said Dorothy, fairly bursting out into tears.

'I believe it. I do believe it. There; what more can I say? Clock House, indeed! What matter what house you live in, so that you can pay the rent of it honestly?'

'But the rent is paid honestly,' said Dorothy, amidst her sobs.

'It's paid, I don't doubt. I dare say the woman's husband and your brother see to that among them. Oh, that my boy, Hugh, as he used to be, should have brought us all to this! But there's no knowing what they won't do among them. Reform, indeed! Murder, sacrilege, adultery, treason, atheism—that's what Reform means; besides every kind of nastiness under the sun.' In which latter category Miss Stanbury intended especially to include bad printer's ink, and paper made of straw.

The reader may as well see the letter, which was as civil a letter as ever one woman wrote to another, so that the collection of the Stanbury correspondence may be made perfect.

> The Close,
> August 6, 186—.

My Dear Niece,

Your letter has not astonished me nearly as much as you expected it would. I am an older woman than you, and, though you will not believe it, I have seen more of the world. I knew that the gentleman would come after the lady. Such gentlemen always do go after their ladies. As for yourself, I can see all that you have done, and pretty nearly hear all that you have said, as plain as a pikestaff. I do you the credit of believing that the plan is none of your making. I know who made the plan, and a very bad plan it is.

As to my former letters and the other man, I understand all about it. You were very angry that I should accuse you of having this man at the house; and you were right to be angry. I respect you for having been angry. But what does all that say as to his coming—now that he has come?

If you will consent to take an old woman's advice, get rid of the whole boiling of them. I say it in firm love and friendship, for I am

Your affectionate aunt,   Jemima Stanbury.

The special vaunted courtesy of this letter consisted, no doubt, in the expression of respect which it contained, and in that declaration of affection with which it terminated. The epithet was one which Miss Stanbury would by no means use promiscuously in writing to her nearest relatives. She had not intended to use it when she commenced her letter to Priscilla. But the respect of which she had spoken had glowed, and had warmed itself into something of temporary love; and feeling at the moment that she was an affectionate aunt, Miss Stanbury had so put herself down in her letter. Having done such a deed she felt that Dorothy, though Dorothy knew nothing about it, ought in her gratitude to listen patiently to anything that she might now choose to say against Priscilla.

But Dorothy was in truth very miserable, and in her misery wrote a long letter that afternoon to her mother which, however, it will not be necessary to place entire among the Stanbury records begging that she might be informed as to the true circumstances of the case. She did not say a word of censure in regard either to her mother or sister; but she expressed an opinion in the mildest words which she could use, that if anything had happened which had compromised their names since their residence at the Clock House, she, Dorothy, had better go home and join them. The meaning of which was that it would not become her to remain in the house in the Close, if the house in the Close would be disgraced by her presence, Poor Dorothy had taught herself to think that the iniquity of roaring lions spread itself very widely.

In the afternoon she made some such proposition to her aunt in ambiguous terms. 'Go home!' said Miss Stanbury. 'Now?'

'If you think it best, Aunt Stanbury'

'And put yourself in the middle of all this iniquity and abomination! I don't suppose you want to know the woman?'

'No, indeed!'

'Or the man?'

'Oh, Aunt Stanbury!'

'It's my belief that no decent gentleman in Exeter would look at you again if you were to go and live among them at Nuncombe Putney while all this is going on. No, no. Let one of you be saved out of it, at least.' Aunt Stanbury had more than once made use of expressions which brought the faintest touch of gentle pink up to her niece's cheeks. We must do Dorothy the justice of saying that she had never dreamed of being looked at by any gentleman, whether decent or indecent. Her life at Nuncombe Putney had been of such a nature, that though she knew that other girls were looked at, and even made love to, and that they got married and had children, no dim vision of such a career for herself had ever presented itself to her eyes. She had known very well that her mother and sister and herself were people apart, ladies, and yet so extremely poor that they could only maintain their rank by the most rigid seclusion. To live, and work unseen, was what the world had ordained for her. Then her call to Exeter had come upon her, and she had conceived that she was henceforth to be the humble companion of a very imperious old aunt. Her aunt, indeed, was imperious, but did not seem to require humility in her companion. All the good things that were eaten and drunk were divided between them with the strictest impartiality. Dorothy's cushion and hassock in the church and in the cathedral were the same as her aunt's. Her bed-room was made very comfortable for her. Her aunt never gave her any orders before company, and always spoke of her before the servants as one whom they were to obey and respect. Gradually Dorothy came to understand the meaning of this, but her aunt would sometimes say things about young men which she did not quite understand. Could it be that her aunt supposed that any young man would come and wish to marry her—her, Dorothy Stanbury? She herself had not quite so strong an aversion to men in general as that which Priscilla felt, but she had not as yet found that any of those whom she had seen at Exeter were peculiarly agreeable to her. Before she went to bed that night her aunt said a word to her which startled her more than she had ever been startled before. On that evening Miss Stanbury had a few friends to drink tea with her. There were Mr and Mrs Crumbie, and Mrs MacHugh of course, and the Cheritons from Alphington, and the Miss Apjohns from Helion Villa, and old Mr Powel all the way from Haldon, and two of the Wrights from their house in the Northernhay, and Mr Gibson; but the Miss Frenches from Heavitree were not there. 'Why don't you have the Miss Frenches, aunt?' Dorothy had asked.

'Bother the Miss Frenches! I'm not bound to have them every time. There's Camilla has been and got herself a band-box on the back of her head a great deal bigger than the place inside where her brains ought to be.' But the band-box at the back of Camilla French's head was not the sole cause of the omission of the two sisters from the list of Miss Stanbury's visitors on this occasion.

The party went off very much as usual. There were two whist tables, for Miss Stanbury could not bear to cut out. At other houses than her own, when there was cutting out, it was quite understood that Miss Stanbury was to be allowed to keep her place. 'I'll go away, and sit out there by myself, if you like,' she would say. But she was never thus banished; and at her own house she usually contrived that there should be no system of banishment. She would play dummy whist, preferring it to the four-handed game; and, when hard driven, and with a meet opponent, would not even despise double-dummy. It was told of her and of Mrs MacHugh that they had played double-dummy for a whole evening together; and they who were given to calumny had declared that the candles on that evening had been lighted very early. On the present occasion a great many sixpenny points were scored, and much tea and cake were consumed. Mr Gibson never played whist nor did Dorothy. That young John Wright and Mary Cheriton should do nothing but talk to each other was a thing of course, as they were to be married in a month or two. Then there was Ida Cheriton, who could not very well be left at home; and Mr Gibson made himself pleasant to Dorothy and Ida Cheriton, instead of making himself pleasant to the two Miss Frenches. Gentlemen in provincial towns quite understand that, from the nature of social circumstances in the provinces, they should always be ready to be pleasant at least to a pair at a time. At a few minutes before twelve they were all gone, and then came the shock.

'Dolly, my dear, what do you think of Mr Gibson?'

'Think of him, Aunt Stanbury?'

'Yes; think of him think of him. I suppose you know how to think?'

'He seems to me always to preach very drawling sermons.'

'Oh, bother his sermons! I don't care anything about his sermons now. He is a very good clergyman, and the Dean thinks very much about him.'

'I am glad of that, Aunt Stanbury.' Then came the shock. 'Don't you think it would be a very good thing if you were to become Mrs Gibson?'

It may be presumed that Miss Stanbury had assured herself that she could not make progress with Dorothy by 'beating about the bush.' There was an inaptitude in her niece to comprehend the advantages of the situations, which made some direct explanation absolutely necessary. Dorothy stood half smiling, half crying, when she heard the proposition, her cheeks suffused with that pink colour, and with both her hands extended with surprise.

'I've been thinking about it ever since you've been here,' said Miss Stanbury.

'I think he likes Miss French,' said Dorothy, in a whisper.

'Which of them? I don't believe he likes them at all. Maybe, if they go on long enough, they may be able to toss up for him. But I don't think it of him. Of course they're after him, but he'll be too wise for them. And he's more of a fool than I take him to be if he don't prefer you to them.' Dorothy remained quite silent. To such an address as this it was impossible that she should reply a word. It was incredible to her that any man should prefer herself to either of the young women in question; but she was too much confounded for the expression even of her humility. 'At any rate you're wholesome, and pleasant and modest,' said Miss Stanbury.

Dorothy did not quite like being told that she was wholesome; but, nevertheless, she was thankful to her aunt.

'I'll tell you what it is,' continued Miss Stanbury; 'I hate all mysteries, especially with those I love. I've saved two thousand pounds, which I've put you down for in my will. Now, if you and he can make it up together, I'll give you the money at once. There's no knowing how often an old woman may alter her will; but when you've got a thing, you've got it. Mr Gibson would know the meaning of a bird in the hand as well as anybody. Now those girls at Heavitree will never have above a few hundreds each, and not that while their mother lives.' Dorothy made one little attempt at squeezing her aunt's hand, wishing to thank her aunt for this affectionate generosity; but she had hardly accomplished the squeeze, when she desisted, feeling strangely averse to any acknowledgment of such a boon as that which had been offered to her. 'And now, good night, my dear. If I did not think you a very sensible young woman, I should not trust you by saying all this.' Then they parted, and Dorothy soon found herself alone in her bedroom.

To have a husband of her own, a perfect gentleman too, and a clergyman and to go to him with a fortune! She believed that two thousand pounds represented nearly a hundred a year. It was a large fortune in those parts according to her understanding of ladies' fortunes. And that she, the humblest of the humble, should be selected for so honourable a position! She had never quite known, quite understood as yet, whether she had made good her footing in her aunt's house in a manner pleasant to her aunt. More than once or twice she had spoken even of going back to her mother, and things had been said which had almost made her think that her aunt had been angry with her. But now, after a month or two of joint residence, her aunt was offering to her two thousand pounds and a husband!

But was it within her aunt's power to offer to her the husband? Mr Gibson had always been very civil to her. She had spoken more to Mr Gibson than to any other man in Exeter. But it had never occurred to her for a moment that Mr Gibson had any special liking for her. Was it probable that he would ever entertain any feeling of that kind for her? It certainly had occurred to her before now that Mr Gibson was sometimes bored by the Miss Frenches but then gentlemen do get bored by ladies.

And at last she asked herself another question: had she any special liking for Mr Gibson? As far as she understood such matters everything was blank there. Thinking of that other question, she went to sleep.

CHAPTER XXIII. COLONEL OSBORNE AND MR BOZZLE RETURN TO LONDON

Hugh Stanbury went down on the Saturday, by the early express to Exeter, on his road to Lessboro'. He took his ticket through to Lessboro', not purposing to stay at Exeter; but, from the exigencies of the various trains, it was necessary that he should remain for half an hour at the Exeter Station. This took place on the Saturday, and Colonel Osborne's visit to the Clock House had been made on the Friday. Colonel Osborne had returned to Lessboro', had slept again at Mrs Clegg's house, and returned to London on the Saturday. It so happened that, he also was obliged to spend half an hour at the Exeter Station, and that his half-hour, and Hugh Stanbury's half-hour, were one and the same. They met, therefore, as a matter of course, upon the platform. Stanbury was the first to see the other, and he found that he must determine on the spur of the moment what he would say, and what he would do. He had received no direct commission from Trevelyan as to his meeting with Colonel Osborne. Trevelyan had declared that, as to the matter of quarrelling, he meant to retain the privilege of doing that for himself; but Stanbury had quite understood that this was only the vague expression of an angry man. The Colonel had taken a glass of sherry, and had lighted a cigar, and was quite comfortable having thrown aside, for a time, that consciousness of the futility of his journey which had perplexed him when Stanbury accosted him.

'What! Mr Stanbury, how do you do? Fine day, isn't it? Are you going up or down?'

'I'm going to see my own people at Nuncombe Putney, a village, beyond Lessboro',' said Hugh.

'Ah indeed.' Colonel Osborne of course perceived it once that as this man was going to the house at which he had just been visiting, it would be better that he should himself explain what he had done. If he were to allow this mention of Nuncombe Putney to pass without saying that he himself had been there, he would be convicted of at least some purpose of secrecy in what he had been doing. 'Very strange,' said he; 'I was at Nuncombe Putney myself yesterday.'

'I know you were,' said Stanbury.

'And how did you know it?' There had been a tone of anger in Stanbury's voice which Colonel Osborne had at once appreciated, and which made him assume a similar one. As they spoke there was a man standing in a corner close by the bookstall, with his eye upon them, and that man was Bozzle, the ex-policeman who was doing his duty with sedulous activity by seeing 'the Colonel' back to London. Now Bozzle did not know Hugh Stanbury, and was angry with himself that, he should be so ignorant. It is the pride of a detective ex-policeman to know everybody that comes in his way.

'Well, I had been so informed. My friend Trevelyan knew that you were there—or that you were going there.'

'I don't care who knew that I was going there,' said the Colonel.

'I won't pretend to understand how that may be, Colonel Osborne; but I think you must be aware, after, what took place in Curzon Street, that it would have been better that you should not have attempted to see Mrs Trevelyan. Whether you have seen her I do not know.'

'What business is it of yours, Mr Stanbury, whether I have seen that lady or not?'

'Unhappily for me, her husband has made it my business.'

'Very unhappily for you, I should say.'

'And the lady is staying at my mother's house.'

'I presume the lady is not a prisoner in your mother's house, and that your mother's hospitality is not so restricted but that her guest may see an old friend under her roof.' This, Colonel Osborne said with an assumed look of almost righteous indignation, which was not at all lost upon Bozzle. They had returned back towards the bookstall, and Bozzle, with his eyes fixed on a copy of the '*D. R.*' which he had just bought, was straining his ears to the utmost to catch what was being said.

'You best know whether you have seen her or not.'

'I have seen her.'

'Then I shall take leave to tell you, Colonel Osborne, that you have acted in a most unfriendly way, and have done that which must tend to keep an affectionate husband apart from his wife.'

'Sir, I don't at all understand this kind of thing addressed to me. The father of the lady you are speaking of has been my most intimate friend for thirty years.' After all, the Coonel was a mean man when he could take pride in his youth, and defend himself on the score of his age, in one and the same proceeding.

'I have nothing further to say,' replied Stanbury.

'You have said too much already, Mr Stanbury.'

'I think not, Colonel Osborne. You have, I fear, done an incredible deal of mischief by going to Nuncombe Putney; and, after all that you have heard on the subject, you must have known that it would be mischievous. I cannot understand how you can force yourself about a man's wife against the man's expressed wish.'

'Sir, I didn't force myself upon anybody. Sir, I went down to see an old friend and a remarkable piece of antiquity. And, when another old friend was in the neighbourhood, close by, one of the oldest friends I have in the world, wasn't I to go and see her? God bless my soul! What business is it of yours? I never heard such impudence in my life!' Let the charitable reader suppose that Colonel Osborne did not know that he was lying—that he really thought, when he spoke, that he had gone down to Lessboro' to see the remarkable piece of antiquity.

'Good morning,' said Hugh Stanbury, turning on his heels and walking away. Colonel Osborne shook himself, inflated his cheeks, and blew forth the breath out of his mouth, put his thumbs up to the armholes of his waistcoat, and walked about the platform as though he thought it to be incumbent on him to show that he was somebody, somebody that ought not to be insulted, somebody, perhaps, whom a very pretty woman might prefer to her own husband, in spite of a small difference in age. He was angry, but not quite so much angry as proud. And he was safe, too. He thought that he was safe. When he should come to account for himself and his actions to his old friend, Sir Marmaduke, he felt that he would be able to show that he had been, in all respects, true to friendship. Sir Marmaduke had unfortunately given his daughter to a jealous, disagreeable fellow, and the fault all lay in that. As for Hugh Stanbury he would simply despise Hugh Stanbury, and have done with it.

Mr Bozzle, though he had worked hard in the cause, had heard but a word or two. Eaves-droppers seldom do hear more than that. A porter had already told him who was Hugh Stanbury, that he was Mr Hugh Stanbury, and that his aunt lived at Exeter. And Bozzle, knowing that the lady about whom he was concerned was living with a Mrs Stanbury at the house he had been watching, put two and two together with his natural cleverness. 'God bless my soul! what business is it of yours?' Those words were nearly all that Bozzle had been able to hear; but even those sufficiently indicated a quarrel. 'The lady' was living with Mrs Stanbury, having been so placed by her husband; and young Stanbury was taking the lady's part! Bozzle began to fear that the husband had not confided in him with that perfect faith which he felt to be essentially necessary to the adequate performance of the duties of his great profession. A sudden thought, however, struck him. Something might be done on the journey up to London. He at once made his way back to the ticket-window and exchanged his ticket second-class for first-class. It was a noble deed, the expense falling all upon his own pocket; for, in the natural course of things, he would have charged his employers with the full first-class fare. He had seen Colonel Osborne seat himself in a carriage, and within two minutes he was occupying the opposite place. The Colonel was aware that he had noticed the man's face lately, but did not know where.

'Very fine summer weather, sir,' said Bozzle.

'Very fine,' said the Colonel, burying himself behind a newspaper.

'They is getting up their wheat nicely in these parts, sir.'

The answer to this was no more than a grunt. But Bozzle was not offended. Not to be offended is the special duty of all policemen, in and out of office; and the journey from Exeter to London was long, and was all before him.

'A very nice little secluded village is Nuncombe Putney,' said Bozzle, as the train was leaving the Salisbury station.

At Salisbury two ladies had left the carriage, no one else had got in, and Bozzle. was alone with the Colonel.

'I dare say,' said the Colonel, 'who by this time had relinquished his shield, and who had begun to compose himself for sleep, or to pretend to compose himself, as soon as he heard Bozzle's voice. He had been looking at Bozzle, and though he had not discovered the man's trade, had told himself that his companion was a thing of dangers a thing to be avoided, by one engaged, as had been he himself, on a special and secret mission.

'Saw you there calling at the Clock House,' said Bozzle.

'Very likely,' said the Colonel, throwing his head well back into the corner, shutting his eyes, and uttering a slight preliminary snore.

'Very nice family of ladies at the Clock House,' said Bozzle. The Colonel answered him by a more developed snore. 'Particularly Mrs T,' said Bozzle.

The Colonel could not stand this. He was so closely implicated with Mrs Trevelyan at the present moment that he could not omit to notice an address so made to him. 'What the devil is that to you, sir?' said he, jumping up and confronting Bozzle in his wrath.

But policemen have always this advantage in their difficulties, that they know to a fraction what the wrath of men is worth, and what it can do. Sometimes it can dismiss a policeman, and sometimes break his head. Sometimes it can give him a long and troublesome job, and sometimes it may be wrath to the death. But in nineteen out of twenty cases it is not a fearful thing, and the policeman knows well when he need not fear it. On the present occasion Bozzle was not at all afraid of Colonel Osborne's wrath.

'Well, sir, not much, indeed, if you come to that. 'Only you was there, sir.'

'Of course I was there,' said the Colonel.

'And a very nice young gentleman is Mr Stanbury,' said Bozzle.

To this Colonel Osborne made no reply, but again had resort to his newspaper in the most formal manner.

'He's a going down to his family, no doubt,' continued Bozzle.

'He may be going to the devil for what I know,' said the Colonel, who could not restrain himself.

'I suppose they're all friends of Mrs T.'s?' asked Bozzle.

'Sir,' said the Colonel, 'I believe that you're a spy.'

'No, Colonel, no; no, no; I'm no spy. I wouldn't demean myself to be such. A spy is a man as has no profession, and nothing to justify his looking into things. Things must be looked into, Colonel; or how's a man to know where he is? or how's a lady to know where she is? But as for spies, except in the way of evidence, I don't think nothing of 'em.' Soon after this, two more passengers entered the train, and nothing more was said between Bozzle and the Colonel.

The Colonel, as soon as he reached London, went home to his lodgings, and then to his club, and did his best to enjoy himself. On the following Monday he intended to start for Scotland. But he could not quite enjoy himself because of Bozzle. He felt that he was being watched; and there is nothing that any man hates so much as that, especially when a lady is concerned. Colonel Osborne knew that his visit to Nuncombe Putney had been very innocent; but he did not like the feeling that even his innocence had been made the subject of observation.

Bozzle went away at once to Trevelyan, whom he found at his chambers. He himself had had no very deep-laid scheme in his addresses to Colonel Osborne. He had begun to think that very little would come of the affair especially after Hugh Stanbury had appeared upon the scene and had felt that there was nothing to be lost by presenting himself before the eyes of the Colonel. It was necessary that he should make a report to his employer, and the report might be made a little more full after a few words with the man whom he had been 'looking into.' 'Well, Mr Trewillian,' he said, seating himself on a chair close against the wall, and holding his hat between the knees 'I've seen the parties, and know pretty much all about it.'

'All I want to know, Mr Bozzle, is, whether Colonel Osborne has been at the Clock House?'

'He has been there, Mr Trewillian. There is no earthly doubt about that. From hour to hour I can tell you pretty nearly where he's been since he left London.' Then Bozzle took out his memorandum-book.

'I don't care about all that,' said Trevelyan.

'I dare say not, sir; but it may be wanted all the same. Any gentleman acting in our way can't be too particular, can't have too many facts. The smallest little tiddly things, and Bozzle as he said this seemed to enjoy immensely the flavour of his own epithet 'the smallest little "tiddly" things do so often turn up trumps when you get your evidence into court.'

'I'm not going to get any evidence into court.'

'Maybe not, sir. A gentleman and lady is always best out of court as long as things can hang on any way, but sometimes things won't hang on no way.'

Trevelyan, who was conscious that the employment of Bozzle was discreditable, and whose affairs in Devonshire were now in the hands of, at any rate, a more honourable ally, was at present mainly anxious to get rid of the ex-policeman. 'I have no doubt you've been very careful, Mr Bozzle,' said he.

'There isn't no one in the business could be more so, Mr Trewillian.'

'And you have found out what it was necessary that I should know. Colonel Osborne did go to the Clock House?'

'He was let in at the front door on Friday the 5th by Sarah French, the housemaid, at 10.37 a.m., and was let out again by the same young woman at 11.44 a.m. Perhaps you'd like to have a copy of the entry, Mr Trewillian?'.

'No, no, no.'

'It doesn't matter. Of course it'll be with me when it's wanted. Who was with him, exactly, at that time, I can't say. There is things, Mr Trewillian, one can't see. But I don't think as he saw neither Mrs Stanbury, nor Miss Stanbury not to speak to. I did just have one word, promiscuous, with Sarah French, after he was gone. Whether the other young lady was with 'em or not, and if so for how long, I can't say. There is things, Mr Trewillian, which one can't see.'

How Trevelyan hated the man as he went on with his odious details, details, not one of which possessed the slightest importance. 'It's all right, I dare say, Mr Bozzle. And now about the account.'

'Quite so, Mr Trewillian. But there was one question—just one question.'

'What question?' said Trevelyan, almost angrily.

'And there's another thing I must tell you, too, Mr Trewillian. I come back to town in the same carriage with the Colonel. I thought it better.'

'You did not tell him who you were?'

'No, Mr Trewillian; I didn't tell him that. I don't think he'd say if you was to ask him that I told him much of anything. No, Mr Trewillian, I didn't tell him nothing. I don't often tell folks much till the time comes. But I thought it better, and I did have a word or two with the gent, just a word or two. He's not so very downy, isn't the Colonel for one that's been at it so long, Mr Trewillian.'

'I dare say not. But if you could just let me have the account, Mr Bozzle—'

'The account? Oh, yes that is necessary; ain't it? These sort of inquiries do come a little expensive, Mr Trewillian; because time goes for so much; and when one has to be down on a thing, sharp, you know, and sure, so that counsel on the other side can't part you from it, though he shakes you like a dog does a rat, and one has to get oneself up ready for all that, you know, Mr Trewillian; as I was saying, one can't count one's shillings when one has such a job as this in hand. Clench your nail—that's what I say; be it even so. Clench your nail— that's what you've got to do.'

'I dare say we shan't quarrel about the money, Mr Bozzle.'

'Oh dear no. I find I never has any words about the money. But there's that one question. There's a young Mr Stanbury has gone down, as knows all about it. What's he up to?'

'He's my particular friend,' said Trevelyan.

'Oh—h. He do know all about it, then?'

'We needn't talk about that, if you please, Mr Bozzle.'

'Because there was words between him and the Colonel upon the platform and very angry words. The young man went at the Colonel quite open-mouthed savage-like. It's not the way such things should be done, Mr Trewillian; and though of course it's not for me to speak—she's your lady—still, when you has got a thing of this kind in hand, one head is better than a dozen. As for myself, Mr Trewillian, I never wouldn't look at a case, not if I knew it, unless I was to have it all to myself. But of course there was no bargain, and so I says nothing.'

After considerable delay the bill was made out on the spot, Mr Bozzle copying down the figures painfully from his memorandum-book, with his head much inclined on one side. Trevelyan asked him, almost in despair, to name the one sum; but this Bozzle declined to do, saying that right was right. He had a scale of pilfering of his own, to which he had easily reconciled his conscience; and beyond that he prided himself on the honesty of his accounts. At last the bill was made out, was paid, and Bozzle was gone. Trevelyan, when he was alone, threw himself back on a sofa, and almost wept in despair. To what a depth of degradation had he not been reduced!

CHAPTER XXIV. NIDDON PARK

As Hugh Stanbury went over to Lessboro', and from thence to Nuncombe Putney, he thought more of himself and Nora Rowley than he did of Mr and Mrs Trevelyan. As to Mrs Trevelyan and Colonel Osborne, he felt that he knew everything that it was necessary that he should know. The man had been there, and had seen Mrs Trevelyan. Of that there could be no doubt. That Colonel Osborne had been wickedly indifferent to the evil consequences of such a visit, and that all the women concerned had been most foolish in permitting him to make it, was his present conviction. But he did not for a moment doubt that the visit had in itself been of all things the most innocent. Trevelyan had sworn that if his wife received the man at Nuncombe Putney, he would never see her again. She had seen him, and this oath would be remembered, and there would be increased difficulties. But these difficulties, whatever they might be, must be overcome. When he had told himself this, then he allowed his mind to settle itself on Nora Rowley.

Hitherto he had known Miss Rowley only as a fashionable girl living with the wife of an intimate friend of his own in London. He had never been staying in the same house with her. Circumstances had never given to him the opportunity of assuming the manner of an intimate friend, justifying him in giving advice, and authorising him to assume that semi-paternal tone which is by far the easiest preliminary to love-making. When a man can tell a young lady what she ought to read, what she ought to do, and whom she ought to know, nothing can be easier than to assure her that, of all her duties, her first duty is to prefer himself to all the world. And any young lady who has consented to receive lessons from such a teacher, will generally be willing to receive this special lesson among others. But Stanbury had hitherto had no such opportunities. In London Miss Rowley had been a fashionable young lady, living in Mayfair, and he had been well, anything but a fashionable young man. Nevertheless, he had seen her often, had sat by her very frequently, was quite sure that he loved her dearly, and had, perhaps, some self-flattering idea in his mind that had he stuck to his honourable profession as a barrister, and were he possessed of some comfortable little fortune of his own, he might, perhaps, have been able, after due siege operations, to make this charming young woman his own. Things were quite changed now. For the present, Miss Rowley certainly could not be regarded as a fashionable London young lady. The house in which he would see her was, in some sort, his own. He would be sleeping under the same roof with her, and would have all the advantages which such a position could give him. He would have no difficulty now in asking, if he should choose to ask; and he thought that she might be somewhat softer, somewhat more likely to yield at Nuncombe Putney, than she would have been in London. She was at Nuncombe in weak circumstances, to a certain degree friendless; with none of the excitement of society around her, with no elder sons buzzing about her and filling her mind, if not her heart, with the glories of luxurious primogeniture. Hugh Stanbury certainly did not dream that any special elder son had as yet been so attracted as to have made a journey to Nuncombe Putney on Nora's behalf. But should he on this account, because she would be, as it were, without means of defence from his attack, should he therefore take advantage of her weakness? She would, of course, go back to her London life after some short absence, and would again, if free, have her chance among the favoured ones of the earth. What had he to offer to her? He had taken the Clock House for his mother, and it would be quite as much as he could do, when Mrs Trevelyan should have left the village, to keep up that establishment and maintain himself in London, quite as much as he could do, even though the favours of the '*D. R.*' should flow upon him with their fullest tides. In such circumstances, would it be honourable in him to ask a girl to love him because he found her defenceless in his mother's house?

'If there bain't another for Nuncombe,' said Mrs. Clegg's Ostler to Mrs Clegg's Boots, as Stanbury was driven off in a gig.

'That be young Stanbury, a-going of whome.'

'They be all a-going for the Clock House. Since the old 'ooman took to thick there house, there be folk a-comin' and a-goin' every day loike.'

'It's along of the madam that they keeps there, Dick,' said the Boots.

'I didn't care if there'd be madams allays. They're the best as is going for trade anyhow,' said the ostler. What the ostler said was true. When there comes to be a feeling that a woman's character is in any way tarnished, there comes another feeling that everybody on the one side may charge double, and that everybody on the other side must pay double, for everything. Hugh Stanbury could not understand why he was charged a shilling a mile, instead of ninepence, for the gig to Nuncombe Putney. He got no satisfactory answer, and had to pay the shilling. The truth was, that gigs to Nuncombe Putney had gone up, since a lady, separated from her husband, with a colonel running after her, had been taken in at the Clock House.

'Here's Hugh!' said Priscilla, hurrying to the front door. And Mrs Stanbury hurried after her. Her son Hugh was the apple of her eye, the best son that ever lived, generous, noble, a thorough man, almost a god!

'Dear, dear, oh dear! Who'd have expected it? God bless you, my boy! Why didn't you write? Priscilla, what is there in the house that he can eat?'

'Plenty of bread and cheese,' said Priscilla, laughing, with her hand inside her brother's arm. For though Priscilla hated all other men, she did not hate her brother Hugh. 'If you wanted things nice to eat directly you got here, you ought to have written.'

'I shall want my dinner, like any other Christian in due time,' said Hugh. 'And how is Mrs Trevelyan and how is Miss Rowley?'

He soon found himself in company with those two ladies, and experienced some immediate difficulty in explaining the cause of his sudden coming. But this was soon put aside by Mrs Trevelyan.

'When did you see my husband?' she asked.

'I saw him yesterday. He was quite well.'

'Colonel Osborne has been here,' she said.

'I know that he has been here. I met him at the station at Exeter. Perhaps I should not say so, but I wish he had remained away.'

'We all wish it,' said Priscilla.

Then Nora spoke. 'But what could we do, Mr Stanbury? It seemed so natural that he should call when he was in the neighbourhood. We have known him so long; and how could we refuse to see him?'

'I will not let any one think that I'm afraid to see any man on earth,' said Mrs Trevelyan. 'If he had ever in his life said a word that he should not have said, a word that would have been an insult, of course it would have been different. But the notion of it is preposterous. Why should I not have seen him?'

'I think he was wrong to come,' said Hugh.

'Of course he was wrong, wickedly wrong,' said Priscilla.

Stanbury, finding that the subject was openly discussed between them, declared plainly the mission that had brought him to Nuncombe. 'Trevelyan heard that he was coming, and asked me to let him know the truth,'

'Now you can tell him the truth,' said Mrs Trevelyan, with something of indignation in her tone, as though she thought that Stanbury had taken upon himself a task of which he ought to be ashamed.

'But Colonel Osborne came specially to pay a visit to Cockchaffington,' said Nora, 'and not to see us. Louis ought to know that.'

'Nora, how can you demean yourself to care about such trash?' said Mrs Trevelyan. 'Who cares why he came here? His visit to me was a thing of course. If Mr Trevelyan disapproves of it, let him say so, and not send secret messengers.'

'Am I a secret messenger?' said Hugh Stanbury.

'There has been a man here, inquiring of the servants,' said Priscilla. So that odious Bozzle had made his foul mission known to them! Stanbury, however, thought it best to say nothing of Bozzle, not to acknowledge that he had ever heard of Bozzle. 'I am sure Mrs Trevelyan does not mean you,' said Priscilla.

'I do not know what I mean,' said Mrs Trevelyan.

'I am so harassed and fevered by these suspicions that I am driven nearly mad.' Then she left the room for a minute and returned with two letters. 'There, Mr Stanbury; I got that note from Colonel Osborne, and wrote to him that reply. You know all about it now. Can you say that I was wrong to see him?'

'I am sure that he was wrong to come,' said Hugh.

'Wickedly wrong,' said Priscilla, again.

'You can keep the letters, and show, them to my husband,' said Mrs Trevelyan; 'then he will know all about it.' But Stanbury declined to keep the letters.

He was to remain the Sunday at Nuncombe Putney and return to London on the Monday. There was, therefore, but one day on which he could say what he had to say to Nora Rowley. When he came down to breakfast on the Sunday morning he had almost made up his mind that he had nothing to say to her. As for Nora, she was in a state of mind much less near to any fixed purpose. She had told herself that she loved this man—had indeed done so in the clearest way, by acknowledging the fact of her love, to another suitor, by pleading to that other suitor the fact of her love as an insuperable reason why he should be rejected. There was no longer any doubt about it to her. When Priscilla had declared that Hugh Stanbury was at the door, her heart had gone into her mouth. Involuntarily she had pressed her hands to her sides, and had held her breath. Why had he come there? Had he come there for her? Oh! if he had come there for her, and if she might dare to forget all the future, how sweet, sweetest of all things in heaven or earth, might be an August evening with him among the lanes! But she, too, had endeavoured to be very prudent. She had told herself that she was quite unfit to be the wife of a poor man, that she would be only a burden round his neck, and not an aid to him. And in so telling herself, she had told herself also that she had been a fool not to accept Mr Glascock. She should have dragged out from her heart the image of this man who had never even whispered a word of love in her ears, and should have constrained herself to receive with affection a man in loving whom there ought to be no difficulty. But when she had been repeating those lessons to herself, Hugh Stanbury had not been in the house. Now he was there, and what must be her answer if he should whisper that word of love? She had an idea that it would be treason in her to disown the love she felt, if questioned concerning her heart by the man to whom it had been given.

They all went to church on the Sunday morning, and up to that time Nora had not been a moment alone with the man. It had been decided that they should dine early, and then ramble out, when the evening would be less hot than the day had been, to a spot called Niddon Park. This was nearly three miles from Nuncombe, and was a beautiful wild slope of ground full of ancient, blighted, blasted, but still half-living oaks, oaks that still brought forth leaves overlooking a bend of the river Teign. Park, in the usual sense of the word, there was none, nor did they who lived round Nuncombe Putney know whether Niddon Park had ever been enclosed. But of all the spots in that lovely neighbourhood, Priscilla Stanbury swore that it was the loveliest; and, as it had never yet been seen by Mrs Trevelyan or her sister, it was determined that they would walk there on this August afternoon. There were four of them and as was natural, they fell into parties of two and two. But Priscilla walked with Nora, and Hugh Stanbury walked with his friend's wife. Nora was talkative, but demure in her manner, and speaking now and again as though she were giving words and not thoughts. She felt that there was something to hide, and was suffering from disappointment that their party should not have been otherwise divided. Had Hugh spoken to her and asked her to be his wife, she could not have accepted him, because she knew that they were both poor, and that she was not fit to keep a poor man's house. She had declared to herself most plainly that that must be her course but yet she was disappointed, and talked in the knowledge that she had something to conceal.

When they were seated beneath an old riven, withered oak, looking down upon the river, they were still divided in the same way. In seating herself she had been very anxious not to disarrange that arrangement, almost equally anxious not to seem to adhere to it with any special purpose. She was very careful that there should be nothing seen in her manner that was in any way special, but in the meantime she was suffering an agony of trouble. He did not care for her in the least. She was becoming sure of that. She had given all her love to a man who had none to give her in return. As she thought of this she almost longed for the offer of that which she knew she could not have accepted had it been offered to her. But she talked on about the scenery, about the weather, descanting on the pleasure of living where such loveliness was within reach. Then there came a pause for a moment. 'Nora' said Priscilla, 'I do not know what you are thinking about, but it is not of the beauty of Niddon Park. Then there came a faint sound as of an hysterical sob, and then a gurgle in the throat, and then a pretence at laughter.

'I don't believe I am thinking of anything at all' said Nora.

After which Hugh insisted on descending to the bank of the river, but, as the necessity of re-climbing the slope was quite manifest, none of the girls would go with him. 'Come, Miss Rowley' said he, 'will you not show them that a lady can go up and down a hill as well as a man?'

'I had rather not go up and down the hill' said she.

Then he understood that she was angry with him; and in some sort surmised the cause of her anger. Not that he believed that she loved him; but it seemed possible to him that she resented the absence of his attention. He went down, and scrambled out on the rocks into the bed of the river, while the girls above looked down upon him, watching the leaps that he made. Priscilla and Mrs Trevelyan called to him, bidding him beware; but Nora called not at all. He was whistling as he made his jumps, but still he heard their voices, and knew that he did not hear Nora's voice. He poised himself on the edge of a rock in the middle of the stream, and looked up the river and down the river, turning himself carefully on his narrow foothold; but he was thinking only of Nora. Could there be anything nobler than to struggle on with her, if she only would be willing? But then she was young; and should she yield to such a request from him, she would not know what she was yielding. He turned again, jumping from rock to rock till he reached the bank, and then made his way again up to the withered oak.

'You would not have repented it if you had come down with me' he said to Nora.

'I am not so sure of that' she answered.

When they started to return she stepped on gallantly with Priscilla; but Priscilla was stopped by some chance, having some word to say to her brother, having some other word to say to Mrs Trevelyan. Could it be that her austerity had been softened, and that in kindness they contrived that Nora should be left some yards behind them with her brother? Whether it were kindness, or an unkind error, so it was. Nora, when she perceived what destiny was doing for her, would not interfere with destiny. If he chose to speak to her she would hear him and would answer him. She knew very well what answer she would give him. She had her answer quite ready at her fingers' ends. There was no doubt about her answer.

They had walked half a mile together and he had spoken of nothing but the scenery. She had endeavoured to appear to be excited. Oh, yes, the scenery of Devonshire was delightful. She hardly wanted anything more to make her happy. If only this misery respecting her sister could be set right!

'And you, you yourself' said he, 'do you mean that there is nothing you want in leaving London?'

'Not much, indeed.'

'It sometimes seemed to me that that kind of life was was very pleasant to you.'

'What kind of life, Mr Stanbury?'

'The life that you were living—going out, being admired, and having the rich and dainty all around you.'

'I don't dislike people because they are rich,' she said.

'No; nor do I; and I despise those who affect to dislike them. But all cannot be rich.'

'Nor all dainty, as you choose to call them.'

'But they who have once been dainty as I call them never like to divest themselves of their daintiness. You have been one of the dainty, Miss Rowley.'

'Have I?'

'Certainly; I doubt whether you would be happy if you thought that your daintiness had departed from you.'

'I hope, Mr Stanbury, that nothing nice and pleasant has departed from me. If I have ever been dainty, dainty I hope. I may remain. I will never, at, any rate, give it up of my own accord'. Why she said this, she could never explain to herself. She had certainly not intended to rebuff him when she had been saying it. But he spoke not a word to her further as they walked home, either of her mode of life or of his own.

CHAPTER XXV. HUGH STANBURY SMOKES HIS PIPE

Nora Rowley, when she went to bed, after her walk to Niddon Park in company with Hugh Stanbury, was full of wrath against him. But she could not own her anger to herself, nor could she even confess to herself though she was breaking her heart that there really existed for her the slightest cause of grief. But why had he been so stern to her? Why had he gone out of his way to be uncivil to her? He had called her 'dainty' meaning to imply by the epithet that she was one of the butterflies of the day, caring for nothing but sunshine, and an opportunity of fluttering her silly wings. She had understood well what he meant. Of course he was right to be cold to her if his heart was cold, but he need not have insulted her by his ill-concealed rebukes. Had he been kind to her, he might have rebuked her as much as he liked. She quite appreciated the delightful intimacy of a loving word of counsel from the man she loved—how nice it is, as it were, to play at marriage, and to hear beforehand something of the pleasant weight of gentle marital authority. But there had been nothing of that in his manner to her. He had told her that she was dainty and had so told it her, as she thought, that she might, learn thereby, that under no circumstances would he have any other tale to tell her. If he had no other tale, why had he not been silent? Did he think that she was subject to his rebuke merely because she lived under his mother's roof? She would soon shew him that her residence at the Clock House gave him no such authority over her. Then amidst her wrath and despair, she cried herself asleep.

While she was sobbing in bed, he was sitting, with a short, black pipe stuck into his mouth, on the corner of the churchyard wall opposite. Before he had left the house he and Priscilla had spoken together for some minutes about Mrs Trevelyan. 'Of course she was wrong to see him' said Priscilla. 'I hesitate to wound her by so saying, because she has been ill-used, though I did tell her so, when she asked me. She could have lost nothing by declining his visit.'

'The worst of it is that Trevelyan swears that he will never receive her again if she received him.'

'He must unswear it,' said Priscilla, 'that is all. It is out of the question that a man should take a girl from her home, and make her his wife, and then throw her off for so little of an offence as this. She might compel him by law to take her back.'

'What would she get by that?'

'Little enough,' said Priscilla; 'and it was little enough she got by marrying him. She would have had bread, and meat, and raiment without being married, I suppose.'

'But it was a love-match.'

'Yes and now she is at Nuncombe Putney, and he is roaming about in London. He has to pay ever so much a year for his love-match, and she is crushed into nothing by it. How long will she have to remain here, Hugh?'

'How can I say? I suppose there is no reason against her remaining as far as you are concerned?'

'For me personally, none. Were she much worse than I think she is, I should not care in the least for myself, if I thought that we were doing her good helping to bring her back. She can't hurt me. I am so fixed, and dry, and established that nothing anybody says will affect me. But mamma doesn't like it.'

'What is it she dislikes?'

'The idea that she is harbouring a married woman, of whom people say, at least, that she has a lover.'

'Is she to be turned out because people are slanderers?'

'Why should mamma suffer because this woman, who is a stranger to her, has been imprudent? If she were your wife, Hugh—'

'God forbid!'

'If we were in any way bound to her, of course we would do our duty. But if it makes mamma unhappy I am sure you will not press it. I think Mrs Merton has spoken to her. And then Aunt Stanbury has written such letters!'

'Who cares for Aunt Jemima?'

'Everybody cares for her except you and I. And now this man who has been here asking the servant questions has upset her greatly. Even your coming has done so, knowing, as she does, that you have come, not to see us, but to make inquiries about Mrs Trevelyan. She is so annoyed by it, that she does not sleep.'

'Do you wish her to be taken away at once?' asked Hugh almost in an angry tone.

'Certainly not. That would be impossible. We have agreed to take her, and must bear with it. And I would not have her moved from this, if I thought that if she stayed awhile it might be arranged that she might return from us direct to her husband.'

'I shall try that, of course now.'

'But if he will not have her, if he be so obstinate, so foolish, and so wicked, do not leave her here longer than you can help. Then Hugh explained that Sir Marmaduke and Lady Rowley were to be in England in the spring, and that it would be very desirable that the poor woman should not be sent abroad to look for a home before that. 'If it must be so, it must' said Priscilla. 'But eight months is a long time.'

Hugh went out to smoke his pipe on the church-wall in a moody, unhappy state of mind. He had hoped to have done so well in regard to Mrs Trevelyan. Till he had met Colonel Osborne, he felt sure, almost sure, that she would have refused to see that pernicious trouble of the peace of families. In this he found that he had been disappointed; but he had not expected that Priscilla would have been so much opposed to the arrangement which he had made about the house, and then he had been buoyed up by the anticipation of some delight in meeting Nora Rowley. There was, at any rate, the excitement of seeing her to keep his spirits from flagging. He had seen her, and had had the opportunity of which he had so long been thinking. He had seen her and had had every possible advantage on his side. What could any man desire better than the privilege of walking home with the girl he loved through country lanes of a summer evening? They had been an hour together or might have been, had he chosen to prolong the interview. But the words which had been spoken between them had had not the slightest interest unless it were that they had tended to make the interval between him and her wider than ever. He had asked her—he thought that he had asked—whether it would grieve her to abandon that delicate, dainty mode of life to which she had been accustomed; and she had replied that she would never abandon it of her own accord. Of course she had intended him to take her at her word.

He blew forth quick clouds of heavy smoke, as he attempted to make himself believe that this was all for the best. What would such a one as he was do with a wife? Or, seeing as he did see, that marriage itself was quite out of the question, how could it be good either for him or her that they should be tied together by a long engagement? Such a future would not at all suit the purpose of his life. In his life absolute freedom would be needed, freedom from unnecessary ties, freedom from unnecessary burdens. His income was most precarious and he certainly would not make it less so by submission to any closer literary thraldom. And he believed himself to be a Bohemian, too much of a Bohemian to enjoy a domestic fireside with children and slippers. To be free to go where he liked, and when he liked, to think as he pleased, to be driven nowhere by conventional rules, to use his days, Sundays as well as Mondays, as he pleased to use them; to turn Republican, if his mind should take him that way or Quaker, or Mormon or Red Indian, if he wished it, and in so turning to do no damage to any one but himself—that was the life which he had planned for himself. His aunt Stanbury had not read his character altogether wrongly, as he thought, when she had once declared that decency and godliness were both distasteful to him. Would it not be destruction to such a one as he was, to fall into an interminable engagement with any girl, let her be ever so sweet?

But yet, he felt as he sat there filling pipe after pipe, smoking away till past midnight, that though he could not bear the idea of trammels, though he was totally unfit for matrimony, either present or in prospect, he felt that he had within his breast a double identity, and that that other division of himself would be utterly crushed if it were driven to divest itself of the idea of love. Whence was to come his poetry, the romance of his life, the springs of clear water in which his ignoble thoughts were to be dipped till they should become pure, if love was to be banished altogether from the list of delights that were possible to him? And then he began to speculate on love—that love of which poets wrote, and of which he found that some sparkle was necessary to give light to his life. Was it not the one particle of divine breath given to man, of which he had heard since he was a boy? And how was this love to be come at, and was it to be a thing of reality, or merely an idea? Was it a pleasure to be attained or a mystery that, charmed by the difficulties of the distance, a distance that never could be so passed, that the thing should really be reached? Was love to be ever a delight, vague as is that feeling of unattainable beauty which far-off mountains give, when you know that you can never place yourself amidst their unseen valleys? And if love could be reached, the love of which the poets sing, and of which his own heart was ever singing, what were to be its pleasures? To press a hand, to kiss a lip, to clasp a waist, to hear even the low voice of the vanquished, confessing loved one as she hides her blushing cheek upon your shoulder—what is it all but to have reached the once mysterious valley of your far-off mountain, and to have found that it is as other valleys, rocks and stones, with a little grass, and a thin stream of running water? But beyond that pressing of the hand, and that kissing of the lips, beyond that short-lived pressure of the plumage which is common to birds and men, what could love do beyond that? There were children with dirty faces and household bills, and a wife, who must, perhaps, always darn the stockings and be sometimes cross. Was love to lead only to this, a dull life, with a woman who had lost the beauty from her cheeks, and the gloss from her hair, and the music from her voice, and the fire from her eye and the grace from her step, and whose waist an arm should no longer be able to span? Did the love of the poets lead to that, and that only? Then, through the cloud of smoke, there came upon him some dim idea of self-abnegation that the mysterious valley among the mountains, the far-off prospect of which was so charming to him, which made the poetry of his life, was, in fact, the capacity of caring more for other human beings than for himself. The beauty of it all was not so much in the thing loved, as in the loving. 'Were she a cripple, hunchbacked, eyeless,' he said to, himself, 'it might be the same. Only she must be a woman.' Then he blew off a great cloud of smoke, and went into bed lost amid poetry, philosophy, love, and tobacco.

It had been arranged overnight that he was to start the next morning at half-past seven, and Priscilla had promised to give him his breakfast before he went. Priscilla, of course, kept her word. She was one of those women who would take a grim pleasure in coming down to make the tea at any possible hour, at five, at four, if it were needed, and who would never want to go to bed again when the ceremony was performed. But when Nora made her appearance—Nora, who had been dainty—both Priscilla and Hugh were surprised. They could not say why she was there nor could Nora tell herself. She had not forgiven him. She had no thought of being gentle and loving to him. She declared to herself that she had no wish of saying good-bye to him once again. But yet she was in the room, waiting for him, when he came down to his breakfast. She had been unable to sleep, and had reasoned with herself as to the absurdity of lying in bed awake, when she preferred to be up and out of the house. It was true that she had not been out of her bed at seven any morning since she had been at Nuncombe Putney; but that was no reason why she should not be more active on this special morning. There was a noise in the house, and she never could sleep when there was a noise. She was quite sure that she was not going down because she wished to see Hugh Stanbury, but she was equally sure that it would be a disgrace to her to be deterred from going down, simply because the man was there. So she descended to the parlour, and was standing near the open window when Stanbury bustled into the room, some quarter of an hour after the proper time. Priscilla was there also, guessing something of the truth, and speculating whether these two young people, should they love each other, would be the better or the worse for such love. There must be marriages if only that the world might go on in accordance with the Creator's purpose. But, as Priscilla could see, blessed were they who were not called upon to assist in the scheme. To her eyes all days seemed to be days of wrath, and all times, times of tribulation. And it was all mere vanity and vexation of spirit. To go on and bear it till one was dead, helping others to bear it, if such help might be of avail, that was her theory of life. To make it pleasant by eating, and drinking, and dancing, or even by falling in love, was, to her mind, a vain crunching of ashes between the teeth. Not to have ill things said of her and of hers, not to be disgraced, not to be rendered incapable of some human effort, not to have actually to starve, such was the extent of her ambition in this world. And for the next she felt so assured of the goodness of God that she could not bring herself to doubt of happiness in a world that was to be eternal. Her doubt was this, whether it was really the next world which would be eternal. Of eternity she did not doubt, but might there not be many worlds? These, things, however, she kept almost entirely to herself. 'You, down!' Priscilla had said.

'Well, yes; I could not sleep when I heard you all moving. And the morning is so fine, and I thought that perhaps you would go out and walk after your brother has gone.' Priscilla promised that she would walk, and then the tea was made.

'Your sister and I are going out for an early walk,' said Nora, when she was greeted by Stanbury. Priscilla said nothing but thought she understood it all.

'I wish I were going with you,' said Hugh. Nora, remembering how very little he had made of his opportunity on the evening before, did not believe him.

The eggs and fried bacon were eaten in a hurry, and very little was said. Then there came the moment for parting. The brother and sister kissed each other, and Hugh took Nora by the hand. 'I hope you make yourself happy here,' he said.

'Oh, yes, if it were only for myself I should want nothing.'

'I will do the best I can with Trevelyan.'

'The best will be to make him and every one understand that the fault is altogether his, and not Emily's.'

'The best will be to make each think that there has been no real fault,' said Hugh.

'There should be no talking of faults,' said Priscilla. 'Let the husband take his wife back as he is bound to do.'

These words occupied hardly a minute in the saying, but during that minute Hugh Stanbury held Nora by the hand. He held it fast. She would not attempt to withdraw it, but neither would she return his pressure by the muscle of a single finger. What right had he to press her hand; or to make any sign of love, any pretence of loving, when he had gone out of his way to tell her that she was not good enough for him? Then he started, and Nora and Priscilla put on their hats and left the house.

'Let us go to Niddon Park,' said Nora.

'To Niddon Park again?'

'Yes; it is so beautiful! And I should like to see it by the morning light. There is plenty of time.'

So they walked to Niddon Park in the morning, as they had done on the preceding evening. Their conversation at first regarded Trevelyan and his wife, and the old trouble; but Nora could not keep herself from speaking of Hugh Stanbury.

'He would not have come,' she said, 'unless Louis had sent him.'

'He would not have come now, I think.'

'Of course not; why should he before Parliament was hardly over, too? But he won't remain in town now, will he?'

'He says somebody must remain and I think he will be in London till near Christmas.'

'How disagreeable! But I suppose he doesn't care. It's all the same to a man like him. They don't shut the clubs up, I dare say. Will he come here at Christmas?'

'Either then or for the New Year—just for a day or two.'

'We shall be gone then, I suppose?' said Nora.

'That must depend on Mr Trevelyan,' said Priscilla.

'What a life for two women to lead to depend upon the caprice of a man who must be mad! Do you think that Mr Trevelyan will care for what your brother says to him?'

'I do not know Mr Trevelyan'.

'He is very fond of your brother, and I suppose men friends do listen to each other. They never seem to listen to women. Don't you think that, after all, they despise women? They look on them as dainty, foolish things.'

'Sometimes women despise men,' said Priscilla.

'Not very often do they? And then women are so dependent on men. A woman can get nothing without a man.'

'I manage to get on somehow,' said Priscilla.

'No, you don't, Miss Stanbury, if you think of it. You want mutton. And who kills the sheep?'

'But who cooks it?'

'But the men-cooks are the best,' said Nora; 'and the men-tailors, and the men to wait at table, and the men poets, and the men-painters, and the men-nurses. All the things that women do, men do better.'

'There are two things they can't do,' said Priscilla.

'What are they?'

'They can't suckle babies, and they can't forget themselves.'

'About the babies, of course not. As for forgetting themselves I am not quite so sure that I can forget myself. That is just where your brother went down last night.'

They had at this moment reached the top of the steep slope below which the river ran brawling among the rocks, and Nora seated herself exactly where she had sat on the previous evening.

'I have been down scores of times,' said Priscilla.

'Let us go now.'

'You wouldn't go when Hugh asked you yesterday.'

'I didn't care then. But do come now if you don't mind the climb.' Then they went down the slope and reached the spot from whence Hugh Stanbury had jumped from rock to rock across the stream. 'You have never been out there, have you?' said Nora.

'On the rocks? Oh, dear, no! I should be sure to fall.'

'But he went; just like a goat.'

'That's one of the things that men can do, I suppose,' said Priscilla. 'But I don't see any great glory in being like a goat.'

'I do. I should like to be able to go, and I think I'll try. It is so mean to be dainty and weak.'

'I don't think it at all dainty to keep dry feet.'

'But he didn't get his feet wet,' said Nora. 'Or if he did, he didn't mind. I can see at once that I should be giddy and tumble down if I tried it.'

'Of course you would.'

'But he didn't tumble down.'

'He has been doing it all his life,' said Priscilla.

'He can't do it up in London. When I think of myself, Miss Stanbury, I am so ashamed. There is nothing that I can do. I couldn't write an article for a newspaper.'

'I think I could. But I fear no one would read it.'

'They read his,' said Nora, 'or else he wouldn't be paid for writing them.' Then they climbed back again up the hill, and during the climbing there were no words spoken. The slope was not much of a hill, was no more than the fall from the low ground of the valley to the course which the river had cut for itself; but it was steep while it lasted; and both the young women were forced to pause for a minute before they could proceed upon their journey. As they walked home Priscilla spoke of the scenery, and of the country, and of the nature of the life which she and her mother and sister had passed at Nuncombe Putney. Nora said but little till they were just entering the village, and then she went back to the subject of her thoughts. 'I would sooner,' said she, 'write for a newspaper than do anything else in the world.'

'Why so?'

'Because it is so noble to teach people everything! And then a man who writes for a newspaper must know so many things himself! I believe there are women who do it, but very few. One or two have done it, I know.'

'Go and tell that to Aunt Stanbury, and hear what she will say about such women.'

'I suppose she is very prejudiced.'

'Yes; she is; but she is a clever woman. I am inclined to think women had better not write for newspapers.'

'And why not?' Nora asked.

'My reasons would take me a week to explain, and I doubt whether I have them very clear in my own head. In the first place there is that difficulty about the babies. Most of them must get married, you know.'

'But not all,' said Nora.

'No; thank God; not all.'

'And if you are not married you might write for a newspaper. At any rate, if I were you, I should be very proud of my brother.'

'Aunt Stanbury is not at all proud of her nephew,' said Priscilla, as they entered the house.

CHAPTER XXVI. A THIRD PARTY IS SO OBJECTIONABLE

Hugh Stanbury went in search of Trevelyan immediately on his return to London, and found his friend at his rooms in Lincoln's Inn.

'I have executed my commission,' said Hugh, endeavouring to speak of what he had done in a cheery voice.

'I am much obliged to you, Stanbury very much; but I do not know that I need trouble you to tell me anything about it.'

'And why not?'

'I have learned it all from that man.'

'What man?'

'From Bozzle. He has come back, and has been with me, and has learned everything.'

'Look here, Trevelyan, when you asked me to go down to Devonshire, you promised me that there should be nothing more about Bozzle. I expect you to put that rascal, and all that he has told you, out of your head altogether. You are bound to do so for my sake, and you will be very wise to do so for your own.'

'I was obliged to see him when he came.'

'Yes, and to pay him, I do not doubt. But that is all done, and should be forgotten.'

'I can't forget it. Is it true or untrue that he found that man down there? Is it true or untrue that my wife received Colonel Osborne at your mother's house? Is it true or untrue that Colonel Osborne went down there with the express object of seeing her? Is it true or untrue that they had corresponded? It is nonsense to bid me to forget all this. You might as well ask me to forget that I had desired her neither to write to him, nor to see him.'

'If I understand the matter,' said Trevelyan, 'you are incorrect in one of your assertions.'

'In which?'

'You must excuse me if I am wrong, Trevelyan; but I don't think you ever did tell your wife not to see this man, or not to write to him?'

'I never told her! I don't understand what you mean.'

'Not in so many words. It is my belief that she has endeavoured to obey implicitly every clear instruction that you have given her.'

'You are wrong absolutely and altogether wrong. Heaven and earth! Do you mean to tell me now, after all that has taken place, that she did not know my wishes?'

'I have not said that. But you, have chosen to place her in such a position, that though your word would go for much with her, she cannot bring herself to respect your wishes.'

'And you call that being dutiful and affectionate!'

'I call it human and reasonable; and I think that it is compatible with duty and affection. Have you consulted her wishes?'

'Always!'

'Consult them now then, and bid her come back to you.'

'No never! As far as I can see, I will never do so. The moment she is away from me this man goes to her, and she receives him. She must have known that she was wrong and you must know it.'

'I do not think that she is half so wrong as you yourself,' said Stanbury. To this Trevelyan made no answer, and they both remained silent some minutes. Stanbury had a communication to make before he went, but it was one which he wished to delay as long as there was a chance that his friend's heart might be softened, one which he need not make if Trevelyan would consent to receive his wife back to his house. There was the day's paper lying on the table, and Stanbury had taken it up and was reading it or pretending to read it.

'I will tell you what I propose to do,' said Trevelyan.

'Well.'

'It is best both for her and for me that we should be apart.'

'I cannot understand how you can be so mad as to say so.'

'You don't understand what I feel. Heaven and earth! To have a man coming and going. But, never mind. You do not see it, and nothing will make you see it. And there is no reason why you should.'

'I certainly do not see it. I do not believe that your wife cares more for Colonel Osborne, except as an old friend of her father's, than she does for the fellow that sweeps the crossing. It is a matter in which I am bound to tell you what I think.'

'Very well. Now, if you have freed your mind, I will tell you my purpose. I am bound to do so, because your people are concerned in it. I shall go abroad.'

'And leave her in England?'

'Certainly. She will be safer here than she can be abroad unless she should choose to go back with her father to the islands.'

'And take the boy?'

'No I could not permit that. What I intend is this. I will give her 800 pounds a year, as long as I have reason to believe that she has no communication whatever, either by word of mouth or by letter, with that man. If she does, I will put the case immediately into the hands of my lawyer, with instructions to him to ascertain from counsel what severest steps I can take.'

'How I hate that word severe, when applied to a woman.'

'I dare say you do when applied to another man's wife. But there will be no severity in my first proposition. As for the child, if I approve of the place in which she lives, as I do at present, he shall remain with her for nine months in the year till he is six years old. Then he must come to me. And he shall come to me altogether if she sees or hears from that man. I believe that 800 pounds a year will enable her to live with all comfort under your mother's roof."

'As to that,' said Stanbury, slowly, 'I suppose I had better tell you at once, that the Nuncombe Putney arrangement cannot be considered as permanent.'

'Why not?'

'Because my mother is timid, and nervous, and altogether unused to the world.'

'That unfortunate woman is to be sent away even from Nuncombe Putney!'

'Understand me, Trevelyan.'

'I understand you. I understand you most thoroughly. Nor do I wonder at it in the least. Do not suppose that I am angry with your mother, or with you, or with your sister. I have no right to expect that they should keep her after that man has made his way into their house. I can well conceive that no honest, high-minded lady would do so.'

'It is not that at all.'

'But it is that. How can you tell me that it isn't? And yet you would have me believe that I am not disgraced!' As he said this Trevelyan got up, and walked about the room, tearing his hair with his hands. He was in truth a wretched man, from whose mind all expectation of happiness, was banished, who regarded his own position as one of incurable ignominy, looking upon himself as one who had been made unfit for society by no fault of his own. What was he to do with the wretched woman who could be kept from the evil of her pernicious vanity by no gentle custody, whom no most distant retirement would make safe from the effects of her own ignorance, folly, and obstinacy? 'When is she to go?' he asked in a low, sepulchral tone as though these new tidings that had come upon him had been fatal laden with doom, and finally subversive of all chance even of tranquillity.

'When you and she may please.'

'That is all very well but let me know the truth. I would not have your mother's house contaminated; but may she remain there for a week?'

Stanbury jumped from his seat with an oath. 'I tell you what it is, Trevelyan if you speak of your wife in that way, I will not listen to you. It is unmanly and untrue to say that her presence can contaminate any house.'

'That is very fine. It may be chivalrous in you to tell me on her behalf that I am a liar and that I am not a man.'

'You drive me to it.'

'But what am I to think when you are forced to declare that this unfortunate woman can not be allowed to remain at your mother's house, a house which has been especially taken with reference to a shelter for her? She has been received with the idea that she would be discreet. She has been indiscreet, past belief, and she is to be turned out most deservedly. Heaven and earth! Where shall I find a roof for her head?' Trevelyan as he said this was walking about the room with his hands stretched up towards the ceiling; and as his friend was attempting to make him comprehend that there was no intention on the part of anyone to banish Mrs Trevelyan from the Clock House, at least for some months to come, not even till after Christmas unless some satisfactory arrangement could be sooner made, the door of the room was opened by the boy, who called himself a clerk, and who acted as Trevelyan's servant in the chambers, and a third person was shown into the room. That third person was Mr Bozzle. As no name was given, Stanbury did not at first know Mr Bozzle, but he had not had his eye on Mr Bozzle for half a minute before he recognised the ex-policeman by the outward attributes and signs of his profession. 'Oh; is that you, Mr Bozzle?' said Trevelyan, as soon as the great man had made his bow of salutation. 'Well what is it?'

'Mr Hugh Stanbury, I think,' said Bozzle, making another bow to the young barrister.

'That's my name,' said Stanbury.

'Exactly so, Mr S. The identity is one as I could prove on oath in any court in England. You was on the railway platform at Exeter on Saturday when we was waiting for the 12 express 'buss, wasn't you now, Mr S?'

'What's that to you?'

'Well as it do happen, it is something to me. And, Mr S, if you was asked that question in any court in England or before even one of the metropolitan bekes, you wouldn't deny it.'

'Why the devil should I deny it? What's all this about, Trevelyan?'

'Of course you can't deny it, Mr S. When I'm down on a fact, I am down on it. Nothing else wouldn't do in my profession.'

'Have you anything to say to me, Mr Bozzle?' asked Trevelyan.

'Well I have; just a word.'

'About your journey to Devonshire?'

'Well in a way it is about my journey to Devonshire. It's all along of the same job, Mr Trewillian.'

'You can speak before my friend here,' said Trevelyan. Bozzle had taken a great dislike to Hugh Stanbury, regarding the barrister with a correct instinct as one who was engaged for the time in the same service with himself and who was his rival in that service. When thus instigated to make as it were a party of three in this delicate and most confidential matter, and to take his rival into his confidence, he shook his head slowly and looked Trevelyan hard in the face. 'Mr Stanbury is my particular friend,' said Trevelyan, 'and knows well the circumstances of this unfortunate affair. You can say anything before him.'

Bozzle shook his head again. 'I'd rayther not, Mr Trewillian,' said he. 'Indeed I'd rayther not. It's something very particular.'

'If you take my advice,' said Stanbury, 'you will not hear him yourself.'

'That's your advice, Mr S.?' asked Mr Bozzle.

'Yes that's my advice. I'd never have anything to do with such a fellow as you as long as I could help it.'

'I dare say not, Mr S.; I dare say not. We're hexpensive, and we're haccurate—neither of which is much in your line, Mr S., if I understand about it rightly.'

'Mr Bozzle, if you've got anything to tell, tell it,' said Trevelyan, angrily.

'A third party is so objectionable,' pleaded Bozzle.

'Never mind. That is my affair.'

'It is your affair, Mr Trewillian. There's not a doubt of that. The lady is your wife.'

'Damnation!' shouted Trevelyan.

'But the credit, sir,' said Bozzle. 'The credit is mine. And here is Mr S. has been down a interfering with me, and doing no 'varsal good, as I'll undertake to prove by evidence before the affair is over.'

'The affair is over,' said Stanbury.

'That's as you think, Mr S. That's where your information goes to, Mr S. Mine goes a little beyond that, Mr S. I've means as you can know nothing about, Mr S. I've irons in the fire, what you're as ignorant on as the babe as isn't born.'

'No doubt you have, Mr Bozzle,' said Stanbury.

'I has. And now if it be that I must speak before a third party, Mr Trewillian, I'm ready. It ain't that I'm no ways ashamed. I've done my duty, and knows how to do it. And let a counsel be ever so sharp, I never yet was so 'posed but what I could stand up and hold my own. The Colonel, Mr Trewillian, got a letter from your lady this morning.'

'I don't believe it,' said Stanbury, sharply.

'Very likely not, Mr S. It ain't in my power to say anything whatever about you believing or not believing. But Mr T.'s lady has wrote the letter; and the Colonel he has received it. You don't look after these things, Mr S. You don't know the ways of 'em. But it's my business. The lady has wrote the letter, and the Colonel why, he has received it.' Trevelyan had become white with rage when Bozzle first mentioned this continued correspondence between his wife and Colonel Osborne. It never occurred to him to doubt the correctness of the policeman's information, and he regarded Stanbury's assertion of incredulity as being simply of a piece with his general obstinacy in the matter. At this moment he began to regret that he had called in the assistance of his friend, and that he had not left the affair altogether in the hands of that much more satisfactory, but still more painful, agent, Mr Bozzle. He had again seated himself, and for a moment or two remained silent on his chair. 'It ain't my fault, Mr Trewillian,' continued Bozzle, 'if this little matter oughtn't never to have been mentioned before a third party.'

'It is of no moment,' said Trevelyan, in a low voice. 'What does it signify who knows it now?'

'Do not believe it, Trevelyan,' said Stanbury.

'Very well, Mr S. Very well. Just as you like. Don't believe it. Only it's true, and it's my business to find them things out. It's my business, and I finds 'em out. Mr Trewillian can do as he likes about it. If it's right, why, then it is right. It ain't for me to say nothing about that. But there's the fact. The lady, she has wrote another letter; and the Colonel why, he has received it. There ain't nothing wrong about the post-office. If I was to say what was inside of that billydou why, then I should be proving what I didn't know; and when it came to standing up in court, I shouldn't be able to hold my own. But as for the letter, the lady wrote it, and the Colonel he received it.'

'That will do, Mr Bozzle,' said Trevelyan.

'Shall I call again, Mr Trewillian?'

'No; yes. I'll send to you, when I want you. You shall hear from me.'

'I suppose I'd better be keeping my eyes open about the Colonel's place, Mr Trewillian?'

'For God's sake, Trevelyan, do not have anything more to do with this man!'

'That's all very well for you, Mr S.,' said Bozzle. 'The lady ain't your wife.'

'Can you imagine anything more disgraceful than all this?' said Stanbury.

'Nothing; nothing; nothing!' answered Trevelyan.

'And I'm to keep stirring, and be on the move?' again suggested Bozzle, who prudently required to be fortified by instructions before he devoted his time and talents even to so agreeable a pursuit as that in which he had been engaged.

'You shall hear from me,' said Trevelyan.

'Very well very well. I wish you good-day, Mr Trewillian. Mr S., yours most obedient. There was one other point, Mr Trewillian.'

'What point?' asked Trevelyan, angrily.

'If the lady was to join the Colonel—'

'That will do, Mr Bozzle,' said Trevelyan, again jumping up from his chair. 'That will do.' So saying, he opened the door, and Bozzle, with a bow, took his departure. 'What on earth am I to do? How am I to save her?' said the wretched husband, appealing to his friend.

Stanbury endeavoured with all his eloquence to prove that this latter piece of information from the spy must be incorrect. If such a letter had been written by Mrs Trevelyan to Colonel Osborne, it must have been done while he, Stanbury, was staying at the Clock House. This seemed to him to be impossible; but he could hardly explain why it should be impossible. She had written to the man before, and had received him when he came to Nuncombe Putney. Why was it even improbable that she should have written to him again? Nevertheless, Stanbury felt sure that she had sent no such letter. 'I think I understand her feelings and her mind,' said he; 'and if so, any such correspondence would be incompatible with her previous conduct.' Trevelyan only smiled at this or pretended to smile. He would not discuss the question; but believed implicitly what Bozzle had told him in spite of all Stanbury's arguments. 'I can say nothing further,' said Stanbury.

'No, my dear fellow. There is nothing further to be said, except this, that I will have my unfortunate wife removed from the decent protection of your mother's roof with the least possible delay. I feel that I owe Mrs Stanbury the deepest apology for having sent such an inmate to trouble her repose.'

'Nonsense!'

'That is what I feel.'

'And I say that it is nonsense. If you had never sent that wretched blackguard down to fabricate lies at Nuncombe Putney, my mother's repose would have been all right. As it is, Mrs Trevelyan can remain where she is till after Christmas. There is not the least necessity for removing her at once. I only meant to say that the arrangement should not be regarded as altogether permanent. I must go to my work now. Goodbye.'

'Good-bye, Stanbury.'

Stanbury paused at the door, and then once more turned round. 'I suppose it is of no use my saying anything further; but I wish you to understand fully that I regard your wife as a woman much ill-used, and I think you are punishing her, and yourself, too, with a cruel severity for an indiscretion of the very slightest kind.'

CHAPTER XXVII. MR TREVELYAN'S LETTER TO HIS WIFE

Trevelyan, when he was left alone, sat for above a couple of hours contemplating the misery of his position, and endeavouring to teach himself by thinking what ought to be his future conduct. It never occurred to him during these thoughts that it would be well that he should at once take back his wife, either as a matter of duty, or of welfare, for himself or for her. He had taught himself to believe that she had disgraced him; and, though this feeling of disgrace made him so wretched that he wished that he were dead, he would allow himself to make no attempt at questioning the correctness of his conviction. Though he were to be shipwrecked for ever, even that seemed to be preferable to supposing that he had been wrong. Nevertheless, he loved his wife dearly, and, in the white heat of his anger endeavoured to be merciful to her. When Stanbury accused him of severity, he would not condescend to defend himself; but he told himself then of his great mercy. Was he not as fond of his own boy as any other father, and had he not allowed her to take the child because he had felt that a mother's love was more imperious, more craving in its nature, than the love of a father? Had that been severe? And had he not resolved to allow her every comfort which her unfortunate position the self-imposed misfortune of her position would allow her to enjoy? She had come to him without a shilling; and yet, bad as her treatment of him had been, he was willing to give enough not only to support her, but her sister also, with every comfort. Severe! No; that, at least, was an undeserved accusation. He had been anything but severe. Foolish he might have been, in taking a wife from a home in which she had been unable to learn the discretion of a matron; too trusting he had been, and too generous but certainly not severe. But, of course, as he said to himself, a young man like Stanbury would take the part of a woman with whose sister he was in love. Then he turned his thoughts upon Bozzle, and there came over him a crushing feeling of ignominy, shame, moral dirt, and utter degradation, as he reconsidered his dealings with that ingenious gentleman. He was paying a rogue to watch the steps of a man whom he hated, to pry into the home secrets, to read the letters, to bribe the servants, to record the movements of this rival, this successful rival, in his wife's affections! It was a filthy thing and yet what could he do? Gentlemen of old, his own grandfather or his father, would have taken such a fellow as Colonel Osborne by the throat and have caned him, and afterwards would have shot him, or have stood to be shot.

All that was changed now, but it was not his fault that it was changed. He was willing enough to risk his life, could any opportunity of risking it in this cause be obtained for him. But were he to cudgel Colonel Osborne, he would be simply arrested, and he would then be told that he had disgraced himself foully by striking a man old enough to be his father!

How was he to have avoided the employment of some such man as Bozzle? He had also employed a gentleman, his friend, Stanbury; and what was the result? The facts were not altered. Even Stanbury did not attempt to deny that there had been a correspondence, and that there had been a visit. But Stanbury was so blind to all impropriety, or pretended such blindness, that he defended that which all the world agreed in condemning. Of what use had Stanbury been to him? He had wanted facts, not advice. Stanbury had found out no facts for him; but Bozzle, either by fair means or foul, did get at the truth. He did not doubt but that Bozzle was right about that letter written only yesterday, and received on that very morning. His wife, who had probably been complaining of her wrongs to Stanbury, must have retired from that conversation to her chamber, and immediately have written this letter to her lover! With such a woman as that what can be done in these days otherwise than by the aid of such a one as Bozzle? He could not confine his wife in a dungeon. He could not save himself from the disgrace of her misconduct by any rigours of surveillance on his own part. As wives are managed nowadays, he could not forbid to her the use of the post-office, could not hinder her from seeing this hypocritical scoundrel, who carried on his wickedness under the false guise of family friendship. He had given her every chance to amend her conduct; but, if she were resolved on disobedience, he had no means of enforcing obedience. The facts, however, it was necessary that he should know.

And now, what should he do? How should he go to work to make her understand that she could not write even a letter without his knowing it; and that if she did either write to the man or see him he would immediately take the child from her, and provide for her only in such fashion as the law should demand from him? For himself, and his own life, he thought that he had determined what he would do. It was impossible that he should continue to live in London. He was ashamed to enter a club. He had hardly a friend to whom it was not an agony to speak. They who knew of him, knew also of his disgrace, and no longer asked him to their houses. For days past he had eaten alone, and sat alone, and walked alone. All study was impossible to him. No pursuit was open to him. He spend his time in thinking of his wife, and of the disgrace which she had brought upon him. Such a life as this, he knew, was unmanly and shameful, and it was absolutely necessary for him that he should in some way change it. He would go out of England, and would travel if only he could so dispose of his wife that she might be safe from any possible communication with Colonel Osborne. If that could be effected, nothing that money could do should be spared for her. If that could not be effected he would remain at home and crush her.

That night before he went to bed he wrote a letter to his wife, which was as follows:

Dear Emily,

I have learned, beyond the shadow of a doubt, that you have corresponded with Colonel Osborne since you have been at Nuncombe Putney, and also that you have seen him there. This has been done in direct opposition to my expressed wishes, and I feel myself compelled to tell you that such conduct is disgraceful to you, and disgracing to me. I am quite at a loss to understand how you can reconcile to yourself so flagrant a disobedience of my instructions, and so perverse a disregard to the opinion of the world at large.

But I do not write now for the sake of finding fault with you. It is too late for me to have any hope that I can do so with good effect, either as regards your credit or my happiness. Nevertheless, it is my duty to protect both you and myself from further shame; and I wish to tell you what are my intentions with that view. In the first place, I warn you that I keep a watch on you. The doing so is very painful to me, but it is absolutely necessary. You cannot see Colonel Osborne, or write to him, without my knowing it. I pledge you my word that in either case—that is, if you correspond with him or see him—I will at once take our boy away from you. I will not allow him to remain, even with a mother, who shall so misconduct herself. Should Colonel Osborne address a letter to you, I desire that you will put it under an envelope addressed to me.

If you obey my commands on this head I will leave our boy with you nine months out of every year till he shall be six years old. Such, at least, is my present idea, though I will not positively bind myself to adhere to it. And I will allow you 800 pounds per year, for your own maintenance and that of your sister. I am greatly grieved to find from my friend Mr Stanbury that your conduct in reference to Colonel Osborne has been such as to make it necessary that you should leave Mrs Stanbury's house. I do not wonder that it should be so. I shall immediately seek for a future home for you, and when I have found one that is suitable, I will have you conveyed to it.

I must now further explain my purposes and I must beg you to remember that I am driven to do so by your direct disobedience to my expressed wishes. Should there be any further communication between you and Colonel Osborne, not only will I take your child away from you, but I will also limit the allowance to be made to you to a bare sustenance. In such case, I shall put the matter into the hands of a lawyer, and shall probably feel myself driven to take steps towards freeing myself from a connection which will be disgraceful to my name.

For myself, I shall live abroad during the greater part of the year. London has become to me uninhabitable, and all English pleasures are distasteful.

Yours affectionately,   LOUIS TREVELYAN.

When he had finished this he read it twice, and believed that he had written, if not an affectionate, at any rate a considerate letter. He had no bounds to the pity which he felt for himself in reference to the injury which was being done to him, and he thought that the offers which he was making, both in respect to his child and the money, were such as to entitle him to his wife's warmest gratitude. He hardly recognised the force of the language which he used when he told her that her conduct was disgraceful, and that she had disgraced his name. He was quite unable to look at the whole question between him and his wife from her point of view. He conceived it possible that such a woman as his wife should be told that her conduct would be watched, and that she should be threatened with the Divorce Court, with an effect that should, upon the whole, be salutary. There be men, and not bad men either, and men neither uneducated, or unintelligent, or irrational in ordinary matters, who seem to be absolutely unfitted by nature to have the custody or guardianship of others. A woman in the hands of such a man can hardly save herself or him from endless trouble. It may be that between such a one and his wife, events shall flow on so evenly that no ruling, no constraint is necessary that even the giving of advice is never called for by the circumstances of the day. If the man be happily forced to labour daily for his living till he be weary, and the wife be laden with many ordinary cares, the routine of life may run on without storms; but for such a one, if he be without work, the management of a wife will be a task full of peril. The lesson may be learned at last; he may after years come to perceive how much and how little of guidance the partner of his life requires at his hands; and he may be taught how that guidance should be given, but in the learning of the lesson there will be sorrow and gnashing of teeth. It was so now with this man. He loved his wife. To a certain extent he still trusted her. He did not believe that she would be faithless to him after the fashion of women who are faithless altogether But he was jealous of authority, fearful of slights, self-conscious, afraid of the world, and utterly ignorant of the nature of a woman's mind.

He carried the letter with him in his pocket throughout the next morning, and in the course of the day he called upon Lady Milborough. Though he was obstinately bent on acting in accordance with his own views, yet he was morbidly desirous of discussing the grievousness of his position with his friends. He went to Lady Milborough, asking for her advice, but desirous simply of being encouraged by her to do that which he was resolved to do on his own judgment.

'Down after her to Nuncombe Putney!' said Lady Milborough, holding up both her hands.

'Yes; he has been there. And she has been weak enough to see him.'

'My dear Louis, take her to Naples at once—at once.'

'It is too late for that now, Lady Milborough.'

'Too late! Oh no. She has been foolish, indiscreet, disobedient—what you will of that kind. But, Louis, don't send her away; don't send your young wife away from you. Those whom God has joined together, let no man put asunder.'

'I cannot consent to live with a wife with whom neither my wishes nor my word have the slightest effect. I may believe of her what I please; but, think what the world will believe! I cannot disgrace myself by living with a woman who persists in holding intercourse with a man whom the world speaks of as her lover.'

'Take her to Naples,' said Lady Milborough, with all the energy of which she was capable.

'I can take her nowhere, nor will I see her, till she has given proof that her whole conduct towards me has been altered. I have written a letter to her, and I have brought it. Will you excuse me if I ask you to take the trouble to read it?'

Then he handed Lady Milborough the letter, which she read very slowly, and with much care.

'I don't think I would—would—would—'

'Would what?' demanded Trevelyan.

'Don't you think that what you say is a little—just a little—prone to make to make the breach perhaps wider?'

'No, Lady Milborough. In the first place, how can it be wider?'

'You might take her back, you know; and then if you could only get to Naples!'

'How can I take her back while she is corresponding with this man?'

'She wouldn't correspond with him at Naples.'

Trevelyan shook his head and became cross. His old friend would not at all do as old friends are expected to do when called upon for advice.

'I think,' said he, 'that what I have proposed is both just and generous.'

'But, Louis, why should there be any separation?'

'She has forced it upon me. She is headstrong, and will not be ruled.'

'But this about disgracing you. Do you think that you must say that?'

'I think I must, because it is true. If I do not tell her the truth, who is there that will do so? It may be bitter now, but I think that it is for her welfare.'

'Dear, dear, dear!'

'I want nothing for myself, Lady Milborough.'

'I am sure of that, Louis.'

'My whole happiness was in my home. No man cared less for going out than I did. My child and my wife were everything to me. I don't suppose that I was ever seen at a club in the evening once throughout a season. And she might have had anything that she liked—anything! It is hard; Lady Milborough; is it not?'

Lady Milborough, who had seen the angry brow, did not dare to suggest Naples again. But yet, if any word might be spoken to prevent this utter wreck of a home, how good a thing it would be! He had got up to leave her, but she stopped him by holding his hand.

'For better, for worse, Louis; remember that.'

'Why has she forgotten it?'

'She is flesh of your flesh, bone of your bone. And for the boy's sake! Think of your boy, Louis. Do not send that letter. Sleep on it, Louis, and think of it.'

'I have slept on it.'

'There is no promise in it of forgiveness after a while. It is written as though you intended that she should never come back to you.'.

'That shall be as she behaves herself.'

'But tell her so. Let there be some one bright spot in what you say to her, on which her mind may fix itself. If she be not altogether hardened, that letter will drive her to despair.'

But Trevelyan would not give up the letter, nor indicate by a word that he would reconsider the question of its propriety. He escaped as soon as he could from Lady Milborough's room, and almost declared as he did so, that he would never enter her doors again. She had utterly failed to see the matter in the proper light. When she talked of Naples she must surely have been unable to comprehend the extent of the ill-usage to which he, the husband, had been subjected. How was it possible that he should live under the same roof with a wife who claimed to herself the right of receiving visitors of whom he disapproved—a visitor, a gentleman, one whom the world called her lover? He gnashed his teeth and clenched his fist as he thought of his old friend's ignorance of the very first law in a married man's code of laws.

But yet when he was out in the streets he did not post his letter at once; but thought of it throughout the whole day, trying to prove the weight of every phrase that he had used. Once or twice his heart almost relented. Once he had the letter in his hand, that he might tear it. But he did not tear it. He put it back into his pocket, and thought again of his grievance. Surely it was his first duty in such an emergency to be firm!

It was certainly a wretched life that he was leading. In the evening he went all alone to an eating-house for his dinner, and then, sitting with a miserable glass of sherry before him, he again read and re-read the epistle which he had written. Every harsh word that it contained was, in some sort, pleasant to his ear. She had hit him hard, and should he not hit her again? And then, was it not his bounden duty to let her know the truth? Yes; it was his duty to be firm.

So he went out and posted the letter.

CHAPTER XXVIII. GREAT TRIBULATION

Trevelyan's letter to his wife fell like a thunderbolt among them at Nuncombe Putney. Mrs Trevelyan was altogether unable to keep it to herself; indeed she made no attempt at doing so. Her husband had told her that she was to be banished from the Clock House because her present hostess was unable to endure her misconduct, and of course she demanded the reasons of the charge that was thus brought against her. When she first read the letter, which she did in the presence of her sister, she towered in her passion.

'Disgraced him! I have never disgraced him. It is he that has disgraced me. Correspondence! Yes he shall see it all. Unjust, ignorant, foolish man! He does not remember that the last instructions he really gave me, were to bid me see Colonel Osborne. Take my boy away! Yes. Of course, I am a woman and must suffer. I will write to Colonel Osborne, and will tell him the truth, and will send my letter to Louis. He shall know how he has ill-treated me! I will not take a penny of his money, not a penny. Maintain you! I believe he thinks that we are beggars. Leave this house because of my conduct! What can Mrs Stanbury have said? What can any of them have said? I will demand to be told. Free himself from the connection! Oh, Nora, Nora! that it should come to this! that I should be thus threatened, who have been as innocent as a baby! If it were not for my child, I think that I should destroy myself!'

Nora said what she could to comfort her sister, insisting chiefly on the promise that the child should not be taken away. There was no doubt as to the husband's power in the mind of either of them; and though, as regarded herself, Mrs Trevelyan would have defied her husband, let his power be what it might, yet she acknowledged to herself that she was in some degree restrained by the fear that she would find herself deprived of her only comfort.

'We must just go where he bids us till papa comes,' said Nora.

'And when papa is here, what help will there be then? He will not let me go back to the islands with my boy. For myself I might die, or get out of his way anywhere. I can see that. Priscilla Stanbury is right when she says that no woman should trust herself to any man. Disgraced! That I should live to be told by my husband that I had disgraced him by a lover!'

There was some sort of agreement made between the two sisters as to the manner in which Priscilla should be interrogated respecting the sentence of banishment which had been passed. They both agreed that it would be useless to make inquiry of Mrs Stanbury. If anything had really been said to justify the statement made in Mr Trevelyan's letter, it must have come from Priscilla, and have reached Trevelyan through Priscilla's brother. They, both of them, had sufficiently learned the ways of the house to be sure that Mrs Stanbury had not been the person active in the matter. They went down, therefore, together, and found Priscilla seated at her desk in the parlour. Mrs Stanbury was also in the room, and it had been presumed between the sisters that the interrogation should be made in that lady's absence; but Mrs Trevelyan was too hot in the matter for restraint, and she at once opened out her budget of grievance.

'I have a letter from my husband,' she said and then paused. But Priscilla, seeing from the fire in her eyes that she was much moved, made no reply, but turned to listen to what might further be said. 'I do not know why I should trouble you with his suspicions,' continued Mrs Trevelyan, 'or read to you what he says about Colonel Osborne.' As she spoke she was holding her husband's letter open in her hands. 'There is nothing in it that you do not know. He says I have corresponded with him. So I have and he shall see the correspondence. He says that Colonel Osborne visited me. He did come to see me and Nora.'

'As any other old man might have done,' said Nora.

'It was not likely that I should openly confess myself to be afraid to see my father's old friend. But the truth is, my husband does not know what a woman is.'

She had begun by declaring that she would not trouble her friend with any statement of her husband's complaints against her; but now she had made her way to the subject, and could hardly refrain herself. Priscilla understood this, and thought that it would be wise to interrupt her by a word that might bring her back to her original purpose. 'Is there anything,' said she, 'which we can do to help you?'

'To help me? No God only can help me. But Louis informs me that I am to be turned out of this house, because you demand that we should go.'

'Who says that?' exclaimed Mrs Stanbury.

'My husband. Listen; this is what he says "I am greatly grieved to hear from my friend Mr Stanbury that your conduct in reference to Colonel Osborne has been such as to make it necessary that you should leave Mrs Stanbury's house." Is that true? Is that true?' In her general mode of carrying herself, and of enduring the troubles of her life, Mrs Trevelyan was a strong woman; but now her grief was too much for her, and she burst out into tears. 'I am the most unfortunate woman that ever was born!' she sobbed out through her tears.

'I never said that you were to go,' said Mrs Stanbury.

'But your son has told Mr Trevelyan that we must go,' said Nora, who felt that her sense of injury against Hugh Stanbury was greatly increased by what had taken place. To her mind he was the person most important in the matter. Why had he desired that they should be sent away from the Clock House? She was very angry with him, and declared to herself that she hated him with all her heart. For this man she had sent away that other lover, a lover who had really loved her! And she had even confessed that it was so!

'There is a misunderstanding about this,' said Priscilla.

'It must be with your brother, then,' said Nora.

'I think not,' said Priscilla: 'I think that it has been with Mr Trevelyan.' Then she went on to explain, with much difficulty, but still with a slow distinctness that was peculiar to her, what had really taken place. 'We have endeavoured,' she said, 'to show you, my mother and I, that we have not misjudged you; but it is certainly true that I told my brother that I did not think the arrangement a good one quite as a permanence.' It was very difficult, and her cheeks were red as she spoke, and her lips faltered. It was an exquisite pain to her to have to give the pain which her words would convey; but there was no help for it as she said to herself more than once at the time, there was nothing to be done but to tell the truth.

'I never said so,' blurted out Mrs Stanbury, with her usual weakness.

'No, mother. It was my saying. In discussing what was best for us all, with Hugh, I told him what I have just now explained.'

'Then of course we must go,' said Mrs Trevelyan, who had gulped down her sobs and was resolved to be firm, to give way to no more tears, to bear all without sign of womanly weakness.

'You will stay with us till your father comes,' said Priscilla.

'Of course you will,' said Mrs Stanbury 'you and Nora. We have got to be such friends, now.'

'No,' said Mrs Trevelyan. 'As to friendship for me, it is out of the question. We must pack up, Nora, and go somewhere. Heaven knows where!'

Nora was now sobbing. 'Why your brother should want to turn us out after he has sent us here !'

'My brother wants nothing of the kind,' said Priscilla. 'Your sister has no better friend than my brother.'

'It will be better, Nora, to discuss the matter no further,' said Mrs Trevelyan. 'We must go away somewhere; and the sooner the better. To be an unwelcome guest is always bad; but to be unwelcome for such a reason as this is terrible.'

'There is no reason,' said Mrs Stanbury; 'indeed there is none.'

'Mrs Trevelyan will understand us better when she is less excited,' said Priscilla. 'I am not surprised that she should be indignant now. I can only say again that we hope you will stay with us till Sir Marmaduke Rowley shall be in England.'

'That is not what your brother means,' said Nora.

'Nor is it what I mean,' said Mrs Trevelyan. 'Nora, we had better go to our own room. I suppose I must write to my husband; indeed, of course I must, that I may send him the the correspondence. I fear I cannot walk out into the street, Mrs Stanbury, and make you quit of me till I hear from him. And if I were to go to an inn at once, people would speak evil of me and I have no money.'

'My dear, how can you think of such a thing!' said Mrs Stanbury.

'But you may be quite sure that we shall be gone within three days or four at the furthest. Indeed, I will pledge myself not to remain longer than that even though I should have to go to the poor-house. Neither I nor my sister will stay in any family to contaminate it. Come, Nora.' And so speaking she sailed out of the room, and her sister followed her.

'Why did you say anything about, it? Oh dear, oh dear! why did you speak to Hugh? See what you have done?'

'I am sorry that I did speak,' replied Priscilla, slowly.

'Sorry! Of course you are sorry; but what good is that?'

'But, mother; I do not think that I was wrong. I feel sure that the real fault in all this is with Mr Trevelyan as it has been all through. He should not have written to her as he has done.'

'I suppose Hugh did tell him.'

'No doubt and I told Hugh; but not after the fashion in which he has told her. I blame myself mostly for this that we ever consented to come to this house. We had no business here. Who is to pay the rent?'

'Hugh insisted upon taking it.'

'Yes and he will pay the rent; and we shall be a drag upon him, as though he had been fool enough to have a wife and a family of his own. And what good have we done? We had not strength enough to say that that wicked man should not see her when he came, for he is a wicked man.'

'If we had done that she would have been as bad then as she is now.'

'Mother, we had no business to meddle either with her badness or her goodness. What had we to do with the wife of such a one as Mr Trevelyan, or with any woman who was separated from her husband?'

'It was Hugh who thought we should be of service to them.'

'Yes and I do not blame him. He is in a position to be of service to people. He can do work and earn money, and has a right to think and to speak. We have a right to think only for ourselves, and we should not have yielded to him. How are we to get back again out of this house to our cottage?'

'They are pulling the cottage down, Priscilla.'

'To some other cottage, mother. Do you not feel while we are living here that we are pretending to be what we are not? After all, Aunt Stanbury was right, though it was not her business to meddle with us. We should never have come here. That poor woman now regards us as her bitter enemies.'

'I meant to do for the best,' said Mrs Stanbury.

'The fault was mine, mother.'

'But you meant it for the best, my dear.'

'Meaning for the best is trash. I don't know that I did mean it for the best. While we were at the cottage we paid our way and were honest. What is it people say of us now?'

'They can't say any harm.'

'They say that we are paid by the husband to keep his wife, and paid again by the lover to betray the husband.'

'Priscilla!'

'Yes it is shocking enough. But that comes of people going out of their proper course. We were too humble and low to have a right to take any part in such a matter. How true it is that while one crouches on the ground, one can never fall.'

The matter was discussed in the Clock House all day, between Mrs Stanbury and Priscilla, and between Mrs Trevelyan and Nora, in their rooms and in the garden; but nothing could come of such discussions. No change could be made till further instructions should have been received from the angry husband; nor could any kind of argument be even invented by Priscilla which might be efficacious in inducing the two ladies to remain at the Clock House, even should Mr Trevelyan allow them to do so. They all felt the intolerable injustice, as it appeared to them, of their subjection to the caprice of an unreasonable and ill-conditioned man; but to all of them it seemed plain enough that in this matter the husband must exercise his own will at any rate, till Sir Marmaduke should be in England. There were many difficulties throughout the day. Mrs Trevelyan would not go down to dinner, sending word that she was ill, and that she would, if she were allowed, have some tea in her own room. And Nora said that she would remain with her sister. Priscilla went to them more than once; and late in the evening they all met in the parlour. But any conversation seemed to he impossible; and Mrs Trevelyan, as she went up to her room at night, again declared that she would rid the house of her presence as soon as possible.

One thing, however, was done on that melancholy day. Mrs Trevelyan wrote to her husband, and enclosed Colonel Osborne's letter to herself, and a copy of her reply. The reader will hardly require to be told that no such further letter had been written by her as that of which Bozzle had given information to her husband. Men whose business it is to detect hidden and secret things, are very apt to detect things which have never been done. What excuse can a detective make even to himself for his own existence if he can detect nothing? Mr Bozzle was an active-minded man, who gloried in detecting, and who, in the special spirit of his trade, had taught himself to believe that all around him were things secret and hidden, which would be within his power of unravelling if only the slightest clue were put in his hand. He lived by the crookednesses of people, and therefore was convinced that straight doings in the world were quite exceptional. Things dark and dishonest, fights fought and races run that they might be lost, plants and crosses, women false to their husbands, sons false to their fathers, daughters to their mothers, servants to their masters, affairs always secret, dark, foul, and fraudulent, were to him the normal condition of life. It was to be presumed that Mrs Trevelyan should continue to correspond with her lover, that old Mrs Stanbury should betray her trust by conniving at the lover's visit, that everybody concerned should be steeped to the hips in lies and iniquity. When, therefore, he found at Colonel Osborne's rooms that the Colonel had received a letter with the Lessboro' post-mark, addressed in the handwriting of a woman, he did not scruple to declare that Colonel Osborne had received, on that morning, a letter from Mr Trevelyan's 'lady.' But in sending to her husband what she called with so much bitterness, 'the correspondence,' Mrs Trevelyan had to enclose simply the copy of one sheet note from herself.

But she now wrote again to Colonel Osborne, and enclosed to her husband, not a copy of what she had written, but the note itself. It was as follows:

Nuncombe Putney,
Wednesday, August 10.

My Dear Colonel Osborne,

'My husband has desired me not to see you, or to write to you, or to hear from you again. I must therefore beg you to enable me to obey him at any rate, till papa comes to England.

Yours truly,   Emily Trevelyan.

And then she wrote to her husband, and in the writing of this letter there was much doubt, much labour, and many changes. We will give it as it was written when completed:

Nuncombe Putney,
August 10.

I have received your letter, and will obey your commands to the best of my power. In order that you may not be displeased by any further unavoidable correspondence between me and Colonel Osborne, I have written to him a note, which I now send to you. I send it that you may forward it. If you do not choose to do so, I cannot be answerable either for his seeing me, or for his writing to me again.

I send also copies of all the correspondence I have had with Colonel Osborne since you turned me out of your house. When he came to call on me, Nora remained with me while he was here. I blush while I write this not for myself, but that I should be so suspected as to make such a statement necessary.

You say that I have disgraced you and myself. I have done neither. I am disgraced but it is you that have disgraced me. I have never spoken a word or done a thing, as regards you, of which I have cause to be ashamed.

I have told Mrs Stanbury that I and Nora will leave her house as soon as we can be made to know where we are to go. I beg that this may be decided instantly, as else we must walk out into the street without a shelter. After what has been said, I cannot remain here.

My sister bids me say that she will relieve you of all burden respecting herself as soon as possible. She will probably be able to find a home with my aunt, Mrs Outhouse, till papa comes to England. As for myself, I can only say that till he comes, I shall do exactly what you order.   Emily Trevelyan.

CHAPTER XXIX. MR AND MRS OUTHOUSE

Both Mr Outhouse and his wife were especially timid in taking upon themselves the cares of other people. Not on that account is it to be supposed that they were bad or selfish. They were both given much to charity, and bestowed both in time and money more than is ordinarily considered necessary even from persons in their position. But what they gave, they gave away from their own quiet hearth. Had money been wanting to the daughters of his wife's brother, Mr Outhouse would have opened such small coffer as he had with a free hand. But he would have much preferred that his benevolence should be used in a way that would bring upon him no further responsibility and no questionings from people whom he did not know and could not understand.

The Rev. Oliphant Outhouse had been Rector of St. Diddulph's-in-the-East for the last fifteen years, having married the sister of Sir Marmaduke Rowley, then simply Mr Rowley, with a colonial appointment in Jamaica of 120 pounds per annum, twelve years before his promotion, while he was a curate in one of the populous borough parishes. He had thus been a London clergyman all his life; but he knew almost as little of London society as though he had held a cure in a Westmoreland valley. He had worked hard, but his work had been altogether among the poor. He had no gift of preaching, and had acquired neither reputation nor popularity. But he could work, and having been transferred because of that capability to the temporary curacy of St. Diddulph's out of one diocese into another, he had received the living from the bishop's hands when it became vacant.

A dreary place was the parsonage of St. Diddulph's-in-the-East for the abode of a gentleman. Mr Outhouse had not, in his whole parish, a parishioner with whom he could consort. The greatest men around him were the publicans, and the most numerous were men employed in and around the docks. Dredgers of mud, navvies employed on suburban canals, excavators, loaders and unloaders of cargo, cattle drivers, whose driving, however, was done mostly on board ship—such and such like were the men who were the fathers of the families of St. Diddulph's-in-the-East. And there was there, not far removed from the muddy estuary of a little stream that makes its black way from the Essex marshes among the houses of the poorest of the poor into the Thames, a large commercial establishment for turning the carcasses of horses into manure. Messrs Flowsem and Blurt were in truth the great people of St. Diddulph's-in-the-East; but the closeness of their establishment was not an additional attraction to the parsonage. They were liberal, however, with their money, and Mr Outhouse was disposed to think, custom perhaps having made the establishment less objectionable to him than it was at first, that St. Diddulph's-in-the-East would be more of a Pandemonium than it now was, if by any sanitary law Messrs Flowsem and Blurt were compelled to close their doors. '*Non olet*,' he would say with a grim smile when the charitable cheque of the firm would come punctually to hand on the first Saturday after Christmas.

But such a house as his would be, as he knew, but a poor residence for his wife's nieces. Indeed, without positively saying that he was unwilling to receive them, he had, when he first heard of the breaking up of the house in Curzon Street, shewn that he would rather not take upon his shoulders so great a responsibility. He and his wife had discussed the matter between them, and had come to the conclusion that they did not know what kind of things might have been done in Curzon Street. They would think no evil, they said; but the very idea of a married woman with a lover was dreadful to them. It might be that their niece was free from blame. They hoped so. And even though her sin had been of ever so deep a dye, they would take her in if it were indeed necessary. But they hoped that such help from them might not be needed. They both knew how to give counsel to a poor woman, how to rebuke a poor man, how to comfort, encourage, or to upbraid the poor. Practice had told them how far they might go with some hope of doing good and at what stage of demoralisation no good from their hands was any longer within the scope of fair expectation. But all this was among the poor. With what words to encourage such a one as their niece Mrs Trevelyan, to encourage her or to rebuke her, as her conduct might seem to make necessary, they both felt that They were altogether ignorant. To them Mrs Trevelyan was a fine lady. To Mr Outhouse, Sir Marmaduke had ever been a fine gentleman, given much to worldly things, who cared more for whist and a glass of wine than for anything else, and who thought that he had a good excuse for never going to church in England because he was called upon, as he said, to show himself in the governor's pew always once on Sundays, and frequently twice, when he was at the seat of his government. Sir Marmaduke manifestly looked upon church as a thing in itself notoriously disagreeable. To Mr Outhouse it afforded the great events of the week. And Mrs Outhouse would declare that to hear her husband preach was the greatest joy of her life. It may be understood therefore that though the family connection between the Rowleys and the Outhouses had been kept up with a semblance of affection, it had never blossomed forth into cordial friendship.

When therefore the clergyman of St. Diddulph's received a letter from his niece, Nora, begging him to take her into his parsonage till Sir Marmaduke should arrive in the course of the spring, and hinting also a wish that her uncle Oliphant should see Mr Trevelyan and if possible arrange that his other niece should also come to the parsonage, he was very much perturbed in spirit. There was a long consultation between him and his wife before anything could be settled, and it may be doubted whether anything would have been settled, had not Mr Trevelyan himself made his way to the parsonage, on the second day of the family conference. Mr and Mrs Outhouse had both seen the necessity of sleeping upon the matter. They had slept upon it, and the discourse between them on the second day was so doubtful in its tone that more sleeping would probably have been necessary had not Mr Trevelyan appeared and compelled them to a decision.

'You must remember that I make no charge against her,' said Trevelyan, after the matter had been discussed for about an hour.

'Then why should she not come back to you?' said Mr Outhouse, timidly.

'Some day she may if she will be obedient. But it cannot be now. She has set me at defiance; and even yet it is too clear from the tone of her letter to me that she thinks that she has been right to do so. How could we live together in amity when she addresses me as a cruel tyrant?'

'Why did she go away at first?' asked Mrs Outhouse.

'Because she would compromise my name by an intimacy which I did not approve. But I do not come here to defend myself, Mrs Outhouse. You probably think that I have been wrong. You are her friend; and to you, I will not even say that I have been right. What I want you to understand is this. She cannot come back to me now. It would not be for my honour that she should do so.'

'But, sir would it not be for your welfare, as a Christian?' asked Mr Outhouse.

'You must not be angry with me, if I say that I will not discuss that just now. I did not come here to discuss it.'

'It is very sad for our poor niece,' said Mrs Outhouse. 'It is very sad for me,' said Trevelyan, gloomily 'very sad, indeed. My home is destroyed; my life is made solitary; I do not even see my own child. She has her boy with her, and her sister. I have nobody.'

'I can't understand, for the life of me; why you should not live together just like any other people,' said Mrs Outhouse, whose woman's spirit was arising in her bosom. 'When people are married, they must put up with something at least, most always.' This she added, lest it might be for a moment imagined that she had had any cause for complaint with her Mr Outhouse.

'Pray excuse me, Mrs Outhouse; but I cannot discuss that. The question between us is this: can you consent to receive your two nieces till their father's return and if so, in what way shall I defray the expense of their living? You will of course understand that I willingly undertake the expense not only of my wife's maintenance and of her sister's also, but that I will cheerfully allow anything that may be required either for their comfort or recreation.'

'I cannot take my nieces into my house as lodgers,' said Mr Outhouse.

'No, not as lodgers; but of course you can understand that it is for me to pay for my own wife. I know I owe you an apology for mentioning it but how else could I make my request to you?'

'If Emily and Nora come here they must come as our guests,' said Mrs Outhouse.

'Certainly,' said the clergyman. 'And if I am told they are in want of a home they shall find one here till their father comes. But I am bound to say that as regards the elder I think her home should be elsewhere.'

'Of course it should,' said Mrs Outhouse. 'I don't know anything about the law, but it seems to me very odd that a young woman should be turned out in this way. You say she has done nothing?'

'I will not argue the matter,' said Trevelyan.

'That's all very well, Mr Trevelyan,' said the lady, 'but she's my own niece, and if I don't stand up for her I don't know who will. I never heard such a thing in my life as a wife being sent away after such a fashion as that. We wouldn't treat a cookmaid so; that we wouldn't. As for coming here, she shall come if she pleases, but I shall always say that it's the greatest shame I ever heard of.'

Nothing came of this visit at last. The lady grew in her anger; and Mr Trevelyan, in his own defence, was driven to declare that his wife's obstinate intimacy with Colonel Osborne had almost driven him out of his senses. Before he left the parsonage he was brought even to tears by his own narration of his own misery whereby Mr Outhouse was considerably softened, although Mrs Outhouse became more and more stout in the defence of her own sex. But nothing at last came of it. Trevelyan insisted on paying for his wife, wherever she might be placed; and when he found that this would not be permitted to him at the parsonage, he was very anxious to take some small furnished house in the neighbourhood, in which the two sisters might live for the next six months under the wings of their uncle and aunt But even Mr Outhouse was moved to pleasantry by this suggestion, as he explained the nature of the tenements which were common at St. Diddulph's. Two rooms, front and back, they might have for about five-and sixpence a week in a house with three other families. 'But perhaps that is not exactly what you'd like,' said Mr Outhouse. The interview ended with no result, and Mr Trevelyan took his leave, declaring to himself that he was worse off than the foxes, who have holes in which to lay their heads, but it must be presumed that his sufferings in this respect were to be by attorney; as it was for his wife, and not for himself, that the necessary hole was now required.

As soon as he was gone Mrs Outhouse answered Nora's letter, and without meaning to be explicit, explained pretty closely what had taken place. The spare bedroom at the parsonage was ready to receive either one or both of the sisters till Sir Marmaduke should be in London, if one or both of them should choose to come. And though there was no nursery at the parsonage, for Mr and Mrs Outhouse had been blessed with no children, still room should be made for the little boy. But they must come as visitors 'as our own nieces,' said Mrs Outhouse. And she went on to say that she would have nothing to do with the quarrel between Mr Trevelyan and his wife. All such quarrels were very bad but as to this quarrel she could take no part either one side or the other. Then she stated that Mr Trevelyan had been at the parsonage, but that no arrangement had been made, because Mr Trevelyan had insisted on paying for their board and lodging.

This letter reached Nuncombe Putney before any reply was received by Mrs Trevelyan from her husband. This was on the Saturday morning, and Mrs Trevelyan had pledged herself to Mrs Stanbury that she would leave the Clock House on the Monday. Of course, there was no need that she should do so. Both Mrs Stanbury and Priscilla would now have willingly consented to their remaining till Sir Marmaduke should be in England. But Mrs Trevelyan's high spirit revolted against this after all that had been said. She thought that she should hear from her husband on the morrow, but the post on Sunday brought no letter from Trevelyan. On the Saturday they had finished packing up so certain was Mrs Trevelyan that some instructions as to her future destiny would be sent to her by her lord.

At last they decided on the Sunday that they would both go at once to St. Diddulph's; or perhaps it would be more correct to say that this was the decision of the elder sister. Nora would willingly have yielded to Priscilla's entreaties, and have remained. But Emily declared that she could not, and would not, stay in the house. She had a few pounds what would suffice for her journey; and as Mr Trevelyan had not thought proper to send his orders to her, she would go without them. Mrs Outhouse was her aunt, and her nearest relative in England. Upon whom else could she lean in this time of her great affliction? A letter, therefore, was written to Mrs Outhouse, saying that the whole party, including the boy and nurse, would be at St. Diddulph's on the Monday evening, and the last cord was put to the boxes.

'I suppose that he is very angry,' Mrs Trevelyan said to her sister, 'but I do not feel that I care about that now. He shall have nothing to complain of in reference to any gaiety on my part. I will see no one. I will have no correspondence. But I will not remain here, after what he has said to me, let him be ever so angry. I declare, as I think of it, it seems to me that no woman was ever so cruelly treated as I have been.' Then she wrote one further line to her husband.

Not having received any orders from you, and having promised Mrs Stanbury that I would leave this house on Monday, I go with Nora to my aunt, Mrs Outhouse, to-morrow.   E. T.

On the Sunday evening the four ladies drank tea together, and they all made an effort to be civil, and even affectionate, to each other. Mrs Trevelyan had at last allowed Priscilla to explain how it had come to pass that she had told her brother that it would be better both for her mother and for herself that the existing arrangements should be brought to an end, and there had come to be an agreement between them that they should all part in amity. But the conversation on the Sunday evening was very difficult.

'I am sure we shall always think of you both with the greatest kindness,' said Mrs Stanbury.

'As for me,' said Priscilla, 'your being with us has been a delight that I cannot describe, only it has been wrong.'

'I know too well,' said Mrs Trevelyan, 'that in our present circumstances we are unable to carry delight with us anywhere.'

'You hardly understand what our life has been,' said Priscilla; 'but the truth is that we had no right to receive you in such a house as this. It has not been our way of living, and it cannot continue to be so. It is not wonderful that people should talk of us. Had it been called your house, it might have been better.'

'And what will you do now?' asked Nora.

'Get out of this place as soon as we can. It is often hard to go back to the right path; but it may always be done or at least attempted.'

'It seems to me that I take misery with me wherever I go,' said Mrs Trevelyan.

'My dear, it has not been your fault,' said Mrs Stanbury.

'I do not like to blame my brother,' said Priscilla, 'because he has done his best to be good to us all and the punishment will fall heaviest upon him, because he must pay for it.'

'He should not be allowed to pay a shilling,' said Mrs Trevelyan.

Then the morning came, and at seven o'clock the two sisters, with the nurse and child, started for Lessboro' Station in Mrs Crocket's open carriage, the luggage having been sent on in a cart. There were many tears shed, and any one looking at the party would have thought that very dear friends were being torn asunder.

'Mother,' said Priscilla, as soon as the parlour door was shut, and the two were alone together, 'we must take care that we never are brought again into such a mistake as that. They who protect the injured should be strong themselves.'

CHAPTER XXX. DOROTHY MAKES UP HER MIND

It was true that most ill-natured things had been said at Lessboro' and at Nuncombe Putney about Mrs Stanbury and the visitors at the Clock House, and that these ill-natured things had spread themselves to Exeter. Mrs Ellison of Lessboro', who was not the most good-natured woman in the world, had told Mrs Merton of Nuncombe that she had been told that the Colonel's visit to the lady had been made by express arrangement between the Colonel and Mrs Stanbury. Mrs Merton, who was very good-natured, but not the wisest woman in the world, had declared that any such conduct on the part of Mrs Stanbury was quite impossible 'What does it matter which it is Priscilla or her mother?' Mrs Ellison had said. 'These are the facts. Mrs Trevelyan has been sent there to be out of the way of this Colonel; and the Colonel immediately comes down and sees her at the Clock House. But when people are very poor they do get driven to do almost anything.'

Mrs Merton, not being very wise, had conceived it to be her duty to repeat this to Priscilla; and Mrs Ellison, not being very good-natured, had conceived it to be hers to repeat it to Mrs MacHugh at Exeter. And then Bozzle's coming had become known.

'Yes, Mrs MacHugh, a policeman in mufti down at Nuncombe! I wonder what our friend in the Close here will think about it! I have always said, you know, that if she wanted to keep things straight at Nuncombe, she should have opened her purse-strings.'

From all which it may be understood, that Priscilla Stanbury's desire to go back to their old way of living had not been without reason.

It may be imagined that Miss Stanbury of the Close did not receive with equanimity the reports which reached her. And, of course, when she discussed the matter either with Martha or with Dorothy, she fell back upon her own early appreciation of the folly of the Clock House arrangement. Nevertheless, she had called Mrs Ellison very bad names, when she learned from her friend Mrs MacHugh what reports were being spread by the lady from Lessboro'.

'Mrs Ellison! Yes; we all know Mrs Ellison. The bitterest tongue in Devonshire, and the falsest! There are some people at Lessboro' who would be well pleased if she paid her way there as well as those poor women do at Nuncombe. I don't think much of what Mrs Ellison says.'

'But it is bad about the policeman,' said Mrs MacHugh.

'Of course it's bad. It's all bad. I'm not saying that it's not bad. I'm glad I've got this other young woman out of it. It's all that young man's doing. If I had a son of my own, I'd sooner follow him to the grave than hear him call himself a Radical.'

Then, on a sudden, there came to the Close news that Mrs Trevelyan and her sister were gone. On the very Monday on which they went, Priscilla sent a note on to her sister, in which no special allusion was made to Aunt Stanbury, but which was no doubt written with the intention that the news should be communicated.

'Gone; are they? As it is past wishing that they hadn't come, it's the best thing they could do now. And who is to pay the rent of the house, now they have gone?' As this was a point on which Dorothy was not prepared to trouble herself at present, she made no answer to the question.

Dorothy at this time was in a state of very great perturbation on her own account. The reader may perhaps remember that she had been much startled by a proposition that had been made to her in reference to her future life. Her aunt had suggested to her that she should become Mrs Gibson. She had not as yet given any answer to that proposition, and had indeed found it to be quite impossible to speak about it at all. But there can be no doubt that the suggestion had opened out to her altogether new views of life. Up to the moment of her aunt's speech to her, the idea of her becoming a married woman had never presented itself to her. In her humility it had not occurred to her that she should be counted as one among the candidates for matrimony. Priscilla had taught her to regard herself—indeed, they had both regarded themselves—as born to eat and drink, as little as might be, and then to die. Now, when she was told that she could, if she pleased, become Mrs Gibson, she was almost lost in a whirl of new and confused ideas. Since her aunt had spoken, Mr Gibson himself had dropped a hint or two which seemed to her to indicate that he also must be in the secret. There had been a party, with a supper, at Mrs Crumbie's, at which both the Miss Frenches had been present. But Mr Gibson had taken her, Dorothy Stanbury, out to supper, leaving both Camilla and Arabella behind him in the drawing-room! During the quarter of an hour afterwards in which the ladies were alone while the gentlemen were eating and drinking, both Camilla and Arabella continued to wreak their vengeance. They asked questions about Mrs Trevelyan, and suggested that Mr Gibson might be sent over to put things right. But Miss Stanbury had heard them, and had fallen upon them with a heavy hand.

'There's a good deal expected of Mr Gibson, my dears,' she said, 'which it seems to me Mr Gibson is not inclined to perform.'

'It is quite indifferent to us what Mr Gibson may be inclined to perform,' said Arabella. 'I'm sure we shan't interfere with Miss Dorothy.'

As this was said quite out loud before all the other ladies, Dorothy was overcome with shame. But her aunt comforted her when they were again at home.

'Laws, my dear; what does it matter? When you're Mrs Gibson, you'll be proud of it all.'

Was it then really written in the book of the Fates that she, Dorothy Stanbury, was to become Mrs Gibson? Poor Dorothy began to feel that she was called upon to exercise an amount of thought and personal decision to which she had not been accustomed. Hitherto, in the things which she had done, or left undone, she had received instructions which she could obey. Had her mother and Priscilla told her positively not to go to her aunt's house, she would have remained at Nuncombe without complaint. Had her aunt since her coming given her orders as to her mode of life— enjoined, for instance, additional church attendances, or desired her to perform menial services in the house—she would have obeyed, from custom, without a word. But when she was told that she was to marry Mr Gibson, it did seem to her to be necessary to do something more than obey. Did she love Mr Gibson? She tried hard to teach herself to think that she might learn to love him. He was a nice-looking man enough, with sandy hair, and a head rather bald, with thin lips, and a narrow nose, who certainly did preach drawling sermons; but of whom everybody said that he was a very excellent clergyman. He had a house and an income, and all Exeter had long since decided that he was a man who would certainly marry. He was one of those men of whom it may be said that they have no possible claim to remain unmarried. He was fair game, and unless he surrendered himself to be bagged before long, would subject himself to just and loud complaint. The Miss Frenches had been aware of this, and had thought to make sure of him among them. It was a little hard upon them that the old maid of the Close, as they always called Miss Stanbury, should interfere with them when their booty was almost won. And they felt it to be the harder because Dorothy Stanbury was, as they thought, so poor a creature. That Dorothy herself should have any doubt as to accepting Mr Gibson, was an idea that never occurred to them. But Dorothy had her doubts. When she came to think of it, she remembered that she had never as yet spoken a word to Mr Gibson, beyond such little trifling remarks as are made over a tea-table. She might learn to love him, but she did not think that she loved him as yet.

'I don't suppose all this will make any difference to Mr Gibson,' said Miss Stanbury to her niece, on the morning after the receipt of Priscilla's note stating that the Trevelyans had left Nuncombe.

Dorothy always blushed when Mr Gibson's name was mentioned, and she blushed now. But she did not at all understand her aunt's allusion. 'I don't know what you mean, aunt,' she said.

'Well, you know, my dear, what they say about Mrs Trevelyan and the Clock House is not very nice. If Mr Gibson were to turn round and say that the connection wasn't pleasant, no one would have a right to complain.'

The faint customary blush on Dorothy's cheeks which Mr Gibson's name had produced now covered her whole face even up to the roots of her hair. 'If he believes bad of mamma, I'm sure, Aunt Stanbury, I don't want to see him again.'

'That's all very fine, my dear, but a man has to think of himself, you know.'

'Of course he thinks of himself. Why shouldn't he? I dare say he thinks of himself more than I do.'

'Dorothy, don't be a fool. A good husband isn't to be caught every day.'

'Aunt Stanbury, I don't want to catch any man.'

'Dorothy, don't be a fool.'

'I must say it. I don't suppose Mr Gibson thinks of me the least in the world.'

'Psha! I tell you he does.'

'But as for mamma and Priscilla, I never could like anybody for a moment who would be ashamed of them.'

She was most anxious to declare that, as far as she knew herself and her own wishes at present, she entertained no partiality for Mr Gibson, no feeling which could become partiality even if Mr Gibson was to declare himself willing to accept her mother and her sister with herself. But she did not dare to say so. There was an instinct within her which made it almost impossible to her to express an objection to a suitor before the suitor had declared himself to be one. She could speak out as touching her mother and her sister but as to her own feelings she could express neither assent or dissent.

'I should like to have it settled soon,' said Miss Stanbury, in a melancholy voice. Even to this Dorothy could make no reply. What did soon mean? Perhaps in the course of a year or two. 'If it could be arranged by the end of this week, it would be a great comfort to me.' Dorothy almost fell off her chair, and was stricken altogether dumb. 'I told you, I think, that Brooke Burgess is coming here?'

'You said he was to come some day.'

'He is to be here on Monday. I haven't seen him for more than twelve years; and now he's to be here next week! Dear, dear! When I think sometimes of all the hard words that have been spoken, and the harder thoughts that have been in people's minds, I often regret that the money ever came to me at all. I could have done without it very well, very well.'

'But all the unpleasantness is over now, aunt.'

'I don't know about that. Unpleasantness of that kind is apt to rankle long. But I wasn't going to give up my rights. Nobody but a coward does that. They talked of going to law and trying the will, but they wouldn't have got much by that. And then they abused me for two years. When they had done and got sick of it, I told them they should have it all back again as soon as I am dead. It won't be long now. This Burgess is the elder nephew, and he shall have it all.'

'Is not he grateful?'

'No. Why should he be grateful? I don't do it for special love of him. I don't want his gratitude; nor anybody's gratitude. Look at Hugh. I did love him.'

'I am grateful, Aunt Stanbury.'

'Are you, my dear? Then show it by being a good wife to Mr Gibson, and a happy wife. I want to get everything settled while Burgess is here. If he is to have it, why should I keep him out of it whilst I live? I wonder whether Mr Gibson would mind coming and living here, Dolly?'

The thing was coming so near to her that Dorothy began to feel that she must, in truth, make up her mind, and let her aunt know also how it had been made up. She was sensible enough to perceive that if she did not prepare herself for the occasion she would find herself hampered by an engagement simply because her aunt had presumed that it was out of the question that she should not acquiesce. She would drift into marriage with Mr Gibson against her will. Her greatest difficulty was the fact that her aunt clearly had no doubt on the subject. And as for herself, hitherto her feelings did not, on either side, go beyond doubts. Assuredly it would be a very good thing for her to become Mrs Gibson, if only she could create for herself some attachment for the man. At the present moment her aunt said nothing more about Mr Gibson, having her mind much occupied with the coming of Mr Brooke Burgess.

'I remember him twenty years ago and more; as nice a boy as you would wish to see. His father was the fourth of the brothers. Dear, dear! Three of them are gone; and the only one remaining is old Barty, whom no one ever loved.'

The Burgesses had been great people in Exeter, having been both bankers and brewers there, but the light of the family had paled; and though Bartholomew

Burgess, of whom Miss Stanbury declared that no one had ever loved him, still had a share in the bank, it was well understood in the city that the real wealth in the firm of Cropper and Burgess belonged to the Cropper family. Indeed the most considerable portion of the fortune that had been realised by old Mr Burgess had come into the possession of Miss Stanbury herself. Bartholomew Burgess had never forgiven his brother's will, and between him and Jemima Stanbury the feud was irreconcileable. The next brother, Tom Burgess, had been a solicitor at Liverpool, and had done well there. But Miss Stanbury knew nothing of the Tom Burgesses as she called them. The fourth brother, Harry Burgess, had been a clergyman, and this Brooke Burgess, Junior, who was now coming to the Close, had been left with a widowed mother, the eldest of a large family. It need not now be told at length how there had been ill-blood also between this clergyman and the heiress. There had been attempts at friendship, and at one time Miss Stanbury had received the Rev. Harry Burgess and all his family at the Close but the attempts had not been successful; and though our old friend had never wavered in her determination to leave the money all back to some one of the Burgess family, and with this view had made a pilgrimage to London some twelve years since, and had renewed her acquaintance with the widow and the children, still there had been no comfortable relations between her and any of the Burgess family. Old Barty Burgess, whom she met in the Close, or saw in the High Street every day of her life, was her great enemy. He had tried his best so at least she was convinced to drive her out of the pale of society, years upon years ago, by saying evil things of her. She had conquered in that combat. Her victory had been complete, and she had triumphed after a most signal fashion. But this triumph did not silence Barty's tongue, nor soften his heart. When she prayed to be forgiven, as she herself forgave others, she always exempted Barty Burgess from her prayers. There are things which flesh and blood cannot do. She had not liked Harry Burgess' widow, nor, for the matter of that, Harry Burgess himself. When she had last seen the children she had not liked any of them much, and had had her doubts even as to Brooke. But with that branch of the family she was willing to try again. Brooke was now coming to the Close, having received, however, an intimation, that if, during his visit to Exeter, he chose to see his Uncle Barty, any such intercourse must be kept quite in the background. While he remained in Miss Stanbury's house he was to remain there as though there were no such person as Mr Bartholomew Burgess in Exeter.

At this time Brooke Burgess was a man just turned thirty, and was a clerk in the Ecclesiastical Record Office, in Somerset House. No doubt the peculiar nature and name of the public department to which he was attached had done something to recommend him to Miss Stanbury. Ecclesiastical records were things greatly to be reverenced in her eyes, and she felt that a gentleman who handled them and dealt with them would probably be sedate, gentlemanlike, and conservative. Brooke

Burgess, when she had last seen him, was just about to enter upon the duties of the office. Then there had come offence, and she had in truth known nothing of him from that day to this. The visitor was to be at Exeter on the following Monday, and very much was done in preparation of his coming. There was to be a dinner party on that very day, and dinner parties were not common with Miss Stanbury. She had, however, explained to Martha that she intended to put her best foot forward. Martha understood perfectly that Mr Brooke Burgess was to be received as the heir of property. Sir Peter Mancrudy, the great Devonshire chemist, was coming to dinner, and Mr and Mrs Powel from Haldon, people of great distinction in that part of the county, Mrs MacHugh of course; and, equally of course, Mr Gibson. There was a deep discussion between Miss Stanbury and Martha as to asking two of the Cliffords, and Mr and Mrs Noel from Doddiscombeleigh. Martha had been very much in favour of having twelve. Miss Stanbury had declared that with twelve she must have two waiters from the greengrocers, and that two waiters would overpower her own domesticities below stairs. Martha had declared that she didn't care about them any more than if they were puppy dogs. But Miss Stanbury had been quite firm against twelve. She had consented to have ten for the sake of artistic arrangement at the table; 'They should be pantaloons and petticoats alternate, you know,' she had said to Martha and had therefore asked the Cliffords. But the Cliffords could not come, and then she had declined to make any further attempt. Indeed, a new idea had struck her. Brooke Burgess, her guest, should sit at one end of the table, and Mr Gibson, the clergyman, at the other. In this way the proper alternation would be effected. When Martha heard this, Martha quite understood the extent of the good fortune that was in store for Dorothy. If Mr Gibson was to be welcomed in that way, it could only be in preparation of his becoming one of the family.

And Dorothy herself became aware that she must make up her mind. It was not so declared to her, but she came to understand that it was very probable that something would occur on the coming Monday which would require her to be ready with her answer on that day. And she was greatly tormented by feeling that if she could not bring herself to accept Mr Gibson should Mr Gibson propose to her, as to which she continued to tell herself that the chance of such a thing must be very remote indeed, but that if he should propose to her, and if she could not accept him, her aunt ought to know that it would be so before the moment came. But yet she could not bring herself to speak to her aunt as though any such proposition were possible.

It happened that during the week, on the Saturday, Priscilla came into Exeter. Dorothy met her sister at the railway station, and then the two walked together two miles and back along the Crediton Road. Aunt Stanbury had consented to Priscilla coming to the Close, even though it was not the day appointed for such visits; but the walk had been preferred, and Dorothy felt that she would be able to ask for counsel from the only human being to whom she could have brought herself to confide the fact that a gentleman was expected to ask her to marry him. But it was not till they had turned upon their walk, that she was able to open her mouth on the subject even to her sister. Priscilla had been very full of their own cares at Nuncombe, and had said much of her determination to leave the Clock House and to return to the retirement of some small cottage. She had already written to Hugh to this effect, and during their walk had said much of her own folly in having consented to so great a change in their mode of life. At last Dorothy struck in with her story.

'Aunt Stanbury wants me to make a change too.'

'What change?' asked Priscilla anxiously.

'It is not my idea, Priscilla, and I don't think that there can be anything in it. Indeed, I'm sure there isn't. I don't see how it's possible that there should be.'

'But what is it, Dolly?'

'I suppose there can't be any harm in my telling you.'

'If it's anything concerning yourself, I should say not. If it concerns Aunt Stanbury, I dare say she'd rather you held your tongue.'

'It concerns me most,' said Dorothy.

'She doesn't want you to leave her, does she?'

'Well; yes; no. By what she said last I shouldn't leave her at all in that way. Only I'm sure it's not possible.'

'I am the worst hand in the world, Dolly, at guessing a riddle.'

'You've heard of that Mr Gibson, the clergyman haven't you?'

'Of course I have.'

'Well—. Mind, you know, it's only what Aunt Stanbury says. He has never so much as opened his lips to me himself, except to say, "How do you do?" and that kind of thing.'

'Aunt Stanbury wants you to marry him?'

'Yes!'

'Well?'

'Of course it's out of the question,' said Dorothy, sadly.

'I don't see why it should be out of the question,' said Priscilla, proudly. 'Indeed, if Aunt Stanbury has said much about it, I should say that Mr Gibson himself must have spoken to her.'

'Do you think he has?'

'I do not believe that my aunt would raise false hopes,' said Priscilla.

'But I haven't any hopes. That is to say, I had never thought about such a thing.'

'But you think about it now, Dolly?'

'I should never have dreamed about it, only for Aunt Stanbury.'

'But, dearest, you are dreaming of it now, are you not?'

'Only because she says that it is to be so. You don't know how generous she is. She says that if it should be so, she will give me ever so much money two thousand pounds!'

'Then I am quite sure that she and Mr Gibson must understand each other.'

'Of course,' said Dorothy, sadly, 'if he were to think of such a thing at all, it would only be because the money would be convenient.'

'Not at all,' said Priscilla, sternly with a sternness that was very comfortable to her listener. 'Not at all. Why should not Mr Gibson love you as well as any man ever loved any woman? You are nice-looking,' Dorothy blushed beneath her hat even at her sister's praise, 'and good-tempered, and lovable in every way. And I think you are just fitted to make a good wife. And you must not suppose, Dolly, that because Mr Gibson wouldn't perhaps, have asked you without the money, that therefore he is mercenary. It so often happens that a gentleman can't marry unless the lady has some money!'

'But he hasn't asked me at all.'

'I suppose he will, dear.'

'I only know what Aunt Stanbury says.'

'You may be sure that he will ask you.'

'And what must I say, Priscilla?'

'What must you say? Nobody can tell you that, dear, but yourself. Do you like him?'

'I don't dislike him.'

'Is that all?'

'I know him so very little, Priscilla. Everybody says he is very good and then it's a great thing, isn't it, that he should be a clergyman?'

'I don't know about that.'

'I think it is. If it were possible that I should ever marry any one, I should like a clergyman so much the best.'

'Then you do know what to say to him.'

'No, I don't, Priscilla. I don't know at all.'

'Look here, dearest. What my aunt offers to you is a very great step in life. If you can accept this gentleman I think you would be happy and I think, also, which should be of more importance for your consideration, that you would make him happy. It is a brighter prospect, dear Dolly, than to live either with us at Nuncombe, or even with Aunt Stanbury as her niece.'

'But if I don't love him, Priscilla?'

'Then give it up, and be as you are, my own, own, dearest sister.'

'So I will,' said Dorothy, and at that time her mind was made up.

CHAPTER XXXI. MR BROOKE BURGESS

The hour at which Mr Brooke Burgess was to arrive had come round, and Miss Stanbury was in a twitter, partly of expectation, and partly, it must be confessed, of fear. Why there should be any fear she did not herself know, as she had much to give and nothing to expect. But she was afraid, and was conscious of it, and was out of temper because she was ashamed of herself. Although it would be necessary that she should again dress for dinner at six, she had put on a clean cap at four, and appeared at that early hour in one of her gowns which was not customarily in use for home purposes at that early hour. She felt that she was 'an old fool' for her pains, and was consequently cross to poor Dorothy. And there were other reasons for some display of harshness to her niece. Mr Gibson had been at the house that very morning, and Dorothy had given herself airs. At least, so Miss Stanbury thought. And during the last three or four days, whenever Mr Gibson's name had been mentioned, Dorothy had become silent, glum, and almost obstructive. Miss Stanbury had been at the trouble of explaining that she was specially anxious to have that little matter of the engagement settled at once. She knew that she was going to behave with great generosity, that she was going to sacrifice, not her money only, of which she did not think much, but a considerable portion of her authority, of which she did think a great deal; and that she was about to behave in a manner which demanded much gratitude. But it seemed to her that Dorothy was not in the least grateful. Hugh had proved himself to be 'a mass of ingratitude,' as she was in the habit of saying. None of the Burgesses had ever shewn to her any gratitude for promises made to them, or, indeed, for any substantial favours conferred upon them. And now Dorothy, to whom a very seventh heaven of happiness had been opened—a seventh heaven, as it must be computed in comparison with her low expectations—now Dorothy was already shewing how thankless she could become. Mr Gibson had not yet declared his passion, but he had freely admitted to Miss Stanbury that he was prepared to do so. Priscilla had been quite right in her suggestion that there was a clear understanding between the clergyman and her aunt.

'I don't think he is come after all,' said Miss Stanbury, looking at her watch. Had the train arrived at the moment that it was due, had the expectant visitor jumped out of the railway carriage into a fly, and had the driver galloped up to the Close, it might have been possible that the wheels should have been at the door as Miss Stanbury spoke.

'It's hardly time yet, aunt.'

'Nonsense; it is time. The train comes in at four. I dare say he won't come at all.'

'He is sure to come, aunt.'

'I've no doubt you know all about it better than any one else. You usually do.' Then five minutes were passed in silence. 'Heaven and earth! what shall I do with these people that are coming? And I told them especially that it was to meet this young man! It's the way I am always treated by everybody that I have about me.'

'The train might be ten minutes late, Aunt Stanbury.'

'Yes and monkeys might chew tobacco. There, there's the omnibus at the "Cock and Bottle"; the omnibus up from the train. Now, of course, he won't come.'

'Perhaps he's walking, Aunt Stanbury.'

'Walking with his luggage on his shoulders? Is that your idea of the way in which a London gentleman goes about? And there are two flies coming up from the train, of course.' Miss Stanbury was obliged to fix the side of her chair very close to the window in order that she might see that part of the Close in which the vehicles of which she had spoken were able to pass.

'Perhaps they are not coming from the train, Aunt Stanbury.'

'Perhaps a fiddlestick! You have lived here so much longer than I have done that, of course, you must know all about it.' Then there was an interval of another ten minutes, and even Dorothy was beginning to think that Mr Burgess was not coming. 'I've given him up now,' said Miss Stanbury. 'I think I'll send and put them all off.' Just at that moment there came a knock at the door. But there was no cab. Dorothy's conjecture had been right. The London gentleman had walked, and his portmanteau had been carried behind him by a boy. 'How did he get here?' exclaimed Miss Stanbury, as she heard the strange voice speaking to Martha downstairs. But Dorothy knew better than to answer the question.

'Miss Stanbury, I am very glad to see you,' said Mr Brooke Burgess, as he entered the room. Miss Stanbury courtesied, and then took him by both hands. 'You wouldn't have known me, I dare say,' he continued. 'A black beard and a bald head do make a difference.'

'You are not bald at all,' said Miss Stanbury.

'I am beginning to be thin enough at the top. I am so glad to come to you, and so much obliged to you for having me! How well I remember the old room!'

'This is my niece, Miss Dorothy Stanbury, from Nuncombe Putney.' Dorothy was about to make some formal acknowledgment of the introduction, when Brooke Burgess came up to her, and shook her hand heartily. 'She lives with me,' continued the aunt.

'And what has become of Hugh?' said Brooke.

'We never talk of him,' said Miss Stanbury gravely.

'I hope there's nothing wrong? I hear of him very often in London.'

'My aunt and he don't agree that's all,' said Dorothy.

'He has given up his profession as a barrister in which he might have lived like a gentleman,' said Miss Stanbury, 'and has taken to writing for a penny newspaper.'

'Everybody does that now, Miss Stanbury.'

'I hope you don't, Mr Burgess.'

'I! Nobody would print anything that I wrote. I don't write for anything, certainly.'

'I'm very glad to hear it,' said Miss Stanbury.

Brooke Burgess, or Mr Brooke, as he came to be called very shortly by the servants in the house, was a good-looking man, with black whiskers and black hair, which, as he said, was beginning to be thin on the top of his head, and pleasant small bright eyes. Dorothy thought that next to her brother Hugh he was the most good-natured looking man she had ever seen. He was rather below the middle height, and somewhat inclined to be stout. But he would boast that he could still walk his twelve miles in three hours, and would add that as long as he could do that he would never recognise the necessity of putting himself on short commons. He had a well-cut nose, not quite aquiline, but tending that way, a chin with a dimple on it, and as sweet a mouth as ever declared the excellence of a man's temper. Dorothy immediately began to compare him with her brother Hugh, who was to her, of all men, the most godlike. It never occurred to her to make any comparison between Mr Gibson and Mr Burgess. Her brother Hugh was the most godlike of men; but there was something godlike also about the new corner. Mr Gibson, to Dorothy's eyes, was by no means divine;

'I used to call you Aunt Stanbury,' said Brooke Burgess to the old lady; 'am I to go on doing it now?'

'You may call me what you like,' said Miss Stanbury. 'Only, dear me! I never did see anybody so much altered.' Before she went up to dress herself for dinner, Miss Stanbury was quite restored to her good humour, as Dorothy could perceive.

The dinner passed off well enough. Mr Gibson, at the head of the table, did, indeed, look very much out of his element, as though he conceived that his position revealed to the outer world those ideas of his in regard to Dorothy, which ought to have been secret for a while longer. There are few men who do not feel ashamed of being paraded before the world as acknowledged suitors, whereas ladies accept the position with something almost of triumph. The lady perhaps regards herself as the successful angler, whereas the gentleman is conscious of some similitude to the unsuccessful fish. Mr Gibson, though he was not yet gasping in the basket, had some presentiment of this feeling, which made his present seat of honour unpleasant to him. Brooke Burgess, at the other end of the table, was as gay as a lark. Mrs MacHugh sat on one side of him, and Miss Stanbury on the other, and he laughed at the two old ladies, reminding them of his former doings in Exeter, how he had hunted Mrs MacHugh's cat, and had stolen Aunt Stanbury's best apricot jam, till everybody began to perceive that he was quite a success. Even Sir Peter Mancrudy laughed at his jokes, and Mrs Powel, from the other side of Sir Peter, stretched her head forward so that she might become one of the gay party.

'There isn't a word of it true,' said Miss Stanbury. 'It's all pure invention, and a great scandal. I never did such a thing in my life.'

'Didn't you though?' said Brooke Burgess. 'I remember it as well as if it was yesterday, and old Dr. Ball, the prebendary, with the carbuncles on his nose, saw it too!'

'Dr. Ball had no carbuncles on his nose,' said Mrs MacHugh. 'You'll say next that I have carbuncles on my nose.'

'He had three. I remember each of them quite well, and so does Sir Peter.'

Then everybody laughed; and Martha, who was in the room, knew that Brooke Burgess was a complete success.

In the meantime Mr Gibson was talking to Dorothy; but Dorothy was endeavouring to listen to the conversation at the other end of the table. 'I found it very dirty on the roads to-day outside the city,' said Mr Gibson.

'Very dirty,' said Dorothy, looking round at Mr Burgess, as she spoke.

'But the pavement in the High Street was dry enough.'

'Quite dry,' said Dorothy. Then there came a peal of laughter from Mrs MacHugh and Sir Peter, and Dorothy wondered whether anybody before had ever made those two steady old people laugh after that fashion.

'I should so like to get a drive with you up to the top of Haldon Hill,' said Mr Gibson. 'When the weather gets fine, that is. Mrs Powel was talking about it.'

'It would be very nice,' said Dorothy.

'You have never seen the view from Haldon Hill yet?' asked Mr Gibson. But to this question Dorothy could make no answer. Miss Stanbury had lifted one of the table-spoons, as though she was going to strike Mr Brooke Burgess with the bowl of it. And this during a dinner party! From that moment Dorothy turned herself round, and became one of the listeners to the fun at the other end of the table; Poor Mr Gibson soon found himself 'nowhere.'

'I never saw a man so much altered in my life,' said Mrs MacHugh, up in the drawing-room.

'I don't remember that he used to be clever.'

'He was a bright boy!' said Miss Stanbury.

'But the Burgesses all used to be such serious, straitlaced people,' said Mrs MacHugh. 'Excellent people,' she added, remembering the source of her friend's wealth; 'but none of them like that.'

'I call him a very handsome man,' said Mrs Powel. 'I suppose he's not married yet?'

'Oh, dear no,' said Miss Stanbury. 'There's time enough for him yet.'

'He'll find plenty here to set their caps at him,' said Mrs MacHugh.

'He's a little old for my girls,' said Mrs Powel, laughing. Mrs Powel was the happy mother of four daughters, of whom the eldest was only twelve.

'There are others who are more forward,' said Mrs MacHugh. 'What a chance it would be for dear Arabella French!'

'Heaven forbid!' said Miss Stanbury.

'And then poor Mr Gibson wouldn't any longer be like the donkey between two bundles of hay,' said Mrs Powel. Dorothy was quite determined that she would never marry a man who was like a donkey between two bundles of hay.

When the gentlemen came up into the drawing-room Dorothy was seated behind the urn and tea-things at a large table, in such a position as to be approached only at one side. There was one chair at her left hand, but at her right hand there was no room for a seat, only room for some civil gentleman to take away full cups and bring them back empty. Dorothy was not sufficiently ready-witted to see the danger of this position till Mr Gibson had seated himself in the chair. Then it did seem cruel to her that she should be thus besieged for the rest of the evening as she had been also at dinner. While the tea was being consumed Mr Gibson assisted at the service, asking ladies whether they would have cake or bread and butter; but when all that was over Dorothy was still in her prison, and Mr Gibson was still the jailer at the gate. She soon perceived that everybody else was chatting and laughing, and that Brooke Burgess was the centre of a little circle which had formed itself quite at a distance from her seat. Once, twice, thrice she meditated an escape, but she had not the courage to make the attempt. She did not know how to manage it. She was conscious that her aunt's eye was upon her, and that her aunt would expect her to listen to Mr Gibson. At last she gave up all hope of moving, and was anxious simply that Mr Gibson should confine himself to the dirt of the paths and the noble prospect from Haldon Hill.

'I think we shall have more rain before we have done with it,' he said. Twice before during the evening he had been very eloquent about the rain.

'I dare say we shall,' said Dorothy. And then there came the sound of loud laughter from Sir Peter, and Dorothy could see that he was poking Brooke Burgess in the ribs. There had never been anything so gay before since she had been in Exeter, and now she was hemmed up in that corner, away from it all, by Mr Gibson!

'This Mr Burgess seems to be different from the other Burgesses,' said Mr Gibson.

'I think he must be very clever,' said Dorothy.

'Well yes; in a sort of a way. What people call a Merry Andrew.'

'I like people who make me laugh and laugh themselves,' said Dorothy.

'I quite agree with you that laughter is a very good thing in its place. I am not at all one of those who would make the world altogether grave. There are serious things, and there must be serious moments.'

'Of course,' said Dorothy.

'And I think that serious conversation upon the whole has more allurements than conversation which when you come to examine it is found to mean nothing. Don't you?'

'I suppose everybody should mean something when he talks.'

'Just so. That is exactly my idea,' said Mr Gibson. 'On all such subjects as that I should be so sorry if you and I did not agree. I really should.' Then he paused, and Dorothy was so confounded by what she conceived to be the dangers of the coming moment that she was unable even to think what she ought to say. She heard Mrs MacHugh's clear, sharp, merry voice, and she heard her aunt's tone of pretended anger, and she heard Sir Peter's continued laughter, and Brooke Burgess as he continued the telling of some story; but her own trouble was too great to allow of her attending to what was going on at the other end of the room. 'There is nothing as to which I am so anxious as that you and I should agree about serious things,' said Mr Gibson.

'I suppose we do agree about going to church,' said Dorothy. She knew that she could have made no speech more stupid, more senseless, more inefficacious but what was she to say in answer to such an assurance?

'I hope so,' said Mr Gibson; 'and I think so. Your aunt is a most excellent woman, and her opinion has very great weight with me on all subjects even as to matters of church discipline and doctrine, in which, as a clergyman, I am of course presumed to be more at home. But your aunt is a woman among a thousand.'

'Of course I think she is very good.'

'And she is so right about this young man and her property. Don't you think so?'

'Quite right, Mr Gibson.'

'Because, you know, to you, of course, being her near relative, and the one she has singled out as the recipient of her kindness, it might have been cause for some discontent.'

'Discontent to me, Mr Gibson!'

'I am quite sure your feelings are what they ought to be. And for myself, if I ever were that is to say, supposing I could be in any way interested. But perhaps it is premature to make any suggestion on that head at present.'

'I don't at all understand what you mean, Mr Gibson.'

'I thought that perhaps I might take this opportunity of expressing-. But, after all, the levity of the moment is hardly in accordance with the sentiments which I should wish to express.'

'I think that I ought to go to my aunt now, Mr Gibson, as perhaps she might want something.' Then she did push back her chair and stand upon her legs-and Mr Gibson, after pausing for a moment, allowed her to escape. Soon after that the visitors went, and Brooke Burgess was left in the drawing-room with Miss Stanbury and Dorothy.

'How well I recollect all the people,' said Brooke; 'Sir Peter, and old Mrs MacHugh; and Mrs Powel who then used to be called the beautiful Miss Noel. And I remember every bit of furniture in the room.'

'Nothing changed except the old woman, Brooke,' said Miss Stanbury.

'Upon my word you are the least changed of all except that you don't seem to be so terrible as you were then.'

'Was I very terrible, Brooke?'

'My mother had told me, I fancy, that I was never to make a noise, and be sure not to break any of the china. You were always very good-natured, and when you gave me a silver watch I could hardly believe the extent of my own bliss.'

'You wouldn't care about a watch from an old woman now, Brooke?'

'You try me. But what rakes you are here! It's past eleven o'clock, and I must go and have a smoke.'

'Have a what?' said Miss Stanbury, with a startled air.

'A smoke. You needn't be frightened, I don't mean in the house.'

'No I hope you don't mean that.'

'But I may take a turn round the Close with a pipe mayn't I?'

'I suppose all young men do smoke now,' said Miss Stanbury, sorrowfully.

'Every one of them; and they tell me that the young women mean to take to it before long.'

'If I saw a young woman smoking, I should blush for my sex; and though she were the nearest and dearest that I had, I would never speak to her never. Dorothy, I don't think Mr Gibson smokes.'

'I'm sure I don't know, aunt.'

'I hope he doesn't. I do hope that he does not. I cannot understand what pleasure it is that men take in making chimneys of themselves, and going about smelling so that no one can bear to come near them.'

Brooke merely laughed at this, and went his way, and smoked his pipe out in the Close, while Martha sat up to let him in when he had finished it. Then Dorothy escaped at once to her room, fearful of being questioned by her aunt about Mr Gibson. She had, she thought now, quite made up her mind. There was nothing in Mr Gibson that she liked. She was by no means so sure as she had been when she was talking to her sister, that she would prefer a clergyman to any one else. She had formed no strong ideas on the subject of lovemaking, but she did think that any man who really cared for her would find some other way of expressing his love than that which Mr Gibson had adopted. And then Mr Gibson had spoken to her about her aunt's money in a way that was distasteful to her. She thought that she was quite sure that if he should ask her, she would not accept him.

She was nearly undressed, nearly safe for the night, when there came a knock at the door, and her aunt entered the room. 'He has come in,' said Miss Stanbury.

'I suppose he has had his pipe, then.'

'I wish he didn't smoke. I do wish he didn't smoke. But I suppose an old woman like me is only making herself a fool to care about such things. If they all do it I can't prevent them. He seems to be a very nice young man in other things; does he not, Dolly?'

'Very nice indeed, Aunt Stanbury.'

'And he has done very well in his office. And as for his saying that he must smoke, I like that a great deal better than doing it on the sly.'

'I don't think Mr Burgess would do anything on the sly, aunt.'

'No, no; I don't think he would. Dear me; he's not at all like what I fancied.'

'Everybody seemed to like him very much.'

'Didn't they. I never saw Sir Peter so much taken. And there was quite a flirtation between him and Mrs MacHugh. And now, my dear, tell me about Mr Gibson.'

'There is nothing to tell, Aunt Stanbury.'

'Isn't there? From what I saw going on, I thought there would be something to tell. He was talking to you the whole evening.'

'As it happened he was sitting next to me of course.'

'Indeed he was sitting next to you so much so that I thought everything would be settled.'

'If I tell you something, Aunt Stanbury, you mustn't be angry with me.'

'Tell me what? What is it you have to tell me?'

'I don't think I shall ever care for Mr Gibson not in that way.'

'Why not, Dorothy?'

'I'm sure he doesn't care for me. And I don't think he means it.'

'I tell you he does mean it. Mean it! Why, I tell you it has all been settled between us. Since I first spoke to you I have explained to him exactly what I intend to do, He knows that he can give up his house and come and live here. I am sure he must have said something about it to you tonight.'

'Not a word, Aunt Stanbury.'

'Then he will.'

'Dear aunt, I do so wish you would prevent it. I don't like him. I don't indeed.'

'Not like him!'

'No I don't care for him a bit, and I never shall. I can't help it, Aunt Stanbury. I thought I would try, but I find it would be impossible. You can't want me to marry a man if I don't love him.'

'I never heard of such a thing in my life. Not love him! And why shouldn't you love him? He's a gentleman. Everybody respects him. He'll have plenty to make you comfortable all your life! And then why didn't you tell me before?'

'I didn't know, Aunt Stanbury. I thought that perhaps—'

'Perhaps what?'

'I could not say all at once that I didn't care for him, when I had never so much as thought about it for a moment before.'

'You haven't told him this?'

'No, I have not told him. I couldn't begin by telling him, you know.'

'Then I must pray that you will think about it again. Have you imagined what a great thing for you it would be to be established for life so that you should never have any more trouble again about a home, or about money, or anything? Don't answer me now, Dorothy, but think of it. It seemed to me that I was doing such an excellent thing for both of you.' So saying Miss Stanbury left the room, and Dorothy was enabled to obey her, at any rate, in one matter. She did think of it. She laid awake thinking of it almost all the night. But the more she thought of it, the less able was she to realise to herself any future comfort or happiness in the idea of becoming Mrs Gibson.

CHAPTER XXXII. THE 'FULL MOON' AT ST. DIDDULPH'S

The receipt of Mrs Trevelyan's letter on that Monday morning was a great surprise both to Mr and Mrs Outhouse. There was no time for any consideration, no opportunity for delaying their arrival till they should have again referred the matter to Mr Trevelyan. Their two nieces were to be with them on that evening, and even the telegraph wires, if employed with such purpose, would not be quick enough to stop their coming. The party, as they knew, would have left Nuncombe Putney before the arrival of the letter at the parsonage of St. Diddulph's. There would have been nothing in this to have caused vexation, had it not been decided between Trevelyan and Mr Outhouse that Mrs Trevelyan was not to find a home at the parsonage. Mr Outhouse was greatly afraid of being so entangled in the matter as to be driven to take the part of the wife against the husband; and Mrs Outhouse, though she was full of indignation against Trevelyan, was at the same time not free from anger in regard to her own niece. She more than once repeated that most unjust of all proverbs, which declares that there is never smoke without fire, and asserted broadly that she did not like to be with people who could not live at home, husbands with wives, and wives with husbands, in a decent, respectable manner. Nevertheless the preparations went on busily, and when the party arrived at seven o'clock in the evening, two rooms had been prepared close to each other, one for the two sisters, and the other for the child and nurse, although poor Mr Outhouse himself was turned out of his own little chamber in order that the accommodation might be given. They were all very hot, very tired, and very dusty, when the cab reached the parsonage. There had been the preliminary drive from Nuncombe Putney to Lessboro'. Then the railway journey from thence to the Waterloo Bridge Station had been long. And it had seemed to them that the distance from the station to St. Diddulph's had been endless. When the cabman was told whither he was to go, he looked doubtingly at his poor old horse, and then at the luggage which he was required to pack on the top of his cab, and laid himself out for his work with a full understanding that it would not be accomplished without considerable difficulty. The cabman made it twelve miles from Waterloo Bridge to St. Diddulph's, and suggested that extra passengers and parcels would make the fare up to ten and six. Had he named double as much Mrs Trevelyan would have assented. So great was the fatigue, and so wretched the occasion, that there was sobbing and crying in the cab, and when at last the parsonage was reached, even the nurse was hardly able to turn her hand to anything. The poor wanderers were made welcome on that evening without a word of discussion as to the cause of their coming. 'I hope you are not angry with us, Uncle Oliphant,' Emily Trevelyan had said, with tears in her eyes. 'Angry with you, my dear, for coming to our house! How could I be angry with you?' Then the travellers were hurried upstairs by Mrs Outhouse, and the master of the parsonage was left alone for a while. He certainly was not angry, but he was ill at ease, and unhappy. His guests would probably remain with him for six or seven months. He had resolutely refused all payment from Mr Trevelyan, but, nevertheless, he was a poor man. It is impossible to conceive that a clergyman in such a parish as St. Diddulph's, without a private income, should not be a poor man. It was but a hand-to-mouth existence which he lived, paying his way as his money came to him, and sharing the proceeds of his parish with the poor. He was always more or less in debt. That was quite understood among the tradesmen. And the butcher who trusted him, though he was a bad churchman, did not look upon the parson's account as he did on other debts. He would often hint to Mr Outhouse that a little money ought to be paid, and then a little money would be paid. But it was never expected that the parsonage bill should be settled. In such a household the arrival of four guests, who were expected to remain for an almost indefinite number of months, could not be regarded without dismay. On that first evening, Emily and Nora did come down to tea, but they went up again to their rooms almost immediately afterwards; and Mr Outhouse found that many hours of solitary meditation were allowed to him on the occasion. 'I suppose your brother has been told all about it,' he said to his wife, as soon as they were together on that evening.

'Yes he has been told. She did not write to her mother till after she had got to Nuncombe Putney. She did not like to speak about her troubles while there was a hope that things might be made smooth.'

'You can't blame her for that, my dear.'

'But there was a month lost, or nearly. Letters go only once a month. And now they can't hear from Marmaduke or Bessy,' Lady Rowley's name was Bessy, 'till the beginning of September.'

'That will be in a fortnight.'

'But what can my brother say to them? He will suppose that they are still down in Devonshire.'

'You don't think he will come at once?'

'How can he, my dear? He can't come without leave, and the expense would be ruinous. They would stop his pay, and there would be all manner of evils. He is to come in the spring, and they must stay here till he comes.' The parson of St. Diddulph's sighed and groaned. Would it not have been almost better that he should have put his pride in his pocket, and have consented to take Mr Trevelyan's money?

On the second morning Hugh Stanbury called at the parsonage, and was closeted for a while with the parson. Nora had heard his voice in the passage, and every one in the house knew who it was that was talking to Mr Outhouse, in the little back parlour that was called a study. Nora was full of anxiety. Would he ask to see them to see her? And why was he there so long? 'No doubt he has brought a message from Mr Trevelyan,' said her sister. 'I dare say he will send word that I ought not to have come to my uncle's house.' Then, at last, both Mr Outhouse and Hugh Stanbury came into the room in which they were all sitting. The greetings were cold and unsatisfactory, and Nora barely allowed Hugh to touch the tip of her fingers. She was very angry with him, and yet she knew that her anger was altogether unreasonable. That he had caused her to refuse a marriage that had so much to attract her was not his sin, not that; but that, having thus overpowered her by his influence, he should then have stopped. And yet Nora had told herself twenty times that it was quite impossible that she should become Hugh Stanbury's wife and that, were Hugh Stanbury to ask her, it would become her to be indignant with him, for daring to make a proposition so outrageous. And now she was sick at heart, because he did not speak to her!

He had, of course, come to St. Diddulph's with a message from Trevelyan, and his secret was soon told to them all. Trevelyan himself was upstairs in the sanded parlour of the Full Moon public-house, round the corner. Mrs Trevelyan, when she heard this, clasped her hands and bit her lips. What was he there for? If he wanted to see her, why did he not come boldly to the parsonage? But it soon appeared that he had no desire to see his wife. 'I am to take Louey to him,' said Hugh Stanbury, 'if you will allow me.'

'What to be taken away from me!' exclaimed the mother. But Hugh assured her that no such idea had been formed; that he would have concerned himself in no such stratagem, and that he would himself undertake to bring the boy back again within an hour. Emily was, of course, anxious to be informed what other message was to be conveyed to her; but there was no other message—no message either of love or of instruction.

'Mr Stanbury,' said the parson, 'has left me something in my hands for you.' This 'something' was given over to her as soon as Stanbury had left the house, and consisted of cheques for various small sums, amounting in all to 200 pounds. 'And he hasn't said what I am to do with it?' Emily asked of her uncle. Mr Outhouse declared that the cheques had been given to him without any instructions on that head. Mr Trevelyan had simply expressed his satisfaction that his wife should be with her uncle and aunt, had sent the money, and had desired to see the child.

The boy was got ready, and Hugh walked with him in his arms round the corner, to the Full Moon. He had to pass by the bar, and the barmaid and the potboy looked at him very hard. 'There's a young 'ooman has to do with that ere little game,' said the potboy 'And it's two to one the young 'ooman has the worst of it,' said the barmaid. 'They mostly does,' said the potboy, not without some feeling of pride in the immunities of his sex. 'Here he is,' said Hugh, as he entered the parlour. 'My boy, there's papa.' The child at this time was more than a year old, and could crawl about and use his own legs with the assistance of a finger to his little hand, and could utter a sound which the fond mother interpreted to mean papa; for with all her hot anger against her husband, the mother was above all things anxious that her child should be taught to love his father's name. She would talk of her separation from her husband as though it must be permanent; she would declare to her sister how impossible it was that they should ever again live together; she would repeat to herself over and over the tale of the injustice that had been done to her, assuring herself that it was out of the question that she should ever pardon the man; but yet, at the bottom of her heart, there was a hope that the quarrel should be healed before her boy would be old enough to understand the nature of quarrelling. Trevelyan took the child on to his knee, and kissed him; but the poor little fellow, startled by his transference from one male set of arms to another, confused by the strangeness of the room, and by the absence of things familiar to his sight, burst out into loud tears. He had stood the journey round the corner in Hugh's arms manfully, and, though he had looked about him with very serious eyes, as he passed through the bar, he had borne that, and his carriage up the stairs; but when he was transferred to his father, whose air, as he took the boy, was melancholy and lugubrious in the extreme, the poor little fellow could endure no longer a mode of treatment so unusual, and, with a grimace which for a moment or two threatened the coming storm, burst out with an infantile howl. 'That's how he has been taught,' said Trevelyan.

'Nonsense,' said Stanbury. 'He's not been taught at all. It's Nature.'

'Nature that he should be afraid of his own father! He did not cry when he was with you.'

'No as it happened, he did not. I played with him when I was at Nuncombe; but, of course, one can't tell when a child will cry, and when it won't.'

'My darling, my dearest, my own son!' said Trevelyan, caressing the child, and trying to comfort him; but the poor little fellow only cried the louder. It was now nearly two months since he had seen his father, and, when age is counted by months only, almost everything may be forgotten in six weeks. 'I suppose you must take him back again,' said Trevelyan, sadly.

'Of course, I must take him back again. Come along, Louey, my boy.'

'It is cruel very cruel,' said Trevelyan. 'No man living could love his child better than I love mine or, for the matter of that, his wife. It is very cruel.'

'The remedy is in your own hands, Trevelyan,' said Stanbury, as he marched off with the boy in his arms.

Trevelyan had now become so accustomed to being told by everybody that he was wrong, and was at the same time so convinced that he was right, that he regarded the perversity of his friends as a part of the persecution to which he was subjected. Even Lady Milborough, who objected to Colonel Osborne quite as strongly as did Trevelyan himself, even she blamed him now, telling him that he had done wrong to separate himself from his wife. Mr Bideawhile, the old family lawyer, was of the same opinion. Trevelyan had spoken to Mr Bideawhile as to the expediency of making some lasting arrangement for a permanent maintenance for his wife; but the attorney had told him that nothing of the kind could be held to be lasting. It was clearly the husband's duty to look forward to a reconciliation, and Mr Bideawhile became quite severe in the tone of rebuke which he assumed. Stanbury treated him almost as though he were a madman. And as for his wife herself when she wrote to him she would not even pretend to express any feeling of affection. And yet, as he thought, no man had ever done more for a wife. When Stanbury had gone with the child, he sat waiting for him in the parlour of the public-house, as miserable a man as one could find.

He had promised himself something that should be akin to pleasure in seeing his boy but it had been all disappointment and pain. What was it that they expected him to do? What was it that they desired? His wife had behaved with such indiscretion as almost to have compromised his honour; and in return for that he was to beg her pardon, confess himself to have done wrong, and allow her to return in triumph! That was the light in which he regarded his own position; but he promised to himself that let his own misery be what it might he would never so degrade him. The only person who had been true to him was Bozzle. Let them all look to it. If there were any further intercourse between his wife and Colonel Osborne, he would take the matter into open court, and put her away publicly, let Mr Bideawhile say what he might. Bozzle should see to that and as to himself, he would take himself out of England and hide himself abroad. Bozzle should know his address, but he would give it to no one else. Nothing on earth should make him yield to a woman who had ill-treated him nothing but confession and promise of amendment on her part. If she would acknowledge and promise, then he would forgive all, and the events of the last four months should never again be mentioned by him. So resolving he sat and waited till Stanbury should return to him.

When Stanbury got back to the parsonage with the boy he had nothing to do but to take his leave. He would fain have asked permission to come again, could he have invented any reason for doing so. But the child was taken from him at once by its mother, and he was left alone with Mr Outhouse. Nora Rowley did not even show herself, and he hardly knew how to express sympathy and friendship for the guests at the parsonage, without seeming to be untrue to his friend Trevelyan. 'I hope all this may come to an end soon,' he said.

'I hope it may, Mr Stanbury,' said the clergyman; 'but to tell you the truth, it seems to me that Mr Trevelyan is so unreasonable a man, so much like a madman indeed, that I hardly know how to look forward to any future happiness for my niece.' This was spoken with the utmost severity that Mr Outhouse could assume.

'And yet no man loves his wife more tenderly.'

'Tender love should show itself by tender conduct, Mr Stanbury. What has he done to his wife? He has blackened her name among all his friends and hers, he has turned her out of his house, he has reviled her and then thinks to prove how good he is by sending her money. The only possible excuse is that he must be mad.'

Stanbury went back to the Full Moon, and retraced his steps with his friend towards Lincoln's Inn. Two minutes took him from the parsonage to the public-house, but during these two minutes he resolved that he would speak his mind roundly to Trevelyan as they returned home. Trevelyan should either take his wife back again at once, or else he, Stanbury, would have no more to do with him. He said nothing till they had threaded together the maze of streets which led them from the neighbourhood of the Church of St. Diddulph's into the straight way of the Commercial Road. Then he began. 'Trevelyan,' said he, 'you are wrong in all this from beginning to end.'

'What do you mean?'

'Just what I say. If there was anything in what your wife did to offend you, a soft word from you would have put it all right.'

'A soft word! How do you know what soft words I used?'

'A soft word now would do it. You have only to bid her come back to you, and let bygones be bygones, and all would be right. Can't you be man enough to remember that you are a man?'

'Stanbury, I believe you want to quarrel with me.'

'I tell you fairly that I think that you are wrong.'

'They have talked you over to their side.'

'I know nothing about sides. I only know that you are wrong.'

'And what would you have me do?'

'Go and travel together for six months.' Here was Lady Milborough's receipt again! 'Travel together for a year if you will. Then come back and live where you please. People will have forgotten it or if they remember it, what matters? No sane person can advise you to go on as you are doing now.'

But it was of no avail. Before they had reached the Bank the two friends had quarrelled and had parted.

Then Trevelyan felt that there was indeed no one left to him but Bozzle. On the following morning he saw Bozzle, and on the evening of the next day he was in Paris.

CHAPTER XXXIII. HUGH STANBURY SMOKES ANOTHER PIPE

Trevelyan was gone, and Bozzle alone knew his address. During the first fortnight of her residence at St. Diddulph's Mrs Trevelyan received two letters from Lady Milborough, in both of which she was recommended, indeed tenderly implored, to be submissive to her husband. 'Anything,' said Lady Milborough, 'is better than separation.' In answer to the second letter Mrs Trevelyan told the old lady that she had no means by which she could shew any submission to her husband, even if she were so minded. Her husband had gone away, she did not know whither, and she had no means by which she could communicate with him. And then came a packet to her from her father and mother, despatched from the islands after the receipt by Lady Rowley of the melancholy tidings of the journey to Nuncombe Putney. Both Sir Marmaduke and Lady Rowley were full of anger against Trevelyan, and wrote as though the husband could certainly be brought back to a sense of his duty, if they only were present. This packet had been at Nuncombe Putney, and contained a sealed note from Sir Marmaduke addressed to Mr Trevelyan. Lady Rowley explained that it was impossible that they should get to England earlier than in the spring. 'I would come myself at once and leave papa to follow,' said Lady Rowley, 'only for the children. If I were to bring them, I must take a house for them, and the expense would ruin us. Papa has written to Mr Trevelyan in a way that he thinks will bring him to reason.'

But how was this letter, by which the husband was to be brought to reason, to be put into the husband's hands? Mrs Trevelyan applied to Mr Bideawhile and to Lady Milborough, and to Stanbury, for Trevelyan's address; but was told by each of them that nothing was known of his whereabouts. She did not apply to Mr Bozzle, although Mr Bozzle was more than once in her neighbourhood; but as yet she knew nothing of Mr Bozzle. The replies from Mr Bideawhile and from Lady Milborough came by the post; but Hugh Stanbury thought that duty required him to make another journey to St. Diddulph's and carry his own answer with him.

And on this occasion Fortune was either very kind to him or very unkind. Whichever it was, he found himself alone for a few seconds in the parsonage parlour with Nora Rowley. Mr Outhouse was away at the time. Emily had gone upstairs for the boy; and Mrs Outhouse, suspecting nothing, had followed her.

'Miss Rowley,' said he, getting up from his seat, 'if you think it will do any good I will follow Trevelyan till I find him.'

'How can you find him? Besides, why should you give up your own business?'

'I would do anything to serve your sister.' This he said with hesitation in his voice, as though he did not dare to speak all that he desired to have spoken.

'I am sure that Emily is very grateful,' said Nora; 'but she would not wish to give you such trouble as that.'

'I would do anything for your sister,' he repeated, 'for your sake, Miss Rowley.' This was the first time that he had ever spoken a word to her in such a strain, and it would be hardly too much to say that her heart was sick for some such expression. But now that it had come, though there was a sweetness about it that was delicious to her, she was absolutely silenced by it.

And she was at once not only silent, but stern, rigid, and apparently cold. Stanbury could not but feel as he looked at her that he had offended her. 'Perhaps I ought not to say as much,' said he; 'but it is so.'

'Mr Stanbury,' said she, 'that is nonsense. It is of my sister, not of me, that we are speaking.'

Then the door was opened and Emily came in with her child, followed by her aunt. There was no other opportunity, and perhaps it was well for Nora and for Hugh that there should have been no other. Enough had been said to give her comfort; and more might have led to his discomposure. As to that matter on which he was presumed to have come to St. Diddulph's, he could do nothing. He did not know Trevelyan's address, but did know that Trevelyan had abandoned the chambers in Lincoln's Inn. And then he found himself compelled to confess that he had quarrelled with Trevelyan, and that they had parted in anger on the day of their joint visit to the East. 'Everybody who knows him must quarrel with him,' said Mrs Outhouse. Hugh when he took his leave was treated by them all as a friend who had been gained. Mrs Outhouse was gracious to him. Mrs Trevelyan whispered a word to him of her own trouble. 'If I can hear anything of him, you may be sure that I will let you know,' he said. Then it was Nora's turn to bid him adieu. There was nothing to be said. No word could be spoken before others that should be of any avail. But as he took her hand in his he remembered the reticence of her fingers on that former day, and thought that he was sure there was a difference.

On this occasion he made his journey back to the end of Chancery Lane on the top of an omnibus; and as he lit his little pipe, disregarding altogether the scrutiny of the public, thoughts passed through his mind similar to those in which he had indulged as he sat smoking on the corner of the churchyard wall at Nuncombe

Putney. He declared to himself that he did love this girl; and as it was so, would it not be better, at any rate more manly, that he should tell her so honestly, than go on groping about with half-expressed words when he saw her, thinking of her and yet hardly daring to go near her, bidding himself to forget her although he knew that such forgetting was impossible, hankering after the sound of her voice and the touch of her hand, and something of the tenderness of returned affection and yet regarding her as a prize altogether out of his reach! Why should she be out of his reach? She had no money, and he had not a couple of hundred pounds in the world. But he was earning an income which would give them both shelter and clothes and bread and cheese.

What reader is there, male or female, of such stories as is this, who has not often discussed in his or her own mind the different sides of this question of love and marriage? On either side enough may be said by any arguer to convince at any rate himself. It must be wrong for a man, whose income is both insufficient and precarious also, not only to double his own cares and burdens, but to place the weight of that doubled burden on other shoulders besides his own, on shoulders that are tender and soft, and ill adapted to the carriage of any crushing weight. And then that doubled burden, that burden of two mouths to be fed, of two backs to be covered, of two minds to be satisfied, is so apt to double itself again and again The two so speedily become four, and six! And then there is the feeling that that kind of semi-poverty, which has in itself something of the pleasantness of independence, when it is borne by a man alone, entails the miseries of a draggle-tailed and querulous existence when it is imposed on a woman who has in her own home enjoyed the comforts of affluence. As a man thinks of all this, if he chooses to argue with himself on that side, there is enough in the argument to make him feel that not only as a wise man but as an honest man, he had better let the young lady alone. She is well as she is, and he sees around him so many who have tried the chances of marriage and who are not well! Look at Jones with his wan, worn wife and his five children, Jones who is not yet thirty, of whom he happens to know that the wretched man cannot look his doctor in the face, and that the doctor is as necessary to the man's house as is the butcher! What heart can Jones have for his work with such a burden as this upon his shoulders? And so the thinker, who argues on that side, resolves that the young lady shall go her own way for him.

But the arguments on the other side are equally cogent, and so much more alluring! And they are used by the same man with reference to the same passion, and are intended by him to put himself right in his conduct in reference to the same dear girl. Only the former line of thoughts occurred to him on a Saturday, when he was ending his week rather gloomily, and this other way of thinking on the same subject has come upon him on a Monday, as he is beginning his week with renewed hope. Does this young girl of his heart love him? And if so, their affection for each other being thus reciprocal, is she not entitled to an expression of her opinion and her wishes on this difficult subject? And if she be willing to run the risk and to encounter the dangers, to do so on his behalf, because she is willing to share everything with him, is it becoming in him, a man, to fear what she does not fear? If she be not willing let her say so. If there be any speaking, he must speak first but she is entitled, as much as he is, to her own ideas respecting their great outlook into the affairs of the world. And then is it not manifestly God's ordinance that a man should live together with a woman? How poor a creature does the man become who has shirked his duty in this respect, who has done nothing to keep the world going, who has been willing to ignore all affection so that he might avoid all burdens, and who has put into his own belly every good thing that has come to him, either by the earning of his own hands or from the bounty and industry of others! Of course there is a risk; but what excitement is there in anything in which there is none? So on the Tuesday he speaks his mind to the young lady, and tells her candidly that there will be potatoes for the two of them sufficient, as he hopes, of potatoes, but no more. As a matter of course the young lady replies that she for her part will be quite content to take the parings for her own eating. Then they rush deliciously into each others arms and the matter is settled. For, though the convictions arising from the former line of argument may be set aside as often as need be, those reached from the latter are generally conclusive. That such a settlement will always be better for the young gentleman and the young lady concerned than one founded on a sterner prudence is more than one may dare to say; but we do feel sure that that country will be most prosperous in which such leaps in the dark are made with the greatest freedom.

Our friend Hugh, as he sat smoking on the knife-board of the omnibus, determined that he would risk everything. If it were ordained that prudence should prevail, the prudence should be hers. Why should he take upon himself to have prudence enough for two, seeing that she was so very discreet in all her bearings? Then he remembered the touch of her hand, which he still felt upon his palm as he sat handling his pipe, and he told himself that after that he was bound to say a word more. And moreover he confessed to himself that he was compelled by a feeling that mastered him altogether. He could not get through an hour's work without throwing down his pen and thinking of Nora Rowley. It was his destiny to love her and there was, to his mind, a mean, pettifogging secrecy, amounting almost to daily lying, in his thus loving her and not telling her that he loved her. It might well be that she should rebuke him; but he thought that he could bear that. It might well be that he had altogether mistaken that touch of her hand. After all it had been the slightest possible motion of no more than one finger. But he would at any rate know the truth. If she would tell him at once that she did not care for him, he thought that he could get over it; but life was not worth having while he lived in this shifty, dubious, and uncomfortable state. So he made up his mind that he would go to St. Diddulph's with his heart in his hand.

In the mean time, Mr Bozzle had been twice to St. Diddulph's and now he made a third journey there, two days after Stanbury's visit. Trevelyan, who, in truth, hated the sight of the man, and who suffered agonies in his presence, had, nevertheless, taught himself to believe that he could not live without his assistance. That it should be so was a part of the cruelty of his lot. Who else was there that he could trust? His wife had renewed her intimacy with Colonel Osborne the moment that she had left him. Mrs Stanbury, who had been represented to him as the most correct of matrons, had at once been false to him and to her trust, in allowing Colonel Osborne to enter her house. Mr and Mrs Outhouse, with whom his wife had now located herself, not by his orders, were, of course, his enemies. His old friend, Hugh Stanbury, had gone over to the other side, and had quarrelled with him purposely, with malice *prepense*, because he would not submit himself to the caprices of the wife who had injured him. His own lawyer had refused to act for him; and his fast and oldest ally, the very person who had sounded in his ear the earliest warning note against that odious villain, whose daily work it was to destroy the peace of families, even Lady Milborough had turned against him! Because he would not follow the stupid prescription which she, with pig-headed obstinacy, persisted in giving, because he would not carry his wife off to Naples, she was ill-judging and inconsistent enough to tell him that he was wrong! Who was then left to him but Bozzle? Bozzle was very disagreeable. Bozzle said things, and made suggestions to him which were as bad as pins stuck into his flesh. But Bozzle was true to his employer, and could find out facts. Had it not been for Bozzle, he would have known nothing of the Colonel's journey to Devonshire. Had it not been for Bozzle, he would never have heard of the correspondence; and, therefore, when he left London, he gave Bozzle a roving commission; and when he went to Paris, and from Paris onwards, over the Alps into Italy, he furnished Bozzle with his address. At this time, in the midst of all his misery, it never occurred to him to inquire of himself whether it might be possible that his old friends were right, and that he himself was wrong. From morning to night he sang to himself melancholy silent songs of inward wailing, as to the cruelty of his own lot in life and, in the mean time, he employed Bozzle to find out for him how far that cruelty was carried.

Mr Bozzle was, of course, convinced that the lady whom he was employed to watch was no better than she ought to be. That is the usual Bozzlian language for broken vows, secrecy, intrigue, dirt, and adultery. It was his business to obtain evidence of her guilt. There was no question to be solved as to her innocency. The Bozzlian mind would have regarded any such suggestion as the product of a green softness, the possession of which would have made him quite unfit for his profession. He was aware that ladies who are no better than they should be are often very clever, so clever, as to make it necessary that the Bozzles who shall at last confound them should be first-rate Bozzles, Bozzles quite at the top of their profession and, therefore, he went about his work with great industry and much caution. Colonel Osborne was at the present moment in Scotland. Bozzle was sure of that. He was quite in the north of Scotland. Bozzle had examined his map, and had found that Wick, which was the Colonel's post-town, was very far north indeed. He had half a mind to run down to Wick, as he was possessed by a certain honest zeal, which made him long to do something hard and laborious; but his experience told him that it was very easy for the Colonel to come up to the neighbourhood of St. Diddulph's, whereas the lady could not go down to Wick, unless she were to decide upon throwing herself into her lover's arms, whereby Bozzle's work would be brought to an end. He, therefore, confined his immediate operations to St. Diddulph's.

He made acquaintance with one or two important persons in and about Mr Outhouse's parsonage. He became very familiar with the postman. He arranged terms of intimacy, I am sorry to say, with the housemaid; and, on the third journey, he made an alliance with the potboy at the 'Full Moon'. The potboy remembered well the fact of the child being brought to 'our 'ouse,' as he called the Full Moon; and he was enabled to say, that the same 'gent as had brought the boy backards and forrards,' had since that been at the parsonage. But Bozzle was quite quick enough to perceive that all this had nothing to do with the Colonel. He was led, indeed, to fear that his 'governor,' as he was in the habit of calling Trevelyan in his half-spoken soliloquies, that his governor was not as true to him as he was to his governor. What business had that meddling fellow Stanbury at St. Diddulph's? for Trevelyan had not thought it necessary to tell his satellite that he had quarrelled with his friend. Bozzle was grieved in his mind when he learned that Stanbury's interference was still to be dreaded; and wrote to his governor, rather severely, to that effect; but, when so writing, he was able to give no further information. Facts, in such cases, will not unravel themselves without much patience on the part of the investigators.

CHAPTER XXXIV. PRISCILLA'S WISDOM

 On the night after the dinner party in the Close, Dorothy was not the only person in the house who laid awake thinking of what had taken place. Miss Stanbury also was full of anxiety, and for hour after hour could not sleep as she remembered the fruitlessness of her efforts on behalf of her nephew and niece.

It had never occurred to her when she had first proposed to herself that Dorothy should become Mrs Gibson that Dorothy herself would have any objection to such a step in life. Her fear had been that Dorothy would have become over-radiant with triumph at the idea of having a husband, and going to that husband with a fortune of her own. That Mr Gibson might hesitate, she had thought very likely. It is thus, in general, that women regard the feelings, desires, and aspirations of other women. You will hardly ever meet an elderly lady who will not speak of her juniors as living in a state of breathless anxiety to catch husbands. And the elder lady will speak of the younger as though any kind of choice in such catching was quite disregarded. The man must be a gentleman or, at least, gentlemanlike and there must be bread. Let these things be given, and what girl won't jump into what man's arms? Female reader, is it not thus that the elders of your sex speak of the younger? When old Mrs Stanbury heard that Nora Rowley had refused Mr Glascock, the thing was to her unintelligible; and it was now quite unintelligible to Miss Stanbury that Dorothy should prefer a single life to matrimony with Mr Gibson.

It must be acknowledged, on Aunt Stanbury's behalf, that Dorothy was one of those yielding, hesitating, submissive young women, trusting others but doubting ever of themselves, as to whom it is natural that their stronger friends should find it expedient to decide for them. Miss Stanbury was almost justified in thinking that unless she were to find a husband for her niece, her niece would never find one for herself. Dorothy would drift into being an old maid, like Priscilla, simply because she would never assert herself, never put her best foot foremost. Aunt Stanbury had therefore taken upon herself to put out a foot; and having carefully found that Mr Gibson was 'willing,' had conceived that all difficulties were over. She would be enabled to do her duty by her niece, and establish comfortably in life, at any rate, one of her brother's children. And now Dorothy was taking upon herself to say that she did not like the gentleman! Such conduct was almost equal to writing for a penny newspaper!

On the following morning, after breakfast, when Brooke Burgess was gone out to call upon his uncle, which he insisted upon doing openly, and not under the rose, in spite of Miss Stanbury's great gravity on the occasion, there was a very serious conversation, and poor Dorothy had found herself to be almost silenced. She did argue for a time; but her arguments seemed, even to herself, to amount to so little! Why shouldn't she love Mr Gibson? That was a question which she found it impossible to answer. And though she did not actually yield, though she did not say that she would accept the man, still, when she was told that three days were to be allowed to her for consideration, and that then the offer would be made to her in form, she felt that, as regarded the anti-Gibson interest, she had not a leg to stand upon. Why should not such an insignificant creature, as was she, love Mr Gibson or any other man, who had bread to give her, and was in some degree like a gentleman? On that night, she wrote the following letter to her sister:

The Close,
Tuesday

Dearest Priscilla,

I do so wish that you could be with me, so that I could talk to you again. Aunt Stanbury is the most affectionate and kindest friend in the world; but she has always been so able to have her own way, because she is both clever and good, that I find myself almost like a baby with her. She has been talking to me again about Mr Gibson; and it seems that Mr Gibson really does mean it. It is certainly very strange; but I do think now that it is true. He is to come on Friday. It seems very odd that it should all be settled for him in that way; but then Aunt Stanbury is so clever at settling things!

He sat next to me almost all the evening yesterday but he didn't say anything about it, except that he hoped I agreed with him about going to church, and all that. I suppose I do; and I am quite sure that if I were to be a clergyman's wife, I should endeavour to do whatever my husband thought right about religion. One ought to try to do so, even if the clergyman is not one's husband. Mr Burgess has come, and he was so very amusing all the evening, that perhaps that was the reason Mr Gibson said so little. Mr Burgess is a very nice man, and I think Aunt Stanbury is more fond of him than of anybody. He is not at all the sort of person that I expected.

But if Mr Gibson does come on Friday, and do really mean it, what am I to say to him? Aunt Stanbury will be very angry if I do not take her advice. I am quite sure that she intends it all for my happiness; and then, of course, she knows so much more about the world than I do. She asks me what it is that I expect. Of course, I do not expect anything. It is a great compliment from Mr Gibson, who is a clergyman, and thought well of by everybody. And nothing could be more respectable. Aunt

Stanbury says that with the money she would give us we should be quite comfortable; and she wants us to live in this house. She says that there are thirty girls round Exeter who would give their eyes for such a chance; and, looking at it in that light, of course, it is a very great thing for me. Only think how poor we have been! And then, dear Priscilla, perhaps he would let me be good to you and dear mamma!

But, of course, he will ask me whether I love him; and what am I to say? Aunt Stanbury says that I am to love him. "Begin to love him at once," she said this morning. I would if I could, partly for her sake, and because I do feel that it would be so respectable. When I think of it, it does seem such a pity that poor I should throw away such a chance. And I must say that Mr Gibson is very good, and most obliging; and everybody says that he has an excellent temper, and that he is a most prudent, well-dispositioned man. I declare, dear Priscilla, when I think of it, I cannot bring myself to believe that such a man should want me to be his wife.

But what ought I to do? I suppose when a girl is in love she is very unhappy if the gentleman does not propose to her. I am sure it would not make me at all unhappy if I were told that Mr Gibson had changed his mind.

Dearest Priscilla, you must write at once; because he is to be here on Friday. Oh, dear; Friday does seem to be so near! And I shall never know what to say to him, either one way or the other.

Your most affectionate sister,   Dorothy Stanbury.

P.S. Give my kindest love to mamma; but you need not tell her unless you think it best.

Priscilla received this letter on the Wednesday morning, and felt herself bound to answer it on that same afternoon. Had she postponed her reply for a day, it would still have been in Dorothy's hands before Mr Gibson could have come to her on the dreaded Friday morning. But still that would hardly give her time enough to consider the matter with any degree of deliberation after she should have been armed with what wisdom Priscilla might be able to send her. The post left Nuncombe Putney at three; and therefore the letter had to be written before their early dinner.

So Priscilla went into the garden and sat hers down under an old cedar that she might discuss the matter with herself in all its bearings. She felt that no woman could be called upon to write a letter that should be of more importance. The whole welfare in life of the person who was dearest to her would probably depend upon it. The weight upon her was so great that she thought for a while she would take counsel with her mother; but she felt sure that her mother would recommend the marriage; and that if she afterwards should find herself bound to oppose it, then her mother would be a miserable woman. There could be no use to her taking counsel with her mother, because her mother's mind was known to her beforehand. The responsibility was thrown upon her, and she alone must bear it.

She tried hard to persuade herself to write at once and tell her sister to marry the man. She knew her sister's heart so well as to be sure that Dorothy would learn to love the man who was her husband. It was almost impossible that Dorothy should not love those with whom she lived. And then her sister was so well adapted to be a wife and a mother. Her temper was so sweet, she was so pure, so unselfish, so devoted, and so healthy withal! She was so happy when she was acting for others; and so excellent in action when she had another one to think for her! She was so trusting and trustworthy that any husband would adore her! Then Priscilla walked slowly into the house, got her prayer-book, and returning to her seat under the tree, read the marriage service. It was one o'clock when she went upstairs to write her letter, and it had not yet struck eleven when she first seated herself beneath the tree. Her letter, when written, was as follows:

Nuncombe Putney,
August 25, 186—.

DEAREST DOROTHY,

I got your letter this morning, and I think it is better to answer it at once, as the time is very short. I have been thinking about it with all my mind, and I feel almost awe-stricken lest I should advise you wrongly. After all, I believe that your own dear sweet truth and honesty would guide you better than anybody else can guide you. You may be sure of this, that whichever way it is, I shall think that you have done right. Dearest sister, I suppose there can be no doubt that for most women a married life is happier than a single one. It is always thought so, as we may see by the anxiety of others to get married; and when an opinion becomes general, I think that the world is most often right. And then, my own one, I feel sure that you are adapted both for the cares and for the joys of married life. You would do your duty as a married woman happily, and would be a comfort to your husband not a thorn in his side, as are so many women.

'But, my pet, do not let that reasoning of Aunt Stanbury's about the thirty young girls who would give their eyes for Mr Gibson, have any weight with you. You should not take him because thirty other young girls would be glad to have him. And do not think too much of that respectability of which you speak. I would never advise my Dolly to marry any man unless she could be respectable in her new position; but that alone should go for nothing. Nor should our poverty. We shall not starve. And even if we did, that would be but a poor excuse.

I can find no escape from this that you should love him before you say that you will take him. But honest, loyal love need not, I take it, be of that romantic kind which people write about in novels and poetry. You need not think him to be perfect, or the best or grandest of men. Your heart will tell you whether he is dear to you. And remember, Dolly, that I shall remember that love itself must begin at some precise time. Though you had not learned to love him when you wrote on Tuesday, you may have begun to do so when you get this on Thursday.

If you find that you love him, then say that you will be his wife. If your heart revolts from such a declaration as being false if you cannot bring yourself to feel that you prefer him to others as the partner of your life then tell him, with thanks for his courtesy, that it cannot be as he would have it.

Yours always and ever most affectionately,   PRISCILLA.

CHAPTER XXXV. MR GIBSON'S GOOD FORTUNE

'I'll bet you half-a-crown, my lad, you're thrown over at last, like the rest of them. There's nothing she likes so much as taking some one up in order that she may throw him over afterwards.' It was thus that Mr Bartholomew Burgess cautioned his nephew Brooke.

'I'll take care that she shan't break my heart, Uncle Barty. I will go my way and she may go hers, and she may give her money to the hospital if she pleases.'

On the morning after his arrival Brooke Burgess had declared aloud in Miss Stanbury's parlour that he was going over to the bank to see his uncle. Now there was in this almost a breach of contract. Miss Stanbury, when she invited the young man to Exeter, had stipulated that there should be no intercourse between her house and the bank. 'Of course, I shall not need to know where you go or where you don't go,' she had written; 'but after all that has passed there must not be any positive intercourse between my house and the bank And now he had spoken of going over to C and B, as he called them, with the utmost indifference. Miss Stanbury had looked very grave, but had said nothing. She had determined to be on her guard, so that she should not be driven to quarrel with Brooke if she could avoid it.

Bartholomew Burgess was a tall, thin, ill-tempered old man, as well-known in Exeter as the cathedral, and respected after a fashion. No one liked him. He said ill-natured things of all his neighbours, and had never earned any reputation for doing good-natured acts. But he had lived in Exeter for nearly seventy years, and had achieved that sort of esteem which comes from long tenure. And he had committed no great iniquities in the course of his fifty years of business. The bank had never stopped payment, and he had robbed no one. He had not swallowed up widows and orphans, and had done his work in the firm of Cropper and Burgess after the old-fashioned safe manner, which leads neither to riches nor to ruin. Therefore he was respected. But he was a discontented, sour old man, who believed himself to have been injured by all his own friends, who disliked his own partners because they had bought that which had, at any rate, never belonged to him and whose strongest passion it was to hate Miss Stanbury of the Close.

'She's got a parson by the hand now,' said the uncle, as he continued his caution to the nephew.

'There was a clergyman there last night.'

'No doubt, and she'll play him off against you, and you against him; and then she'll throw you both over. I know her.'

'She has got a right to do what she likes with her own, Uncle Barty.'

'And how did she get it? Never mind. I'm not going to set you against her, if you're her favourite for the moment. She has a niece with her there hasn't she?'

'One of her brother's daughters.'

'They say she's going to make that clergyman marry her.'

'What, Mr Gibson?'

'Yes. They tell me he was as good as engaged to another girl, one of the Frenches of Heavitree. And therefore dear Jemima could do nothing better than interfere. When she has succeeded in breaking the girl's heart—'

'Which girl's heart, Uncle Barty?'

'The girl the man was to have married; when that's done she'll throw Gibson over. You'll see. She'll refuse to give the girl a shilling. She took the girl's brother by the hand ever so long, and then she threw him over. And she'll throw the girl over too, and send her back to the place she came from. And then she'll throw you over.'

'According to you, she must be the most malicious old woman that ever was allowed to live!'

'I don't think there are many to beat her, as far as malice goes. But you'll find out for yourself. I shouldn't be surprised if she were to tell you before long that you were to marry the niece.'

'I shouldn't think that such very hard lines either,' said Brooke Burgess.

'I've no doubt you may have her if you like,' said Barty, 'in spite of Mr Gibson. Only I should recommend you to take care and get the money first.'

When Brooke went back to the house in the Close, Miss Stanbury was quite fussy in her silence. She would have given much to have been told something about Barty, and, above all, to have learned what Barty had said about herself. But she was far too proud even to mention the old man's name of her own accord. She was quite sure that she had been abused. She guessed, probably with tolerable accuracy, the kind of things that had been said of her, and suggested to herself what answer Brooke would make to such accusations. But she had resolved to cloak it all in silence, and pretended for awhile not to remember the young man's declared intention when he left the house. 'It seems odd to me,' said Brooke, 'that Uncle Barty should always live alone as he does. He must have a dreary time of it.'

'I don't know anything about your Uncle Barty's manner of living.'

'No I suppose not. You and he are not friends.'

'By no means, Brooke.'

'He lives there all alone in that poky bank-house, and nobody ever goes near him. I wonder whether he has any friends in the city?'

'I really cannot tell you anything about his friends. And, to tell you the truth, Brooke, I don't want to talk about your uncle. Of course, you can go to see him when you please, but I'd rather you didn't tell me of your visits afterwards.'

'There is nothing in the world I hate so much as a secret,' said he. He had no intention in this of animadverting upon Miss Stanbury's secret enmity, nor had he purposed to ask any question as to her relations with the old man. He had alluded to his dislike of having secrets of his own. But she misunderstood him.

'If you are anxious to know—' she said, becoming very red in the face.

'I am not at all curious to know. You quite mistake me.'

'He has chosen to believe or to say that he believed that I wronged him in regard to his brother's will. I nursed his brother when he was dying as I considered it to be my duty to do. I cannot tell you all that story. It is too long, and too sad. Romance is very pretty in novels, but the romance of a life is always a melancholy matter. They are most happy who have no story to tell.'

'I quite believe that.'

'But your Uncle Barty chose to think indeed, I hardly know what he thought. He said that the will was a will of my making. When it was made I and his brother were apart; we were not even on speaking terms. There had been a quarrel, and all manner of folly. I am not very proud when I look back upon it. It is not that I think myself better than others; but your Uncle Brooke's will was made before we had come together again. When he was ill it was natural that I should go to him after all that had passed between us. Eh, Brooke?'

'It was womanly.'

'But it made no difference about the will. Mr Bartholomew Burgess might have known that at once, and must have known it afterwards. But he has never acknowledged that he was wrong, never even yet.'

'He could not bring himself to do that, I should say.'

'The will was no great triumph to me. I could have done without it. As God is my judge, I would not have lifted up my little finger to get either a part or the whole of poor Brooke's money. If I had known that a word would have done it, I would have bitten my tongue before it should have been spoken.' She had risen from her seat, and was speaking with a solemnity that almost filled her listener with awe. She was a woman short of stature; but now, as she stood over him, she seemed to be tall and majestic. 'But when the man was dead,' she continued, 'and the will was there the property was mine, and I was bound in duty to exercise the privileges and bear the responsibilities which the dead man had conferred upon me. It was Barty, then, who sent a low attorney to me, offering me a compromise. What had I to compromise? Compromise! No. If it was not mine by all the right the law could give, I would sooner have starved than have had a crust of bread out of the money.' She had now clenched both her fists, and was shaking them rapidly as she stood over him, looking down upon him.

'Of course it was your own.'

'Yes. Though they asked me to compromise, and sent messages to me to frighten me, both Barty and your Uncle Tom; ay, and your father too, Brooke; they did not dare to go to law. To law, indeed! If ever there was a good will in the world, the will of your Uncle Brooke was good. They could talk, and malign me, and tell lies as to dates, and strive to make my name odious in the county; but they knew that the will was good. They did not succeed very well in what they did attempt.'

'I would try to forget it all now, Aunt Stanbury.'

'Forget it! How is that to be done? How can the mind forget the history of its own life? No I cannot forget it. I can forgive it.'

'Then why not forgive it?'

'I do. I have. Why else are you here?'

'But forgive old Uncle Barty also!'

'Has he forgiven me? Come now. If I wished to forgive him, how should I begin? Would he be gracious if I went to him? Does he love me, do you think or hate me? Uncle Barty is a good hater. It is the best point about him. No, Brooke, we won't try the farce of a reconciliation after a long life of enmity. Nobody would believe us, and we should not believe each other.'

'Then I certainly would not try.'

'I do not mean to do so. The truth is, Brooke, you shall have it all when I'm gone, if you don't turn against me. You won't take to writing for penny newspapers, will you, Brooke?' As she asked the question she put one of her hands softly on his shoulder.

'I certainly shan't offend in that way.'

'And you won't be a Radical?'

'No, not a Radical.'

'I mean a man to follow Beales and Bright, a republican, a putter-down of the Church, a hater of the Throne. You won't take up that line, will you, Brooke?'

'It isn't my way at present, Aunt Stanbury. But a man shouldn't promise.'

'Ah me! It makes me sad when I think what the country is coming to. I'm told there are scores of members of Parliament who don't pronounce their *h*'s. When I was young, a member of Parliament used to be a gentleman and they've taken to ordaining all manner of people. It used to be the case that when you met a clergyman you met a gentleman. By-the-bye, Brooke, what do you think of Mr Gibson?'

'Mr Gibson! To tell the truth, I haven't thought much about him yet.'

'But you must think about him. Perhaps you haven't thought about my niece, Dolly Stanbury?'

'I think she's an uncommonly nice girl.'

'She's not to be nice for you, young man. She's to be married to Mr Gibson.'

'Are they engaged?'

'Well, no; but I intend that they shall be. You won't begrudge that I should give my little savings to one of my own name?'

'You don't know me, Aunt Stanbury, if you think that I should begrudge anything that you might do with your money.'

'Dolly has been here a month or two. I think it's three months since she came, and I do like her. She's soft and womanly, and hasn't taken up those vile, filthy habits which almost all the girls have adopted. Have you seen those Frenches with the things they have on their heads?'

'I was speaking to them yesterday.'

'Nasty sluts! You can see the grease on their foreheads when they try to make their hair go back in the dirty French fashion. Dolly is not like that is she?'

'She is not in the least like either of the Miss Frenches.'

'And now I want her to become Mrs Gibson. He is quite taken.'

'Is he?'

'Oh dear, yes. Didn't you see him the other night at dinner and afterwards? Of course he knows that I can give her a little bit of money, which always goes for something, Brooke. And I do think it would be such a nice thing for Dolly.'

'And what does Dolly think about it?'

'There's the difficulty. She likes him well enough; I'm sure of that. And she has no stuck-up ideas about herself. She isn't one of those who think that almost nothing is good enough for them. But—'

'She has an objection.'

'I don't know what it is. I sometimes think she is so bashful and modest she doesn't like to talk of being married even to an old woman like me.'

'Dear me! That's not the way of the age is it, Aunt Stanbury?'

'It's coming to that, Brooke, that the girls will ask the men soon. Yes and that they won't take a refusal either. I do believe that Camilla French did ask Mr Gibson.'

'And what did Mr Gibson say?'

'Ah I can't tell you that. He knows too well what he's about to take her. He's to come here on Friday at eleven, and you must be out of the way. I shall be out of the way too. But if Dolly says a word to you before that, mind you make her understand that she ought to accept Gibson.'

'She's too good for him, according to my thinking.'

'Don't you be a fool. How can any young woman be too good for a gentleman and a clergyman? Mr Gibson is a gentleman. Do you know, only you must not mention this, that I have a kind of idea we could get Nuncombe Putney for him. My father had the living, and my brother; and I should like it to go on in the family.'

No opportunity came in the way of Brooke Burgess to say anything in favour of Mr Gibson to Dorothy Stanbury. There did come to be very quickly a sort of intimacy between her and her aunt's favourite; but she was one not prone to talk about her own affairs. And as to such an affair as this, a question as to whether she should or should not give herself in marriage to her suitor, she, who could not speak of it even to her own sister without a blush, who felt confused and almost confounded when receiving her aunt's admonitions and instigations on the subject, would not have endured to hear Brooke Burgess speak on the matter. Dorothy did feel that a person easier to know than Brooke had never come in her way. She had already said as much to him as she had spoken to Mr Gibson in the three months that she had made his acquaintance. They had talked about Exeter, and about Mrs MacHugh, and the cathedral, and Tennyson's poems, and the London theatres, and Uncle Barty, and the family quarrel. They had become quite confidential with each other on some matters. But on this heavy subject of Mr Gibson and his proposal of marriage not a word had been said. When Brooke once mentioned Mr Gibson on the Thursday morning, Dorothy within a minute had taken an opportunity of escaping from the room.

But circumstances did give him an opportunity of speaking to Mr Gibson. On the Wednesday afternoon both he and Mr Gibson were invited to drink tea at Mrs French's house on that evening. Such invitations at Exeter were wont to be given at short dates, and both the gentlemen had said that they would go. Then Arabella French had called in the Close and had asked Miss Stanbury and Dorothy. It was well understood by Arabella that Miss Stanbury herself would not drink tea at Heavitree. And it may be that Dorothy's company was not in truth desired. The ladies both declined. 'Don't you stay at home for me, my dear,' Miss Stanbury said to her niece. But Dorothy had not been out without her aunt since she had been at Exeter, and understood perfectly that it would not be wise to commence the practice at the house of the Frenches. 'Mr Brooke is coming, Miss Stanbury; and Mr Gibson,' Miss French said. And Miss Stanbury had thought that there was some triumph in her tone. 'Mr Brooke can go where he pleases, my dear,' Miss Stanbury replied. 'And as for Mr Gibson, I am not his keeper.' The tone in which Miss Stanbury spoke would have implied great imprudence, had not the two ladies understood each other so thoroughly, and had not each known that it was so.

There was the accustomed set of people in Mrs French's drawing-room, the Crumbies, and the Wrights, and the Apjohns. And Mrs MacHugh came also knowing that there would be a rubber. 'Their naked shoulders don't hurt me,' Mrs MacHugh said, when her friend almost scolded her for going to the house. 'I'm not a young man. I don't care what they do to themselves.' 'You might say as much if they went naked altogether,' Miss Stanbury had replied in anger. 'If nobody else complained, I shouldn't,' said Mrs MacHugh. Mrs MacHugh got her rubber; and as she had gone for her rubber, on a distinct promise that there should be a rubber, and as there was a rubber, she felt that she had no right to say ill-natured things. 'What does it matter to me,' said Mrs MacHugh, 'how nasty she is? She's not going to be my wife.' 'Ugh!' exclaimed Miss Stanbury, shaking her head both in anger and disgust.

Camilla French was by no means so bad as she was painted by Miss Stanbury, and Brooke Burgess rather liked her than otherwise. And it seemed to him that Mr Gibson did not at all dislike Arabella, and felt no repugnance at either the lady's noddle or shoulders now that he was removed from Miss Stanbury's influence. It was clear enough also that Arabella had not given up the attempt, although she must have admitted to herself that the claims of Dorothy Stanbury were very strong. On this evening it seemed to have been specially permitted to Arabella, who was the elder sister, to take into her own hands the management of the case.

Beholders of the game had hitherto declared that Mr Gibson's safety was secured by the constant coupling of the sisters. Neither would allow the other to hunt alone. But a common sense of the common danger had made some special strategy necessary, and Camilla hardly spoke a word to Mr Gibson during the evening. Let us hope that she found some temporary consolation in the presence of the stranger.

'I hope you are going to stay with us ever so long, Mr Burgess?' said Camilla.

'A month. That is ever so long isn't it? Why I mean to see all Devonshire within that time. I feel already that I know Exeter thoroughly and everybody in it.'

'I'm sure we are very much flattered.'

'As for you, Miss French, I've heard so much about you all my life, that I felt that I knew you before I came here.'

'Who can have spoken to you about me?'

'You forget how many relatives I have in the city. Do you think my Uncle Barty never writes to me?'

'Not about me.'

'Does he not? And do you suppose I don't hear from Miss Stanbury?'

'But she hates me. I know that.'

'And do you hate her?'

'No, indeed. I've the greatest respect for her. But she is a little odd; isn't she, now, Mr Burgess? We all like her ever so much; and we've known her ever so long, six or seven years since we were quite young things. But she has such queer notions about girls.'

'What sort of notions?'

'She'd like them all to dress just like herself; and she thinks that they should never talk to young men. If she was here she'd say I was flirting with you, because we're sitting together.'

'But you are not; are you?'

'Of course I am not.'

'I wish you would,' said Brooke.

'I shouldn't know how to begin. I shouldn't, indeed. I don't know what flirting means, and I don't know who does know. When young ladies and gentlemen go out, I suppose they are intended to talk to each other.'

'But very often they, don't, you know.'

'I call that stupid,' said Camilla. 'And yet, when they do, all the old maids say that the girls are flirting. I'll tell you one thing, Mr Burgess. I don't care what any old maid says about me. I always talk to people that I like, and if they choose to call me a flirt, they may. It's my opinion that still waters run the deepest.'

'No doubt the noisy streams are very shallow,' said Brooke.

'You may call me a shallow stream if you like, Mr Burgess.'

'I meant nothing of the kind.'

'But what do you call Dorothy Stanbury? That's what I call still water. She runs deep enough.'

'The quietest young lady I ever saw in my life.'

'Exactly. So quiet, but so clever. What do you think of Mr Gibson?'

'Everybody is asking me what I think of Mr Gibson.'

'You know what they say. They say he is to marry Dorothy Stanbury. Poor man! I don't think his own consent has ever been asked yet but, nevertheless, it's settled.'

'Just at present he seems to me to be what shall I say? I oughtn't to say flirting with your sister; ought I?'

'Miss Stanbury would say so if she were here, no doubt. But the fact is, Mr Burgess, we've known him almost since we were infants, and of course we take an interest in his welfare. There has never been anything more than that. Arabella is nothing more to him than I am. Once, indeed—but, however that does not signify. It would be nothing to us, if he really liked Dorothy Stanbury. But as far as we can see, and we do see a good deal of him, there is no such feeling on his part. Of course we haven't asked. We should not think of such a thing. Mr Gibson may do just as he likes for us. But I am not quite sure that Dorothy Stanbury is just the girl that would make him a good wife. Of course when you've known a person seven or eight years you do get anxious about his happiness. Do you know, we think her perhaps a little sly.'

In the meantime, Mr Gibson was completely subject to the individual charms of Arabella. Camilla had been quite correct in a part of her description of their intimacy. She and her sister had known Mr Gibson for seven or eight years; but nevertheless the intimacy could not with truth be said to have commenced during the infancy of the young ladies, even if the word were used in its legal sense. Seven or eight years, however, is a long acquaintance; and there was, perhaps, something of a real grievance in this Stanbury intervention. If it be a recognised fact in society that young ladies are in want of husbands, and that an effort on their part towards matrimony is not altogether impossible, it must be recognised also that failure will be disagreeable, and interference regarded with animosity. Miss Stanbury the elder was undoubtedly interfering between Mr Gibson and the Frenches; and it is neither manly nor womanly to submit to interference with one's dearest prospects. It may, perhaps, be admitted that the Miss Frenches had shown too much open ardour in their pursuit of Mr Gibson. Perhaps there should have been no ardour and no pursuit. It may be that the theory of womanhood is right which forbids to women any such attempts, which teaches them that they must ever be the pursued, never the pursuers. As to that there shall be no discourse at present. But it must be granted that whenever the pursuit has been attempted, it is not in human nature to abandon it without an effort. That the French girls should be very angry with Miss Stanbury, that they should put their heads together with the intention of thwarting her, that they should think evil things of poor Dorothy, that they should half despise Mr Gibson, and yet resolve to keep their hold upon him as a chattel and a thing of value that was almost their own, was not perhaps much to their discredit.

'You are a good deal at the house in the Close now,' said Arabella, in her lowest voice, in a voice so low that it was almost melancholy.

'Well; yes. Miss Stanbury, you know, has always been a staunch friend of mine. And she takes an interest in my little church.' People say that girls are sly; but men can be sly, too, sometimes.

'It seems that she has taken you so much away from us, Mr Gibson.'

'I don't know why you should say that, Miss French.'

'Perhaps I am wrong. One is apt to be sensitive about one's friends. We seem to have known you so well. There is nobody else in Exeter that mamma regards as she does you. But, of course, if you are happy with Miss Stanbury that is everything.'

'I am speaking of the old lady,' said Mr Gibson, who, in spite of his slyness, was here thrown a little off his guard.

'And I am speaking of the old lady too,' said Arabella. 'Of whom else should I be speaking?'

'No, of course not.'

'Of course,' continued Arabella, 'I hear what people say about the niece. One cannot help what one hears, you know, Mr Gibson; but I don't believe that, I can assure you.' As she said this, she looked into his face, as though waiting for an answer; but Mr Gibson had no answer ready. Then Arabella told herself that if anything was to be done it must be done at once. What use was there in beating round the bush, when the only chance of getting the game was to be had by dashing at once into the thicket. 'I own I should be glad,' she said, turning her eyes away from him, 'if I could hear from your own mouth that it is not true.'

Mr Gibson's position was one not to be envied. Were he willing to tell the very secrets of his soul to Miss French with the utmost candour, he could not answer her question either one way or the other, and he was not willing to tell her any of his secrets. It was certainly the fact, too, that there had been tender passages between him and Arabella. Now, when there have been such passages, and the gentleman is cross-examined by the lady, as Mr Gibson was being cross-examined at the present moment, the gentleman usually teaches himself to think that a little falsehood is permissible. A gentleman can hardly tell a lady that he has become tired of her, and has changed his mind. He feels the matter, perhaps, more keenly even than she does; and though, at all other times he may be a very Paladin in the cause of truth, in such strait as this he does allow himself some latitude.

'You are only joking, of course,' he said.

'Indeed, I am not joking. I can assure you, Mr Gibson, that the welfare of the friends whom I really love can never be a matter of joke to me. Mrs Crumbie says that you positively are engaged to marry Dorothy Stanbury.'

'What does Mrs Crumbie know about it?'

'I dare say nothing; It is not so is it?'

'Certainly not.'

'And there is nothing in it is there?'

'I wonder why people make these reports,' said Mr Gibson, prevaricating.

'It is a fabrication from beginning to end, then?' said Arabella, pressing the matter quite home. At this time she was very close to him, and though her words were severe, the glance from her eyes was soft. And the scent from her hair was not objectionable to him as it would have been to Miss Stanbury. And the mode of her head-dress was not displeasing to him. And the folds of her dress, as they fell across his knee, were welcome to his feelings. He knew that he was as one under temptation, but he was not strong enough to bid the tempter avaunt. 'Say that it is so, Mr Gibson!'

'Of course, it is not so,' said Mr Gibson lying.

'I am so glad. For, of course, Mr Gibson, when we heard it we thought a great deal about it. A man's happiness depends so much on whom he marries doesn't it? And a clergyman's more than anybody else's. And we didn't think she was quite the sort of woman that you would like. You see, she has had no advantages, poor thing!

She has been shut up in a little country cottage all her life, just a labourer's hovel, no more, and though it wasn't her fault, of course, and we all pitied her, and were so glad when Miss Stanbury brought her to the Close—still, you know, though one was very glad of her as an acquaintance, yet, you know, as a wife and for such a dear, dear friend.' She went on, and said many other things with equal enthusiasm, and then wiped her eyes, and then smiled and laughed. After that she declared that she was quite happy, so happy; and so she left him. The poor man, after the falsehood had been extracted from him, said nothing more; but sat, in patience, listening to the raptures and enthusiasm of his friend. He knew that he had disgraced himself; and he knew also that his disgrace would be known, if Dorothy Stanbury should accept his offer on the morrow. And yet how hardly he had been used! What answer could he have given compatible both with the truth and with his own personal dignity?

About half an hour afterwards, he was walking back to Exeter with Brooke Burgess, and then Brooke did ask him a question or two.

'Nice girls those Frenches, I think,' said Brooke.

'Very nice,' said Mr Gibson.

'How Miss Stanbury does hate them,' says Brooke.

'Not hate them, I hope,' said Mr Gibson.

'She doesn't love them does she?'

'Well, as for love, yes; in one sense I hope she does. Miss Stanbury, you know, is a woman who expresses herself strongly.'

'What would she say, if she were told that you and I were going to marry those two girls? We are both favourites, you know.'

'Dear me! What a very odd supposition,' said Mr Gibson.

'For my part, I don't think I shall,' said Brooke.

'I don't suppose I shall either,' said Mr Gibson, with a gravity which was intended to convey some smattering of rebuke.

'A fellow might do worse, you know,' said Brooke. 'For my part, I rather like girls with chignons, and all that sort of get-up. But the worst of it is, one can't marry two at a time.'

'That would be bigamy,' said Mr Gibson. 'Just so,' said Brooke.

CHAPTER XXXVI.MISS STANBURY'S WRATH

Punctually at eleven o'clock on the Friday morning Mr Gibson knocked at the door of the house in the Close. The reader must not imagine that he had ever wavered in his intention with regard to Dorothy Stanbury, because he had been driven into a corner by the pertinacious ingenuity of Miss French. He never for a moment thought of being false to Miss Stanbury, the elder. Falseness of that nature would have been ruinous to him, would have made him a marked man in the city all his days, and would probably have reached even to the bishop's ears. He was neither bad enough, nor audacious enough, nor foolish enough, for such perjury as that. And, moreover, though the wiles of Arabella had been potent with him, he very much preferred Dorothy Stanbury. Seven years of flirtation with a young lady is more trying to the affection than any duration of matrimony. Arabella had managed to awaken something of the old glow, but Mr Gibson, as soon as he was alone, turned from her mentally in disgust. No! Whatever little trouble there might be in his way, it was clearly his duty to marry Dorothy Stanbury. She had the sweetest temper in the world, and blushed with the prettiest blush! She would have, moreover, two thousand pounds on the day she married, and there was no saying what other and greater pecuniary advantages might follow. His mind was quite made up; and during the whole morning he had been endeavouring to drive all disagreeable reminiscences of Miss French from his memory, and to arrange the words with which he would make his offer to Dorothy. He was aware that he need not be very particular about his words, as Dorothy, from the bashfulness of her nature, would be no judge of eloquence at such a time. But still, for his own sake, there should be some form of expression, some propriety of diction. Before eleven o'clock he had it all by heart, and had nearly freed himself from the uneasiness of his falsehood to Arabella. He had given much serious thought to the matter, and had quite resolved that he was right in his purpose, and that he could marry Dorothy with a pure conscience, and with a true promise of a husband's love. 'Dear Dolly!' he said to himself, with something of enthusiasm as he walked across the Close. And he looked up to the house as he came to it. There was to be his future home. There was not one of the prebends who had a better house. And there was a dovelike softness about Dorothy's eyes, and a winning obedience in her manner, that were charming. His lines had fallen to him in very pleasant places. Yes he would go up to her and take her at once by the hand, and ask her whether she would be his, now and for ever. He would not let go her hand, till he had brought her so close to him that she could hide her blushes on his shoulder. The whole thing had been so well conceived, had become so clear to his mind, that he felt no hesitation or embarrassment as he knocked at the door. Arabella French would, no doubt, hear of it soon. Well she must hear of it. After all she could do him no injury.

He was shewn up at once into the drawing-room, and there he found Miss Stanbury the elder.

'Oh, Mr Gibson!' she said at once.

'Is anything the matter with dear Dorothy?'

'She is the most obstinate, pig-headed young woman I ever came across since the world began.'

'You don't say so! But what is it, Miss Stanbury?'

'What is it? Why just this. Nothing on earth that I can say to her will induce her to come down and speak to you.'

'Have I offended her?'

'Offended a fiddlestick! Offence indeed! An offer from an honest man, with her friends' approval, and a fortune at her back as though she had been born with a gold spoon in her mouth! And she tells me that she can't, and won't, and wouldn't, and shouldn't, as though I were asking her to walk the streets. I declare I don't know what has come to the young women or what it is they want. One would have thought that butter wouldn't melt in her mouth.'

'But what is the reason, Miss Stanbury?'

'Oh, reason! You don't suppose people give reasons in these days. What reason have they when they dress themselves up with bandboxes on their sconces? Just simply the old reason "I do not like thee, Dr. Fell; why I cannot tell."'

'May I not see her myself, Miss Stanbury?'

'I can't make her come downstairs to you. I've been at her the whole morning, Mr Gibson, ever since daylight pretty nearly. She came into my room before I was up and told me she'd made up her mind. I've coaxed, and scolded, and threatened, and cried but if she'd been a milestone it couldn't have been of less use. I told her she might go back to Nuncombe, and she just went off to pack up.'

'But she's not to go?'

'How can I say what such a young woman will do? I'm never allowed a way of my own for a moment. There's Brooke Burgess been scolding me at that rate I didn't know whether I stood on my head or my heels. And I don't know now.'

Then there was a pause, while Mr Gibson was endeavouring to decide what would now be his best course of action. 'Don't you think she'll ever come round, Miss Stanbury?'

'I don't think she'll ever come any way that anybody wants her to come, Mr Gibson.'

'I didn't think she was at all like that,' said Mr Gibson, almost in tears.

'No nor anybody else. I have been seeing it come all the same. It's just the Stanbury perversity. If I'd wanted to keep her by herself, to take care of me, and had set my back up at her if she spoke to a man, and made her understand that she wasn't to think of getting married, she'd have been making eyes at every man that came into the house. It's just what one gets for going out of one's way. I did think she'd be so happy, Mr Gibson, living here as your wife. She and I between us could have managed for you so nicely.'

Mr Gibson was silent for a minute or two, during which he walked up and down the room contemplating, no doubt, the picture of married life which Miss Stanbury had painted for him, a picture which, as it seemed, was not to be realised. 'And what had I better do, Miss Stanbury?' he asked at last.

'Do! I don't know what you're to do. I'm groom enough to bring a mare to water, but I can't make her drink.'

'Will waiting be any good?'

'How can I say? I'll tell you one thing not to do. Don't go and philander with those girls at Heavitree. It's my belief that Dorothy has been thinking of them. People talk to her, of course.'

'I wish people would hold their tongues. People are so indiscreet. People don't know how much harm they may do.'

'You've given them some excuse, you know, Mr Gibson.'

This was very ill-natured, and was felt by Mr Gibson to be so rude, that he almost turned upon his patroness in anger. He had known Dolly for not more than three months, and had devoted himself to her, to the great anger of his older friends. He had come this morning true to his appointment, expecting that others would keep their promises to him, as he was ready to keep those which he had made, and now he was told that it was his fault! 'I do think that's rather hard, Miss Stanbury,' he said.

'So you have,' said she 'nasty, slatternly girls, without an idea inside their noddles. But it's no use your scolding me.'

'I didn't mean to scold, Miss Stanbury.'

'I've done all that I could.'

'And you think she won't see me for a minute?'

'She says she won't. I can't bid Martha carry her down.'

'Then, perhaps, I had better leave you for the present,' said Mr Gibson, after another pause. So he went, a melancholy, blighted man. Leaving the Close, he passed through into Southernhay, and walked across by the new streets towards the Heavitree road. He had no design in taking this route, but he went on till he came in sight of the house in which Mrs French lived. As he walked slowly by it, he looked up at the windows, and something of a feeling of romance came across his heart. Were his young affections buried there, or were they not? And, if so, with which of those fair girls were they buried? For the last two years, up to last night, Camilla had certainly been in the ascendant. But Arabella was a sweet young woman; and there had been a time when those tender passages were going on in which he had thought that no young woman ever was so sweet. A period of romance, an era of enthusiasm, a short-lived, delicious holiday of hot-tongued insanity had been permitted to him in his youth but all that was now over. And yet here he was, with three strings to his bow, so he told himself, and he had not as yet settled for himself the great business of matrimony. He was inclined to think, as he walked on, that he would walk his life alone, an active, useful, but a melancholy man. After such experiences as his, how should he ever again speak of his heart to a woman? During this walk, his mind recurred frequently to Dorothy Stanbury; and, doubtless, he thought that he had often spoken of his heart to her. He was back at his lodgings before three, at which hour he ate an early dinner, and then took the afternoon cathedral service at four. The evening he spent at home, thinking of the romance of his early days. What would Miss Stanbury have said, had she seen him in his easy chair behind the *Exeter Argus*, with a pipe in his mouth?

In the meantime, there was an uncomfortable scene in progress between Dorothy and her aunt. Brooke Burgess, as desired, had left the house before eleven, having taken upon himself, when consulted, to say in the mildest terms, that he thought that, in general, young women should not be asked to marry if they did not like to, which opinion had been so galling to Miss Stanbury that she had declared that he had so scolded her, that she did not know whether she was standing on her head or her heels. As soon as Mr Gibson left her, she sat herself down, and fairly cried. She had ardently desired this thing, and had allowed herself to think of her desire as of one that would certainly be accomplished. Dorothy would have been so happy as the wife of a clergyman! Miss Stanbury's standard for men and women was not high. She did not expect others to be as self sacrificing, as charitable, and as good as herself. It was not that she gave to herself credit for such virtues; but she thought of herself as one who, from the peculiar circumstances of life, was bound to do much for others. There was no end to her doing good for others if only the others would allow themselves to be governed by her. She did not think that Mr Gibson was a great divine; but she perceived that he was a clergyman, living decently—of that secret pipe Miss Stanbury knew nothing—doing his duty punctually, and, as she thought, very much in want of a wife. Then there was her niece, Dolly soft, pretty, feminine, without a shilling, and much in want of some one to comfort and take care of her. What could be better than such a marriage! And the overthrow to the girls with the big chignons would be so complete! She had set her mind upon it, and now Dorothy said that it couldn't, and it wouldn't, and it shouldn't be accomplished! She was to be thrown over by this chit of a girl, as she had been thrown over by the girl's brother! And, when she complained, the girl simply offered to go away!

At about twelve Dorothy came creeping down into the room in which her aunt was sitting, and pretended to occupy herself on some piece of work. For a considerable time, for three minutes perhaps, Miss Stanbury did not speak. She resolved that she would not speak to her niece again at least, not for that day. She would let the ungrateful girl know how miserable she had been made. But at the close of the three minutes her patience was exhausted. 'What are you doing there?' she said.

'I am quilting your cap, Aunt Stanbury.'

'Put it down. You shan't do anything for me. I won't have you touch my things any more. I don't like pretended service.'

'It is not pretended, Aunt Stanbury.'

'I say it is pretended. Why did you pretend to me that you would have him when you had made up your mind against it all the time?'

'But I hadn't made up my mind.'

'If you had so much doubt about it, you might have done what I wanted you.'

'I couldn't, Aunt Stanbury.'

'You mean you wouldn't. I wonder what it is you do expect.'

'I don't expect anything, Aunt Stanbury.'

'No; and I don't expect anything. What an old fool I am ever to look for any comfort. Why should I think that anybody would care for me?'

'Indeed, I do care for you.'

'In what sort of way do you show it? You're just like your brother Hugh. I've disgraced myself to that man promising what I could not perform. I declare it makes me sick when I think of it. Why did you not tell me at once?' Dorothy said nothing further, but sat with the cap on her lap. She did not dare to resume her needle, and she did not like to put the cap aside, as by doing so it would seem as though she had accepted her aunt's prohibition against her work. For half an hour she sat thus, during which time Miss Stanbury dropped asleep. She woke with a start, and began to scold again. 'What's the good of sitting there all the day, with your hands before you, doing nothing?'

But Dorothy had been very busy. She had been making up her mind, and had determined to communicate her resolution to her aunt. 'Dear aunt,' she said, 'I've been thinking of something.'

'It's too late now,' said Miss Stanbury.

'I see I've made you very unhappy.'

'Of course you have.'

'And you think that I'm ungrateful. I'm not ungrateful, and I don't think that Hugh is.'

'Never mind Hugh.'

'Only because it seems so hard that you should take so much trouble about us, and that then there should be so much vexation.'

'I find it very hard.'

'So I think that I'd better go back to Nuncombe.'

'That's what you call gratitude.'

'I don't like to stay here and make you unhappy. I can't think that I ought to have done what you asked me, because I did not feel at all in that way about Mr Gibson. But as I have only disappointed you, it will be better that I should go home. I have been very happy here very.'

'Bother!' exclaimed Miss Stanbury.

'I have, and I do love you, though you won't believe it. But I am sure I oughtn't to remain to make you unhappy. I shall never forget all that you have done for me; and though you call me ungrateful, I am not. But I know that I ought not to stay, as I cannot do what you wish. So, if you please, I will go back to Nuncombe.'

'You'll not do anything of the kind,' said Miss Stanbury.

'But it will be better.'

'Yes, of course; no doubt. I suppose you're tired of us all.'

'It is not that I'm tired, Aunt Stanbury. It isn't that at all.' Dorothy had now become red up to the roots of her hair, and her eyes were full of tears. 'But I cannot stay where people think that I am ungrateful. If you please, Aunt Stanbury, I will go.' Then, of course, there was a compromise. Dorothy did at last consent to remain in the Close, but only on condition that she should be forgiven for her sin in reference to Mr Gibson, and be permitted to go on with her aunt's cap.

CHAPTER XXXVII. MONT CENIS

The night had been fine and warm, and it was now noon on a fine September day when the train from Paris reached St. Michael, on the route to Italy by Mont Cenis; as all the world knows St. Michael is, or was a year or two back, the end of the railway travelling in that direction. At the time Mr Fell's grand project of carrying a line of rails over the top of the mountain was only in preparation, and the journey from St. Michael to Susa was still made by the diligences those dear old continental coaches which are now nearly as extinct as our own, but which did not deserve death so fully as did our abominable vehicles. The *coupé* of a diligence, or, better still, the banquette, was a luxurious mode of travelling as compared with anything that our coaches offered. There used indeed to be a certain halo of glory round the occupant of the box of a mail-coach. The man who had secured that seat was supposed to know something about the world, and to be such a one that the passengers sitting behind him would be proud to be allowed to talk to him. But the prestige of the position was greater than the comfort. A night on the box of a mail-coach was but a bad time, and a night inside a mail-coach was a night in purgatory. Whereas a seat up above, on the banquette of a diligence passing over the Alps, with room for the feet, and support for the back, with plenty of rugs and plenty of tobacco, used to be on the Mont Cenis, and still is on some other mountain passes, a very comfortable mode of seeing a mountain route. For those desirous of occupying the *coupé*, or the three front seats of the body of the vehicle, it must be admitted that difficulties frequently arose; and that such difficulties were very common at St. Michael. There would be two or three of those enormous vehicles preparing to start for the mountain, whereas it would appear that twelve or fifteen passengers had come down from Paris armed with tickets assuring them that this preferable mode of travelling should be theirs. And then assertions would be made, somewhat recklessly, by the officials, to the effect that all the diligence was *coupé*. It would generally be the case that some middle-aged Englishman who could not speak French would go to the wall, together with his wife. Middle-aged Englishmen with their wives, who can't speak French, can nevertheless be very angry, and threaten loudly, when they suppose themselves to be ill-treated. A middle-aged Englishman, though he can't speak a word of French, won't believe a French official who tells him that the diligence is all *coupé*, when he finds himself with his unfortunate partner in a roundabout place behind with two priests, a dirty man who looks like a brigand, a sick maid-servant, and three agricultural labourers.

The attempt, however, was frequently made, and thus there used to be occasionally a little noise round the bureau at St. Michael.

On the morning of which we are speaking, two Englishmen had just made good their claim, each independently of the other, each without having heard or seen the other, when two American ladies, coming up very tardily, endeavoured to prove their rights. The ladies were without other companions, and were not fluent with their French, but were clearly entitled to their seats. They were told that the conveyance was all *coupé*, but perversely would not believe the statement. The official shrugged his shoulders and signified that his ultimatum had been pronounced. What can an official do in such circumstances, when more *coupé* passengers are sent to him than the *coupés* at his command will hold? 'But we have paid for the *coupé*,' said the elder American lady, with considerable indignation, though her French was imperfect, for American ladies understand their rights. 'Bah; yes; you have paid and you shall go. What would you have?' 'We would have what we have paid for,' said the American lady. Then the official rose from his stool and shrugged his shoulders again, and made a motion with both his hands, intended to shew that the thing was finished. 'It is a robbery,' said the elder American lady to the younger. 'I should not mind, only you are so unwell.' 'It will not kill me, I dare say,' said the younger. Then one of the English gentlemen declared that his place was very much at the service of the invalid and the other Englishman declared that his also was at the service of the invalid's companion. Then, and not till then, the two men recognised each other. One was Mr Glascock, on his way to Naples, and the other was Mr Trevelyan, on his way he knew not whither.

Upon this, of course, they spoke to each other. In London they had been well acquainted, each having been an intimate guest at the house of old Lady Milborough. And each knew something of the other's recent history. Mr Glascock was aware, as was all the world, that Trevelyan had quarrelled with his wife; and Trevelyan was aware that Mr Glascock had been spoken of as a suitor to his own sister-in-law. Of that visit which Mr Glascock had made to Nuncombe Putney, and of the manner in which Nora had behaved to her lover, Trevelyan knew nothing. Their greetings spoken, their first topic of conversation was, of course, the injury proposed to be done to the American ladies, and which would now fall upon them. They went into the waiting-room together, and during such toilet as they could make there, grumbled furiously. They would take post horses over the mountain, not from any love of solitary grandeur, but in order that they might make the company pay for its iniquity. But it was soon apparent to them that they themselves had no ground of complaint, and as everybody was very civil, and as a seat in the banquette over the heads of the American ladies was provided for them, and as the man from the bureau came and apologised, they consented to be pacified, and ended, of course, by tipping half-a-dozen of the servants about the yard. Mr Glascock had a man of his own with him, who was very nearly being put on to the same seat with his master as an extra civility; but this inconvenience was at last avoided. Having settled these little difficulties, they went into breakfast in the buffet.

There could be no better breakfast than used to be given in the buffet at the railway terminus at St. Michael. The company might occasionally be led into errors about that question of *coupé* seats, but in reference to their provisions, they set an example which might be of great use to us here in England. It is probably the case that breakfasts for travellers are not so frequently needed here as they are on the Continent; but, still, there is often to be found a crowd of people ready to eat if only the wherewithal were there. We are often told in our newspapers that England is disgraced by this and by that; by the unreadiness of our army, by the unfitness of our navy, by the irrationality of our laws, by the immobility of our prejudices, and what not; but the real disgrace of England is the railway sandwich—that whited sepulchre, fair enough outside, but so meagre, poor, and spiritless within, such a thing of shreds and parings, such a dab of food, telling us that the poor bone whence it was scraped had been made utterly bare before it was sent into the kitchen for the soup pot. In France one does get food at the railway stations, and at St. Michael the breakfast was unexceptional.

Our two friends seated themselves near to the American ladies, and were, of course, thanked for their politeness. American women are taught by the habits of their country to think that men should give way to them more absolutely than is in accordance with the practices of life in Europe. A seat in a public conveyance in the States, when merely occupied by a man, used to be regarded by any woman as being at her service as completely as though it were vacant. One woman indicating a place to another would point with equal freedom to a man or a space. It is said that this is a little altered now, and that European views on this subject are spreading themselves. Our two ladies, however, who were pretty, clever-looking, and attractive even after the night's journey, were manifestly more impressed with the villainy of the French officials than they were with the kindness of their English neighbours.

'And nothing can be done to punish them?' said the younger of them to Mr Glascock.

'Nothing, I should think,' said he. 'Nothing will, at any rate.'

'And you will not get back your money?' said the elder who, though the elder, was probably not much above twenty.

'Well no. Time is money, they say. It would take thrice the value of the time in money, and then one would probably fail. They have done very well for us, and I suppose there are difficulties.'

'It couldn't have taken place in our country,' said the younger lady. 'All the same, we are very much obliged to you. It would not have been nice for us to have to go up into the banquette.'

'They would have put you into the interior.'

'And that would have been worse. I hate being put anywhere as if I were a sheep. It seems so odd to us, that you here should be all so tame.'

'Do you mean the English, or the French, or the world in general on this side of the Atlantic?'

'We mean Europeans,' said the younger lady, who was better after her breakfast. 'But then we think that the French have something of compensation, in their manners, and their ways of life, their climate, the beauty of their cities, and their general management of things.'

'They are very great in many ways, no doubt,' said Mr Glascock.

'They do understand living better than you do,' said the elder.

'Everything is so much brighter with them,' said the younger.

'They contrive to give a grace to every-day existence,' said the elder.

'There is such a welcome among them for strangers,' said the younger.

'Particularly in reference to places taken in the *coupé*,' said Trevelyan, who had hardly spoken before.

'Ah, that is an affair of honesty,' said the elder. 'If we want honesty, I believe we must go back to the stars and stripes.'

Mr Glascock looked up from his plate almost aghast. He said nothing, however, but called for the waiter, and paid for his breakfast. Nevertheless, there was a considerable amount of travelling friendship engendered between the ladies and our two friends before the diligence had left the railway yard. They were two Miss Spaldings, going on to Florence, at which place they had an uncle, who was minister from the States to the kingdom of Italy; and they were not at all unwilling to receive such little civilities as gentlemen can give to ladies when travelling. The whole party intended to sleep at Turin that night, and they were altogether on good terms with each other when they started on the journey from St. Michael.

'Clever women those,' said Mr Glascock, as soon as they had arranged their legs and arms in the banquette.

'Yes, indeed.'

'American women always are clever and are almost always pretty.'

'I do not like them,' said Trevelyan who in these days was in a mood to like nothing. 'They are exigent and then they are so hard. They want the weakness that a woman ought to have.'

'That comes from what they would call your insular prejudice. We are accustomed to less self-assertion on the part of women than is customary with them. We prefer women to rule us by seeming to yield. In the States, as I take it, the women never yield, and the men have to fight their own battles with other tactics.'

'I don't know what their tactics are.'

'They keep their distance. The men live much by themselves, as though they knew they would not have a chance in the presence of their wives and daughters. Nevertheless they don't manage these things badly. You very rarely hear of an American being separated from his wife.'

The words were no sooner out of his mouth, than Mr Glascock knew, and remembered, and felt what he had said. There are occasions in which a man sins so deeply against fitness and the circumstances of the hour, that it becomes impossible for him to slur over his sin as though it had not been committed. There are certain little peccadilloes in society which one can manage to throw behind one perhaps with some difficulty, and awkwardness; but still they are put aside, and conversation goes on, though with a hitch. But there are graver offences, the gravity of which strikes the offender so seriously that it becomes impossible for him to seem even to ignore his own iniquity. Ashes must be eaten publicly, and sackcloth worn before the eyes of men. It was so now with poor Mr Glascock. He thought about it for a moment whether or no it was possible that he should continue his remarks about the American ladies, without betraying his own consciousness of the thing that he had done; and he found that it was quite impossible. He knew that he was red up to his hairs, and hot, and that his blood tingled. His blushes, indeed, would not be seen in the seclusion of the banquette; but he could not overcome the heat and the tingling. There was silence for about three minutes, and then he felt that it would be best for him to confess his own fault. 'Trevelyan,' he said, 'I am very sorry for the allusion that I made. I ought to have been less awkward, and I beg your pardon.'

'It does not matter,' said Trevelyan. 'Of course I know that everybody is talking of it behind my back. I am not to expect that people will be silent because I am unhappy.'

'Nevertheless I beg your pardon,' said the other.

There was but little further conversation between them till they reached Lanslebourg, at the foot of the mountain, at which place they occupied themselves with getting coffee for the two American ladies. The Miss Spaldings took their coffee almost with as much grace as though it had been handed to them by Frenchmen. And indeed they were very gracious, as is the nature of American ladies in spite of that hardness of which Trevelyan had complained. They assume an intimacy readily, with no appearance of impropriety, and are at their ease easily. When, therefore, they were handed out of their carriage by Mr Glascock, the bystanders at Lanslebourg might have thought that the whole party had been travelling together from New York. 'What should we have done if you hadn't taken pity on us?' said the elder lady. 'I don't think we could have climbed up into that high place; and look at the crowd that have come out of the interior. A man has some advantages after all.'

'I am quite in the dark as to what they are,' said Mr Glascock.

'He can give up his place to a lady, and can climb up into a banquette.'

'And he can be a member of Congress,'said the younger. 'I'd sooner be senator from Massachusetts than be the Queen of England.'

'So would I,' said Mr Glascock. 'I'm glad we can agree about one thing.'

The two gentlemen agreed to walk up the mountain together, and with some trouble induced the conductor to permit them to do so. Why conductors of diligences should object to such relief to their horses the ordinary Englishman can hardly understand. But in truth they feel so deeply the responsibility which attaches itself to their shepherding of their sheep, that they are always fearing lest some poor lamb should go astray on the mountain side. And though the road be broad and very plainly marked, the conductor never feels secure that his passenger will find his way safely to the summit. He likes to know that each of his flock is in his right place, and disapproves altogether of an erratic spirit. But Mr Glascock at last prevailed, and the two men started together up the mountain. When the permission has been once obtained the walker may be sure that his guide and shepherd will not desert him.

'Of course I know,' said Trevelyan, when the third twist up the mountain had been overcome, 'that people talk about me and my wife. It is a part of the punishment for the mistake that one makes.'

'It is a sad affair altogether.'

'The saddest in the world. Lady Milborough has no doubt spoken to you about it.'

'Well yes; she has.'

'How could she help it? I am not such a fool as to suppose that people are to hold their tongues about me more than they do about others. Intimate as she is with you, of course she has spoken to you.'

'I was in hopes that something might have been done by this time.'

'Nothing has been done. Sometimes I think I shall put an end to myself, it makes me so wretched.'

'Then why don't you agree to forget and forgive and have done with it?'

'That is so easily said, so easily said.' After this they walked on in silence for a considerable distance. Mr Glascock was not anxious to talk about Trevelyan's wife, but he did wish to ask a question or two about Mrs Trevelyan's sister, if only this could be done without telling too much of his own secret. 'There's nothing I think so grand as walking up a mountain,' he said after a while.

'It's all very well,' said Trevelyan, in a tone which seemed to imply that to him in his present miserable condition all recreations, exercises, and occupations were mere leather and prunella.

'I don't mean, you know, in the Alpine Club way, said Glascock. 'I'm too old and too stiff for that. But when the path is good, and the air not too cold, and when it is neither snowing, nor thawing, nor raining, and when the sun isn't hot, and you've got plenty of time, and know that you can stop any moment you like and be pushed up by a carriage, I do think walking up a mountain is very fine if you've got proper shoes, and a good stick, and it isn't too soon after dinner. There's nothing like the air of Alps.' And Mr Glascock renewed his pace, and stretched himself against the hill at the rate of three miles an hour.

'I used to be very fond of Switzerland,' said Trevelyan, 'but I don't care about it now. My eye has lost all its taste.'

'It isn't the eye,' said Glascock.

'Well; no. The truth is that when one is absolutely unhappy one cannot revel in the imagination. I don't believe in the miseries of poets.'

'I think myself,' said Glascock, 'that a poet should have a good digestion. By-the-bye, Mrs Trevelyan and her sister went down to Nuncombe Putney, in Devonshire.'

'They did go there.'

'Have they moved since? A very pretty place is Nuncombe Putney.'

'You have been there, then?'

Mr Glascock blushed again. He was certainly an awkward man, saying things that he ought not to say, and telling secrets which ought not to have been told. 'Well yes. I have been there as it happens.'

'Just lately do you mean?'

Mr Glascock paused, hoping to find his way out of the scrape, but soon perceived that there was no way out. He could not lie, even in an affair of love, and was altogether destitute of those honest subterfuges, subterfuges honest in such position of which a dozen would have been at once at the command of any woman, and with one of which, sufficient for the moment, most men would have been able to arm themselves. 'Indeed, yes,' he said, almost stammering as he spoke. 'It was lately since your wife went there.' Trevelyan, though he had been told of the possibility of Mr Glascock's courtship, felt himself almost aggrieved by this man's intrusion on his wife's retreat. Had he not sent her there that she might be private; and what right had any one to invade such privacy? 'I suppose I had better tell the truth at once,' said Mr Glascock. 'I went to see Miss Rowley.'

'Oh, indeed.'

'My secret will be safe with you, I know.'

'I did not know that there was a secret,' said Trevelyan. 'I should have thought that they would have told me.'

'I don't see that. However, it doesn't matter much. I got nothing by my journey. Are the ladies still at Nuncombe Putney?'

'No, they have moved from there to London.'

'Not back to Curzon Street?'

'Oh dear, no. There is no house in Curzon Street for them now.' This was said in a tone so sad that it almost made Mr Glascock weep. 'They are staying with an aunt of theirs out to the east of the city.'

'At St. Diddulph's?'

'Yes with Mr Outhouse, the clergyman there. You can't conceive what it is not to be able to see your own child; and yet, how can I take the boy from her?'

'Of course not. He's only a baby.'

'And yet all this is brought on me solely by her obstinacy. God knows, however, I don't want to say a word against her. People choose to say that I am to blame, and they may say so for me. Nothing that any one may say can add anything to the weight that I have to bear.' Then they walked to the top of the mountain in silence, and in due time were picked up by their proper shepherd and carried down to Susa at a pace that would give an English coachman a concussion of the brain.

Why passengers for Turin, who reach Susa dusty, tired, and sleepy, should be detained at that place for an hour and a half instead of being forwarded to their beds in the great city, is never made very apparent. All travelling officials on the continent of Europe are very slow in their manipulation of luggage; but as they are equally correct we will find the excuse for their tardiness in the latter quality. The hour and a half, however, is a necessity, and it is very grievous. On this occasion the two Miss Spaldings ate their supper, and the two gentlemen waited on them. The ladies had learned to regard at any rate Mr Glascock as their own property, and received his services, graciously indeed, but quite as a matter of course. When he was sent from their peculiar corner of the big, dirty refreshment room to the supper-table to fetch an apple, and then desired to change it because the one which he had brought was spotted, he rather liked it. And when he sat down with his knees near to theirs, actually trying to eat a large Italian apple himself simply because they had eaten one and discussed with them the passage over the Mont Cenis, he began to think that Susa was, after all, a place in which an hour and a half might be whiled away without much cause for complaint.

'We only stay one night at Turin,' said Caroline Spalding, the elder.

'And we shall have to start at ten to get through to Florence to-morrow,' said Olivia, the younger. 'Isn't it cruel, wasting all this time when we might be in bed?'

'It is not for me to complain of the cruelty,' said Mr Glascock.

'We should have fared infinitely worse if we hadn't met you,' said Caroline Spalding.

'But our republican simplicity won't allow us to assert that even your society is better than going to bed, after a journey of thirty hours,' said Olivia.

In the meantime Trevelyan was roaming about the station moodily by himself, and the place is one not apt to restore cheerfulness to a moody man by any resources of its own. When the time for departure came Mr Glascock sought him and found him; but Trevelyan had chosen a corner for himself in a carriage, and declared that he would rather avoid the ladies for the present. 'Don't think me uncivil to leave you,' he said, 'but the truth is, I don't like American ladies.'

'I do rather,' said Mr Glascock.

'You can say that I've got a headache,' said Trevelyan. So Mr Glascock returned to his friends, and did say that Mr Trevelyan had a headache. It was the first time that a name had been mentioned between them.

'Mr Trevelyan! What a pretty name. It sounds like a novel,' said Olivia.

'A very clever man,' said Mr Glascock, 'and much liked by his own circle. But he has had trouble, and is unhappy.'

'He looks unhappy,' said Caroline.

'The most miserable looking man I ever saw in my life,' said Olivia. Then it was agreed between them as they went up to Trompetta's hotel, that they would go on together by the ten o'clock train to Florence.

CHAPTER XXXVIII. VERDICT OF THE JURY 'MAD, MY LORD'

Trevelyan was left alone at Turin when Mr Glascock went on to Florence with his fair American friends. It was imperatively necessary that he should remain at Turin, though he had no business there of any kind whatever, and did not know a single person in the city. And of all towns in Italy Turin has perhaps less of attraction to offer to the solitary visitor than any other. It is new and parallelogrammatic as an American town is very cold in cold weather, very hot in hot weather, and now that it has been robbed of its life as a capital is as dull and uninteresting as though it were German or English. There is the Armoury, and the river Po, and a good hotel. But what are these things to a man who is forced to live alone in a place for four days, or perhaps a week? Trevelyan was bound to remain at Turin till he should hear from Bozzle. No one but Bozzle knew his address; and he could do nothing till Bozzle should have communicated to him tidings of what was being done at St. Diddulph's.

There is perhaps no great social question so imperfectly understood among us at the present day as that which refers to the line which divides sanity from insanity. That this man is sane and that other unfortunately mad we do know well enough; and we know also that one man may be subject to various hallucinations—may fancy himself to be a teapot, or what not—and yet be in such a condition of mind as to call for no intervention either on behalf of his friends, or of the law; while another may be in possession of intellectual faculties capable of lucid exertion for the highest purposes, and yet be so mad that bodily restraint upon him is indispensable. We know that the sane man is responsible for what he does, and that the insane man is irresponsible; but we do not know, we only guess wildly, at the state of mind of those who now and again act like madmen, though no court or council of experts has declared them to be mad. The bias of the public mind is to press heavily on such men till the law attempts to touch them, as though they were thoroughly responsible; and then, when the law interferes, to screen them as though they were altogether irresponsible. The same juryman who would find a man mad who has murdered a young woman, would in private life express a desire that the same young man should be hung, crucified, or skinned alive, if he had moodily and without reason broken faith to the young woman in lieu of killing her. Now Trevelyan was, in truth, mad on the subject of his wife's alleged infidelity. He had abandoned everything that he valued in the world, and had made himself wretched in every affair of life, because he could not submit to acknowledge to himself the possibility of error on his own part. For that, in truth, was the condition of his mind. He had never hitherto believed that she had been false to her vow, and had sinned against him irredeemably; but he had thought that in her regard for another man she had slighted him; and, so thinking, he had subjected her to a severity of rebuke which no high-spirited woman could have borne. His wife had not tried to bear it, in her indignation had not striven to cure the evil. Then had come his resolution that she should submit, or part from him; and, having so resolved, nothing could shake him. Though every friend he possessed was now against him including even Lady Milborough he was certain that he was right. Had not his wife sworn to obey him, and was not her whole conduct one tissue of disobedience? Would not the man who submitted to this find himself driven to submit to things worse? Let her own her fault, let her submit, and then she should come back to him.

He had not considered, when his resolutions to this effect were first forming themselves, that a separation between a man and his wife once effected cannot be annulled, and as it were cured, so as to leave no cicatrice behind. Gradually, as he spent day after day in thinking on this one subject, he came to feel that even were his wife to submit, to own her fault humbly, and to come back to him, this very coming back would in itself be a new wound. Could he go out again with his wife on his arm to the houses of those who knew that he had repudiated her because of her friendship with another man? Could he open again that house in Curzon Street, and let things go on quietly as they had gone before? He told himself that it was impossible, that he and she were ineffably disgraced, that, if reunited, they must live buried out of sight in some remote distance. And he told himself, also, that he could never be with her again night or day without thinking of the separation. His happiness had been shipwrecked.

Then he had put himself into the hands of Mr Bozzle, and Mr Bozzle had taught him that women very often do go astray. Mr Bozzle's idea of female virtue was not high, and he had opportunities of implanting his idea on his client's mind. Trevelyan hated the man. He was filled with disgust by Bozzle's words, and was made miserable by Bozzle's presence. Yet he came gradually to believe in Bozzle. Bozzle alone believed in him. There were none but Bozzle who did not bid him to submit himself to his disobedient wife. And then, as he came to believe in Bozzle, he grew to be more and more assured that no one but Bozzle could tell him facts. His chivalry, and love, and sense of woman's honour, with something of manly pride on his own part, so he told himself, had taught him to believe it to be impossible that his wife should have sinned. Bozzle, who knew the world, thought otherwise. Bozzle, who had no interest in the matter, one way or the other, would find out facts. What if his chivalry, and love, and manly pride had deceived him?

There were women who sinned. Then he prayed that his wife might not be such a woman; and got up from his prayers almost convinced that she was a sinner.

His mind was at work upon it always. Could it be that she was so base as this, so vile a thing, so abject, such dirt, pollution, filth? But there were such cases. Nay, were they not almost numberless? He found himself reading in the papers records of such things from day to day, and thought that in doing so he was simply acquiring experience necessary for himself. If it were so, he had indeed done well to separate himself from a thing so infamous. And if it were not so, how could it be that that man had gone to her in Devonshire? He had received from his wife's hands a short note addressed to the man, in which the man was desired by her not to go to her, or to write to her again, because of her husband's commands. He had shown this to Bozzle, and Bozzle had smiled. 'It's just the sort of thing they does,' Bozzle had said. 'Then they writes another by post.' He had consulted Bozzle as to the sending on of that letter, and Bozzle had been strongly of opinion that it should be forwarded, a copy having been duly taken and attested by himself. It might be very pretty evidence by-and-by. If the letter were not forwarded, Bozzle thought that the omission to do so might be given in evidence against his employer. Bozzle was very careful, and full of 'evidence.' The letter therefore was sent on to Colonel Osborne. 'If there's billy-dous going between 'em we shall nobble 'em,' said Bozzle. Trevelyan tore his hair in despair, but believed that there would be billy-dous.

He came to believe everything; and, though he prayed fervently that his wife might not be led astray, that she might be saved at any rate from utter vice, yet he almost came to hope that it might be otherwise—not, indeed, with the hope of the sane man, who desires that which he tells himself to be for his advantage; but with the hope of the insane man, who loves to feed his grievance, even though the grief should be his death. They who do not understand that a man may be brought to hope that which of all things is the most grievous to him, have not observed with sufficient closeness the perversity of the human mind. Trevelyan would have given all that he had to save his wife; would, even now, have cut his tongue out before he would have expressed to anyone save to Bozzle a suspicion that she could in truth have been guilty; was continually telling himself that further life would be impossible to him, if he, and she, and that child of theirs, should be thus disgraced; and yet he expected it, believed it, and, after a fashion, he almost hoped it.

He was to wait at Turin till tidings should come from Bozzle, and after that he would go on to Venice; but he would not move from Turin till he should have received his first communication from England. When he had been three days at Turin they came to him, and, among other letters in Bozzle's packet, there was a letter addressed in his wife's handwriting. The letter was simply directed to Bozzle's house. In what possible way could his wife have found out ought of his dealings with Bozzle, where Bozzle lived, or could have learned that letters intended for him should be sent to the man's own residence? Before, however, we inspect the contents of Mr Bozzle's dispatch, we will go back and see how Mrs Trevelyan had discovered the manner of forwarding a letter to her husband.

The matter of the address was, indeed, very simple. All letters for Trevelyan were to be redirected from the house in Curzon Street, and from the chambers in Lincoln's Inn, to the Acrobats' Club; to the porter of the Acrobats' Club had been confided the secret, not of Bozzle's name, but of Bozzle's private address, No. 55, Stony Walk, Union Street, Borough. Thus all letters reaching the Acrobats' were duly sent to Mr Bozzle's house. It may be remembered that Hugh Stanbury, on the occasion of his last visit to the parsonage of St. Diddulph's, was informed that Mrs Trevelyan had a letter from her father for her husband, and that she knew not whither to send it. It may well be that, had the matter assumed no interest in Stanbury's eyes than that given to it by Mrs Trevelyan's very moderate anxiety to have the letter forwarded, he would have thought nothing about it; but having resolved, as he sat upon the knifeboard of the omnibus—the reader will, at any rate, remember those resolutions made on the top of the omnibus while Hugh was smoking his pipe—having resolved that a deed should be done at St. Diddulph's, he resolved also that it should be done at once. He would not allow the heat of his purpose to be cooled by delay. He would go to St. Diddulph's at once, with his heart in his hand. But it might, he thought, be as well that he should have an excuse for his visit. So he called upon the porter at the Acrobats', and was successful in learning Mr Trevelyan's address. 'Stony Walk, Union Street, Borough,' he said to himself, wondering; then it occurred to him that Bozzle, and Bozzle only among Trevelyan's friends, could live at Stony Walk in the Borough. Thus armed, he set out for St. Diddulph's and, as one of the effects of his visit to the East, Sir Marmaduke's note was forwarded to Louis Trevelyan at Turin.

CHAPTER XXXIX. MISS NORA ROWLEY IS MALTREATED

Hugh Stanbury, when he reached the parsonage, found no difficulty in making his way into the joint presence of Mrs Outhouse, Mrs Trevelyan, and Nora. He was recognised by the St. Diddulph's party as one who had come over to their side, as a friend of Trevelyan who had found himself constrained to condemn his friend in spite of his friendship, and was consequently very welcome. And there was no difficulty about giving the address. The ladies wondered how it came to pass that Mr Trevelyan's letters should be sent to such a locality, and Hugh expressed his surprise also. He thought it discreet to withhold his suspicions about Mr Bozzle, and simply expressed his conviction that letters sent in accordance with the directions given by the club-porter would reach their destination. Then the boy was brought down, and they were all very confidential and very unhappy together. Mrs Trevelyan could see no end to the cruelty of her position, and declared that her father's anger against her husband was so great that she anticipated his coming with almost more of fear than of hope. Mrs Outhouse expressed an opinion that Mr Trevelyan must surely be mad; and Nora suggested that the possibility of such perversity on the part of a man made it almost unwise in any woman to trust herself to the power of a husband, 'But there are not many like him, thank God,' said Mrs Outhouse, bridling in her wrath. Thus they were very friendly together, and Hugh was allowed to feel that he stood upon comfortable terms in the parsonage; but he did not as yet see how he was to carry out his project for the present day.

At last Mrs Trevelyan went away with the child. Hugh felt that he ought to go, but stayed courageously. He thought he could perceive that Nora suspected the cause of his assiduity; but it was quite evident that Mrs Outhouse did not do so. Mrs Outhouse, having reconciled herself to the young man, was by no means averse to his presence. She went on talking about the wickedness of Trevelyan, and her brother's anger, and the fate of the little boy, till at last the little boy's mother came back into the room. Then Mrs Outhouse went. They must excuse her for a few minutes, she said. If only she would have gone a few minutes sooner, how well her absence might have been excused. Nora understood it all now; and though she became almost breathless, she was not surprised, when Hugh got up from his chair and asked her sister to go away. 'Mrs Trevelyan,' he said, 'I want to speak a few words to your sister, I hope you will give me the opportunity.'

'Nora!' exclaimed Mrs Trevelyan.

'She knows nothing about it,' said Hugh.

'Am I to go?' said Mrs Trevelyan to her sister. But Nora said never a word. She sat perfectly fixed, not turning her eyes from the object on which she was gazing.

'Pray, pray do,' said Hugh.

'I cannot think that it will be for any good,' said Mrs Trevelyan; 'but I know that she may be trusted. And I suppose it ought to be so, if you wish it.'

'I do wish it, of all things,' said Hugh, still standing up, and almost turning the elder sister out of the room by the force of his look and voice. Then, with another pause of a moment, Mrs Trevelyan rose from her chair and left the room, closing the door after her.

Hugh, when he found that the coast was clear for him, immediately began his task with a conviction that not a moment was to be lost. He had told himself a dozen times that the matter was hopeless, that Nora had shown him by every means in her power that she was indifferent to him, that she with all her friends would know that such a marriage was out of the question; and he had in truth come to believe that the mission which he had in hand was one in which success was not possible. But he thought that it was his duty to go on with it. 'If a man love a woman, even though it be the king and the beggar-woman reversed though it be a beggar and a queen, he should tell her of it. If it be so, she has a right to know it and to take her choice. And he has a right to tell her, and to say what he can for himself.' Such was Hugh's doctrine in the matter; and, acting upon it, he found himself alone with his mistress.

'Nora,' he said, speaking perhaps with more energy than the words required, 'I have come here to tell you that I love you, and to ask you to be my wife.'

Nora, for the last ten minutes, had been thinking that this would come, that it would come at once; and yet she was not at all prepared with an answer. It was now weeks since she had confessed to herself frankly that nothing else but this this one thing which was now happening, this one thing which had now happened, that nothing else could make her happy, or could touch her happiness. She had refused a man whom she otherwise would have taken, because her heart had been given to Hugh Stanbury. She had been bold enough to tell that other suitor that it was so, though she had not mentioned the rival's name. She had longed for some expression of love from this man when they had been at Nuncombe together, and had been fiercely angry with him because no such expression had come from him. Day after day, since she had been with her aunt, she had told herself that she was a broken-hearted woman, because she had given away all that she had to give and had received nothing in return. Had he said a word that might have given her hope, how happy could she have been in hoping. Now he had come to her with a plain-spoken offer, telling her that he loved her, and asking her to be his wife, and she was altogether unable to answer. How could she consent to be his wife, knowing as she did that there was no certainty of an income on which they could live? How could she tell her father and mother that she had engaged herself to marry a man who might or might not make 400 pounds a year, and who already had a mother and sister depending on him?

In truth, had he come more gently to her, his chance of a happy answer of an answer which might be found to have in it something of happiness would have been greater. He might have said a word which she could not but have answered softly and then from that constrained softness other gentleness would have followed, and so he would have won her in spite of her discretion. She would have surrendered gradually, accepting on the score of her great love all the penalties of a long and precarious engagement. But when she was asked to come and be his wife, now and at once, she felt that in spite of her love it was impossible that she should accede to a request so sudden, so violent, so monstrous. He stood over her as though expecting an instant answer; and then, when she had sat dumb before him for a minute, he repeated his demand. 'Tell me, Nora, can you love me? If you knew how thoroughly I have loved you, you would at least feel something for me.'

To tell him that she did not love him was impossible to her. But how was she to refuse him without telling him either a lie, or the truth? Some answer she must give him; and as to that matter of marrying him, the answer must be a negative. Her education had been of that nature which teaches girls to believe that it is a crime to marry a man without an assured income. Assured morality in a husband is a great thing. Assured good temper is very excellent. Assured talent, religion, amiability, truth, honesty, are all desirable. But an assured income is indispensable. Whereas, in truth, the income may come hereafter; but the other things, unless they be there already, will hardly be forthcoming. 'Mr Stanbury,' she said, 'your suddenness has quite astounded me.'

'Ah, yes; but how should I not be sudden? I have come here on purpose to say this to you. If I do not say it now—'

'You heard what Emily said.'

'No, what did she say?'

'She said that it would not be for good that you should speak to me thus.'

'Why not for good? But she is unhappy, and looks gloomily at things.'

'Yes, indeed.'

'But all the world need not be sad for ever because she has been unfortunate.'

'Not all the world, Mr Stanbury, but you must not be surprised if it affects me.'

'But would that prevent your loving me if you did love me? But, Nora, I do not expect you to love me not yet. I do not say that I expect it ever. But if you would—. Nora, I can do no more than tell you the simple truth. Just listen to me for a minute. You know how I came to be intimate with you all in Curzon Street. The first day I saw you I loved you; and there has come no change yet. It is months now since I first knew that I loved you. Well; I told myself more than once when I was down at Nuncombe for instance that I had no right to speak to you. What right can a poor devil like me have, who lives from hand to mouth, to ask such a girl as you to be his wife? And so I said nothing though it was on my lips every moment that I was there.' Nora remembered at the moment how she had looked to his lips, and had not seen the words there. 'But I think there is something unmanly in this. If you cannot give me a grain of hope, if you tell me that there never can be hope, it is my misfortune. It will be very grievous, but I will bear it. But that will be better than puling and moping about without daring to tell my tale. I am not ashamed of it. I have fallen in love with you, Nora, and I think it best to come for an answer.'

He held out his arms as though he thought that she might perhaps come to him. Indeed he had no idea of any such coming on her part; but she, as she looked at him, almost thought that it was her duty to go. Had she a right to withhold herself from him, she who loved him so dearly? Had he stepped forward and taken her in his arms, it might be that all power of refusal would soon have been beyond her power.

'Mr Stanbury,' she said, 'you have confessed yourself that it is impossible.'

'But do you love me, do you think that it is possible that you should ever love me?'

'You know, Mr Stanbury, that you should not say anything further. You know that it cannot be.'

'But do you love me?'

'You are ungenerous not to take an answer without driving me to be uncourteous.'

'I do not care for courtesy. Tell me the truth. Can you ever love me? With one word of hope I will wait, and work, and feel myself to be a hero. I will not go till you tell me that you cannot love me.'

'Then I must tell you so.'

'What is it you will tell me, Nora? Speak it. Say it. If I knew that a girl disliked me, nothing should make me press myself upon her. Am I odious to you, Nora?'

'No; not odious, but very, very unfair.'

'I will have the truth if I be ever so unfair,' he said. And by this time probably some inkling of the truth had reached his intelligence. There was already a tear in Nora's eye, but he did not pity her. She owed it to him to tell him the truth, and he would have it from her if it was to be reached. 'Nora,' he said, 'listen to me again. All my heart and soul are in this. It is everything to me. If you can love me you are bound to say so. By Jove, I will believe you do, unless you swear to me that it is not so!' He was now holding her by the hand and looking closely into her face.

'Mr Stanbury,' she said, 'let me go; pray, pray let me go.'

'Not till you say that you love me. Oh, Nora, I believe that you love me. You do; yes; you do love me. Dearest, dearest Nora, would you not say a word to make me the happiest man in the world?' And now he had his arm round her waist.

'Let me go,' she said, struggling through her tears and covering her face with her hands. 'You are very, very wicked. I will never speak to you again. Nay, but you shall let me go!' And then she was out of his arms and had escaped from the room before he had managed to touch her face with his lips.

As he was thinking how he also might escape now, might escape and comfort himself with his triumph, Mrs Outhouse returned to the chamber. She was very demure, and her manner towards him was considerably changed since she had left the chamber. 'Mr Stanbury,' she said, 'this kind of thing mustn't go any further indeed, at least not in my house.'

'What kind of thing, Mrs Outhouse?'

'Well, what my elder niece has told me. I have not seen Miss Rowley since she left you. I am quite sure she has behaved with discretion.'

'Indeed she has, Mrs Outhouse.'

'The fact is my nieces are in grief and trouble, and this is no time or place for love-making. I am sorry to be uncivil, but I must ask you not to come here any more.'

'I will stay away from this house, certainly, if you bid me.'

'I am very sorry; but I must bid you. Sir Marmaduke will be home in the spring, and if you have anything to say to him of course you can see him.'

Then Hugh Stanbury took his leave of Mrs Outhouse; but as he went home, again on the knifeboard of an omnibus, he smoked the pipe of triumph rather than the pipe of contemplation.

CHAPTER XL. 'C. G.'

The Miss Spaldings were met at the station at Florence by their uncle, the American Minister, by their cousin, the American Secretary of Legation, and by three or four other dear friends and relations, who were there to welcome the newcomers to sunny Italy. Mr Glascock, therefore, who ten minutes since had been, and had felt himself to be, quite indispensable to their comfort, suddenly became as though he were nothing and nobody. Who is there that has not felt these sudden disruptions to the intimacies and friendships of a long journey? He bowed to them, and they to him, and then they were whirled away in their grandeur. He put himself into a small, open hackney-carriage, and had himself driven to the York Hotel, feeling himself to be deserted and desolate. The two Miss Spaldings were the daughters of a very respectable lawyer at Boston, whereas Mr Glascock was heir to a peerage, to an enormous fortune, and to one of the finest places in England. But he thought nothing of this at the time. As he went, he was meditating which young woman was the most attractive, Nora Rowley or Caroline Spalding. He had no doubt but that Nora was the prettier, the pleasanter in manner, the better dressed, the more engaging in all that concerned the outer woman; but he thought that he had never met any lady who talked better than Caroline Spalding. And what was Nora Rowley's beauty to him? Had she not told him that she was the property of some one else; or, for the matter of that, what was Miss Spalding to him? They had parted, and he was going on to Naples in two days. He had said some half-defined word as to calling at the American Embassy, but it had not been taken up by either of the ladies. He had not pressed it, and so they had parted without an understanding as to a future meeting.

The double journey, from Turin to Bologna and from Bologna to Florence, is very long, and forms ample time for a considerable intimacy. There had, too, been a long day's journeying together before that; and with no women is a speedy intimacy so possible, or indeed so profitable, as with Americans. They fear nothing, neither you nor themselves; and talk with as much freedom as though they were men. It may, perhaps, be assumed to be true as a rule, that women's society is always more agreeable to men than that of other men except for the lack of ease. It undoubtedly is so when the women be young and pretty. There is a feeling, however, among pretty women in Europe that such freedom is dangerous, and it is withheld. There is such danger, and more or less of such withholding is expedient; but the American woman does not recognise the danger; and, if she withhold the grace of her countenance and the pearls of her speech, it is because she is not desirous of the society which is proffered to her. These two American sisters had not withholden their pearls from Mr Glascock. He was much their senior in age; he was gentle in his manners, and they probably recognised him to be a safe companion. They had no idea who he was, and had not heard his name when they parted from him. But it was not probable that they should have been with him so long, and that they should leave him without further thought of him, without curiosity, or a desire to know more of him. They had seen 'C. G.' in large letters, on his dressing-bag, and that was all they had learned as to his identity. He had known their names well, and had once called Olivia by hers, in the hurry of speaking to her sister. He had apologised, and there had been a little laugh, and a discussion about the use of Christian names such as is very conducive to intimacy between gentlemen and ladies. When you can talk to a young lady about her own Christian name, you are almost entitled for the nonce to use it.

Mr Glascock went to his hotel, and was very moody and desolate. His name was very soon known there, and he received the honours due to his rank and station. 'I should like to travel in America,' he said to himself, 'if I could be sure that no one would find out who I was.' He had received letters at Turin, stating that his father was better, and, therefore, he intended to remain two days at Florence. The weather was still very hot, and Florence in the middle of September is much preferable to Naples.

That night, when the two Miss Spaldings were alone together, they discussed their fellow-traveller thoroughly. Something, of course, had been said about him to their uncle the minister, to their aunt the minister's wife, and to their cousin the secretary of legation. But travellers will always observe that the dear new friends they have made on their journey are not interesting to the dear old friends whom they meet afterwards. There may be some touch of jealousy in this; and then, though you, the traveller, are fully aware that there has been something special in the case which has made this new friendship more peculiar than others that have sprung up in similar circumstances, fathers and brothers and wives and sisters do not see it in that light. They suspect, perhaps, that the new friend was a bagman, or an opera dancer, and think that the affair need not be made of importance. The American Minister had cast his eye on Mr Glascock during that momentary parting, and had not thought much of Mr Glascock. 'He was, certainly, a gentleman,' Caroline had said. 'There are a great many English gentlemen,' the minister had replied.

'I thought you would have asked him to call,' Olivia said to her sister. 'He did offer.'

'I know he did. I heard it.'

'Why didn't you tell him he might come?'

'Because we are not in Boston, Livy. It might be the most horrible thing in the world to do here in Florence; and it may make a difference, because Uncle Jonas is minister.'

'Why should that make a difference? Do you mean that one isn't to see one's own friends? That must be nonsense.'

'But he isn't a friend, Livy.'

'It seems to me as if I'd known him for ever. That soft, monotonous voice, which never became excited and never disagreeable, is as familiar to me as though I had lived with it all my life.'

'I thought him very pleasant.'

'Indeed, you did, Carry. And he thought you pleasant too. Doesn't it seem odd? You were mending his glove for him this very afternoon, just as if he were your brother.'

'Why shouldn't I mend his glove?'

'Why not, indeed? He was entitled to have everything mended after getting us such a good dinner at Bologna. By-the-bye, you never paid him.'

'Yes, I did when you were not by.'

'I wonder who he is! C. G.! That fine man in the brown coat was his servant, you know. I thought at first that C. G. must have been cracked, and that the tall man was his keeper.'

'I never knew any one less like a madman.'

'No but the man was so queer. He did nothing, you know. We hardly saw him, if you remember, at Turin. All he did was to tie the shawls at Bologna. What can any man want with another man about with him like that, unless he is cracked either in body or mind?'

'You'd better ask C. G. yourself.'

'I shall never see C. G. again, I suppose. I should like to see him again. I guess you would too, Carry. Eh?'

'Of course, I should why not?'

'I never knew a man so imperturbable, and who had yet so much to say for himself. I wonder what he is! Perhaps he's on business, and that man was a kind of a clerk.'

'He had livery buttons on,' said Carry.

'And does that make a difference?'

'I don't think they put clerks into livery, even in England.'

'Nor yet mad doctors,' said Olivia. 'Well, I like him very much; and the only thing against him is that he should have a man, six feet high, going about with him doing nothing.'

'You'll make me angry, Livy, if you talk in that way. It's uncharitable.'

'In what way?'

'About a mad doctor.'

'It's my belief,' said Olivia, 'that he's an English swell, a lord, or a duke and it's my belief, too, that he's in love with you.'

'It's my belief, Livy, that you're a regular ass;' and so the conversation was ended on that occasion.

On the next day, about noon, the American Minister, as a part of the duty which he owed to his country, read in a publication of that day, issued for the purpose, the names of the new arrivals at Florence. First and foremost was that of the Honourable Charles Glascock, with his suite, at the York Hotel, en route to join his father, Lord Peterborough, at Naples. Having read the news first to himself, the minister read it out loud in the presence of his nieces.

'That's our friend C. G.,' said Livy.

'I should think not,' said the minister, who had his own ideas about an English lord.

'I'm sure it is, because of the tall man with the buttons,' said Olivia.

'It's very unlikely,' said the secretary of legation. 'Lord Peterborough is a man of immense wealth, very old, indeed. They say he is dying at Naples. This man is his eldest son.'

'Is that any reason why he shouldn't have been civil to us?' asked Olivia.

'I don't think he is the sort of man likely to sit up in the banquette; and he would have posted over the Alps. Moreover, he had his suite with him.'

'His suite was Buttons,' said Olivia. 'Only fancy, Carry, we've been waited on for two days by a lord as is to be, and didn't know it! And you have mended the tips of his lordship's glove!' But Carry said nothing at all.

Late on that same evening, they met Mr Glascock close to the Duomo, under the shade of the Campanile. He had come out as they had done, to see by moonlight that loveliest of all works made by man's hands. They were with the minister, but Mr Glascock came up and shook hands with them.

'I would introduce you to my uncle, Mr Spalding,' said Olivia 'only as it happens we have never yet heard your name.'

'My name is Mr Glascock,' said he, smiling. Then the introduction was made; and the American Minister took off his hat, and was very affable.

'Only think, Carry,' said Olivia, when they were alone that evening, 'if you were to become the wife of an English lord!'

CHAPTER XLI. SHEWING WHAT TOOK PLACE AT ST DIDDULPH'S

Nora Rowley, when she escaped from the violence of her lover, at once rushed up to her own room, and managed to fasten herself in before she had been seen by any one. Her eider sister had at once gone to her aunt when, at Hugh's request, she had left the room, thinking it right that Mrs Outhouse should know what was being done in her own house. Mrs Outhouse had considered the matter patiently for a while, giving the lovers the benefit of her hesitation, and had then spoken her mind to Stanbury, as we have already heard. He had, upon the whole, been so well pleased with what had occurred, that he was not in the least angry with the parson's wife when he left the parsonage. As soon as he was gone Mrs Outhouse was at once joined by her elder niece, but Nora remained for a while alone in her room.

Had she committed herself; and if so, did she regret it? He had behaved very badly to her, certainly, taking her by the hand and putting his arm round her waist. And then had he not even attempted to kiss her? He had done all this, although she had been resolute in refusing to speak to him one word of kindness though she had told him with all the energy and certainty of which she was mistress, that she would never be his wife. If a girl were to be subjected to such treatment as this when she herself had been so firm, so discreet, so decided, then indeed it would be unfit that a girl should trust herself with a man. She had never thought that he had been such a one as that, to ill-use her, to lay a hand on her in violence, to refuse to take an answer. She threw herself on the bed and sobbed, and then hid her face and was conscious that in spite of this acting before herself she was the happiest girl alive. He had behaved very badly of course, he had behaved most wickedly, and she would tell him so some day. But was he not the dearest fellow living? Did ever man speak with more absolute conviction of love in every tone of his voice? Was it not the finest, noblest heart that ever throbbed beneath a waistcoat? Had not his very wickedness come from the overpowering truth of his affection for her? She would never quite forgive him because it had been so very wrong; but she would be true to him for ever and ever. Of course they could not marry. What! would she go to him and be a clog round his neck, and a weight upon him for ever, bringing him down to the gutter by the burden of her own useless and unworthy self? No. She would never so injure him. She would not even hamper him by an engagement. But yet she would be true to him. She had an idea that in spite of all her protestations which, as she looked back upon them, appeared to her to have been louder than they had been, that through the teeth of her denials, something of the truth had escaped from her. Well let it be so. It was the truth, and why should he not know it? Then she pictured to herself a long romance, in which the heroine lived happily on the simple knowledge that she had been beloved. And the reader may be sure that in this romance Mr Glascock with his splendid prospects filled one of the characters.

She had been so wretched at Nuncombe Putney when she had felt herself constrained to admit to herself that this man for whom she had sacrificed herself did not care for her, that she could not now but enjoy her triumph. After she had sobbed upon the bed, she got up and walked about the room smiling; and she would now press her hands to her forehead, and then shake her tresses, and then clasp her own left hand with her right, as though he were still holding it. Wicked man! Why had he been so wicked and so violent? And why, why, why had she not once felt his lips upon her brow?

And she was pleased with herself. Her sister had rebuked her because she had refused to make her fortune by marrying Mr Glascock; and, to own the truth, she had rebuked herself on the same score when she found that Hugh Stanbury had not had a word of love to say to her. It was not that she regretted the grandeur which she had lost, but that she should, even within her own thoughts, with the consciousness of her own bosom, have declared herself unable to receive another man's devotion because of her love for this man who neglected her. Now she was proud of herself. Whether it might be accounted as good or ill-fortune that she had ever seen Hugh Stanbury, it must at any rate be right that she should be true to him now that she had seen him, and had loved him. To know that she loved and that she was not loved again had nearly killed her. But such was not her lot. She too had been successful with her quarry, and had struck her game, and brought down her dear. He had been very violent with her, but his violence had at least made the matter clear. He did love her. She would be satisfied with that, and would endeavour so to live that that alone should make life happy for her. How should she get his photograph and a lock of his hair? and when again might she have the pleasure of placing her own hand within his great, rough, violent grasp? Then she kissed the hand which he had held, and opened the door of her room, at which her sister was now knocking.

'Nora, dear, will you not come down?'

'Not yet, Emily. Very soon I will.'

'And what has happened, dearest?'

'There is nothing to tell, Emily.'

'There must be something to tell. What did he say to you?'

'Of course you know what he said.'

'And what answer did you make?'

'I told him that it could not be.'

'And did he take that as final, Nora?'

'Of course not. What man ever takes a No as final?'

'When you said No to Mr Glascock he took it.'

'That was different, Emily.'

'But how different? I don't see the difference, except that if you could have brought yourself to like Mr Glascock, it would have been the greatest thing in the world for you, and for all of them.'

'Would you have me take a man, Emily, that I didn't care one straw for, merely because he was a lord? You can't mean that.'

'I'm not talking about Mr Glascock now, Nora.'

'Yes, you are. And what's the use. He is gone, and there's an end of it.'

'And is Mr Stanbury gone?'

'Of course.'

'In the same way?' asked Mrs Trevelyan.

'How can I tell about his ways? No; it is not in the same way. There! He went in a very different way.'

'How was it different, Nora?'

'Oh, so different. I can't tell you how. Mr Glascock will never come back again.'

'And Mr Stanbury will?' said the elder sister. Nora made no reply, but after a while nodded her head. 'And you want him to come back?' She paused again, and again nodded her head. 'Then you have accepted him?'

'I have not accepted him. I have refused him. I have told him that it was impossible.'

'And yet you wish him back again!' Nora again nodded her head. 'That is a state of things I cannot at all understand,' said Mrs Trevelyan, 'and would not believe unless you told me so yourself.'

'And you think me very wrong, of course. I will endeavour to do nothing wrong, but it is so. I have not said a word of encouragement to Mr Stanbury; but I love him with all my heart. Ought I to tell you a lie when you question me? Or is it natural that I should never wish to see again a person whom I love better than all the world? It seems to me that a girl can hardly be right if she have any choice of her own. Here are two men, one rich and the other poor. I shall fall to the ground between them. I know that. I have fallen to the ground already. I like the one I can't marry. I don't care a straw for the one who could give me a grand house. That is falling to the ground. But I don't see that it is hard to understand, or that I have disgraced myself.'

'I said nothing of disgrace, Nora.'

'But you looked it.'

'I did not intend to look it, dearest.'

He knew he was right.

'And remember this, Emily, I have told you everything because you asked me. I do not mean to tell anybody else, at all. Mamma would not understand me. I have not told him, and I shall not.'

'You mean Mr Stanbury?'

'Yes; I mean Mr Stanbury. As to Mr Glascock, of course I shall tell mamma that. I have no secret there. That is his secret, and I suppose mamma should know it. But I will have nothing told about the other. Had I accepted him, or even hinted to him that I cared for him, I would tell mamma at once.'

After that there came something of a lecture, or something, rather, of admonition, from Mrs Outhouse. That lady did not attempt to upbraid, or to find any fault; but observed that as she understood that Mr Stanbury had no means whatever, and as Nora herself had none, there had better be no further intercourse between them, till, at any rate, Sir Marmaduke and Lady Rowley should be in London.'so I told him that he must not come here any more, my dear,' said Mrs Outhouse.

'You are quite right, aunt. He ought not to come here.'

'I am so glad that you agree with me.'

'I agree with you altogether. I think I was bound to see him when he asked to see me; but the thing is altogether out of the question. I don't think he'll come any more, aunt.' Then Mrs Outhouse was quite satisfied that no harm had been done.

A month had now passed since anything had been heard at St. Diddulph's from Mr Trevelyan, and it seemed that many months might go on in the same dull way. When Mrs Trevelyan first found herself in her uncle's house, a sum of two hundred pounds had been sent to her; and since that she had received a letter from her husband's lawyer saying that a similar amount would be sent to her every three months, as long as she was separated from her husband. A portion of this she had given over to Mr Outhouse; but this pecuniary assistance by no means comforted that unfortunate gentleman in his trouble. 'I don't want to get into debt,' he said, 'by keeping a lot of people whom I haven't the means to feed. And I don't want to board and lodge my nieces and their family at so much a head. It's very hard upon me either way.' And so it was. All the comfort of his home was destroyed, and he was driven to sacrifice his independence by paying his tradesmen with a portion of Mrs Trevelyan's money. The more he thought of it all, and the more he discussed the matter with his wife, the more indignant they became with the truant husband. 'I can't believe,' he said, 'but what Mr Bideawhile could make him come back, if he chose to do his duty.'

'But they say that Mr Trevelyan is in Italy, my dear.'

'And if I went to Italy, might I leave you to starve, and take my income with me?'

'He doesn't leave her quite to starve, my dear.'

'But isn't a man bound to stay with his wife? I never heard of such a thing never. And I'm sure that there must be something wrong. A man can't go away and leave his wife to live with her uncle and aunt. It isn't right.'

'But what can we do?'

Mr Outhouse was forced to acknowledge that nothing could be done. He was a man to whom the quiescence of his own childless house was the one pleasure of his existence. And of that he was robbed because this wicked madman chose to neglect all his duties, and leave his wife without a house to shelter her.'supposing that she couldn't have come here, what then?' said Mr Outhouse. 'I did tell him, as plain as words could speak, that we couldn't receive them.' 'But here they are,' said Mrs Outhouse, 'and here they must remain till my brother comes to England.' 'It's the most monstrous thing that I ever heard of in all my life,' said Mr Outhouse. 'He ought to be locked up, that's what he ought.'

It was hard, and it became harder, when a gentleman, whom Mr Outhouse certainly did not wish to see, called upon him about the latter end of September. Mr Outhouse was sitting alone, in the gloomy parlour of his parsonage, for his own study had been given up to other things, since this great inroad had been made upon his family; he was sitting alone on one Saturday morning, preparing for the duties of the next day, with various manuscript sermons lying on the table around him, when he was told that a gentleman had called to see him. Had Mr Outhouse been an incumbent at the West-end of London, or had his maid been a West-end servant, in all probability the gentleman's name would have been demanded; but Mr Outhouse was a man who was not very ready in foreseeing and preventing misfortunes, and the girl who opened the door was not trained to discreet usages in such matters. As she announced the fact that there was a gentleman, she pointed to the door, to show that the gentleman was there; and before Mr Outhouse had been able to think whether it would be prudent for him to make some preliminary inquiry, Colonel Osborne was in the room. Now, as it happened, these two men had never hitherto met each other, though one was the brother-in-law of Sir Marmaduke Rowley, and the other had been his very old friend. 'My name, Mr Outhouse, is Colonel Osborne,' said the visitor, coming forward, with his hand out. The clergyman, of course, took his hand, and asked him to be seated. 'We have known each other's names very long,' continued the Colonel, 'though I do not think we have ever yet had an opportunity of becoming acquainted.'

'No,' said Mr Outhouse; 'we have never been acquainted, I believe.' He might have added, that he had no desire whatever to make such acquaintance; and his manner, over which he himself had no control, did almost say as much. Indeed, this coming to his house of the suspected lover of his niece appeared to him to be a heavy addition to his troubles; for, although he was disposed to take his niece's part against her husband to any possible length, even to the locking up of the husband as a madman, if it were possible, nevertheless he had almost as great a horror of the Colonel, as though the husband's allegations as to the lover had been true as gospel. Because Trevelyan had been wrong altogether, Colonel Osborne was not the less wrong. Because Trevelyan's suspicions were to Mr Outhouse wicked and groundless, he did not the less regard the presumed lover to be an iniquitous roaring lion, going about seeking whom he might devour. Elderly, unmarried men of fashion generally, and especially colonels, and majors, and members of parliament, and such like, were to him as black sheep or roaring lions. They were *fruges consumere nati*; men who stood on club doorsteps talking naughtily and doing nothing, wearing sleek clothing, for which they very often did not pay, and never going to church. It seemed to him in his ignorance that such men had none of the burdens of this world upon their shoulders, and that, therefore, they stood in great peril of the burdens of the next. It was, doubtless, his special duty to deal with men in such peril; but those wicked ones with whom he was concerned were those whom he could reach. Now, the Colonel Osbornes of the earth were not to be got at by any clergyman, or, as far as Mr Outhouse could see, by any means of grace. That story of the rich man and the camel seemed to him to be specially applicable to such people. How was such a one as Colonel Osborne to be shewn the way through the eye of a needle? To Mr Outhouse, his own brother-in-law, Sir Marmaduke, was almost of the same class for he frequented clubs when in London, and played whist, and talked of the things of the world such as the Derby, and the *levées*, and West-end dinner parties as though they were all in all to him. He, to be sure, was weighted with so large a family that there might be hope for him. The eye of the needle could not be closed against him as a rich man; but he savoured of the West-end, and was worldly, and consorted with such men as this Colonel Osborne. When Colonel Osborne introduced himself to Mr Outhouse, it was almost as though Apollyon had made his way into the parsonage of St. Diddulph's.

'Mr Outhouse,' said the Colonel, 'I have thought it best to come to you the very moment that I got back to town from Scotland.' Mr Outhouse bowed, and was bethinking himself slowly what manner of speech he would adopt. 'I leave town again to-morrow for Dorsetshire. I am going down to my friends, the Brambers, for partridge shooting.' Mr Outhouse knitted his thick brows, in further inward condemnation. Partridge shooting! yes this was September, and partridge shooting would be the probable care and occupation of such a man at such a time. A man without a duty in the world! Perhaps, added to this there was a feeling that, whereas Colonel Osborne could shoot Scotch grouse in August, and Dorsetshire partridges in September, and go about throughout the whole year like a roaring lion, he, Mr Outhouse, was forced to remain at St. Diddulph's-in-the-East, from January to December, with the exception of one small parson's week spent at Margate, for the benefit of his wife's health. If there was such a thought, or, rather, such a feeling, who will say that it was not natural? 'But I could not go through London without seeing you,' continued the Colonel. 'This is a most frightful infatuation of Trevelyan!'

'Very frightful, indeed,' said Mr Outhouse.

'And, on my honour as a gentleman, not the slightest cause in the world.'

'You are old enough to be the lady's father,' said Mr Outhouse, managing in that to get one blow at the gallant Colonel.

'Just so. God bless my soul!' Mr Outhouse shrunk visibly at this profane allusion to the Colonel's soul. 'Why, I've known her father ever so many years. As you say, I might almost be her father myself.' As far as age went, such certainly might have been the case, for the Colonel was older than Sir Marmaduke. 'Look here, Mr Outhouse, here is a letter I got from Emily.'

'From Mrs Trevelyan?'

'Yes, from Mrs Trevelyan; and as well as I can understand, it must have been sent to me by Trevelyan himself. Did you ever hear of such a thing? And now I'm told he has gone away, nobody knows where, and has left her here.'

'He has gone away, nobody knows where.'

'Of course, I don't ask to see her.'

'It would be imprudent, Colonel Osborne; and could not be permitted in this house.'

'I don't ask it. I have known Emily Trevelyan since she was an infant, and have always loved her. I'm her godfather, for aught I know, though one forgets things of that sort.' Mr Outhouse again knit his eyebrows and shuddered visibly.'she and I have been fast friends and why not? But, of course, I can't interfere.'

'If you ask me, Colonel Osborne, I should say that you can do nothing in the matter except to remain away from her. When Sir Marmaduke is in England, you can see him, if you please.'

'See him? Of course, I shall see him. And, by George, Louis Trevelyan will have to see him, too! I shouldn't like to have to stand up before Rowley if I had treated a daughter of his in such a fashion. You know Rowley, of course?'

'Oh, yes; I know him.'

'He's not the sort of man to bear this sort of thing. He'll about tear Trevelyan in pieces if he gets hold of him. God bless my soul—' the eyebrows went to work again 'I never heard of such a thing in all my life! Does he pay anything for them, Mr Outhouse?'

This was dreadful to the poor clergyman. 'That is a subject which we surely need not discuss,' said he. Then he remembered that such speech on his part was like to a subterfuge, and he found it necessary to put himself right. 'I am repaid for the maintenance here of my nieces, and the little boy, and their attendants. I do not know why the question should be asked, but such is the fact.'

'Then they are here by agreement between you and him?'

'No, sir; they are not. There is no such agreement. But I do not like these interrogatives from a stranger as to matters which should be private.'

'You cannot wonder at my interest, Mr Outhouse.'

'You had better restrain it, sir, till Sir Marmaduke arrives. I shall then wash my hands of the affair.'

'And she is pretty well—Emily, I mean?'

'Mrs Trevelyan's health is good.'

'Pray tell her though I could not, might not, ask to see her, I came to inquire after her the first moment that I was in London. Pray tell her how much I feel for her; but she will know that. When Sir Marmaduke is here, of course, we shall meet. When she is once more under her father's wing, she need not be restrained by any absurd commands from a husband who has deserted her. At present, of course, I do not ask to see her.'

'Of course, you do not, Colonel Osborne.'

'And give my love to Nora, dear little Nora! There can be no reason why she and I should not shake hands.'

'I should prefer that it should not be so in this house,' said the clergyman, who was now standing in expectation that his unwelcome guest would go.

'Very well, so be it. But you will understand I could not be in London without coming and asking after them.' Then the Colonel at last took his leave, and Mr Outhouse was left to his solitude and his sermons.

Mrs Outhouse was very angry when she heard of the visit. 'Men of that sort,' she said, 'think it a fine thing and talk about it. I believe the poor girl is as innocent as I am, but he isn't innocent. He likes it.'

'"It is easier,"' said Mr Outhouse solemnly, '"for a camel to go through the eye of a needle, than for a rich man to enter the kingdom of God."'

'I don't know that he is a rich man,' said Mrs Outhouse; 'but he wouldn't have come here if he had been honest.'

Mrs Trevelyan was told of the visit, and simply said that of course it was out of the question that she should have seen Colonel Osborne. Nevertheless she seemed to think it quite natural that he should have called, and defended him with some energy when her aunt declared that he had been much to blame. 'He is not bound to obey Mr Trevelyan because I am,' said Emily.

'He is bound to abstain from evil doing,' said Mrs Outhouse; 'and he oughtn't to have come. There; let that be enough, my dear. Your uncle doesn't wish to have it talked about.' Nevertheless it was talked about between the two sisters. Nora was of opinion that Colonel Osborne had been wrong, whereas Emily defended him. 'It seems to me to have been the most natural thing in life,' said she.

Had Colonel Osborne made the visit as Sir Marmaduke's friend, feeling himself to be an old man, it might have been natural. When a man has come to regard himself as being, on the score of age, about as fit to be a young lady's lover as though he were an old woman instead of an old man, which some men will do when they are younger even than was Colonel Osborne, he is justified in throwing behind him as utterly absurd the suspicions of other people. But Colonel Osborne cannot be defended altogether on that plea.

CHAPTER XLII. MISS STANBURY AND MR GIBSON BECOME TWO

There came to be a very gloomy fortnight at Miss Stanbury's house in the Close. For two or three days after Mr Gibson's dismissal at the hands of Miss Stanbury herself, Brooke Burgess was still in the house, and his presence saved Dorothy from the full weight of her aunt's displeasure. There was the necessity of looking after Brooke, and scolding him, and of praising him to Martha, and of dispraising him, and of seeing that he had enough to eat, and of watching whether he smoked in the house, and of quarrelling with him about everything under the sun, which together so employed Miss Stanbury that she satisfied herself with glances at Dorothy which were felt to be full of charges of ingratitude. Dorothy was thankful that it should be so, and bore the glances with abject submission.

And then there was a great comfort to her in Brooke's friendship. On the second day after Mr Gibson had gone she found herself talking to Brooke quite openly upon the subject. 'The fact was, Mr Burgess, that I didn't really care for him. I know he's very good and all that, and of course Aunt Stanbury meant it all for the best. And I would have done it if I could, but I couldn't.' Brooke patted her on the back not in the flesh but in the spirit and told her that she was quite right. And he expressed an opinion too that it was not expedient to yield too much to Aunt Stanbury. 'I would yield to her in anything that was possible to me,' said Dorothy. 'I won't,' said he; 'and I don't think I should do any good if I did. I like her, and I like her money. But I don't like either well enough to sell myself for a price.'

A great part too of the quarrelling which went on from day to day between Brooke and Miss Stanbury was due to the difference of their opinions respecting Dorothy and her suitor. 'I believe you put her up to it,' said Aunt Stanbury.

'I neither put her up nor down, but I think that she was quite right.'

'You've robbed her of a husband, and she'll never have another chance. After what you've done you ought to take her yourself.'

'I shall be ready tomorrow,' said Brooke.

'How can you tell such a lie?' said Aunt Stanbury.

But after two or three days Brooke was gone to make a journey through the distant parts of the county, and see the beauties of Devonshire. He was to be away for a fortnight, and then come back for a day or two before he returned to London. During that fortnight things did not go well with poor Dorothy at Exeter.

'I suppose you know your own business best,' her aunt said to her one morning. Dorothy uttered no word of reply. She felt it to be equally impossible to suggest either that she did or that she did not know her own business best, 'There may be reasons which I don't understand,' exclaimed Aunt Stanbury; 'but I should like to know what it is you expect.'

'Why should I expect anything, Aunt Stanbury?'

'That's nonsense! Everybody expects something. You expect to have your dinner by-and-by don't you?'

'I suppose I shall,' said Dorothy, to whom it occurred at the moment that such expectation was justified by the fact that on every day of her life hitherto some sort of a dinner had come in her way.

'Yes and you think it comes from heaven, I suppose.'

'It comes by God's goodness, and your bounty, Aunt Stanbury.'

'And how will it come when I'm dead? Or how will it come if things should go in such a way that I can't stay here any longer? You don't ever think of that.'

'I should go back to mamma, and Priscilla.'

'Psha! As if two mouths were not enough to eat all the meal there is in that tub. If there was a word to say against the man, I wouldn't ask you to have him; if he drank or smoked, or wasn't a gentleman, or was too poor, or anything you like. But there's nothing. It's all very well to tell me you don't love him, but why don't you love him? I don't like a girl to go and throw herself at a man's head, as those Frenches have done; but when everything has been prepared for you and made proper, it seems to me to be like turning away from good victuals.' Dorothy could only offer to go home if she had offended her aunt, and then Miss Stanbury had scolded her for making the offer. As this kind of thing went on at the house in the Close for a fortnight, during which there was no going out, and no society at home, Dorothy began to be rather tired of it.

At the end of the fortnight, on the morning of the day on which Brooke Burgess was expected back, Dorothy, slowly moving into the sitting room with her usual melancholy air, found Mr Gibson talking to her aunt. 'There she is herself,' said Miss Stanbury, jumping up briskly; 'and now you can speak to her. Of course I have no authority none in the least. But she knows what my wishes are.' And, having so spoken, Miss Stanbury left the room.

It will be remembered that hitherto no word of affection had been whispered by Mr Gibson into Dorothy's ears. When he came before to press his suit she had been made aware of his coming, and had fled, leaving her answer with her aunt. Mr Gibson had then expressed himself as somewhat injured in that no opportunity of pouring forth his own eloquence had been permitted to him. On that occasion Miss Stanbury, being in a snubbing humour, had snubbed him. She had in truth scolded him almost as much as she had scolded Dorothy, telling him that he went about the business in hand as though butter wouldn't melt in his mouth. 'You're stiff as a chair-back,' she had said to him, with a few other compliments, and these amenities had for a while made him regard the establishment at Heavitree as being, at any rate, pleasanter than that in the Close. But since that, cool reflection had come. The proposal was not that he should marry Miss Stanbury, senior, who certainly could be severe on occasions, but Miss Stanbury, junior, whose temper was as sweet as primroses in March. That which he would have to take from Miss Stanbury, senior, was a certain sum of money, as to which her promise was as good as any bond in the world. Things had come to such a pass with him in Exeter—from the hints of his friend the Prebend, from a word or two which had come to him from the Dean, from certain family arrangements proposed to him by his mother and sisters—things had come to such a pass that he was of a mind that he had better marry some one. He had, as it were, three strings to his bow. There were the two French strings, and there was Dorothy. He had not breadth of genius enough to suggest to himself that yet another woman might be found. There was a difficulty on the French score even about Miss Stanbury; but it was clear to him that, failing her, he was due to one of the two Miss Frenches. Now it was not only that the Miss Frenches were empty-handed, but he was beginning to think himself that they were not as nice as they might have been in reference to the arrangement of their head-gear. Therefore, having given much thought to the matter, and remembering that he had never yet had play for his own eloquence with Dorothy, he had come to Miss Stanbury asking that he might have another chance. It had been borne in upon him that he had perhaps hitherto regarded Dorothy as too certainly his own, since she had been offered to him by her aunt as being a prize that required no eloquence in the winning; and he thought that if he could have an opportunity of amending that fault, it might even yet be well with his suit. So he prepared himself, and asked permission, and now found himself alone with the young lady.

'When last I was in this house, Miss Stanbury,' he began, 'I was not fortunate enough to be allowed an opportunity of pleading my cause to yourself.' Then he paused, and Dorothy was left to consider how best she might answer him. All that her aunt had said to her had not been thrown away upon her. The calls upon that slender meal-tub at home she knew were quite sufficient. And Mr Gibson was, she believed, a good man. And how better could she dispose of herself in life? And what was she that she should scorn the love of an honest gentleman? She would take him, she thought if she could. But then there came upon her, unconsciously, without work of thought, by instinct rather than by intelligence, a feeling of the closeness of a wife to her husband. Looking at it in general she could not deny that it would be very proper that she should become Mrs Gibson. But when there came upon her a remembrance that she would be called upon for demonstration of her love, that he would embrace her, and hold her to his heart, and kiss her, she revolted and shuddered. She believed that she did not want to marry any man, and that such a state of things would not be good for her. 'Dear young lady,' continued Mr Gibson, 'you will let me now make up for the loss which I then experienced?'

'I thought it was better not to give you trouble,' said Dorothy.

'Trouble, Miss Stanbury! How could it be trouble? The labour we delight in physics pain. But to go back to the subject-matter. I hope you do not doubt that my affection for you is true, and honest, and genuine.'

'I don't want to doubt anything, Mr Gibson; but—'

'You needn't, dearest Miss Stanbury; indeed you needn't. If you could read my heart you would see written there true love very plainly, very plainly. And do you not think it a duty that people should marry?' It may be surmised that he had here forgotten some connecting link which should have joined without abruptness the declaration of his own love, and his social view as to the general expediency of matrimony. But Dorothy did not discover the hiatus.

'Certainly when they like each other, and if their friends think it proper.'

'Our friends think it proper, Miss Stanbury—may I say Dorothy? all of them. I can assure you that on my side you will he welcomed by a mother and sisters only too anxious to receive you with open arms. And as regards your own relations, I need hardly allude to your revered aunt. As to your own mother and sister and your brother, who, I believe, gives his mind chiefly to other things I am assured by Miss Stanbury that no opposition need be feared from them. Is that true, dearest Dorothy?'

'It is true.'

'Does not all that plead in my behalf? Tell me, Dorothy.'

'Of course it does.'

'And you will be mine?' As far as eloquence could be of service, Mr Gibson was sufficiently eloquent. To Dorothy his words appeared good, and true, and affecting.

All their friends did wish it. There were many reasons why it should be done. If talking could have done it, his talking was good enough. Though his words were in truth cold, and affected, and learned by rote, they did not offend her; but his face offended her; and the feeling was strong within her that if she yielded, it would soon be close to her own. She couldn't do it. She didn't love him, and she wouldn't do it. Priscilla would not grudge her her share out of that meagre meal-tub. Had not Priscilla told her not to marry the man if she did not love him? She found that she was further than ever from loving him. She would not do it.'say that you will be mine,' pleaded Mr Gibson, coming to her with both his hands outstretched.

'Mr Gibson, I can't,' she said. She was sobbing now, and was half choked by tears.

'And why not, Dorothy?'

'I don't know, but I can't. I don't feel that I want to be married at all.'

'But it is honourable.'

'It's no use, Mr Gibson; I can't, and you oughtn't to ask me any more.'

'Must this be your very last answer?'

'What's the good of going over it all again and again. I can't do it.'

'Never, Miss Stanbury?'

'No never.'

'That is cruel, very cruel. I fear that you doubt my love.'

'It isn't cruel, Mr Gibson. I have a right to have my own feelings, and I can't. If you please, I'll go away now.' Then she went, and he was left standing alone in the room. His first feeling was one of anger. Then there came to be mixed with that a good deal of wonder and then a certain amount of doubt. He had during the last fortnight discussed the matter at great length with a friend, a gentleman who knew the world, and who took upon himself to say that he specially understood female nature. It was by advice from this friend that he had been instigated to plead his own cause. 'Of course she means to accept you,' the friend had said. 'Why the mischief shouldn't she? But she has some flimsy, old-fashioned country idea that it isn't maidenly to give in at first. You tell her roundly that she must marry you.' Mr Gibson was just reaching that roundness which his friend had recommended when the lady left him and he was alone.

Mr Gibson was no doubt very much in love with Dorothy Stanbury. So much we may take for granted. He, at least, believed that he was in love with her. He would have thought it wicked to propose to her had he not been in love with her. But with his love was mingled a certain amount of contempt which had induced him to look upon her as an easy conquest. He had been perhaps a little ashamed of himself for being in love with Dorothy, and had almost believed the Frenches when they had spoken of her as a poor creature, a dependant, one born to be snubbed as a young woman almost without an identity of her own. When, therefore, she so pertinaciously refused him, he could not but be angry. And it was natural that he should be surprised. Though he was to have received a fortune with Dorothy, the money was not hers. It was to be hers or rather theirs only if she would accept him. Mr Gibson thoroughly understood this point. He knew that Dorothy had nothing of her own. The proposal made to her was as rich as though he had sought her down at Nuncombe Putney, with his preferment, plus the 2000 pounds, in his own pocket. And his other advantages were not hidden from his own eyes. He was a clergyman, well thought of, not bad-looking certainly, considerably under forty—a man, indeed, who ought to have been, in the eyes of Dorothy, such an Orlando as she would have most desired. He could not therefore but wonder. And then came the doubt. Could it be possible that all those refusals were simply the early pulses of hesitating compliance produced by maidenly reserve? Mr Gibson's friend had expressed a strong opinion that almost any young woman would accept any young man if he put his 'com 'ether' upon her strong enough. For Mr Gibson's friend was an Irishman. As to Dorothy the friend had not a doubt in the world. Mr Gibson, as he stood alone in the room after Dorothy's departure, could not share his friend's certainty; but he thought it just possible that the pulsations of maidenly reserve were yet at work. As he was revolving these points in his mind, Miss Stanbury entered the room.

'It's all over now,' she said.

'As how, Miss Stanbury?'

'As how! She's given you an answer; hasn't she?'

'Yes, Miss Stanbury, she has given me an answer. But it has occurred to me that young ladies are sometimes perhaps a little—'

'She means it, Mr Gibson; you may take my word for that. She is quite in earnest. She can take the bit between her teeth as well as another, though she does look so mild and gentle. She's a Stanbury all over.'

'And must this be the last of it, Miss Stanbury?'

'Upon my word, I don't know what else you can do unless you send the Dean and Chapter to talk er over. She's a pig-headed, foolish young woman but I can't help that. The truth is, you didn't make enough of her at first, Mr Gibson. You thought the plum would tumble into your mouth.'

This did seem cruel to the poor man. From the first day in which the project had been opened to him by Miss Stanbury, he had yielded a ready acquiescence in spite of those ties which he had at Heavitree and had done his very best to fall into her views. 'I don't think that is at all fair, Miss Stanbury,' he said, with some tone of wrath in his voice.

'It's true quite true. You always treated her as though she were something beneath you.' Mr Gibson stood speechless, with his mouth open.'so you did. I saw it all. And now she's had spirit enough to resent it. I don't wonder at it; I don't, indeed. It's no good your standing there any longer. The thing is done.'

Such intolerable ill-usage Mr Gibson had never suffered in his life. Had he been untrue, or very nearly untrue, to those dear girls at Heavitree for this? 'I never treated her as anything beneath me,' he said at last.

'Yes, you did. Do you think that I don't understand? Haven't I eyes in my head, and ears? I'm not deaf yet, nor blind. But there's an end of it. If any young woman ever meant anything, she means it. The truth is, she don't like you.'

Was ever a lover despatched in so uncourteous a way! Then, too, he had been summoned thither as a lover, had been specially encouraged to come there as a lover, had been assured of success in a peculiar way, had had the plum actually offered to him! He had done all that this old woman had bidden him—something, indeed, to the prejudice of his own heart; he had been told that the wife was ready for him; and now, because this foolish young woman didn't know her own mind—this was Mr Gibson's view of the matter—he was reviled and abused, and told that he had behaved badly to the lady. 'Miss Stanbury,' he said, 'I think that you are forgetting yourself.'

'Highty, tighty!' said Miss Stanbury. 'Forgetting myself! I shan't forget you in a hurry, Mr Gibson.'

'Nor I you, Miss Stanbury. Good morning, Miss Stanbury.' Mr Gibson, as he went from the hall-door into the street, shook the dust off his feet, and resolved that for the future he and Miss Stanbury should be two. There would arise great trouble in Exeter; but, nevertheless, he and Miss Stanbury must be two. He could justify himself in no other purpose after such conduct as he had received.

CHAPTER XLIII. LABURNUM COTTAGE

There had been various letters passing, during the last six weeks, between Priscilla Stanbury and her brother, respecting the Clock House at Nuncombe Putney. The ladies at Nuncombe had, certainly, gone into the Clock House on the clear understanding that the expenses of the establishment were to be incurred on behalf of Mrs Trevelyan. Priscilla had assented to the movement most doubtingly. She had disliked the idea of taking the charge of a young married woman who was separated from her husband, and she had felt that a going down after such an uprising, a fall from the Clock House back to a cottage, would be very disagreeable. She had, however, allowed her brother's arguments to prevail, and there they were. The annoyance which she had anticipated from the position of their late guest had fallen upon them: it had been felt grievously, from the moment in which Colonel Osborne called at the house; and now that going back to the cottage must be endured. Priscilla understood that there had been a settlement between Trevelyan and Stanbury as to the cost of the establishment so far, but that must now be at an end. In their present circumstances, she would not continue to live there, and had already made inquiries as to some humble roof for their shelter. For herself she would not have cared had it been necessary for her to hide herself in a hut for herself, as regarded any feeling as to her own standing in the village. For herself, she was ashamed of nothing. But her mother would suffer, and she knew what Aunt Stanbury would say to Dorothy. To Dorothy at the present moment, if Dorothy should think of accepting her suitor, the change might be very deleterious; but still it should be made. She could not endure to live there on the very hard-earned proceeds of her brother's pen, proceeds which were not only hard-earned, but precarious. She gave warning to the two servants who had been hired, and consulted with Mrs Crocket as to a cottage, and was careful to let it be known throughout Nuncombe Putney that the Clock House was to be abandoned. The Clock House had been taken furnished for six months, of which half were not yet over; but there were other expenses of living there much greater than the rent, and go she would. Her mother sighed and assented; and Mrs Crocket, having strongly but fruitlessly advised that the Clock House should be inhabited at any rate for the six months, promised her assistance. 'It has been a bad business, Mrs Crocket,' said Priscilla; 'and all we can do now is to get out of it as well as we can. Every mouthful I eat chokes me while I stay there.' 'It ain't good, certainly, miss, not to know as you're all straight the first thing as you wakes in the morning,' said

Mrs Crocket who was always able to feel when she woke that everything was straight with her.

Then there came the correspondence between Priscilla and Hugh. Priscilla was at first decided, indeed, but mild in the expression of her decision. To this, and to one or two other missives couched in terms of increasing decision, Hugh answered with manly, self-asserting, overbearing arguments. The house was theirs till Christmas; between this and then he would think about it. He could very well afford to keep the house on till next Midsummer, and then they might see what had best be done. There was plenty of money, and Priscilla need not put herself into a flutter. In answer to that word flutter, Priscilla wrote as follows:

Clock House,
September 16, 186—

Dear Hugh,

I know very well how good you are, and how generous, but you must allow me to have feelings as well as yourself. I will not consent to have myself regarded as a grand lady out of your earnings. How should I feel when some day I heard that you had run yourself into debt? Neither mamma nor I could endure it. Dorothy is provided for now, at any rate for a time, and what we have is enough for us. You know I am not too proud to take anything you can spare us, when we are ourselves placed in a proper position; but I could not live in this great house, while you are paying for everything, and I will not. Mamma quite agrees with me, and we shall go out of it on Michaelmas-day. Mrs Crocket says she thinks she can get you a tenant for the three months, out of Exeter, if not for the whole rent, at least for part of it. I think we have already got a small place for eight shillings a week, a little out of the village, on the road to Cockchaffington. You will remember it. Old Soames used to live there. Our old furniture will be just enough. There is a mite of a garden, and Mrs Crocket says she thinks we can get it for seven shillings, or perhaps for six and sixpence, if we stay there. We shall go in on the 29th. Mrs Crocket will see about having somebody to take care of the house.

Your most affectionate sister,   Priscilla.

On the receipt of this letter, Hugh proceeded to Nuncombe. At this time he was making about ten guineas a week, and thought that he saw his way to further work. No doubt the ten guineas were precarious; that is, the 'Daily Record' might discontinue his services tomorrow, if the 'Daily Record' thought fit to do so. The greater part of his earnings came from the 'D. R.,' and the editor had only to say that things did not suit any longer, and there would be an end of it. He was not as a lawyer or a doctor with many clients who could not all be supposed to withdraw their custom at once; but leading articles were things wanted with at least as much regularity as physic or law; and Hugh Stanbury, believing in himself, did not think it probable that an editor, who knew what he was about, would withdraw his patronage. He was proud of his weekly ten guineas, feeling sure that a weekly ten guineas would not as yet have been his had he stuck to the Bar as a profession. He had calculated, when Mrs Trevelyan left the Clock House, that two hundred a year would enable his mother to continue to reside there, the rent of the place furnished, or half-furnished, being only eighty; and he thought that he could pay the two hundred easily. He thought so still, when he received Priscilla's last letter; but he knew something of the stubbornness of his dear sister, and he, therefore, went down to Nuncombe Putney, in order that he might use the violence of his logic on his mother.

He had heard of Mr Gibson from both Priscilla and from Dorothy, and was certainly desirous that 'dear old Dolly,' as he called her, should be settled comfortably. But when dear old Dolly wrote to him declaring that it could not be so, that Mr Gibson was a very nice gentleman, of whom she could not say that she was particularly fond, 'though I really do think that he is an excellent man, and if it was any other girl in the world, I should recommend her to take him,' and that she thought that she would rather not get married, he wrote to her the kindest brotherly letter in the world, telling her that she was a 'brick,' and suggesting to her that there might come some day some one who would suit her taste better than Mr Gibson. 'I'm not very fond of parsons myself,' said Hugh, 'but you must not tell that to Aunt Stanbury.' Then he suggested that as he was going down to Nuncombe, Dorothy should get leave of absence and come over and meet him at the Clock House. Dorothy demanded the leave of absence somewhat imperiously, and was at home at the Clock House when Hugh arrived.

'And so that little affair couldn't come off?' said Hugh at their first family meeting.

'It was a pity,' said Mrs Stanbury, plaintively. She had been very plaintive on the subject. What a thing it would have been for her, could she have seen Dorothy so well established!

'There's no help for spilt milk, mother,' said Hugh. Mrs Stanbury shook her head.

'Dorothy was quite right,' said Priscilla.

'Of course she was right,' said Hugh. 'Who doubts her being right? Bless my soul! "What's any girl to do if she don't like a man except to tell him so?" I honour you, Dolly, not that I ever should have doubted you. You're too much of a chip of the old block to say you liked a man when you didn't.'

'He is a very excellent young man,' said Mrs Stanbury.

'An excellent fiddlestick, mother. Loving and liking don't go by excellence. Besides, I don't know about his being any better than anybody else, just because he's a clergyman.'

'A clergyman is more likely to be steady than other men,' said the mother.

'Steady, yes; and as selfish as you please.'

'Your father was a clergyman, Hugh.'

'I don't mean to say that they are not as good as others; but I won't have it that they are better. They are always dealing with the Bible, till they think themselves apostles. But when money comes up; or comfort, or for the matter of that either, a pretty woman with a little money, then they are as human as the rest of us.'

If the truth had been told on that occasion, Hugh Stanbury would have had to own that he had written lately two or three rather stinging articles in the *Daily Record*, as 'to the assumed merits and actual demerits of the clergy of the Church of England.' It is astonishing how fluent a man is on a subject when he has lately delivered himself respecting it in this fashion.

Nothing on that evening was said about the Clock House, or about Priscilla's intentions. Priscilla was up early on the next morning, intending to discuss it in the garden with Hugh before breakfast; but Hugh was aware of her purpose and avoided her. It was his intention to speak first to his mother; and though his mother was, as he knew, very much in awe of her daughter, he thought that he might carry his point, at any rate for the next three months, by forcing an assent from the elder lady. So he managed to waylay Mrs Stanbury before she descended to the parlour.

'We can't afford it, my dear, indeed we can't,' said Mrs Stanbury.

'That's not the question, mother. The rent must be paid up to Christmas, and you can live here as cheap as you can anywhere.'

'But Priscilla—'

'Oh, Priscilla! Of course we know what Priscilla says. Priscilla has been writing to me about it in the most sensible manner in the world; but what does it all come to? If you are ashamed of taking assistance from me, I don't know who is to do anything for anybody. You are comfortable here?'

'Very comfortable; only Priscilla feels—'

'Priscilla is a tyrant, mother; and a very stern one. Just make up your mind to stay here till Christmas. If I tell you that I can afford it, surely that ought to be enough.' Then Dorothy entered the room, and Hugh appealed to her. Dorothy had come to Nuncombe only on the day before, and had not been consulted on the subject. She had been told that the Clock House was to be abandoned, and had been taken down to inspect the cottage in which old Soames had lived but her opinion had not been asked. Priscilla had quite made up her mind, and why should she ask an opinion of any one? But now Dorothy's opinion was demanded. 'It's what I call the rhodomontade of independence,' said Hugh.

'I suppose it is very expensive,' suggested Dorothy.

'The house must be paid for,' said Hugh 'and if I say that I've got the money, is not that enough? A miserable, dirty little place, where you'll catch your death of lumbago, mother.'

'Of course it's not a comfortable house;' said Mrs Stanbury who, of herself, was not at all indifferent to the comforts of her present residence.

'And it is very dirty,' said Dorothy.

'The nastiest place I ever saw in my life. Come, mother; if I say that I can afford it, ought not that to be enough for you? If you think you can't trust me, there's an end of everything, you now.' And Hugh, as he thus expressed himself, assumed an air of injured virtue.

Mrs Stanbury had very nearly yielded, when Priscilla came in among them. It was impossible not to continue the conversation, though Hugh would much have preferred to have forced an assent from his mother before he opened his mouth on the subject to his sister. 'My mother agrees with me,' said he abruptly, 'and so does Dolly, that it will be absurd to move away from this house at present.'

'Mamma!' exclaimed Priscilla.

'I don't think I said that, Hugh,' murmured Dorothy, softly.

'I am sure I don't want anything for myself,' said Mrs Stanbury.

'It's I that want it,' said Hugh. 'And I think that I've a right to have my wishes respected, so far as that goes.'

'My dear Hugh,' said Priscilla, 'the cottage is already taken, and we shall certainly go into it. I spoke to Mrs Crocket yesterday about a cart for moving the things. I'm sure mamma agrees with me. What possible business can people have to live in such a house as this with about twenty-four shillings a week for every thing? I won't do it. And as the thing is settled, it is only making trouble to disturb it.'

'I suppose, Priscilla,' said Hugh, 'you'll do as your mother chooses?'

'Mamma chooses to go. She has told me so already.'

'You have talked her into it.'

'We had better go, Hugh,' said Mrs Stanbury. 'I'm sure we had better go.'

'Of course we shall go,' said Priscilla. 'Hugh is very kind and very generous, but he is only giving trouble for nothing about this. Had we not better go down to breakfast?'

And so Priscilla carried the day. They went down to breakfast, and during the meal Hugh would speak to nobody. When the gloomy meal was over he took his pipe and walked out to the cottage. It was an untidy-looking, rickety place, small and desolate, with a pretension about it of the lowest order, a pretension that was evidently ashamed of itself. There was a porch. And the one sitting-room had what the late Mr Soames had always called his bow window. But the porch looked as though it were tumbling down, and the bow window looked as though it were tumbling out. The parlour and the bedroom over it had been papered but the paper was torn and soiled, and in sundry places was hanging loose. There was a miserable little room called a kitchen to the right as you entered the door, in which the grate was worn out, and behind this was a shed with a copper. In the garden there remained the stumps and stalks of Mr Soames's cabbages, and there were weeds in plenty, and a damp hole among some elder bushes called an arbour. It was named Laburnum Cottage, from a shrub that grew at the end of the house. Hugh Stanbury shuddered as he stood smoking among the cabbage-stalks. How could a man ask such a girl as Nora Rowley to be his wife, whose mother lived in a place like this? While he was still standing in the garden, and thinking of Priscilla's obstinacy and his own ten guineas a week, and the sort of life which he lived in London where he dined usually at his club, and denied himself nothing in the way of pipes, beer, and beef-steaks, he heard a step behind him, and turning round, saw his elder sister.

'Hugh,' she said, 'you must not be angry with me.'

'But I am angry with you.'

'I know you are; but you are unjust. I am doing what I am sure is right.'

'I never saw such a beastly hole as this in all my life.'

'I don't think it beastly at all. You'll find that I'll make it nice. Whatever we want here you shall give us. You are not to think that I am too proud to take anything at your hands. It is not that.'

'It's very like it.'

'I have never refused anything that is reasonable, but it is quite unreasonable that we should go on living in such a place as that, as though we had three or four hundred a year of our own. If mamma got used to the comfort of it, it would be hard then upon her to move. You shall give her what you can afford, and what is reasonable; but it is madness to think of living there. I couldn't do it.'

'You're to have your way at any rate, it seems.'

'But you must not quarrel with me, Hugh. Give me a kiss. I don't have you often with me; and yet you are the only man in the world that I ever speak to, or even know. I sometimes half think that the bread is so hard and the water so bitter, that life will become impossible. I try to get over it; but if you were to go away from me in anger, I should be so beaten for a week or two that I could do nothing.'

'Why won't you let me do anything?'

'I will whatever you please. But kiss me.' Then he kissed her, as he stood among Mr Soames's cabbage-stalks. 'Dear Hugh; you are such a god to me!'

'You don't treat me like a divinity.'

'But I think of you as one when you are absent. The gods were never obeyed when they showed themselves. Let us go and have a walk. Come; shall we get as far as Ridleigh Mill?'

Then they started together, and all unpleasantness was over between them when they returned to the Clock House.

CHAPTER XLIV. BROOKE BURGESS TAKES LEAVE OF EXETER

The time had arrived at which Brooke Burgess was to leave Exeter. He had made his tour through the county, and returned to spend his two last nights at Miss Stanbury's house. When he came back Dorothy was still at Nuncombe, but she arrived in the Close the day before his departure. Her mother and sister had wished her to stay at Nuncombe. 'There is a bed for you now, and a place to be comfortable in,' Priscilla had said, laughing, 'and you may as well see the last of us.' But Dorothy declared that she had named a day to her aunt, and that she would not break her engagement. 'I suppose you can stay if you like,' Priscilla had urged. But Dorothy was of opinion that she ought not to stay. She said not a word about Brooke Burgess; but it may be that it would have been matter of regret to her not to shake hands with him once more. Brooke declared to her that had she not come back he would have gone over to Nuncombe to see her; but: Dorothy did not consider herself entitled to believe that.

On the morning of the last day Brooke went over to his uncle's office. 'I've come to say Good-bye, Uncle Barty,' he said.

'Good-bye, my boy. Take care of yourself.'

'I mean to try.'

'You haven't quarrelled with the old woman have you? said Uncle Barty.

'Not yet—that is to say, not to the knife.'

'And you still believe that you are to have her money?'

'I believe nothing one way or the other. You may be sure of this, I shall never count it mine till I've got it; and I shall never make myself so sure of it, as to break my heart because I don't get it. I suppose I've got as good a right to it as anybody else, and I don't see why I shouldn't take it if it come in my way.'

'I don't think it ever will,' said the old man, after a pause.

'I shall be none the worse,' said Brooke.

'Yes, you will. You'll be a broken-hearted man. And she means to break your heart. She does it on purpose. She has no more idea of leaving you her money than I have. Why should she?'

'Simply because she takes the fancy.'

'Fancy! Believe me, there is very little fancy about it. There isn't one of the name she wouldn't ruin if she could. She'd break all our hearts if she could get at them. Look at me and my position. I'm little more than a clerk in the concern. By God I'm not so well off as a senior clerk in many a bank. If there came a bad time, I must lose as the others would lose, but a clerk never loses. And my share in the business is almost a nothing. It's just nothing compared to what it would have been, only for her.'

Brooke had known that his uncle was a disappointed, or at least a discontented man; but he had never known much of the old man's circumstances, and certainly had not expected to hear him speak in the strain that he had now used. He had heard often that his Uncle Barty disliked Miss Stanbury, and had not been surprised at former sharp, biting little words spoken to reference to that lady's character. But he had not expected such a tirade of abuse as the banker had now poured out. 'Of course I know nothing about the bank,' said he; 'but I did not suppose that she had had anything to do with it.'

'Where do you think the money came from that she has got? Did you ever hear that she had anything of her own? She never had a penny, never a penny. It came out of this house. It is the capital on which this business was founded, and on which it ought to be carried on to this day. My brother had thrown her off; by heavens, yes had thrown her off. He had found out what she was and had got rid of her.'

'But he left her his money.'

'Yes she got near him when he was dying, and he did leave her his money —his money, and my money, and your father's money.'

'He could have given her nothing, Uncle Barty, that wasn't his own.'

'Of course that's true it's true in one way. You might say the same of a man who was cozened into leaving every shilling away from his own children. I wasn't in Exeter when the will was made. We none of us were here. But she was here; and when we came to see him die, there we found her. She had had her revenge upon him, and she means to have it on all of us. I don't believe she'll ever leave you a shilling, Brooke. You'll find her out yet, and you'll talk of her to your nephews as I do to you.'

Brooke made some ordinary answer to this, and bade is uncle adieu. He had allowed himself to entertain a half chivalrous idea that he could produce a reconciliation between Miss Stanbury and his uncle Barty; and since he had been at Exeter he had said a word, first to the one and then to the other, hinting at the subject but his hints had certainly not been successful. As he walked from the bank into the High Street he could not fail to ask himself whether there were any grounds for the terrible accusations which he had just heard from his uncle's lips. Something of the same kind, though in form much less violent, had been repeated to him very often by others of the family. Though he had as a boy known Miss Stanbury well, he had been taught to regard her as an ogress. All the Burgesses had regarded Miss Stanbury as an ogress since that unfortunate will had come to light. But she was an ogress from whom something might be gained and the ogress had still persisted in saying that a Burgess should be her heir. It had therefore come to pass that Brooke had been brought up half to revere her and half to abhor her. 'She is a dreadful woman,' said his branch of the family, 'who will not scruple at anything evil. But as it seems that you may probably reap the advantage of the evil that she does, it will become you to put up with her iniquity.' As he had become old enough to understand the nature of her position, he had determined to judge for himself; but his judgment hitherto simply amounted to this, that Miss Stanbury was a very singular old woman, with a kind heart and good instincts, but so capricious withal that no sensible man would risk his happiness on expectations formed on her promises. Guided by this opinion, he had resolved to be attentive to her and, after a certain fashion, submissive; but certainly not to become her slave. She had thrown over her nephew. She was constantly complaining to him of her niece. Now and again she would say a very bitter word to him about himself. When he had left Exeter on his little excursion, no one was so much in favour with her as Mr Gibson. On his return he found that Mr Gibson had been altogether discarded, and was spoken of in terms of almost insolent abuse. 'If I were ever so humble to her,' he had said to himself, 'it would do no good; and there is nothing I hate so much as humility.' He had thus determined to take the goods the gods provided, should it ever come to pass that such godlike provision was laid before him out of Miss Stanbury's coffers but not to alter his mode of life or put himself out of his way in obedience to her behests, as a man might be expected to do who was destined to receive so rich a legacy. Upon this idea he had acted, still believing the old woman to be good, but believing at the same time that she was very capricious. Now he had heard what his Uncle Bartholomew Burgess had had to say upon the matter, and he could not refrain from asking himself whether his uncle's accusations were true.

In a narrow passage between the High Street and the Close he met Mr Gibson. There had come to be that sort of intimacy between the two men which grows from closeness of position rather than from any social desire on either side, and it was natural that Burgess should say a word of farewell. On the previous evening Miss Stanbury had relieved her mind by turning Mr Gibson into ridicule in her description to Brooke of the manner in which the clergyman had carried on his love affair; and she had at the same time declared that Mr Gibson had been most violently impertinent to herself. He knew, therefore, that Miss Stanbury and Mr Gibson had become two, and would on this occasion have passed on without a word relative to the old lady had Mr Gibson allowed him to do so. But Mr Gibson spoke his mind freely.

'Off to-morrow, are you?' he said. 'Good-bye. I hope we may meet again; but not in the same house, Mr Burgess.'

'There or anywhere, I shall be very happy,' said Brooke.

'Not there, certainly. While you were absent Miss Stanbury treated me in such a way that I shall certainly never put my foot in her house again.'

'Dear me! I thought that you and she were such great friends.'

'I knew her very well, of course and respected her. She is a good churchwoman, and is charitable in the city; but she has got such a tongue in her head that there is no bearing it when she does what she calls giving you a bit of her mind.'

'She has been indulgent to me, and has not given me much of it.'

'Your time will come, I've no doubt,' continued Mr Gibson. 'Everybody has always told me that it would be so. Even her oldest friends knew it. You ask Mrs MacHugh, or Mrs French, at Heavitree.'

'Mrs French!' said Brooke, laughing. 'That would hardly be fair evidence.'

'Why not? I don't know a better judge of character in all Exeter than Mrs French. And she and Miss Stanbury have been intimate all their lives. Ask your uncle at the bank.'

'My uncle and Miss Stanbury never were friends,' said Brooke.

'Ask Hugh Stanbury what he thinks of her. But don't suppose I want to say a word against her. I wouldn't for the world do such a thing. Only, as we've met there and all that, I thought it best to let you know that she had treated me in such a way, and has been altogether so violent, that I never will go there again.' So saying, Mr Gibson passed on, and was of opinion that he had spoken with great generosity of the old woman who had treated him so badly.

In the afternoon Brooke Burgess went over to the further end of the Close, and called on Mrs MacHugh; and from thence he walked across to Heavitree, and called on the Frenches. It may be doubted whether he would have been so well behaved to these ladies had they not been appealed to by Mr Gibson as witnesses to the character of Miss Stanbury. He got very little from Mrs MacHugh. That lady was kind and cordial, and expressed many wishes that she might see him again in Exeter. When he said a few words about Mr Gibson, Mrs MacHugh only laughed, and declared that the gentleman would soon find a plaister for that sore. 'There are more fishes than one in the sea,' she said.

'But I'm afraid they've quarrelled, Mrs MacHugh.'

'So they tell me. What should we have to talk about here if somebody didn't quarrel sometimes? She and I ought to get up a quarrel for the good of the public, only they know that I never can quarrel with anybody. I never see anybody interesting enough to quarrel with.' But Mrs MacHugh said nothing about Miss Stanbury, except that she sent over a message with reference to a rubber of whist for the next night but one.

He found the two French girls sitting with their mother, and they all expressed their great gratitude to him for coming to say good-bye before he went. 'It is so very nice of you, Mr Burgess,' said Camilla, 'and particularly just at present.'

'Yes, indeed,' said Arabella, 'because you know things have been so unpleasant.'

'My dears, never mind about that,' said Mrs French. 'Miss Stanbury has meant everything for the best, and it is all over now.'

'I don't know what you mean by its being all over, mamma,' said Camilla. 'As far as I can understand, it has never been begun.'

'My dear, the least said the soonest mended,' said Mrs French.

'That's of course, mamma,' said Camilla; 'but yet one can't hold one's tongue altogether. All the city is talking about it, and I dare say Mr Burgess has heard as much as anybody else.'

'I've heard nothing at all,' said Brooke.

'Oh yes, you have,' continued Camilla. Arabella conceived herself at this moment to be situated in so delicate a position, that it was best that her sister should talk about it, and that she herself should hold her tongue with the exception, perhaps, of a hint here and there which might be of assistance; for Arabella completely understood that the prize was now to be hers, if the prize could be rescued out of the Stanbury clutches. She was aware, no one better aware, how her sister had interfered with her early hopes, and was sure, in her own mind, that all her disappointment had come from fratricidal rivalry on the part of Camilla. It had never, however, been open to her to quarrel with Camilla. There they were, linked together, and together they must fight their battles. As two pigs may be seen at the same trough, each striving to take the delicacies of the banquet from the other, and yet enjoying always the warmth of the same dunghill in amicable contiguity, so had these young ladies lived in sisterly friendship, while each was striving to take a husband from the other. They had understood the position, and, though for years back they had talked about Mr Gibson, they had never quarrelled; but now, in these latter days of the Stanbury interference, there had come tacitly to be something of an understanding between them that, if any fighting were still possible on the subject, one must be put forward and the other must yield. There had been no spoken agreement, but Arabella quite understood that she was to be put forward. It was for her to take up the running, and to win, if possible, against the Stanbury filly. That was her view, and she was inclined to give Camilla credit for acting in accordance with it with honesty and zeal. She felt, therefore, that her words on the present occasion ought to be few. She sat back in her corner of the sofa, and was intent on her work, and shewed by the pensiveness of her brow that there were thoughts within her bosom of which she was not disposed to speak. 'You must have heard a great deal,' said Carnilla, laughing. 'You must know how poor Mr Gibson has been abused, because he wouldn't—'

'Camilla, don't be foolish,' said Mrs French.

'Because he wouldn't what?' asked Brooke. 'What ought he to have done that he didn't do?'

'I don't know anything about ought,' said Camilla. 'That's a matter of taste altogether.'

'I'm the worst hand in the world at a riddle,' said Brooke.

'How sly you are,' continued Camilla, laughing; 'as if dear Aunt Stanbury hadn't confided all her hopes to you.'

'Camilla, dear don't,' said Arabella.

'But when a gentleman is hunted, and can't be caught, I don't think he ought to be abused to his face.'

'But who hunted him, and who abused him?' asked Brooke.

'Mind, I don't mean to say a word against Miss Stanbury, Mr Burgess. We've known her and loved her all our lives haven't we, mamma?'

'And respected her,' said Arabella.

'Quite so,' continued Camilla. 'But you know, Mr Burgess, that she likes her own way.'

'I don't know anybody that does not,' said Brooke.

'And when she's disappointed, she shows it. There's no doubt she is disappointed now, Mr Burgess.'

'What's the good of going on, Camilla?' said Mrs French. Arabella sat silent in her corner, with a conscious glow of satisfaction, as she reflected that the joint disappointment of the elder and the younger Miss Stanbury had been caused by a tender remembrance of her own charms. Had not dear Mr Gibson told her, in the glowing language of truth, that there was nothing further from his thoughts than the idea of taking Dorothy Stanbury for his wife?

'Well, you know,' continued Camilla, 'I think that when a person makes an attempt, and comes by the worst of it, that person should put up with the defeat, and not say all manner of ill-natured things. Everybody knows that a certain gentleman is very intimate in this house.'

Don't, dear,' said Arabella, in a whisper.

'Yes, I shall,' said Camilla. 'I don't know why people should hold their tongues, when other people talk so loudly. I don't care a bit what anybody says about the gentleman and us. We have known him for ever so many years, and mamma is very fond of him.'

'Indeed I am, Camilla,' said Mrs French.

'And for the matter of that, so am I very,' said Camilla, laughing bravely. 'I don't care who knows it.'

'Don't be so silly, child,' said Arabella. Camilla was certainly doing her best, and Arabella was grateful.

'We don't care what people may say,' continued Camilla again. 'Of course we heard, as everybody else heard too, that a certain gentleman was to be married to a certain lady. It was nothing to us whether he was married or not.'

'Nothing at all,' said Arabella.

'We never spoke ill of the young lady. We did not interfere. If the gentleman liked the young lady, he was quite at liberty to marry her, as far as we were concerned. We had been in the habit of seeing him here, almost as a brother, and perhaps we might feel that a connection with that particular young lady would take him from us; but we never hinted so much even as that to him or to anyone else. Why should we? It was nothing to us. Now it turns out that the gentleman never meant anything of the kind, whereupon he is pretty nearly kicked out of the house, and all manner of ill-natured things are said about us everywhere.' By this time Camilla had become quite excited, and was speaking with much animation.

'How can you be so foolish, Camilla?' said Arabella.

'Perhaps I am foolish,' said Camilla, 'to care what anybody says.'

'What can it all be to Mr Burgess?' said Mrs French.

'Only this, that as we all like Mr Burgess, and as he is almost one of the family in the Close, I think he ought to know why we are not quite so cordial as we used to be. Now that the matter is over I have no doubt things will get right again. And as for the young lady, I'm sure we feel for her. We think it was the aunt who was indiscreet.'

'And then she has such a tongue,' said Arabella.

Our friend Brooke, of course, knew the whole truth knew the nature of Mr Gibson's failure, and knew also how Dorothy had acted in the affair. He was inclined, moreover, to believe that the ladies who were now talking to him were as well instructed on the subject as was he himself. He had heard, too, of the ambition of the two young ladies now before him, and believed that that ambition was not yet dead. But he did not think it incumbent on him to fight a battle even on behalf of Dorothy. He might have declared that Dorothy, at least, had not been disappointed, but he thought it better to be silent about Dorothy. 'Yes,' he said, 'Miss Stanbury has a tongue; but I think it speaks as much good as it does evil, and perhaps that is a great deal to say for any lady's tongue.'

'We never speak evil of anybody,' said Camilla; 'never. It is a rule with us.' Then Brooke took his leave, and the three ladies were cordial and almost affectionate in their farewell greetings.

Brooke was to start on the following morning before anybody would be up except Martha, and Miss Stanbury was very melancholy during the evening. 'We shall miss him very much; shall we not?' she said, appealing to Dorothy. 'I am sure you will miss him very much,' said Dorothy. 'We are so stupid here alone,' said Miss Stanbury. 'When they had drank their tea, she sat nearly silent for half an hour, and then summoned him up into her own room.'so you are going, Brooke?' she said.

'Yes; I must go now. They would dismiss me if I stayed an hour longer.'

'It was good of you to come to the old woman; and you must let me hear of you from time to time.'

'Of course I'll write.'

'And, Brooke—'

'What is it, Aunt Stanbury?'

'Do you want any money, Brooke?'

'No none, thank you. I've plenty for a bachelor.'

'When you think of marrying, Brooke, mind you tell me.'

'I'll be sure to tell you but I can't promise yet when that will be.' She said nothing more to him, though she paused once more as though she were going to speak. She kissed him and bade him good-bye, saying that she would not go down-stairs again that evening. He was to tell Dorothy to go to bed. And so they parted.

But Dorothy did not go to bed for an hour after that. When Brooke came down into the parlour with his message she intended to go at once, and put up her work, and lit her candle, and put out her hand to him, and said good-bye to him. But, for all that, she remained there for an hour with him. At first she said very little, but by degrees her tongue was loosened, and she found herself talking with a freedom which she could hardly herself understand. She told him how thoroughly she believed her aunt to be a good woman, how sure she was that her aunt was at any rate honest. 'As for me,' said Dorothy, 'I know that I have displeased her about Mr Gibson and I would go away, only that I think she would be so desolate.' Then Brooke begged her never to allow the idea of leaving Miss Stanbury to enter her head. Because Miss Stanbury was capricious, he said, not on that account should her caprices either be indulged or permitted. That was his doctrine respecting Miss Stanbury, and he declared that, as regarded himself, he would never be either disrespectful to her or submissive. 'It is a great mistake,' he said, 'to think that anybody is either an angel or a devil.' When Dorothy expressed an opinion that with some people angelic tendencies were predominant, and with others diabolic tendencies, he assented; but declared that it was not always easy to tell the one tendency from the other. At last, when Dorothy had made about five attempts to go, Mr Gibson's name was mentioned. 'I am very glad that you are not going to be Mrs Gibson,' said he.

'I don't know why you should be glad.'

'Because I should not have liked your husband—not as your husband.'

'He is an excellent man, I'm sure,' said Dorothy.

'Nevertheless I am very glad. But I did not think you would accept him, and I congratulate you on your escape. You would have been nothing to me as Mrs Gibson.'

'Shouldn't I?' said Dorothy, not knowing what else to say.

'But now I think we shall always be friends.'

'I'm sure I hope so, Mr Burgess. But indeed I must go now. It is ever so late, and you will hardly get any sleep. Good night.' Then he took her hand, and pressed it very warmly, and referring to a promise before made to her, he assured her that he would certainly make acquaintance with her brother as soon as he was back in London. Dorothy, as she went up to bed, was more than ever satisfied with herself, in that she had not yielded in reference to Mr Gibson.

CHAPTER XLV.TREVELYAN AT VENICE

Trevelyan passed on moodily and alone from Turin to Venice, always expecting letters from Bozzle, and receiving from time to time the dispatches which that functionary forwarded to him, as must be acknowledged, with great punctuality. For Mr Bozzle did his work, not only with a conscience, but with a will. He was now, as he had declared more than once, altogether devoted to Mr Trevelyan's interest; and as he was an active, enterprising man, always on the alert to be doing something, and as he loved the work of writing dispatches, Trevelyan received a great many letters from Bozzle. It is not exaggeration to say that every letter made him for the time a very wretched man. This ex-policeman wrote of the wife of his bosom, of her who had been the wife of his bosom, and who was the mother of his child, who was at this very time the only woman whom he loved with an entire absence of delicacy. Bozzle would have thought reticence on his part to he dishonest. We remember Othello's demand of Iago. That was the demand which Bozzle understood that Trevelyan had made of him, and he was minded to obey that order. But Trevelvan, though he had in truth given the order, was like Othello also in this that he would have preferred before all the prizes of the world to have had proof brought home to him exactly opposite to that which he demanded. But there was nothing so terrible to him as the grinding suspicion that he was to be kept in the dark. Bozzle could find out facts. Therefore he gave, in effect, the same order that Othello gave and Bozzle went to work determined to obey it. There came many dispatches to Venice, and at last there came one, which created a correspondence which shall be given here at length. The first is a letter from Mr Bozzle to his employer:

55, Stony Walk,
Union Street,
Borough,
September 29, 186—, 4.30 p.m.

HOND. SIR,

Since I wrote yesterday morning, something has occurred which, it may be, and I think it will, will help to bring this melancholy affair to a satisfactory termination and conclusion. I had better explain, Mr Trewilyan, how I have been at work from the beginning about watching the Colonel. I couldn't do nothing with the porter at the Albany, which he is always mostly muzzled with beer, and he wouldn't have taken my money, not on the square. So, when it was tellegrammed to me as the Colonel was on the move in the North, I put on two boys as knows the Colonel, at eighteenpence a day, at each end, one Piccadilly end, and the other Saville Row end, and yesterday morning, as quick as ever could be, after the Limited Express Edinburgh Male Up was in, there comes the Saville Row End Boy here to say as the Colonel was lodged safe in his downey. Then I was off immediate myself to St. Diddulph's, because I knows what it is to trust to inferiors when matters gets delicate. Now, there hadn't been no letters from the Colonel, nor none to him as I could make out, though that mightn't be so sure. She might have had 'em addressed to A. Z., or the like of that, at any of the Post-offices as was distant, as nobody could give the notice to 'em all. Barring the money, which I know ain't an object when the end is so desirable, it don't do to be too ubiketous, because things will go astray. But I've kept my eye uncommon open, and I don't think there have been no letters since that last which was sent, Mr Trewilyan, let any of 'em, parsons or what not, say what they will. And I don't see as parsons are better than other folk when they has to do with a lady as likes her fancy-man.

Trevelyan, when he had read as far as this, threw down the letter and tore his hair in despair. 'My wife,' he exclaimed, 'Oh, my wife!' But it was essential that he should read Bozzle's letter, and he persevered.

Well; I took to the ground myself as soon as ever I heard that the Colonel was among us, and I hung out at the Full Moon. They had been quite on the square with me at the Full Moon, which I mention, because, of course, it has to be remembered, and it do come up as a hitem. And I'm proud, Mr Trewilyan, as I did take to the ground myself; for what should happen but I see the Colonel as large as life ringing at the parson's bell at 1.47 p.m. He was let in at 1.49, and he was let out at 2.17. He went away in a cab which it was kept, and I followed him till he was put down at the Arcade, and I left him having his 'ed washed and greased at Trufitt's rooms, half-way up. It was a wonder to me when I see this, Mr Trewilyan, as he didn't have his 'ed done first, as they most of 'em does when they're going to see their ladies; but I couldn't make nothing of that, though I did try to put too and too together, as I always does.

What he did at the parson's, Mr Trewilyan, I won't say I saw, and I won't say I know. It's my opinion the young woman there isn't on the square, though she's been remembered too, and is a hitem of course. And, Mr Trewilyan, it do go against the grain with me when they're remembered and ain't on the square. I doesn't expect too much of Human Nature, which is poor, as the saying goes; but when they're remembered and ain't on the square after that, it's too bad for Human Nature. It's more than poor. It's what I calls beggarly.

He ain't been there since, Mr Trewilyan, and he goes out of town to-morrow by the 1.15 p.m. express to Bridport. So he lets on; but of course I shall see to that. That he's been at St. Diddulph's, in the house from 1.47 to 2.17, you may take as a fact. There won't be no shaking of that, because I have it in my mem. book, and no Counsel can get the better of it. Of course he went there to see her, and it's my belief he did. The young woman as was remembered says he didn't, but she isn't on the square. They never is when a lady wants to see her gentleman, though they comes round afterwards, and tells up everything when it comes before his ordinary lordship.

If you ask me, Mr Trewilyan, I don't think it's ripe yet for the court, but we'll have it ripe before long. I'll keep a look-out, because it's just possible she may leave town. If she do, I'll be down upon them together, and no mistake.

Yours most respectful,   S. Bozzle.

Every word in the letter had been a dagger to Trevelyan, and yet he felt himself to be under an obligation to the man who had written it. No one else would or could make facts known to him. If she were innocent, let him know that she were innocent, and he would proclaim her innocence, and believe in her innocence and sacrifice himself to her innocence, if such sacrifice were necessary. But if she were guilty, let him also know that. He knew how bad it was, all that bribing of postmen and maidservants, who took his money, and her money also, very likely. It was dirt, all of it. But who had put him into the dirt? His wife had, at least, deceived him had deceived him and disobeyed him, and it was necessary that he should know the facts. Life without a Bozzle would now have been to him a perfect blank.

The Colonel had been to the parsonage at St. Diddulph's, and had been admitted! As to that he had no doubt. Nor did he really doubt that his wife had seen the visitor. He had sent his wife first into a remote village on Dartmoor, and there she had been visited by her lover! How was he to use any other word? Iago, oh, Iago! The pity of it, Iago! Then, when she had learned that this was discovered, she had left the retreat in which he had placed her without permission from him and had taken herself to the house of a relative of hers. Here she was visited again by her lover! Oh, Iago; the pity of it, Iago! And then there had been between them an almost constant correspondence. So much he had ascertained as fact; but he did not for a moment believe that Bozzle had learned all the facts. There might be correspondence, or even visits, of which Bozzle could learn nothing. How could Bozzle know where Mrs Trevelyan was during all those hours which Colonel Osborne passed in London? That which he knew, he knew absolutely, and on that he could act; but there was, of course, much of which he knew nothing. Gradually the truth would unveil itself, and then he would act. He would tear that Colonel into fragments, and throw his wife from him with all the ignominy which the law made possible to him.

But in the meantime he wrote a letter to Mr Outhouse. Colonel Osborne, after all that had been said, had been admitted at the parsonage, and Trevelyan was determined to let the clergyman know what he thought about it. The oftener he turned the matter in his mind, as he walked slowly up and down the piazza of St. Mark, the more absurd it appeared to him to doubt that his wife had seen the man. Of course she had seen him. He walked there nearly the whole night, thinking of it, and as he dragged himself off at last to his inn, had almost come to have but one desire namely, that he should find her out, that the evidence should be conclusive, that it should be proved, and so brought to an end. Then he would destroy her, and destroy that man and afterwards destroy himself, so bitter to him would be his ignominy. He almost revelled in the idea of the tragedy he would make. It was three o'clock before he was in his bedroom, and then he wrote his letter to Mr Outhouse before he took himself to his bed. It was as follows:

Venice,

Oct. 4, 186—.

SIR

Information of a certain kind, on which I can place a firm reliance, has reached me, to the effect that Colonel Osborne has been allowed to visit at your house during the sojourn of my wife under your roof. I will thank you to inform me whether this be true; as, although I am confident of my facts, it is necessary, in reference to my ulterior conduct, that I should have from you either an admission or a denial of my assertion. It is of course open to you to leave my letter unanswered. Should you think proper to do so, I shall know also how to deal with that fact.

As to your conduct in admitting Colonel Osborne into your house while my wife is there after all that has passed, and all that you know that has passed I am quite unable to speak with anything like moderation of feeling. Had the man succeeded in forcing himself into your residence, you should have been the first to give me notice of it. As it is, I have been driven to ascertain the fact from other sources. I think that you have betrayed the trust that a husband has placed in you, and that you will find from the public voice that you will be regarded as having disgraced yourself as a clergyman.

In reference to my wife herself, I would wish her to know, that after what has now taken place, I shall not feel myself justified in leaving our child longer in her hands, even tender as are his years. I shall take steps for having him removed. What further I shall do to vindicate myself, and extricate myself as far as may be possible from the slough of despond in which I have been submerged, she and you will learn in due time.

Your obedient servant,   L. TREVELYAN.

A letter addressed "*poste restante*, Venice," will reach me here.

If Trevelyan was mad when he wrote this letter, Mr Outhouse was very nearly as mad when he read it. He had most strongly desired to have nothing to do with his wife's niece when she was separated from her husband. He was a man honest, charitable, and sufficiently affectionate; but he was timid, and disposed to think ill of those whose modes of life were strange to him. Actuated by these feelings, he would have declined to offer the hospitality of his roof to Mrs Trevelyan, had any choice been left to him. But there had been no choice. She had come thither unasked, with her boy and baggage, and he could not send her away. His wife had told him that it was his duty to protect these women till their father came, and he recognised the truth of what his wife said. There they were, and there they must remain throughout the winter. It was hard upon him, especially as the difficulties and embarrassments as to money were so disagreeable to him, but there was no help for it. His duty must be done though it were ever so painful. Then that horrid Colonel had come. And now had come this letter, in which he was not only accused of being an accomplice between his married niece and her lover, but was also assured that he should be held up to public ignominy and disgrace. Though he had often declared that Trevelyan was mad, he would not remember that now. Such a letter as he had received should have been treated by him as the production of a madman. But he was not sane enough himself to see the matter in that light. He gnashed his teeth, and clenched his fist, and was almost beside himself as he read the letter a second time.

There had been a method in Trevelyan's madness; for, though he had declared to himself that without doubt Bozzle had been right in saying that as the Colonel had been at the parsonage, therefore, as a certainty, Mrs Trevelyan had met the Colonel there, yet he had not so stated in his letter. He had merely asserted that Colonel Osborne had been at the house, and had founded his accusation upon that alleged fact. The alleged fact had been in truth a fact. So far Bozzle had been right. The Colonel had been at the parsonage; and the reader knows how far Mr Outhouse had been to blame for his share in the matter! He rushed off to his wife with the letter, declaring at first that Mrs Trevelyan, Nora, and the child, and the servant, should be sent out of the house at once. But at last Mrs Outhouse succeeded in showing him that he would not be justified in ill-using them because Trevelyan had ill-used him. 'But I will write to him,' said Mr Outhouse. 'He shall know what I think about it.' And he did write his letter that day, in spite of his wife's entreaties that he would allow the sun to set upon his wrath. And his letter was as follows:

St. Diddulph's,
October 8, 186—.

Sɪʀ,

I have received your letter of the 4th, which is more iniquitous, unjust, and ungrateful, than anything I ever before saw written. I have been surprised from the first at your gross cruelty to your unoffending wife; but even that seems to me more intelligible than your conduct in writing such words as those which you have dared to send to me.

For your wife's sake, knowing that she is in a great degree still in your power, I will condescend to tell you what has happened. When Mrs Trevelyan found herself constrained to leave Nuncombe Putney by your aspersions on her character, she came here, to the protection of her nearest relatives within reach, till her father and mother should be in England. Sorely against my will I received them into my home, because they had been deprived of other shelter by the cruelty or madness of him who should have been their guardian. Here they are, and here they shall remain till Sir Marmaduke Rowley arrives. The other day, on the 29th of September, Colonel Osborne, who is their father's old friend, called, not on them, but on me. I may truly say that I did not wish to see Colonel Osborne. They did not see him, nor did he ask to see them. If his coming was a fault, and I think it was a fault, they were not implicated in it. He came, remained a few minutes, and went without seeing any one but myself. That is the history of Colonel Osborne's visit to my house.

I have not thought fit to show your letter to your wife, or to make her acquainted with this further proof of your want of reason. As to the threats which you hold out of removing her child from her, you can of course do nothing except by law. I do not think that even you will be sufficiently audacious to take any steps of that description. Whatever protection the law may give her and her child from your tyranny and misconduct cannot be obtained till her father shall be here.

I have only further to request that you will not address any further communication to me. Should you do so, it will be refused.

Yours, in deep indignation,   Oʟɪᴘʜᴀɴᴛ Oᴜᴛʜᴏᴜꜱᴇ.

Trevelyan had also written two other letters to England, one to Mr Bideawhile, and the other to Bozzle. In the former he acquainted the lawyer that he had discovered that his wife still maintained her intercourse with Colonel Osborne, and that he must therefore remove his child from her custody. He then inquired what steps would be necessary to enable him to obtain possession of his little boy. In the letter to Bozzle he sent a cheque, and his thanks for the ex-policeman's watchful care. He desired Bozzle to continue his precautions, and explained his intentions about his son. Being somewhat afraid that Mr Bideawhile might not be zealous on his behalf, and not himself understanding accurately the extent of his power with regard to his own child, or the means whereby he might exercise it, he was anxious to obtain assistance from Bozzle also on this point; he had no doubt that Bozzle knew all about it. He had great confidence in Bozzle. But still he did not like to consult the ex policeman. He knew that it became him to have some regard for his own dignity. He therefore put the matter very astutely to Bozzle asking no questions, but alluding to his difficulty in a way that would enable Bozzle to offer advice.

And where was he to get a woman to take charge of his child? If Lady Milborough would do it, how great would be the comfort! But he was almost sure that Lady Milborough would not do it. All his friends had turned against him, and Lady Milborough among the number. There was nobody left to him, but Bozzle. Could he entrust Bozzle to find some woman for him who would take adequate charge of the little fellow, till he himself could see to the child's education? He did not put this question to Bozzle in plain terms; but he was very astute, and wrote in such a fashion that Bozzle could make a proposal, if any proposal were within his power.

The answer from Mr Outhouse came first. To this Mr Trevelyan paid very little attention. It was just what he expected. Of course, Mr Outhouse's assurance about Colonel Osborne went for nothing. A man who would permit intercourse in his house between a married lady and her lover, would not scruple to deny that he had permitted it. Then came Mr Bideawhile's answer, which was very short. Mr Bideawhile said that nothing could be done about the child till Mr Trevelyan should return to England and that he could give no opinion as to what should be done then till he knew more of the circumstances. It was quite clear to Trevelyan that he must employ some other lawyer. Mr Bideawhile had probably been corrupted by Colonel Osborne. Could Bozzle recommend a lawyer?

From Bozzle himself there came no other immediate reply than, 'his duty, and that he would make further inquiries.'

CHAPTER XLVI. THE AMERICAN MINISTER

In the second week in October, Mr Glascock returned to Florence, intending to remain there till the weather should have become bearable at Naples. His father was said to be better, but was in such a condition as hardly to receive much comfort from his son's presence. His mind was gone, and he knew no one but his nurse; and, though Mr Glascock was unwilling to put himself altogether out of the reach of returning at a day's notice, he did not find himself obliged to remain in Naples during the heat of the autumn. So Mr Glascock returned to the hotel at Florence, accompanied by the tall man who wore the buttons. The hotel-keeper did not allow such a light to remain long hidden under a bushel, and it was soon spread far and wide that the Honourable Charles Glascock and his suite were again in the beautiful city.

And the fact was soon known to the American Minister and his family. Mr Spalding was a man who at home had been very hostile to English interests. Many American gentlemen are known for such hostility. They make anti-English speeches about the country, as though they thought that war with England would produce certain triumph to the States, certain increase to American trade, and certain downfall to a tyranny which no Anglo-Saxon nation ought to endure. But such is hardly their real opinion. There, in the States, as also here in England, you shall from day to day hear men propounding, in very loud language, advanced theories of political action, the assertion of which is supposed to be necessary to the end which they have in view. Men whom we know to have been as mild as sucking doves in the political aspiration of their whole lives, suddenly jump up, and with infuriated gestures declare themselves the enemies of everything existing. When they have obtained their little purpose or have failed to do so they revert naturally into their sucking-dove elements. It is so with Americans as frequently as with ourselves and there is no political subject on which it is considered more expedient to express pseudo-enthusiasm than on that of the sins of England. It is understood that we do not resent it. It is presumed that we regard it as the Irishman regarded his wife's cuffs. In the States a large party, which consists chiefly of those who have lately left English rule, amid who are keen to prove to themselves how wise they have been in doing so, is pleased by this strong language against England; and, therefore, the strong language is spoken. But the speakers, who are, probably, men knowing something of the world, mean it not at all; they have no more idea of war with England than they have of war with all Europe; and their respect for England and for English opinion is unbounded. In their political tones of speech and modes of action they strive to be as English as possible. Mr Spalding's aspirations were of this nature. He had uttered speeches against England which would make the hair stand on end on the head of an uninitiated English reader. He had told his countrymen that Englishmen hugged their chains, and would do so until American hammers had knocked those chains from off their wounded wrists and bleeding ankles. He had declared that, if certain American claims were not satisfied, there was nothing left for Americans to do but to cross the ferry with such a sheriff's officer as would be able to make distraint on the great English household. He had declared that the sheriff's officer would have very little trouble. He had spoken of Canada as an outlying American territory, not yet quite sufficiently redeemed from savage life to be received into the Union as a State. There is a multiplicity of subjects of this kind ready to the hand of the American orator. Mr Spalding had been quite successful, and was now Minister at Florence; but, perhaps, one of the greatest pleasures coming to him from his prosperity was the enjoyment of the society of well-bred Englishmen in the capital to which he had been sent. When, therefore, his wife and nieces pointed out to him the fact that it was manifestly his duty to call upon Mr Glascock after what had passed between them on that night under the Campanile, he did not rebel for an instant against the order given to him. His mind never reverted for a moment to that opinion which had gained for him such a round of applause, when expressed on the platform of the Temperance Hall at Nubbly Creek, State of Illinois, to the effect that the English aristocrat, thorough-born and thorough-bred, who inherited acres and title from his father, could never be fitting company for a thoughtful Christian American citizen. He at once had his hat brushed, and took up his best gloves and umbrella, and went off to Mr Glascock's hotel. He was strictly enjoined by the ladies to fix a day on which Mr Glascock would come and dine at the American embassy.

'"C. G." has come back to see you,' said Olivia to her elder sister. They had always called him 'C. G.' since the initials had been seen on the travelling bag.

'Probably,' said Carry. 'There is so very little else to bring people to Florence, that there can hardly be any other reason for his coming. They do say it's terribly hot at Naples just now; but that can have had nothing to do with it.'

'We shall see,' said Livy. 'I'm sure he's in love with you. He looked to me just like a proper sort of lover for you, when I saw his long legs creeping up over our heads into the banquette.'

'You ought to have been very much obliged to his long legs so sick as you were at the time.'

'I like him amazingly,' said Livy, 'legs and all. I only hope Uncle Jonas won't bore him, so as to prevent his coming.'

'His father is very ill,' said Carry, 'and I don't suppose we shall see him at all.'

But the American Minister was successful. He found Mr Glascock sitting in his dressing-gown, smoking a cigar, and reading a newspaper. The English aristocrat seemed very glad to see his visitor, and assumed no airs at all. The American altogether forgot his speech at Nubbly Creek, and found the aristocrat's society to be very pleasant. He lit a cigar, and they talked about Naples, Rome, and Florence. Mr Spalding, when the marbles of old Rome were mentioned, was a little too keen in insisting on the merits of Story, Miss Hosmer, and Hiram Powers, and hardly carried his listener with him in the parallel which he drew between Greenough and Phidias; and he was somewhat repressed by the apathetic curtness of Mr Glascock's reply, when he suggested that the victory gained by the gunboats at Vicksburg, on the Mississippi, was vividly brought to his mind by an account which he had just been reading of the battle of Actium; but he succeeded in inducing Mr Glascock to accept an invitation to dinner for the next day but one, and the two gentlemen parted on the most amicable terms.

Everybody meets everybody in Florence every day. Carry and Livy Spalding had met Mr Glascock twice before the dinner at their uncle's house, so that they met at dinner quite as intimate friends. Mrs Spalding had very large rooms, up three flights of stairs, on the Lungarno. The height of her abode was attributed by Mrs Spalding to her dread of mosquitoes. She had not yet learned that people in Florence require no excuse for being asked to walk up three flights of stairs. The rooms, when they were reached, were very lofty, floored with what seemed to be marble, and were of a nature almost to warrant Mrs Spalding in feeling that nature had made her more akin to an Italian countess than to a matron of Nubbly Creek, State of Illinois, where Mr Spalding had found her and made her his own. There was one other Englishman present, Mr Harris Hyde Granville Gore, from the Foreign Office, now serving temporarily at the English Legation in Florence; and an American, Mr Jackson Unthank, a man of wealth and taste, who was resolved on having such a collection of pictures at his house in Baltimore that no English private collection should in any way come near to it; and a Tuscan, from the Italian Foreign Office, to whom nobody could speak except Mr Harris Hyde Granville Gore, who did not indeed seem to enjoy the efforts of conversation which were expected of him. The Italian, who had a handle to his name—he was a Count Buonarosci—took Mrs Spalding into dinner. Mrs Spalding had been at great trouble to ascertain whether this was proper, or whether she should not entrust herself to Mr Glascock. There were different points to be considered in the matter. She did not quite know whether she was in Italy or in America. She had glimmerings on the subject of her privilege to carry her own nationality into her own drawing-room. And then she was called upon to deal between an Italian Count with an elder brother, and an English Honourable, who had no such encumbrance. Which of the two was possessed of the higher rank? 'I've found it all out, Aunt Mary,' said Livy. 'You must take the Count.' For Livy wanted to give her sister every chance. 'How have you found it out?' said the aunt. 'You may be sure it is so,' said Livy.

And the lady in her doubt yielded the point. Mrs Spalding, as she walked along the passage on the Count's arm, determined that she would learn Italian. She would have given all Nubbly Creek to have been able to speak a word to Count Buonarosci. To do her justice, it must be admitted that she had studied a few words. But her courage failed her, and she could not speak them. She was very careful, however, that Mr H. H. G. Gore was placed in the chair next to the Count.

'We are very glad to see you here,' said Mr Spalding, addressing himself especially to Mr Glascock, as he stood up at his own seat at the round table. 'In leaving my own country, sir, there is nothing that I value more than the privilege of becoming acquainted with those whose historic names and existing positions are of such inestimable value to the world at large.' In saying this, Mr Spalding was not in the least insincere, nor did his conscience at all prick him in reference to that speech at Nubbly Creek. On both occasions he half thought as he spoke or thought that he thought so. Unless it be on subjects especially endeared to us the thoughts of but few of us go much beyond this.

Mr Glascock, who sat between Mrs Spalding and her niece, was soon asked by the elder lady whether he had been in the States. No; he had not been in the States. 'Then you must come, Mr Glascock,' said Mrs Spalding, 'though I will not say, dwelling as we now are in the metropolis of the world of art, that we in our own homes have as much of the outer beauty of form to charm the stranger as is to be found in other lands. Yet I think that the busy lives of men, and the varied institutions of a free country, must always have an interest peculiarly their own.' Mr Glascock declared that he quite agreed with her, and expressed a hope that he might some day find himself in New York.

'You wouldn't like it at all,' said Carry; 'because you are an aristocrat. I don't mean that it would be your fault.'

'Why should that prevent my liking it even if I were an aristocrat?'

'One half of the people would run after you, and the other half would run away from you,' said Carry.

'Then I'd take to the people who ran after me, and would not regard the others.'

'That's all very well but you wouldn't like it. And then you would become unfair to what you saw. When some of our speechifying people talked to you about our institutions through their noses, you would think that the institutions themselves must be bad. And we have nothing to show except our institutions.'

'What are American institutions? asked Mr Glascock.

'Everything is an institution. Having iced water to drink in every room of the house is an institution. Having hospitals in every town is an institution. Travelling altogether in one class of railway cars is an institution. Saying sir, is an institution. Teaching all the children mathematics is an institution. Plenty of food is an institution. Getting drunk is an institution in a great many towns. Lecturing is an institution. There are plenty of them, and some are very good but you wouldn't like it.'

'At any rate, I'll go and see,' said Mr Glascock.

'If you do, I hope we may be at home,' said Miss Spalding.

Mr Spalding, in the mean time, with the assistance of his countryman, the man of taste, was endeavouring to explain a certain point in American politics to the count. As, in doing this, they called upon Mr Gore to translate every speech they made into Italian, and as Mr Gore had never offered his services as an interpreter, and as the Italian did not quite catch the subtle meanings of the Americans in Mr Gore's Tuscan version, and did not in the least wish to understand the things that were explained to him, Mr Gore and the Italian began to think that the two Americans were bores. 'The truth is, Mr Spalding,' said Mr Gore, 'I've got such a cold in my head, that I don't think I can explain it any more.' Then Livy Spalding laughed aloud, and the two American gentlemen began to eat their dinner. 'It sounds ridiculous, don't it?' said Mr Gore, in a whisper.

'I ought not to have laughed, I know,' said Livy.

'The very best thing you could have done. I shan't be troubled any more now. The fact is, I know just nine words of Italian. Now there is a difficulty in having to explain the whole theory of American politics to an Italian, who doesn't want to know anything about it, with so very small a repertory of words at one's command.'

'How well you did it!'

'Too well. I felt that. So well that, unless I had stopped it, I shouldn't have been able to say a word to you all through dinner. Your laughter clenched it, and Buonarosci and I will be grateful to you for ever.'

After the ladies went there was rather a bad half hour for Mr Glascock. He was button-holed by the minister, and found it oppressive before he was enabled to escape into the drawing-room. 'Mr Glascock,' said the minister, 'an English gentleman, sir, like you, who has the privilege of an hereditary seat in your parliament'—Mr Glascock was not quite sure whether he were being accused of having an hereditary seat in the House of Commons, but he would not stop to correct any possible error on that point—'and who has been born to all the gifts of fortune, rank, and social eminence, should never think that his education is complete till he has visited our great cities in the west.' Mr Glascock hinted that he by no means conceived his education to be complete; but the minister went on without attending to this. 'Till you have seen, sir, what men can do who are placed upon the earth with all God's gifts of free intelligence, free air, and a free soil, but without any of those other good things which we are accustomed to call the gifts of fortune, you can never become aware of the infinite ingenuity of man.' There had been much said before, but just at this moment Mr Gore and the American left the room, and the Italian followed them briskly. Mr Glascock at once made a decided attempt to bolt; but the minister was on the alert, and was too quick for him. And he was by no means ashamed of what he was doing. He had got his guest by the coat, and openly declared his intention of holding him. 'Let me keep you for a few minutes, sir,' said he, 'while I dilate on this point in one direction. In the drawing-room female spells are too potent for us male orators. In going among us, Mr Glascock, you must not look for luxury or refinement, for you will find them not. Nor must you hope to encounter the highest order of erudition. The lofty summits of acquired knowledge tower in your country with an altitude we have not reached yet.' 'It's very good of you to say so,' said Mr Glascock. 'No, sir. In our new country and in our new cities we still lack the luxurious perfection of fastidious civilisation. But, sir, regard our level. That's what I say to every unprejudiced Britisher that comes among us; look at our level. And when you have looked at our level, I think that you will confess that we live on the highest table-land that the world has yet afforded to mankind. You follow my meaning, Mr Glascock?' Mr Glascock was not sure that he did, but the minister went on to make that meaning clear. 'It is the multitude that with us is educated. Go into their houses, sir, and see how they thumb their books. Look at the domestic correspondence of our helps and servants, and see how they write and spell. We haven't got the mountains, sir, but our table-lands are the highest on which the bright sun of our Almighty God has as yet shone with its illuminating splendour in this improving world of ours! It is because we are a young people, sir with nothing as yet near to us of the decrepitude of age. The weakness of age, sir, is the penalty paid by the folly of youth. We are not so wise, sir, but what we too shall suffer from its effects as years roll over our heads.' There was a great deal more, but at last Mr Glascock did escape into the drawing-room.

'My uncle has been saying a few words to you perhaps,' said Carry Spalding.

'Yes; he has,' said Mr Glascock.

'He usually does,' said Carry Spalding.

CHAPTER XLVII. ABOUT FISHING, AND NAVIGATION, AND HEAD-DRESSES

The feud between Miss Stanbury and Mr Gibson raged violently in Exeter, and produced many complications which were very difficult indeed of management. Each belligerent party felt that a special injury had been inflicted upon it. Mr Gibson was quite sure that he had been grossly misused by Miss Stanbury the elder, and strongly suspected that Miss Stanbury the younger had had a hand in this misconduct. It had been positively asserted to him, at least so he thought, but in this was probably in error, that the lady would accept him if he proposed to her. All Exeter had been made aware of the intended compact. He, indeed, had denied its existence to Miss French, comforting himself, as best he might, with the reflection that all is fair in love and war; but when he counted over his injuries he did not think of this denial. All Exeter, so to say, had known of it. And yet, when he had come with his proposal, he had been refused without a moment's consideration, first by the aunt, and then by the niece and, after that, had been violently abused, and at last turned out of the house! Surely, no gentleman had ever before been subjected to ill-usage so violent! But Miss Stanbury the elder was quite as assured that the injury had been done to her. As to the matter of the compact itself, she knew very well that she had been as true as steel. She had done everything in her power to bring about the marriage. She had been generous in her offers of money. She had used all her powers of persuasion on Dorothy, and she had given every opportunity to Mr Gibson. It was not her fault if he had not been able to avail himself of the good things which she had put in his way. He had first been, as she thought, ignorant and arrogant, fancying that the good things ought to be made his own without any trouble on his part, and then awkward, not knowing how to take the trouble when trouble was necessary. And as to that matter of abusive language and turning out of the house, Miss Stanbury was quite convinced that she was sinned against, and not herself the sinner. She declared to Martha, more than once, that Mr Gibson had used such language to her that, coming out of a clergyman's mouth, it had quite dismayed her. Martha, who knew her mistress, probably felt that Mr Gibson had at least received as good as he gave; but she had made no attempt to set her mistress right on that point.

But the cause of Miss Stanbury's sharpest anger was not to be found in Mr Gibson's conduct either before Dorothy's refusal of his offer, or on the occasion of his being turned out of the house. A base rumour was spread about the city that Dorothy Stanbury had been offered to Mr Gibson, that Mr Gibson had civilly declined the offer, and that hence had arisen the wrath of the Juno of the Close. Now this was not to be endured by Miss Stanbury. She had felt even in the moment of her original anger against Mr Gibson that she was bound in honour not to tell the story against him. She had brought him into the little difficulty, and she at least would hold her tongue. She was quite sure that Dorothy would never boast of her triumph. And Martha had been strictly cautioned as indeed, also, had Brooke Burgess. The man had behaved like an idiot, Miss Stanbury said; but he had been brought into a little dilemma, and nothing should be said about it from the house in the Close. But when the other rumour reached Miss Stanbury's ears, when Mrs Crumbie condoled with her on her niece's misfortune, when Mrs MacHugh asked whether Mr Gibson had not behaved rather badly to the young lady, then our Juno's celestial mind was filled with a divine anger. But even then she did not declare the truth. She asked a question of Mrs Crumbie, and was enabled, as she thought, to trace the falsehood to the Frenches. She did not think that Mr Gibson could on a sudden have become so base a liar. 'Mr Gibson fast and loose with my niece?' she said to Mrs MacHugh. 'You have not got the story quite right, my dear friend. Pray, believe me there has been nothing of that sort.' 'I dare say not,' said Mrs MacHugh, 'and I'm sure I don't care. Mr Gibson has been going to marry one of the French girls for the last ten years, and I think he ought to make up his mind and do it at last.'

'I can assure you he is quite welcome as far as Dorothy is concerned,' said Miss Stanbury.

Without a doubt the opinion did prevail throughout Exeter that Mr Gibson, who had been regarded time out of mind as the property of the Miss Frenches, had been angled for by the ladies in the Close, that he had nearly been caught, but that he had slipped the hook out of his mouth, and was now about to subside quietly into the net which had been originally prepared for him. Arabella French had not spoken loudly on the subject, but Camilla had declared in more than one house that she had most direct authority for stating that the gentleman had never dreamed of offering to the young lady. 'Why he should not do so if he pleases, I don't know,' said Camilla. 'Only the fact is that he has not pleased. The rumour of course has reached him, and, as we happen to be very old friends we have authority for denying it altogether.' All this came round to Miss Stanbury, and she was divine in her wrath.

'If they drive me to it,' she said to Dorothy, 'I'll have the whole truth told by the bellman through the city, or I'll publish it in the *County Gazette*.'

'Pray don't say a word about it, Aunt Stanbury.'

'It is those odious girls. He's there now every day.'

'Why shouldn't he go there, Aunt Stanbury?'

'If he's fool enough, let him go. I don't care where he goes. But I do care about these lies. They wouldn't dare to say it only they think my mouth is closed. They've no honour themselves, but they screen themselves behind mine.'

'I'm sure they won't find themselves mistaken in what they trust to,' said Dorothy, with a spirit that her aunt had not expected from her. Miss Stanbury at this time had told nobody that the offer to her niece had been made and repeated and finally rejected, but she found it very difficult to hold her tongue.

In the meantime Mr Gibson spent a good deal of his time at Heavitree. It should not perhaps be asserted broadly that he had made up his mind that marriage would be good for him; but he had made up his mind, at least, to this, that it was no longer to be postponed without a balance of disadvantage. The Charybdis in the Close drove him helpless into the whirlpool of the Heavitree Scylla. He had no longer an escape from the perils of the latter shore. He had been so mauled by the opposite waves, that he had neither spirit nor skill left to him to keep in the middle track. He was almost daily at Heavitree, and did not attempt to conceal from himself the approach of his doom.

But still there were two of them. He knew that he must become a prey, but was there any choice left to him as to which siren should have him? He had been quite aware in his more gallant days, before he had been knocked about on that Charybdis rock, that he might sip, and taste, and choose between the sweets. He had come to think lately that the younger young lady was the sweeter. Eight years ago indeed the passages between him and the elder had been tender; but Camilla had then been simply a romping girl, hardly more than a year or two beyond her teens. Now, with her matured charms, Camilla was certainly the more engaging, as far as outward form went. Arabella's cheeks were thin and long, and her front teeth had come to show themselves. Her eyes were no doubt still bright, and what she had of hair was soft and dark. But it was very thin in front, and what there was of supplemental mass behind the bandbox by which Miss Stanbury was so much aggrieved was worn with an indifference to the lines of beauty, which Mr Gibson himself found to be very depressing. A man with a fair burden on his back is not a grievous sight; but when we see a small human being attached to a bale of goods which he can hardly manage to move, we feel that the poor fellow has been cruelly over-weighted. Mr Gibson certainly had that sensation about Arabella's chignon. And as he regarded it in a nearer and a dearer light as a chignon that might possibly become his own, as a burden which in one sense he might himself be called upon to bear, as a domestic utensil of which he himself might be called upon to inspect, and, perhaps, to aid the shifting on and the shifting off, he did begin to think that that side of the Scylla gulf ought to be avoided if possible. And probably this propensity on his part, this feeling that he would like to reconsider the matter dispassionately before he gave himself up for good to his old love, may have been increased by Camilla's apparent withdrawal of her claims. He felt mildly grateful to the Heavitree household in general for accepting him in this time of his affliction, but he could not admit to himself that they had a right to decide upon him in private conclave, and allot him either to the one or to the other nuptials without consultation with himself. To be swallowed up by Scylla he now recognised as his doom; but he thought he ought to be asked on which side of the gulf he would prefer to go down. The way in which Camilla spoke of him as a thing that wasn't hers, but another's; and the way in which Arabella looked at him, as though he were hers and could never be another's, wounded his manly pride. He had always understood that he might have his choice, and he could not understand that the little mishap which had befallen him in the Close was to rob him of that privilege.

He used to drink tea at Heavitree in those days. On one evening on going in he found himself alone with Arabella. 'Oh, Mr Gibson,' she said, 'we weren't sure whether you'd come. And mamma and Camilla have gone out to Mrs Camadge's.' Mr Gibson muttered some word to the effect that he hoped he had kept nobody at home; and, as he did so, he remembered that he had distinctly said that he would come on this evening. 'I don't know that I should have gone,' sad Arabella, 'because I am not quite not quite myself at present. No, not ill; not at all. Don't you know what it is, Mr Gibson, to be to be to be not quite yourself?' Mr Gibson said that he had very often felt like that. 'And one can't get over it can one?' continued Arabella. 'There comes a presentiment that something is going to happen, and a kind of belief that something has happened, though you don't know what; and the heart refuses to be light, and the spirit becomes abashed, and the mind, though it creates new thoughts, will not settle itself to its accustomed work. I suppose it's what the novels have called Melancholy.'

'I suppose it is,' said Mr Gibson. 'But there's generally some cause for it. Debt for instance.'

'It's nothing of that kind with me. Its no debt, at least, that can be written down in the figures of ordinary arithmetic. Sit down, Mr Gibson, and we will have some tea.' Then, as she stretched forward to ring the bell, he thought that he never in his life had seen anything so unshapely as that huge wen at the back of her head. '*Monstrum horrendum, informe, ingens*!' He could not help quoting the words to himself. She was dressed with some attempt at being smart, but her ribbons were soiled, and her lace was tawdry, and the fabric of her dress was old and dowdy. He was quite sure that he would feel no pride in calling her Mrs Gibson, no pleasure in having her all to himself at his own hearth. 'I hope we shall escape the bitterness of Miss Stanbury's tongue if we drink tea *tête-à-tête*,' she said, with her sweetest smile.

'I don't suppose she'll know anything about it.'

'She knows about everything, Mr Gibson. It's astonishing what she knows. She has eyes and ears everywhere. I shouldn't care, if she didn't see and hear so very incorrectly. I'm told now that she declares— but it doesn't signify.'

'Declares what?' asked Mr Gibson.

'Never mind. But wasn't it odd how all Exeter believed that you were going to be married in that house, and to live there all the rest of your life, and be one of Miss Stanbury's slaves. I never believed it, Mr Gibson.' This she said with a sad smile, that ought to have brought him on his knees, in spite of the chignon.

'One can't help these things,' said Mr Gibson.

'I never could have believed it, not even if you had not given me an assurance so solemn, and so sweet, that there was nothing in it.' The poor man had given the assurance, and could not deny the solemnity and the sweetness. 'That was a happy moment for us, Mr Gibson; because, though we never believed it, when it was dinned into our ears so frequently, when it was made such a triumph in the Close, it was impossible not to fear that there might be something in it.' He felt that he ought to make some reply, but he did not know what to say. He was thoroughly ashamed of the lie he had told, but he could not untell it. 'Camilla reproached me afterwards for asking you,' whispered Arabella, in her softest, tenderest voice.'she said that it was unmaidenly. I hope you did not think it unmaidenly, Mr Gibson?'

'Oh dear, no, not at all,' said he.

Arabella French was painfully alive to the fact that she must do something. She had her fish on the hook; but of what use is a fish on your hook, if you cannot land him? When could she have a better opportunity than this of landing the scaly darling out of the fresh and free waters of his bachelor stream, and sousing him into the pool of domestic life, to be ready there for her own household purposes? 'I had known you so long, Mr Gibson,' she said, 'and had valued your friendship so so deeply.' As he looked at her, he could see nothing but the shapeless excrescence to which his eyes had been so painfully called by Miss Stanbury's satire. It is true that he had formerly been very tender with her, but she had not then carried about with her that distorted monster. He did not believe himself to be at all bound by anything which had passed between them in circumstances so very different. But yet he ought to say something. He ought to have said something; but he said nothing. She was patient, however, very patient; and she went on playing him with her hook. 'I am so glad that I did not go out to-night with mamma. It has been such a pleasure to me to have this conversation with you. Camilla, perhaps, would say that I am unmaidenly.'

'I don't think so.'

'That is all that I care for, Mr Gibson. If you acquit me, I do not mind who accuses. I should not like to suppose that you thought me unmaidenly. Anything would be better than that; but I can throw all such considerations to the wind when true true friendship is concerned. Don't you think that one ought, Mr Gibson?'

If it had not been for the thing at the back of her head, he would have done it now. Nothing but that gave him courage to abstain. It grew bigger and bigger, more shapeless, monstrous, absurd, and abominable, as he looked at it. Nothing should force upon him the necessity of assisting to carry such an abortion through the world. 'One ought to sacrifice everything to friendship,' said Mr Gibson, 'except self-respect.'

He meant nothing personal. Something special, in the way of an opinion, was expected of him; and, therefore, he had striven to say something special. But she was in tears in a moment. 'Oh, Mr Gibson,' she exclaimed; 'oh, Mr Gibson!'

'What is the matter, Miss French?'

'Have I lost your respect? Is it that that you mean?'

'Certainly not, Miss French.'

'Do not call me Miss French, or I shall be sure that you condemn me. Miss French sounds so very cold. You used to call me Bella.' That was quite true; but it was long ago, thought Mr Gibson, before the monster had been attached. 'Will you not call me Bella now?'

He thought that he had rather not; and yet, how was he to avoid it? On a sudden he became very crafty. Had it not been for the sharpness of his mother-wit, he would certainly have been landed at that moment. 'As you truly observed just now,' he said, 'the tongues of people are so malignant. There are little birds that hear everything.'

'I don't care what the little birds hear,' said Miss French, through her tears. 'I am a very unhappy girl—I know that; and I don't care what anybody says. It is nothing to me what anybody says. I know what I feel.' At this moment there was some dash of truth about her. The fish was so very heavy on hand that, do what she would, she could not land him. Her hopes before this had been very low, hopes that had once been high; but they had been depressed gradually; and, in the slow, dull routine of her daily life, she had learned to bear disappointment by degrees, without sign of outward suffering, without consciousness of acute pain. The task of her life had been weary, and the wished-for goal was ever becoming more and more distant; but there had been still a chance, and she had fallen away into a lethargy of lessening expectation, from which joy, indeed, had been banished, but in which there had been nothing of agony. Then had come upon the whole house at

Heavitree the great Stanbury peril, and, arising out of that, had sprung new hopes to Arabella, which made her again capable of all the miseries of a foiled ambition. She could again be patient, if patience might be of any service; but in such a condition an eternity of patience is simply suicidal. She was willing to work hard, but how could she work harder than she had worked. Poor young woman perishing beneath an incubus which a false idea of fashion had imposed on her!

'I hope I have said nothing that makes you unhappy,' pleaded Mr Gibson. 'I'm sure I haven't meant it.'

'But you have,' she said. 'You make me very unhappy. You condemn me. I see you do. And if I have done wrong it had been all because—Oh dear, oh dear, oh dear!'

'But who says you have done wrong?'

'You won't call me Bella because you say the little birds will hear it. If I don't care for the little birds, why should you?'

There is no question more difficult than this for a gentleman to answer. Circumstances do not often admit of its being asked by a lady with that courageous simplicity which had come upon Miss French in this moment of her agonising struggle; but nevertheless it is one which, in a more complicated form, is often put, and to which some reply, more or less complicated, is expected. 'If I, a woman, can dare, for your sake, to encounter the public tongue, will you, a man, be afraid?' The true answer, if it could be given, would probably be this; 'I am afraid, though a man, because I have much to lose and little to get. You are not afraid, though a woman, because you have much to get and little to lose.' But such an answer would be uncivil, and is not often given. Therefore men shuffle and lie, and tell themselves that in love—love here being taken to mean all antenuptial contests between man and woman— everything is fair. Mr Gibson had the above answer in his mind, though he did not frame it into words. He was neither sufficiently brave nor sufficiently cruel to speak to her in such language. There was nothing for him, therefore, but that he must shuffle and lie.

'I only meant,' said he, 'that I would not for worlds do anything to make you uneasy.'

She did not see how she could again revert to the subject of her own Christian name. She had made her little tender, loving request, and it had been refused. Of course she knew that it had been refused as a matter of caution. She was not angry with him because of his caution, as she had expected him to be cautious. The barriers over which she had to climb were no more than she had expected to find in her way, but they were so very high and so very difficult! Of course she was aware that he would escape if he could. She was not angry with him on that account. Anger could not have helped her. Indeed, she did not price herself highly enough to make her feel that she would be justified in being angry. It was natural enough that he shouldn't want her. She knew herself to be a poor, thin, vapid, tawdry creature, with nothing to recommend her to any man except a sort of second-rate, provincial-town fashion which, infatuated as she was, she attributed in a great degree to the thing she carried on her head. She knew nothing. She could do nothing. She possessed nothing. She was not angry with him because he so evidently wished to avoid her. But she thought that if she could only be successful she would be good and loving and obedient and that it was fair for her at any rate to try. Each created animal must live and get its food by the gifts which the Creator has given to it, let those gifts be as poor as they may, let them be even as distasteful as they may to other members of the great created family. The rat, the toad, the slug, the flea, must each live according to its appointed mode of existence. Animals which are parasites by nature can only live by attaching themselves to life that is strong. To Arabella, Mr Gibson would be strong enough, and it seemed to her that it she could fix herself permanently upon his strength, that would be her proper mode of living. She was not angry with him because he resisted the attempt, but she had nothing of conscience to tell her that she should spare him as long as there remained to her a chance of success. And should not her plea of excuse, her justification be admitted? There are tormentors as to which no man argues that they are iniquitous, though they be very troublesome. He either rids himself of them, or suffers as quiescently as he may.

'We used to be such great friends, she said, still crying, 'and I am afraid you don't like me a bit now.'

'Indeed, I do I have always liked you. But—'

'But what? Do tell me what the but means. I will do anything that you bid me.'

Then it occurred to him that if, after such a promise, he were to confide to her his feeling that the chignon which she wore was ugly and unbecoming, she would probably be induced to change her mode of head-dress. It was a foolish idea, because, had he followed it out, he would have seen that compliance on her part in such a matter could only be given with the distinct understanding that a certain reward should be the consequence. When an unmarried gentleman calls upon an unmarried lady to change the fashion of her personal adornments, the unmarried lady has a right to expect that the unmarried gentleman means to make her his wife. But Mr Gibson had no such meaning; and was led into error by the necessity for sudden action. When she offered to do anything that he might bid her do, he could not take up his hat and go away he looked up into his face, expecting that he would give her some order and he fell into the temptation that was spread for him.

'If I might say a word,' he began.

'You may say anything,' she exclaimed.

'If I were you I don't think—'

'You don't think what, Mr Gibson?'

He found it to be a matter very difficult of approach. 'Do you know, I don't think the fashion that has come up about wearing your hair quite suits you—not so well as the way you used to do it.' She became on a sudden very red in the face, and he thought that she was angry. Vexed she was, but still, accompanying her vexation, there was a remembrance that she was achieving victory even by her own humiliation. She loved her chignon; but she was ready to abandon even that for him. Nevertheless she could not speak for a moment or two, and he was forced to continue his criticism. 'I have no doubt those things are very becoming and all that, and I dare say they are comfortable.'

'Oh, very,' she said.

'But there was a simplicity that I liked about the other.'

Could it be then that for the last five years he had stood aloof from her because she had arrayed herself in fashionable attire? She was still very red in the face, still suffering from wounded vanity, still conscious of that soreness which affects us all when we are made to understand that we are considered to have failed there, where we have most thought that we excelled. But her womanly art enabled her quickly to conceal the pain. 'I have made a promise,' she said, 'and you will find that I will keep it.'

'What promise?' asked Mr Gibson.

'I said that I would do as you bade me, and so I will. I would have done it sooner if I had known that you wished it. I would never have worn it at all if I had thought that you disliked it.'

'I think that a little of them is very nice,' said Mr Gibson. Mr Gibson was certainly an awkward man. But there are men so awkward that it seems to be their especial province to say always the very worst thing at the very worst moment.

She became redder than ever as she was thus told of the hugeness of her favourite ornament. She was almost angry now. But she restrained herself, thinking perhaps of how she might teach him taste in days to come as he was teaching her now. 'I will change it tomorrow,' she said with a smile. 'You come and see to-morrow.'

Upon this he got up and took his hat and made his escape, assuring her that he would come and see her on the morrow. She let him go now without any attempt at further tenderness. Certainly she had gained much during the interview. He had as good as told her in what had been her offence, and of course, when she had remedied that offence, he could hardly refuse to return to her. She got up as soon as she was alone, and looked at her head in the glass, and told herself that the pity would be great. It was not that the chignon was in itself a thing of beauty, but that it imparted so unmistakable an air of fashion! It divested her of that dowdiness which she feared above all things, and enabled her to hold her own among other young women, without feeling that she was absolutely destitute of attraction. There had been a certain homage paid to it, which she had recognised and enjoyed. But it was her ambition to hold her own, not among young women, but among clergymen's wives, and she would certainly obey his orders. She could not make the attempt now because of the complications; but she certainly would make it before she laid her head on the pillow—and would explain to Camilla that it was a little joke between herself and Mr Gibson.

CHAPTER XLVIII. MR GIBSON IS PUNISHED

Miss Stanbury was divine in her wrath, and became more and more so daily as new testimony reached her of dishonesty on the part of the Frenches and of treachery on the part of Mr Gibson. And these people, so empty, so vain, so weak, were getting the better of her, were conquering her, were robbing her of her prestige and her ancient glory, simply because she herself was too generous to speak out and tell the truth! There was a martyrdom to her in this which was almost unendurable.

Now there came to her one day at luncheon time, on the day succeeding that on which Miss French had promised to sacrifice her chignon, a certain Mrs Clifford from Budleigh Salterton, to whom she was much attached. Perhaps the distance of Budleigh Salterton from Exeter added somewhat to this affection, so that Mrs Clifford was almost closer to our friend's heart even than Mrs MacHugh, who lived just at the other end of the cathedral. And in truth Mrs Clifford was a woman more serious in her mode of thought than Mrs MacHugh, and one who had more in common with Miss Stanbury than that other lady. Mrs Clifford had been a Miss Noel of Doddiscombe Leigh, and she and Miss Stanbury had been engaged to be married at the same time each to a man of fortune. One match had been completed in the ordinary course of matches. What had been the course of the other we already know. But the friendship had been maintained on very close terms. Mrs MacHugh was a Gallio at heart, anxious chiefly to remove from herself and from her friends also all the troubles of life, and make things smooth and easy. She was one who disregarded great questions; who cared little or nothing what people said of her; who considered nothing worth the trouble of a fight. *Epicuri de grege porca*. But there was nothing swinish about Mrs Clifford of Budleigh Salterton. She took life thoroughly in earnest. She was a Tory who sorrowed heartily for her country, believing that it was being brought to ruin by the counsels of evil men. She prayed daily to be delivered from dissenters, radicals, and wolves in sheep's clothing by which latter bad name she meant especially a certain leading politician of the day who had, with the cunning of the devil, tempted and perverted the virtue of her own political friends. And she was one who thought that the slightest breath of scandal on a young woman's name should be stopped at once. An antique, pure-minded, anxious, self-sacrificing matron was Mrs Clifford, and very dear to the heart of Miss Stanbury.

After lunch was over on the day in question Mrs Clifford got Miss Stanbury into some closet retirement, and there spoke her mind as to the things which were being said. It had been asserted in her presence by Camilla French that she, Camilla, was authorised by Mr Gibson to declare that he had never thought of proposing to Dorothy Stanbury, and that Miss Stanbury had been 'labouring under some strange misapprehension in the matter.' 'Now, my dear, I don't care very much for the young lady in question,' said Mrs Clifford, alluding to Camilla French.

'Very little, indeed, I should think,' said Miss Stanbury, with a shake of her head.

'Quite true, my dear, but that does not make the words out of her mouth the less efficacious for evil. She clearly insinuated that you had endeavoured to make up a match between this gentleman and your niece, and that you had failed.' So much was at least true. Miss Stanbury felt this, and felt also that she could not explain the truth, even to her dear old friend. In the midst of her divine wrath she had acknowledged to herself that she had brought Mr Gibson into his difficulty, and that it would not become her to tell any one of his failure. And in this matter she did not herself accuse Mr Gibson. She believed that the lie originated with Camilla French, and it was against Camilla that her wrath raged the fiercest.

'She is a poor, mean, disappointed thing,' said Miss Stanbury.

'Very probably, but I think I should ask her to hold her tongue about Miss Dorothy,' said Mrs Clifford.

The consultation in the closet was carried on for about half-an-hour, and then Miss Stanbury put on her bonnet and shawl and descended into Mrs Clifford's carriage. The carriage took the Heavitree road, and deposited Miss Stanbury at the door of Mrs French's house. The walk home from Heavitree would be nothing, and Mrs Clifford proceeded on her way, having given this little help in counsel, and conveyance to her friend. Mrs French was at home, and Miss Stanbury was shown up into the room in which, the three ladies were sitting.

The reader will doubtless remember the promise which Arabella had made to Mr Gibson. That promise she had already fulfilled to the amazement of her mother and sister; and when Miss Stanbury entered the room the elder daughter of the family was seen without her accustomed head-gear. If the truth is to be owned, Miss Stanbury gave the poor young woman no credit for her new simplicity, but put down the deficiency to the charge of domestic slatternliness. She was unjust enough to declare afterwards that she had found Arabella French only half dressed at between three and four o'clock in the afternoon! From which this lesson may surely be learned: that though the way down Avernus may be, and customarily is, made with great celerity, the return journey, if made at all, must be made slowly. A young woman may commence in chignons by attaching any amount of an edifice to her head; but the reduction should be made by degrees. Arabella's edifice had, in Miss Stanbury's eyes, been the ugliest thing in art that she had known; but, now, its absence offended her, and she most untruly declared that she had come upon the young woman in the middle of the day just out of her bed-room and almost in her dressing-gown.

And the whole French family suffered a diminution of power from the strange phantasy which had come upon Arabella. They all felt, in sight of the enemy, that they had to a certain degree lowered their flag. One of the ships, at least, had shown signs of striking, and this element of weakness made itself felt through the whole fleet. Arabella, herself, when she saw Miss Stanbury, was painfully conscious of her head, and wished that she had postponed the operation till the evening. She smiled with a faint watery smile, and was aware that something ailed her.

The greetings at first were civil, but very formal, as are those between nations which are nominally at peace, but which are waiting for a sign at which each may spring at the other's throat. In this instance the Juno from the Close had come quite prepared to declare her *casus belli* as complete, and to fling down her gauntlet, unless the enemy should at once yield to her everything demanded with an abject submission. 'Mrs French,' she said, 'I have called to-day for a particular purpose, and I must address myself chiefly to Miss Camilla.'

'Oh, certainly,' said Mrs French.

'I shall be delighted to hear anything from you, Miss Stanbury,' said Camilla not without an air of bravado. Arabella said nothing, but she put her hand up almost convulsively to the back of her head.

'I have been told to-day by a friend of mine, Miss Camilla,' began Miss Stanbury, 'that you declared yourself, in her presence, authorised by Mr Gibson to make a statement about my niece Dorothy.'

'May I ask who was your friend?' demanded Mrs French.

'It was Mrs Clifford, of course,' said Camilla. 'There is nobody else would try to make difficulties.'

'There need be no difficulty at all, Miss Camilla,' said Miss Stanbury, 'if you will promise me that you will not repeat the statement. It can't be true.'

'But it is true,' said Camilla.

'What is true?' asked Miss Stanbury, surprised by the audacity of the girl.

'It is true that Mr Gibson authorised us to state what I did state when Mrs Clifford heard me.'

'And what was that?'

'Only this, that people had been saying all about Exeter that he was going to be married to a young lady, and that as the report was incorrect, and as he had never had the remotest idea in his mind of making the young lady his wife.' Camilla, as she said this, spoke with a great deal of emphasis, putting forward her chin and shaking her head, 'and as he thought it was uncomfortable both for the young lady and for himself, and as there was nothing in it, the least in the world, nothing at all, no glimmer of a foundation for the report, it would be better to have it denied everywhere. That is what I said; and we had authority from the gentleman himself. Arabella can say the same, and so can mamma, only mamma did not hear him.' Nor had Camilla heard him, but that incident she did not mention.

The circumstances were, in Miss Stanbury's judgment, becoming very remarkable. She did not for a moment believe Camilla. She did not believe that Mr Gibson had given to either of the Frenches any justification for the statement just made. But Camilla had been so much more audacious than Miss Stanbury had expected, that that lady was for a moment struck dumb. 'I'm sure, Miss Stanbury,' said Mrs French, 'we don't want to give any offence to your niece—very far from it.'

'My niece doesn't care about it two straws,' said Miss Stanbury. 'It is I that care. And I care very much. The things that have been said have been altogether false.'

'How false, Miss Stanbury?' asked Camilla.

'Altogether false; as false as they can be.'

'Mr Gibson must know his own mind,' said Camilla.

'My dear, there's a little disappointment,' said Miss French, 'and it don't signify.'

'There's no disappointment at all,' said Miss Stanbury, 'and it does signify very much. Now that I've begun, I'll go to the bottom of it. If you say that Mr Gibson told you to make these statements, I'll go to Mr Gibson. I'll have it out somehow.'

'You may have what you like out for us, Miss Stanbury,' said Camilla.

'I don't believe Mr Gibson said anything of the kind.'

'That's civil,' said Camilla.

'But why shouldn't he?' asked Arabella.

'There were the reports, you know,' said Mrs French.

'And why shouldn't he deny them when there wasn't a word of truth in them?' continued Camilla. 'For my part, I think the gentleman is bound for the lady's sake to declare that there's nothing in it when there is nothing in it.' This was more than

Miss Stanbury could bear. Hitherto the enemy had seemed to have the best of it. Camilla was firing broadside after broadside, as though she was assured of victory. Even Mrs French was becoming courageous; and Arabella was forgetting the place where her chignon ought to have been. 'I really do not know what else there is for me to say,' remarked Camilla, with a toss of her head, 'and an air of impudence that almost drove poor Miss Stanbury frantic.

It was on her tongue to declare the whole truth, but she refrained. She had schooled herself on this subject vigorously. She would not betray Mr Gibson.' Had she known all the truth or had she believed Camilla French's version of the story there would have been no betrayal. But looking at the matter with such knowledge as she had at present, she did not even yet feel herself justified in declaring that Mr Gibson had offered his hand to her niece, and had been refused. She was, however, sorely tempted. 'Very well, ladies,' she said. 'I shall now see Mr Gibson, and ask him whether he did give you authority to make such statements as you have been spreading abroad everywhere.' Then the door of the room was opened, and in a moment Mr Gibson was among them. He was true to his promise, and had come to see Arabella with her altered headdress, but he had come at this hour thinking that escape in the morning would be easier and quicker than it might have been in the evening. His mind had been full of Arabella and her head-dress even up to the moment of his knocking at the door; but all that was driven out of his brain at once when he saw Miss Stanbury.

'Here is Mr Gibson himself,' said Mrs French.

'How do you do, Mr Gibson?' said Miss Stanbury, with a very stately courtesy. They had never met since the day on which he had been, as he stated, turned out of Miss Stanbury's house. He now bowed to her; but there was no friendly greeting, and the Frenches were able to congratulate themselves on the apparent loyalty to themselves of the gentleman who stood among them. 'I have come here, Mr Gibson,' continued Miss Stanbury, 'to put a small matter right in which you are concerned.'

'It seems to me to be the most insignificant thing in the world,' said Camilla.

'Very likely,' said Miss Stanbury. 'But it is not insignificant to me. Miss Camilla French has asserted publicly that you have authorised her to make a statement about my niece Dorothy.'

Mr Gibson looked into Camilla's face doubtingly, inquisitively, almost piteously.' 'You had better let her go on,' said Camilla.'she will make a great many mistakes, no doubt, but you had better let her go on to the end.'

'I have made no mistake as yet, Miss Camilla. She so asserted, Mr Gibson, in the hearing of a friend of mine, and she repeated the assertion here in this room to me just before you came in. She says that you have authorised her to declare that—that—that; I had better speak it out plainly at once.'

'Much better,' said Camilla.

'That you never entertained an idea of offering your hand to my niece.' Miss Stanbury paused, and Mr Gibson's jaw fell visibly. But he was not expected to speak as yet; and Miss Stanbury continued her accusation. 'Beyond that, I don't want to mention my niece's name, if it can be avoided.'

'But it can't be avoided,' said Camilla.

'If you please, I will continue. Mr Gibson will understand me. I will not, if I can help it, mention my niece's name again, Mr Gibson. But I still have that confidence in you that I do not think that you would have made such a statement in reference to yourself and any young lady unless it were some young lady who had absolutely thrown herself at your head.' And in saying this she paused, and looked very hard at Camilla.

'That's just what Dorothy Stanbury has been doing,' said Camilla.

'She has been doing nothing of the kind, and you know she hasn't,' said Miss Stanbury, raising her arm as though she were going to strike her opponent. 'But I am quite sure, Mr Gibson, that you never could have authorised these young ladies to make such an assertion publicly on your behalf. Whatever there may have been of misunderstanding between you and me, I can't believe that of you.' Then she paused for a reply. 'If you will be good enough to set us right on that point, I shall be obliged to you.'

Mr Gibson's position was one of great discomfort. He had given no authority to anyone to make such a statement. He had said nothing about Dorothy Stanbury to Camilla; but he had told Arabella, when hard pressed by that lady, that he did not mean to propose to Dorothy. He could not satisfy Miss Stanbury because he feared Arabella. He could not satisfy the Frenches because he feared Miss Stanbury. 'I really do not think,' said he, 'that we ought to talk about a young lady in this way.'

'That's my opinion too,' said Camilla; 'but Miss Stanbury will.'

'Exactly so. Miss Stanbury will,' said that lady. 'Mr Gibson, I insist upon it, that you tell me whether you did give any such authority to Miss Camilla French, or to Miss French.'

'I wouldn't answer her, if I were you,' said Camilla.

'I really don't think this can do any good,' said Mrs French.

'And it is so very harassing to our nerves,' said Arabella.

'Nerves! Pooh!' exclaimed Miss Stanbury. 'Now, Mr Gibson, I am waiting for an answer.'

'My dear Miss Stanbury, I really think it better the situation is so peculiar, and, upon my word, I hardly know how not to give offence, which I wouldn't do for the world.'

'Do you mean to tell me that you won't answer my question?' demanded Miss Stanbury.

'I really think that I had better hold my tongue,' pleaded Mr Gibson.

'You are quite right, Mr Gibson,' said Camilla.

'Indeed, it is wisest,' said Mrs French.

'I don't see what else he can do,' said Arabella.

Then was Miss Stanbury driven altogether beyond her powers of endurance. 'If that be so,' said she, 'I must speak out, though I should have preferred to hold my tongue. Mr Gibson did offer to my niece the week before last twice, and was refused by her. My niece, Dorothy, took it into her head that she did not like him; and, upon my word, I think she was right. We should have said nothing about this, not a word; but when these false assertions are made on Mr Gibson's alleged authority, and Mr Gibson won't deny it, I must tell the truth.' Then there was silence among them for a few seconds, and Mr Gibson struggled hard, but vainly, to clothe his face in a pleasant smile. 'Mr Gibson, is that true?' said Miss Stanbury. But Mr Gibson made no reply. 'It is as true as heaven,' said Miss Stanbury, striking her hand upon the table. 'And now you had better, all of you, hold your tongues about my niece, and she will hold her tongue about you. And as for Mr Gibson, anybody who wants him after this is welcome to him for us. Good-morning, Mrs French; good-morning, young ladies.' And so she stalked out of the room, and out of the house, and walked back to her house in the Close.

'Mamma,' said Arabella as soon as the enemy was gone, 'I have got such a headache that I think I will go upstairs.'

'And I will go with you, dear,' said Camilla.

Mr Gibson, before he left the house, confided his secret to the maternal ears of Mrs French. He certainly had been allured into making an offer to Dorothy Stanbury, but was ready to atone for this crime by marrying her daughter Camilla as soon as might be convenient. He was certainly driven to make this declaration by intense cowardice—not to excuse himself, for in that there could be no excuse—but how else should he dare to suggest that he might as well leave the house? 'Shall I tell the dear girl?' asked Mrs French. But Mr Gibson requested a fortnight, in which to consider how the proposition had best be made.

CHAPTER XLIX. MR BROOKE BURGESS AFTER SUPPER

Brooke Burgess was a clerk in the office of the Ecclesiastical Commissioners in London, and as such had to do with things very solemn, grave, and almost melancholy. He had to deal with the rents of episcopal properties, to correspond with clerical claimants, and to be at home with the circumstances of underpaid vicars and perpetual curates with much less than 300 pounds a-year; but yet he was as jolly and pleasant at his desk as though he were busied about the collection of the malt tax, or wrote his letters to admirals and captains instead of to deans and prebendaries. Brooke Burgess had risen to be a senior clerk, and was held in some respect in his office; but it was not perhaps for the amount of work he did, nor yet on account of the gravity of his demeanour, nor for the brilliancy of his intellect. But if not clever, he was sensible; though he was not a dragon of official virtue, he had a conscience and he possessed those small but most valuable gifts by which a man becomes popular among men. And thus it had come to pass in all those battles as to competitive merit which had taken place in his as in other public offices, that no one had ever dreamed of putting a junior over the head of Brooke Burgess. He was tractable, easy, pleasant, and therefore deservedly successful. All his brother clerks called him Brooke except the young lads who, for the first year or two of their service, still denominated him Mr Burgess.

'Brooke,' said one of his juniors, coming into his room and standing before the fireplace with a cigar in his mouth, 'have you heard who is to be the new Commissioner?'

'Colenso, to be sure,' said Brooke.

'What a lark that would be. And I don't see why he shouldn't. But it isn't Colenso. The name has just come down.'

'And who is it?'

'Old Proudie, from Barchester.'

'Why, we had him here years ago, and he resigned.'

'But he's to come on again now for a spell. It always seems to me that the bishops ain't a bit of use here. They only get blown up, and snubbed, and shoved into corners by the others.'

'You young reprobate, to talk of shoving an archbishop into a corner.'

'Well don't they? It's only for the name of it they have them. There's the Bishop of Broomsgrove; he's always sauntering about the place, looking as though he'd be so much obliged if somebody would give him something to do. He's always smiling, and so gracious just as if he didn't feel above half sure that he had any right to be where he is, and he thought that perhaps somebody was going to kick him.'

'And so old Proudie is coming up again,' said Brooke.

'It certainly is very much the same to us whom they send. He'll get shoved into a corner, as you call it, only that he'll go into the corner without any shoving.' Then there came in a messenger with a card, and Brooke learned that Hugh Stanbury was waiting for him in the stranger's room. In performing the promise made to Dorothy, he had called upon her brother as soon as he was back in London, but had not found him. This now was the return visit.

'I thought I was sure to find you here,' said Hugh. 'Pretty nearly sure from eleven till five,' said Brooke. 'A hard stepmother like the Civil Service does not allow one much chance of relief. I do get across to the club sometimes for a glass of sherry and a biscuit but here I am now, at any rate; and I'm very glad you have come.' Then there was some talk between them about affairs at Exeter; but as they were interrupted before half an hour was over their heads by a summons brought for Burgess from one of the secretaries, it was agreed that they should dine together at Burgess's club on the following day. 'We can manage a pretty good beef-steak,' said Brooke, 'and have a fair glass of sherry. I don't think you can get much more than that anywhere nowadays unless you want a dinner for eight at three guineas a head. The magnificence of men has become so intolerable now that one is driven to be humble in one's self-defence.' Stanbury assured his acquaintance that he was anything but magnificent in his own ideas, that cold beef and beer was his usual fare, and at last allowed the clerk to wait upon the secretary.

'I wouldn't have any other fellow to meet you,' said Brooke as they sat at their dinners, 'because in this way we can talk over the dear old woman at Exeter. Yes, our fellow does make good soup, and it's about all that he does do well. As for getting a potato properly boiled, that's quite out of the question. Yes, it is a good glass of sherry. I told you we'd a fairish tap of sherry on. Well, I was there, backwards and forwards, for nearly six weeks.'

'And how did you get on with the old woman?'

'Like a house on fire,' said Brooke.

'She didn't quarrel with you?'

'No upon the whole she did not. I always felt that it was touch and go. She might or she might not. Every now and then she looked at me, and said a sharp word, as though it was about to come. But I had determined when I went there altogether to disregard that kind of thing.'

'It's rather important to you is it not?'

'You mean about her money?'

'Of course, I mean about her money,' said Stanbury.

'It is important and so it was to you.'

'Not in the same degree, or nearly so. And as for me, it was not on the cards that we shouldn't quarrel. I am so utterly a Bohemian in all my ideas of life, and she is so absolutely the reverse, that not to have quarrelled would have been hypocritical on my part or on hers. She had got it into her head that she had a right to rule my life; and, of course, she quarrelled with me when I made her understand that she should do nothing of the kind. Now, she won't want to rule you.'

'I hope not.'

'She has taken you up,' continued Stanbury, 'on altogether a different understanding. You are to her the representative of a family to whom she thinks she owes the restitution of the property which she enjoys. I was simply a member of her own family, to which she owes nothing. She thought it well to help one of us out of what she regarded as her private purse, and she chose me. But the matter is quite different with you.'

'She might have given everything to you, as well as to me,' said Brooke.

'That's not her idea. She conceives herself bound to leave all she has back to a Burgess, except anything she may save as she says, off her own back, or out of her own belly. She has told me so a score of times.'

'And what did you say?'

'I always told her that, let her do as she would, I should never ask any question about her will.'

'But she hates us all like poison except me,' said Brooke. 'I never knew people so absurdly hostile as are your aunt and my uncle Barty. Each thinks the other the most wicked person in the world.'

'I suppose your uncle was hard upon her once.'

'Very likely. He is a hard man and has, very warmly, all the feelings of an injured man. I suppose my uncle Brooke's will was a cruel blow to him. He professes to believe that Miss Stanbury will never leave me a shilling.'

'He is wrong, then,' said Stanbury.

'Oh yes he's wrong, because he thinks that that's her present intention. I don't know that he's wrong as to the probable result.'

'Who will have it, then?'

'There are ever so many horses in the race,' said Brooke. 'I'm one.'

'You're the favourite,' said Stanbury.

'For the moment I am. Then there's yourself.'

'I've been scratched, and am altogether out of the betting.'

'And your sister,' continued Brooke.

'She's only entered to run for the second money; and, if she'll trot over the course quietly, and not go the wrong side of the posts, she'll win that.'

'She may do more than that. Then there's Martha.'

'My aunt will never leave her money to a servant. What she may give to Martha would come from her own savings.'

'The next is a dark horse, but one that wins a good many races of this kind. He's apt to come in with a fatal rush at the end.'

'Who is it?'

'The hospitals. When an old lady finds in her latter days that she hates everybody, and fancies that the people around her are all thinking of her motley, she's uncommon likely to indulge herself a little bit of revenge, and solace herself with large-handed charity.'

'But she's so good a woman at heart,' said Hugh.

'And what can a good woman do better than promote hospitals?'

'She'll never do that. She's too strong. It's a maudlin sort of thing, after all, for a person to leave everything to a hospital.'

'But people are maudlin when they're dying,' said Brooke, 'or even when they think they're dying. How else did the Church get the estates, of which we are now distributing so bountifully some of the last remnants down at our office? Come into the next room, and we'll have a smoke.'

They had their smoke, and then they went at half-price to the play; and, after the play was over, they eat three or four dozen of oysters between them. Brooke Burgess was a little too old for oysters at midnight in September; but he went through his work like a man. Hugh Stanbury's powers were so great, that he could have got up and done the same thing again, after he had been an hour in bed, without any serious inconvenience.

But, in truth, Brooke Burgess had still another word or two to say before he went to his rest, They supped somewhere near the Haymarket, and then he offered to walk home with Stanbury, to his chambers in Lincoln's Inn. 'Do you know that Mr Gibson at Exeter?' he asked, as they passed through Leicester Square.

'Yes; I knew him. He was a sort of tame-cat parson at my aunt's house, in my days.'

'Exactly but I fancy that has come to an end now. Have you heard anything about him lately?'

'Well yes I have,' said Stanbury, feeling that dislike to speak of his sister which is common to most brothers when in company with other men.

'I suppose you've heard of it, and, as I was in the middle of it all, of course I couldn't but know all about it too. Your aunt wanted him to marry your sister.'

'So I was told.'

'But your sister didn't see it,' said Brooke.

'So I understand,' said Stanbury. 'I believe my aunt was exceedingly liberal,' and meant to do the best she could for poor Dorothy; but, if she didn't like him, I suppose she was right not to have him,' said Hugh.

'Of course she was right,' said Brooke, with a good deal of enthusiasm.

'I believe Gibson to be a very decent sort of fellow,' said Stanbury.

'A mean, paltry dog,' said Brooke. There had been a little whisky-toddy after the oysters, and Mr Burgess was perhaps moved to a warmer expression of feeling than he might have displayed had he discussed this branch of the subject before supper. 'I knew from the first that she would have nothing to say to him. He is such a poor creature!'

'I always thought well of him,' said Stanbury, 'and was inclined to think that Dolly might have done worse.'

'It is hard to say what is the worst a girl might do; but I think she might do, perhaps, a little better.'

'What do you mean?' said Hugh.

'I think I shall go down, and ask her to take myself.'

'Do you mean it in earnest?'

'I do,' said Brooke. 'Of course, I hadn't a chance when I was there. She told me—'

'Who told you, Dorothy?'

'No, your aunt she told me that Mr Gibson was to marry your sister. You know your aunt's way. She spoke of it as though the thing were settled as soon as she had got it into her own head; and she was as hot upon it as though Mr Gibson had been an archbishop. I had nothing to do then but to wait and see.'

'I had no idea of Dolly being fought for by rivals.'

'Brothers never think much of their sisters,' said Brooke Burgess.

'I can assure you I think a great deal of Dorothy,' said Hugh. 'I believe her to be as sweet a woman as God ever made. She hardly knows that she has a self belonging to herself.'

'I'm sure she doesn't,' said Brooke.

'She is a dear, loving, sweet-tempered creature, who is only too ready to yield in all things.'

'But she wouldn't yield about Gibson,' said Brooke.

'How did she and my aunt manage?'

'Your sister simply said she couldn't and then that she wouldn't. I never thought from the first moment that she'd take that fellow. In the first place he can't say boo to a goose.'

'But Dolly wouldn't want a man to say boo.'

'I'm not so sure of that, old fellow. At any rate I mean to try myself. Now what'll the old woman say?'

'She'll be pleased as Punch, I should think,' said Stanbury.

'Either that or else she'll swear that she'll never speak another word to either of us. However, I shall go on with it.'

'Does Dorothy know anything of this?' asked Stanbury.

'Not a word,' said Brooke. 'I came away a day or so after Gibson was settled; and as I had been talked to all through the affair by both of them, I couldn't turn round and offer myself the moment he was gone. You won't object will you?'

'Who; I?' said Stanbury. 'I shall have no objection as long as Dolly pleases herself. Of course you know that we haven't as much as a brass farthing among us?'

'That won't matter if the old lady takes it kindly,' said Brooke. Then they parted, at the corner of Lincoln's Inn Fields, and Hugh as he went up to his own rooms, reflected with something of wonderment on the success of Dorothy's charms. She had always been the poor one of the family, the chick out of the nest which would most require assistance from the stronger birds; but it now appeared that she would become the first among all the Stanburys. Wealth had first flowed down upon the Stanbury family from the will of old Brooke Burgess; and it now seemed probable that poor Dolly would ultimately have the enjoyment of it all.